The Price of Pride

The Price of Pride

Donna MacQuigg

Five Star • Waterville, Maine

First Edition
First Printing: May 2006

Published in 2006 in conjunction with Tekno Books.

Set in 11 pt. Plantin by Christina S. Huff.

Printed in the United States on permanent paper.

Library of Congress Cataloging-in-Publication Data

MacQuigg, Donna.
   The price of pride / Donna MacQuigg.—1st ed.
      p. cm.
    ISBN 1-59414-464-8 (hc : alk. paper)
     1. Murder—Investigation—Fiction.   2. Marshals—Fiction.
   3. Women journalists—Fiction.   4. Cattle stealing—Fiction.
   I. Title.
   PS3613.A283P75 2006
    813´.6—dc22
                                           2005033732

To my mother who never doubted me,
and to Misty, the best horse I ever had.
I miss you both.

Prologue

Territory of New Mexico—1892

Emily Brighton shivered and added several small chunks of wood to the pot-bellied stove in the corner of her dress shop. She didn't usually work this late, but Mrs. Pruitt had offered her an additional ten dollars if she could get the gown ready for a fitting by Wednesday.

Emily leaned over her table to straighten the cloth she was cutting, then moved the oil lamp a little closer. She snipped away, smiling when she heard the little bell over her door. "Zachary, is that you?"

"Evening, Miss Brighton," came a man's voice.

Her heart hammered against her chest. She looked up and saw a man standing just inside the doorway that separated her workroom from her shop. His features were obscured by a cloth sack with three holes, two for his eyes and one for his mouth. His dark coat was dusted with a light covering of snow. She had the fleeting thought that he looked like a well-dressed scarecrow wearing a black bowler. She swallowed past the lump in her throat, recognizing the man's perfectly tailored coat.

"What do you want?" she managed to say, concealing her sewing shears behind her apron as she took a step back. "If you've come for money, the cash box is up front. Take it and get out."

"You've been doing a lot of talking around town, saying things you shouldn't be saying, about things you don't know anything about."

"You can't threaten me. I know who you are, and I'm not the only one who knows what you've been doing. Zachary will be here any second, so I advise you to leave."

"I advise you to leave," he repeated, mimicking her voice. "You sure do have a fancy way of saying things." He moved closer, then stepped around the table, forcing her to step back, trapping her against the storage shelf piled high with bolts of material.

"Please," she begged, hating the way her voice wavered. "I don't want any trouble. If you leave now, I shan't press charges."

His low, cynical laughter sent terror shooting up her spine. He took another step toward her, so close his breath could be felt against her cheek. She turned her face away.

"Don't you worry none, Miss Brighton . . . Emily." His hand slipped around her waist, his other hand closing over her breast. "All you need to do is forget what you think you know."

"I-I'm warning you, I'll scream."

"Go ahead, there's no one out tonight. It's too cold." In one fluid motion he pulled her roughly into his arms, one hand rubbing her backside.

"Get out," she demanded, drawing the last of her courage.

"I'll leave, but first, I want one little tumble, come on, sweetheart, just—"

"Never," she hissed. They struggled for a moment until she sank her shears into his forearm.

"Why, you little bitch." He reached for her, but she struck out again, slicing the heel of his hand.

Enraged, he grabbed her wrist and twisted it ruthlessly.

She cried out and dropped the shears. Before she could scream, he clamped a bloodied palm over her nose and mouth.

"Shush," he murmured close to her ear.

"What the hell are you doing?" came a familiar, deep voice.

Emily's eyes widened as they fused with Zachary's. Praise God, he had come.

Her assailant swore violently, and then threw her against the shelf. Pain exploded in her head as she sank down to the floor, too dazed to move. She thought she heard a gunshot, but it sounded very far away. As darkness engulfed her, she folded her fingers over a button she had torn from the scarecrow's coat.

Chapter One

"Oh, God, Ira. You're driving me crazy."

Ira Farrell, U.S. Marshal of Carefree, Arizona, gazed down at the woman writhing beneath him. She'd called him her wild stallion in a moment of lustful insanity. Her eyes glittered green, her lips were full and swollen from his kisses. Yet theirs wasn't an act of love, but one of need.

And he knew she needed him too. That's why Mrs. Ginger Carson, owner of the boarding house, was perfect for him. No demands, no commitments, nothing but a good tumble whenever her husband was out of town selling his snake oil.

The seductive redhead raised her hips, digging her nails into his back when she found her release, bucking beneath him. He could hold back no longer. With a low groan he pulled out just in the nick of time. Slowly, he rolled off of her. Raking his fingers through his thick tawny hair, he relaxed back against the pillows.

"Ira," Ginger breathed as she rolled into the crook of his arm. "You are, without a doubt, the best ride in town. But, I'd like it better if you weren't so considerate."

He laughed dryly. "I reckon you're right, but I'm not willing to take any chances."

"What would it matter? I'd much prefer to raise your child than I would Billy's."

"Yeah, but what would you tell him when his son grew to

six feet and he's barely over five?" Ira shook his head. "You like me because I bathe regularly and pay my rent on time."

She lifted herself up on an elbow and brushed a lock of hair from his forehead. "That's part of it, but not all." Her warm fingers drifted down his cheek, skipping to the hard muscles of his chest, inching lower over the rippled plain of his belly.

Ira caught her hand, drew it up and placed a quick kiss in her palm, then left the bed to dress. He grabbed his trousers and tugged them on, sitting down on the edge of the bed to put on his socks and boots.

"I've got rounds to make," he muttered. No sooner had he said the words than someone knocked on the door.

"Marshal Farrell?" a boy's voice called from the other side.

"Just a minute," Ira answered, shrugging on his shirt before he opened the door a crack.

"Telegram came for you, Marshal. John said I should bring it right over."

Ira took the paper and glanced at it for several long moments. Zachary was dead and the family wanted him to come home. A crushing pain threatened his composure, but, as usual, he quickly regained control. He'd become an expert at concealing his emotions—learned how as a child, he thought bitterly.

Carefully, he folded the telegram then slipped it in the inside pocket of his gold-brocade vest. He finished dressing, took out his wallet and placed several bills on the dresser. "Put that on my account."

"Will I see you tonight?" Ginger purred, stretching out full length on the bed, completely at ease with her nudity. "Billy's out of town the rest of the week."

Ira turned and strapped on his engraved, ivory-handled

cream-colored

Colt .45, then lifted his cream-colored Stetson from the peg by the door and put it on. "I'll be gone a few weeks, Ginger."

"A few weeks?" she protested. "Why . . . where are you going?"

"Home."

"Morning, Marshal Farrell," Carmen said with a nod as Ira walked into the mayor's office then removed his hat. "Did you want to see the mayor?"

"Yeah. It's important. Is he in?"

"My, by your expression, it must be serious." Carmen gave him a wistful smile. "He came in just a little bit ago, Marshal. I'll let him know you're here." The moment she opened the door, the mayor waved her away.

"Ira, come in, come in," Mayor James stated while he opened the bottom drawer of his desk. He produced a bottle and poured two small glasses of whiskey. "I was expecting you to come by as soon as you got word. Figured you could use a drink."

Ira raised one dark brow. "Are you reading my telegrams before I do?"

"Now, now, don't get your feathers in a ruffle. It's my job as mayor to know what's happening in my town. I was simply on my way to the office when Joey asked if I knew where you were. The boy said he had a real important telegram for you . . . something about one of your brothers dying. Naturally I was concerned. And certainly the boy didn't mean no harm. I'm real sorry about your brother."

Ira accepted the mayor's answer and the glass of whiskey. "What else is on your mind?" he asked as he sank down in an overstuffed leather chair. "I don't reckon that look you've got is just about my brother."

"Well, on one hand it is, and on the other it isn't, but I fig-

12

ured you'd be wanting some time off to visit your family. And I thought I could call in a favor while you're up there. I could use your services to help solve something that's been bothering me." The mayor took a sip of his drink. "A month ago, my niece's husband went to Santa Fe—"

"Bob Phillips? I thought he was a deputy in Albuquerque."

"He was until President Harrison made him a marshal. Acting on some rumors about cattle rustling, Bob went up to Santa Fe. Sally, my niece, got a telegram a week later. Bob said he had some information that would close the case early and to expect him home within a week."

"I can see by your expression that he never made it," Ira stated flatly, glad to have something else to think about other than Zach. Ira thought back. He'd met Bob Phillips once. He seemed like a nice guy, not the type to rush in or do anything foolish.

"Sally got the body back in a sealed coffin," the mayor added. "The sheriff over there in Santa Fe—a man named Cooper Finch—delivered it personally. Said Bob had been attacked by a mountain lion."

"It's possible. I've seen a few up there by Jack's Creek." Ira took a drink. "But you don't believe Sheriff Finch," Ira said with a wary glance.

"Do you know him?" the mayor asked.

"Don't even recognize the name," Ira answered honestly. "I haven't been home in almost ten years." He took another sip of his drink, trying not to let old memories surface. "Did they look at the body?"

The mayor grimaced. "No. The sheriff suggested that they just bury him, that he didn't want my niece to have any nightmares, seeing that they didn't find him for several days after he'd been mauled."

"That's understandable. Did they take him to the under-taker?"

The mayor shook his head. "Nope. No one saw the body before it was buried."

"Then there's just the sheriff's report, and no proof of what killed him."

"Ira, like you, I'm a suspicious man. I'm thinking that if Bob learned something about the cattle rustling, he just might have been murdered."

Ira finished the last of his drink, then stood. "Our ranch is damn near four hours away from town. Like I said, I've been gone a long time. I don't know many folks up there any-more."

"I don't see that as a problem. After you've paid your re-spects and spent some time with your family, you could stay in town for a while. Ask a few questions about Bob and see who you spook. Bob was just an unknown . . . someone who wouldn't be missed. You, on the other hand, well . . . let's put it this way: perhaps your reputation will make the good citi-zens of Santa Fe a little nervous."

Ira met the mayor's steady gaze. "And nervous men make mistakes."

"Isn't that what you always say?" The mayor shook his grey head. "I'm real sorry about your brother, but I've got a little something to make the trip worth your while." The mayor opened his drawer and took out a long white envelope, giving it to Ira. "This is for you."

Ira opened it, revealing five one-hundred-dollar bills. "What's this for?"

The mayor sat back in his swivel chair with a satisfied smile. "Let's just say it's a little insurance. Some pay for working on your time off. Me and the town council don't want you to like it too much in Santa Fe and end up staying to help your brothers with the ranch. We want you back here in Carefree."

Ira gave a dry laugh and tucked the envelope into the inside pocket of his vest. "No chance of that happening, but thanks just the same."

"Yeah, well, take care, and my condolences to your family."

"Sarah, thank you for coming."

"What is it, Peter? You look so serious." Sarah Brighton accepted the offered seat in the solicitor's office. "You don't have something scandalous to put in the paper, do you?"

She returned his soft smile. As the only female journalist for the *St. Louis Herald*, he understood she was always looking for more exciting stories than those she wrote for the city's society page.

"It concerns your cousin, Sarah. I'm sure you're aware that a year ago, acting on your advice, Emily asked me to handle her legal affairs as she was planning to open a dress shop out west. I know the two of you weren't terribly close, but I just received word that there's been a horrible accident." He came around his desk and sat in the empty chair next to hers, placing his hand on her shoulder. "I'm sorry, but I'm afraid there's no easy way to say this. She's dead, Sarah. She perished in a fire yesterday."

Sarah's face grew pale before his eyes. When she spoke, her voice was barely over a whisper. "Poor Emily. She had her whole life ahead of her."

"I know it's a shock, but that's not the only reason I wanted to meet with you." Peter gave her a moment, then handed her a telegram, watching while she read. She'd changed since he saw her a few years ago—grown up to be quite an attractive young woman from the eighteen-year-old who had asked his advice on how a single woman should handle her finances.

He'd thought it odd at the time, but the more he got to know her—her ambitious nature, her determination to be any man's equal—the more he understood, especially now that her financial future was well on its way to being secure. Though she had the same, almost innocent, blue eyes, she appeared much more sophisticated with her golden hair drawn back into a neat chignon, tucked under her fancy feathered hat.

"I received that today from Mr. Silas Pruitt, a banker in Santa Fe. Apparently he's representing your cousin's estate, got my name from some papers in a lockbox, and that she listed him as the executor of her estate."

"You're not serious," she replied with a disbelieving frown. "I thought—"

"Don't worry. Nothing's changed, Sarah. Emily's trust is safe. I suspect Mr. Pruitt is speaking about her account in his bank. I doubt his claim is valid, and even so, he'd have to prove it. The man has asked that we settle her outstanding debts."

"Outstanding debts?" she repeated incredulously. "There must be some mistake." She was quiet for several moments while a multitude of emotions flickered in the depth of her vibrant eyes. She stood stiffly. "I need some time . . . to digest the news of my cousin's death, and to think how best to deal with Mr. Pruitt."

"Of course, I won't answer his telegram until you ask me to."

"You're going where?" Randall Watson asked. His dark brows furrowed together as he continued his inspection of a thick, black ledger on his desk. They'd had conversations like this before, Sarah thought, when she wanted to cover a certain story that he thought more fitting for a man to investigate. He'd brushed her off without ever looking at her. Though it appeared that her employer wasn't going to put aside the ledger, from his next sentence, she knew he'd heard. "New Mexico isn't even a state yet. Why, I doubt it's fit for a lady to travel that far without an escort."

Sarah gave an impatient sigh. "Mr. Watson, I'm capable of taking care of myself. All I'm asking is for a few weeks to settle some important matters."

He gave a disgruntled snort then returned to his ledger. "Out of the question."

She'd known he'd say that, and hoped she was making the right decision as she placed a folded piece of paper on top of the ledger. "Then please accept my resignation."

Much to Sarah's relief, her journey had been uneventful. A good thing in reality, she thought, but it would have been exciting to have a few hostiles chase the train for a ways. Why, even the sleepy little town of Santa Fe was rather disappointing . . . almost too civilized. Gas lamps perched on boardwalks, no different from several other towns they'd passed by. She smiled at three little Mexican boys when they converged upon her, all speaking at once, and all offering to take her satchels to the Santa Fe Boarding House, each outbidding the other's fee.

A little while later, Sarah opened the door to her room. Peter had been thorough with his arrangements. Everything she'd asked him to do had been done with his usual efficiency. From train tickets to the cozy room, she hadn't had to worry about a thing. As far as her identity, he had even supplied the necessary documents to prove that she was the wife of Andrew Wellington, an English merchant seeking a new

17

market in the West, traveling by stage to acquire new business contacts along the way.

She took out the paper and glanced at it, giving a bittersweet smile at her falsified title. *Mrs. Andrew Wellington.* It wasn't the first time she'd traveled under a different name. She had learned quickly that married ladies were not so vigorously pursued, at least in the cities she frequented, as were spinsters. As a journalist, she had enough sexual barriers to break down without being considered single men's prey. But, that hardly mattered now. As Mrs. Wellington, none would be the wiser about her intentions to investigate her cousin's accident.

She decided to unpack later, unwilling to be late for her prearranged meeting with Silas Pruitt. As she stepped outside, she braced herself against a cold wind and began walking.

Most of the buildings were constructed out of mud. *Adobe* buildings, she remembered reading, were both warming in the winter and cooling in the summer. Some of the shops had false wooden fronts painted in various colors, describing their purposes. Very few of the shops were made entirely of wood. She nodded at several attractive Mexican women as she continued down the street, captivated by the bright colors of their full flowing skirts.

A life-sized wooden Indian stood before the mercantile, and several horses were tied at the hitching post before it. She quickly inspected their western-style saddles, thinking that they'd be relatively heavy compared to the English style she used when riding. She continued on her way, enjoying the sights and sounds, when she realized she was standing before the burned-out ruin of a shop.

She swallowed past a sudden tightness in her throat and forced a glance upward. The scorched sign read, *Emily's*

Dress Shop. A sick knot formed in her stomach as she cautiously peered inside the broken window, surprised that most of the damage was confined to the roof and the furnishings of the establishment.

"Mrs. Wellington?"

Sarah turned to see a stout, balding man in a too-tight suit. He held out his hand.

"I'm Silas Pruitt, the owner of the bank. I've been expecting you." He motioned across the street. "I saw you through the window."

She shook his hand, warm even through her glove, then slipped her hand back into the mink muff that matched the trim on the collar and cuffs of her emerald-green traveling suit. She cleared her throat, forcing a slight smile. "I assume you received my telegram?"

"Yes, ma'am, I did indeed. So you and Miss Brighton were cousins?"

"That's correct."

He looked a little uncomfortable. "I didn't know that Miss Brighton had any living relatives." He shifted nervously then motioned toward the bank. "Shall we?"

Her curiosity mounting, she followed Silas into his office, accepting a chair. "According to Mr. Hoffman," Sarah began, "you said Emily named you as administer of her personal affairs?"

"Well, not exactly, Mrs. Wellington. Perhaps I didn't make myself clear. You see, Miss Emily had a lockbox in my bank. When she died, I, as the bank owner, looked to see if she had any kin. That's where I found Mr. Hoffman's name. I assure you, I was only honoring her wishes when I released her personal things to . . . well, it's rather complicated." He took his seat behind a huge mahogany desk.

"I have time, Mr. Pruitt."

"Well, the Farrells were real close to Miss Emily. She and Zachary Farrell were planning to marry."

"I fail to see what this has to do with Emily's things," she replied, a little confused.

"Well, I gave what we could salvage from the shop and her personal belongings to Cole Farrell." Once more the portly banker cleared his throat and looked rather uncomfortable. "Did I mention that Zachary died in the fire with Miss Emily?"

"Dear Lord," Sarah gasped, pressing a lace handkerchief to her mouth for a moment. "How dreadful."

"You look kind of pale, Mrs. Wellington. May I get you a glass of water?"

"Thank you, but I'm quite all right."

"Had we known—"

"We?" she inquired.

"Ah, yes . . . the town council and I make all the important decisions together." He cleared his throat. "As I was saying, had we known Miss Emily had family back East, we could have sent the body, but since we didn't know . . . we . . . *I* assumed she was alone, so we let the Farrells bury her on their ranch alongside Zachary."

Sarah remained calm, thankful that the muff kept him from seeing how her hands trembled.

"You're still looking kind of peaked, Mrs. Wellington. Are you sure I can't get you something?"

"No, thank you." She took a moment to gather her thoughts. "Mr. Pruitt, I'm here to reconcile any expenses for my cousin's funeral and rectify any other debts she may have accrued."

"Oh, there's no need for that. After I checked her account more closely, she had quite enough money to settle things at the mercantile with some left over." Again, he cleared his throat, unaware of the spots of color that formed on his jowls. "I apologize for the misunderstanding. I was going to send another telegram, but then I got yours, and, well, here you are." He opened a drawer and gave her an envelope. "Like I said, Miss Emily's and Zach's personal things are up at the Broken Arrow Ranch. Miss Emily's account information is in there. When you're ready, give that to Mrs. Jenkins, and she'll close the account for you."

Sarah took the envelope, opened it and briefly scanned the contents before tucking it in her reticule. "I realize this might sound peculiar, but was Zachary Farrell any relation to Ira Farrell, Marshal Ira Farrell, the man who supposedly tamed the southwestern territory of Arizona?"

Silas Pruitt looked rather surprised. "One and the same. Do you know him?"

Sarah shook her head. "I assure you, Mr. Pruitt, men who gun other men down in the middle of the street are not part of my social circle. I read something outrageous about him in the *St. Louis Herald*." She smoothed a wrinkle from her skirt, still somewhat shaken. "I'd like to visit my cousin's grave."

"I'll have someone take you up there as soon as possible."

"Thank you, but that won't be necessary. However, directions to the ranch would be helpful. In the meantime"—she stood and he stood with her—"I'd like to begin rebuilding."

"Ah . . . rebuilding?" he stammered.

"Yes. Is there a problem?" she asked with more confidence than she felt. After all, she had only moments ago decided to do so.

"No . . . no, not at all. I supposed . . . I mean . . . I just assumed it would be sold. In fact, the town council and I are prepared to make you a generous offer, considering the building's practically ruined."

"How thoughtful. However, it didn't look too badly damaged." She gave Silas a slight smile, watching him closely. "Emily and I were taught sewing by the same person. From her letters, her shop was flourishing."

"I'm not sure I understand," he murmured, appearing a little dumbstruck.

"I've no intention of selling . . . not just yet. Therefore, the sooner it's repaired, the sooner I can make my decision. Will you assist me in finding a carpenter?" she repeated.

He cleared his throat. "Certainly. I shall see to it immediately."

"Thank you. Now about those directions to my cousin's final resting place."

"Yes, ma'am." He took out a little pad of paper and quickly drew a map, handing it to her as he escorted her to the door. "You should really reconsider and allow me to have someone act as escort, Mrs. Wellington. This isn't St. Louis. It's not safe for a woman to travel alone, especially in the mountains."

Chapter Two

The sun had barely peeked over the rolling, wooded hills of Santa Fe when Ira Farrell purposefully shed his sheepskin coat at the outskirts of town. It had been a difficult ride—not the distance or the terrain, but the solitude—solitude filled with memories of his childhood and how hard it had been to protect his brothers from their father.

Ten years, and though he knew the old man had treated his brothers differently, Ira still felt guilty for leaving when he did. He headed his horse down the well-worn path, grateful for the diversion. Though quite early in the morning, many a face turned his way, getting a good look at the United States Marshal's badge pinned over his heart.

For a moment he thought to stop at the sheriff's office and formally announce his arrival and his intentions, but after several people openly stared, even pulled their children out of his way, he knew word of his appearance would spread quickly enough.

A lot had changed since he'd left his hometown. Santa Fe was bigger, swarming with all types of people. Cowboys, women and children, Mexicans and even a few Navajos began to fill the streets as a whole variety of proprietors opened their shops to begin the day. He turned his big roan gelding down Main Street, noticing right away the scorched adobe of Emily's Dress Shop. The barbershop next to it seemed to have suffered no damage. Nor had the

Land Office on the other side—a benefit of being made of mud.

He glanced across the wide street at the bank, and next to it, the mercantile. Much to his surprise, the little boarding house that his mother's friend used to run was gone, replaced by a two-story hotel complete with a third-story false front. There were several other new streets and side streets that also bustled with activities that he'd have to explore, then he spotted one he remembered well. It led to the immoral side of town and the Crystal Slipper Saloon. He smiled at a memory, and then continued down Main Street, touching the brim of his hat as Silas Pruitt turned from speaking with a man and watched him ride by.

Following Mayor James's suggestion, Ira found a public place to have some breakfast, giving the town gossips something to ponder before he headed north to the mountains.

Sarah settled into the saddle and arranged the material of her split skirt so it wouldn't bunch up under her knees. Though the sun was shining, Mr. Pruitt had warned that the mountains were always colder, especially in October, and prone to sudden and furious storms. With this in mind, she dressed accordingly with a short, red fox fur–trimmed, fitted coat in the same rusty-brown as her wool riding skirt, and a matching bonnet. Her tall black boots were also lined and worn in combination with her soft knitted stockings. She was quite comfortable, feeling secure with her two-shot Smith & Wesson derringer tucked into her coat pocket.

After she pulled on a pair of fur-lined black leather gloves, she gathered up the reins and cued the horse into a lively trot, pleased all her childhood lessons in horsemanship were finally paying off. Very quickly she left the bustling town behind, heading down the road Mr. Pruitt had pointed out.

Even though her reasons for visiting were grim, her heart jumped excitedly with the thought that in only a few short hours, she would meet Cole Farrell and get her first glimpse of a real American cowboy.

Ira pulled his hat down more firmly on his forehead and then tugged his knitted scarf and the collar of his coat up over his ears. His memory had served him well—the mountains of New Mexico were damned cold this time of year. Though there was still plenty of daylight, the breeze wafting though the trees was laced with smatterings of snow. Once more he thought of his past—of good times he'd spent with his brothers—memories dampened by his father. Cole and Adam would be grown men, and Zach—Zach was gone, and the reason for this trip.

Ira pushed his dismal thoughts aside. There was no turning back now. He'd stayed away too long, and now it was too late.

Sarah made the right turn at the fork. Shorter cedars and *piñons* gave way to towering ponderosa pines and several varieties of thickly spaced spruce. The road was no longer smooth, but rocky and more rutted. Forced to pull the horse to a walk, she gave the mare a little more rein and leaned with her as they had to maneuver several steep inclines.

The air was crisp and sweet, tinged with the earthy scent of pine, and the sky was a dazzling blue, dotted with a few puffy, grey clouds to the north. Once in a while, she caught sight of several white-tailed deer as they cautiously watched her approach, then bounded gracefully away. She halted the mare, and after tugging her collar up a little higher, lifted the miniature watch pinned to her coat. Half-past eleven. Plenty of daylight left. She gathered her reins and urged the mare up the winding road.

Another hour went by. The clouds grew wispy, until there was very little blue sky left. At one particular point the trees gave way, exposing a breathtaking view, and she stopped to absorb its splendor and made a few sketches on a pad she carried in her saddlebags. *Distant mountain peaks were capped in a sparkling pristine snow, the clouds settling down on them like the wintry breath of God,* she wrote next to her sketch.

The sound of running water up ahead confirmed that she was going the right direction. She relaxed a little and, as she continued on, was immersed in the beautiful scenery. Occasionally the crisp mountain breeze caused the pines to shudder, sending little puffs of white powder swirling into the air. Enchanted by the majestic beauty, she was nearly unseated when her mare shied. A wolf stood on a rocky formation several yards ahead.

She heard a rustling. At the same time a man on horseback crashed out of the trees and galloped past. Her mare reared, slipping and sliding on the mud and snow. Sarah rolled from the mare's back with a startled scream. The thick padding of pine needles and aspen leaves broke her fall.

Choking back another scream, she scrambled to her feet, clutching her derringer. One quick glance confirmed her worst fear. Her horse was galloping down the trail. Thankfully, the intruder had disappeared into the trees. But the wolf remained on the rock, his long red tongue lolling from the side of his mouth, and his tail . . . or the stub that once was a tail, wagging furiously. He wasn't very lean. In fact he was rather fat and a bit short, but then she'd never seen a real wolf. She swallowed, afraid to look away from its eerie black eyes.

"Sh-sh-shoo," she said, trembling.

"He won't hurt you, ma'am," came a deep voice from behind her.

She spun, the two-shot derringer still in hand. A man sat on an enormous horse. The man's features were partially obscured by a cream-colored Stetson and a blue, knitted scarf.

"You could have killed me," she replied scornfully.

"Are you all right?" he asked, pushing his hat back off his forehead. He wore what she thought was a rather perplexed frown as he stepped down from his horse. He was beardless, with tiny laugh lines at the corners of very captivating grey-blue eyes. His tan sheepskin coat with the wool collar was pulled up high. Oddly enough, he bent down and clapped his gloved hands together. "Buster, come here, boy."

She watched the animal bound over to the man then sit. It stared adoringly up at its master. The man scratched the dog's ears as if he hadn't seen the animal for a long time. "Hey, boy. How are you?"

"He shouldn't be allowed to run loose," she snapped, still too frightened to be sociable. "It isn't safe."

"For him or you?" the man countered, standing to face her. "I'm sorry he scared you."

She ignored his sarcasm. The man was tall. Somewhat intimidating.

"You can put away that shooter. Neither Buster nor I will hurt you." His smile was instant and friendlier that she would have expected had their roles been reversed.

"I like it right where it is." She didn't give him time to speak, or care that his smile faded. "Is it your habit to run down travelers?"

Once more he gave her a skeptical glance. "Ma'am?"

"You heard me." She waved the derringer toward the place where the horse and rider had come through the trees, then quickly aimed it back at the stranger. "You very nearly killed me, crashing through the trees like that and galloping past as if I weren't even here. It's a wonder I didn't break a bone." She dusted bits of debris from her coat, all the while pointing the gun at his chest.

"I'm sorry, ma'am," he said, frowning. "But, you're not making any sense. I was at the river when I heard you scream."

"Then who just tried to run me down?" she demanded with a defiant tilt of her chin. "If it wasn't you, who was it?"

"Did you get a look at him?" the man asked, glancing down the trail.

"I was too busy trying to control my horse to notice his attire." She didn't care that he looked puzzled. She did care that the cold was starting to seep into her boots and freeze her toes. "Oh, never mind. It's too cold to worry about him. I'm trying to find Mr. Cole Farrell and . . ." she dug into her pocket and quickly withdrew the paper. ". . . the Broken Arrow Ranch." She kept her weapon poised, stuffing the paper back into her pocket. "Do you know him?"

"Yes, ma'am, I—"

"Then if it isn't too much of an imposition," she interrupted, "I'd appreciate the use of your horse."

"My horse?" he repeated.

She gave an impatient sigh. "I'll see that Mr. Farrell sends someone back for you immediately."

"That won't be necessary. Ira Farrell, ma'am, at your service."

He had never moved the whole time they were talking, and now she knew why. He had obviously been held at gunpoint before. Her frown deepened as she took in the details of his appearance. Though he was good-looking enough, she had expected a more rugged face, perhaps a handlebar moustache, and although he wore a heavy winter coat that made his shoulders appear massive, it wasn't the same as she'd pictured him—short, wearing a white shirt with a droopy string bow tie. Instead of bulky, wooly leggings she was sure Cole Farrell wore, this man wore thigh-hugging shotgun chaps.

As she inspected his manly form, the image of her short gunfighter vanished, replaced by the handsome rogue before her. She let her gaze slide lower, curious to see if he wore a matching pair of pearl-handled Colt .45s, nestled in richly carved holsters. No, he had only one pistol strapped to his right hip, and the gun didn't appear very large or as intimidating as some she'd seen. But on this man, she doubted it needed to be.

Sleeping butterflies stirred awake in the pit of her stomach.

Her gaze continued downward, along the leather stretched tight around very manly thighs, then even lower. His leggings kept her from seeing his footwear, and she wondered if they were the stove-top style that were a gunslinger's favorite, or a shorter, more serviceable boot. Either way, she was almost sure they were void of spur straps and spurs.

"You cannot be Ira Farrell," she said, a little breathlessly. "I mean I was expecting someone much shor—older, not as . . . well," she paused, searching for the word, ". . . refined."

She inwardly scolded herself for sounding like a smitten schoolgirl. He had no way of knowing that she had pictured him much differently. No more than five feet, three inches tall. And a man who probably earned his overstated reputation because he was smaller and faster than the miscreants he faced.

But this man wasn't anything like what she had pictured.

"I'll take that as a compliment." His deep voice startled her back to reality.

Her head snapped up at the same moment warm color crept up her neck into her cheeks. Dear God, by his amused tone, and the slight smile tugging at the corners of his mouth, she knew she'd been caught staring. Acutely conscious of his dancing grey eyes, she cleared her throat, stalling while the butterflies settled. "I only have your word that you are who you say you are."

"Yes, ma'am. Now, if you'd put down that shooter, I'd be happy to escort you to the ranch." His expression was guarded, his eyes flickering from her face to the weapon she held in her hand.

"Then it's nearby?" she asked, hoping to sound more friendly, yet unwilling to completely trust him.

"Yes, ma'am," he said patiently. "Just a mile or two up the trail. Are they expecting you?"

"No. I've only just arrived from St. Louis," Sarah confirmed.

"Are you out here all alone?" he asked, frowning.

"I've no need for an escort. I assure you, I can take care of myself. I'm an excellent shot."

Much to her surprise, he relaxed his stance, pulled up his scarf, and then turned to swing up on his horse. He touched the brim of his hat. "Well, since you've no need of my help, I'll be heading back to the ranch." He paused and she could have sworn he was mocking her behind the scarf—sure of it the moment he spoke. "When you're ready for some help, just fire that little peashooter into the air. Someone's bound to hear."

"You don't mean to leave me out here?"

"I offered to take you to the ranch." He turned his horse to leave.

"How do I know you really are who you say you are? I don't see a badge," she said desperately. "You could be a cattle rustler. Why, just a moment ago, one of your kind nearly killed me."

He stopped his horse and looked at her over his shoulder. "One of my *kind?*" he repeated.

She swallowed hard, sensing she had offended him. But, he stopped, and that was all that mattered. Her feet were positively frozen now, and she had a tight knot forming in the pit of her stomach. "Yes. A-a hooligan."

He seemed to ponder that for a moment, and then added, "I reckon you'll have to trust me."

"I-I'm not in the habit of trusting strange men, especially those of unknown character."

His glinting grey eyes mocked her. "If you start walking in that direction, you'll be at the ranch in about an hour. I'll make sure there's hot coffee on the stove, and a warm fire in the hearth. You're going to need 'em both."

Ira gathered up his reins and made it look as if he was going to ride away. He had no intention of leaving her there, but he wasn't willing to let her know that. Not just yet. He'd ride to the trees and if she didn't call him back, he'd relent even if it did bruise his pride. But the young woman brazenly stepped up and caught Dakota's reins. She was as small as a child from his view on his horse, yet apparently had no fear of being stepped on by his horse. By the defiant angle of her chin and the rebellious gleam in her vibrant blue eyes, she wasn't about to let him ride off without her. He liked her spunk, that and the bronze-gold color of her hair.

No man in his right mind wouldn't have noticed that right away, derringer or no derringer.

Just then Dakota lowered his head and nuzzled the fur collar around her neck, blowing softly several times before he tried to take a little nibble.

31

"Stop that," she scolded, pushing the gelding's nose out of her face. "If you think you're going to ride away and leave me out here to freeze to death, you're sorely mistaken. I'm warning you, I will not hesitate to shoot."

Ira met her steady gaze as she pointed the gun back at his chest. "Let me get this straight. You're willing to gun me down for my horse?"

Some of the color left her cheeks. "No, of course not. I simply meant that—"

Just then muffled men's voices drew closer. If possible, she stiffened even more, her chin quivering ever so slightly. But she held her ground, then glanced in the direction the sound came. "Someone's coming."

He shrugged. "Maybe it's some more rustlers," he said, enjoying the way Dakota wouldn't leave her alone. Cole's voice carried over the treetops when he called Buster's name. "We're over here, Cole."

"Cole . . . Cole Farrell?" Sarah asked, with a tinge of color showing on her cheeks.

"Yup. My brother," Ira added with another lazy smile.

She dodged his horse's muzzle, and then quickly shoved her derringer into her pocket. She forced a strained smile. "Then you really must be Marshal Farrell." She let go of his reins to get away from Dakota's unwelcome advances, swiping at the horse slobber on her collar. "It seems I've made a dreadful mistake."

She paused, and he knew she was waiting for him to accept her apology, but he liked having the advantage. In fact, he even enjoyed watching her struggle with the right words. She sure was a pretty little thing, what with her cheeks and the tip of her nose pink from the cold. And she was stylish too, with that fancy fur and feathered bonnet tipped at a saucy angle on a pile of copper curls.

"I shouldn't have threatened you. Please accept my sincere apology."

Ira leaned his forearms on the saddle horn and shook his head. "That didn't sound very sincere, considering that just a few minutes ago you wanted to shoot me and take my horse."

A spark of anger momentarily narrowed her eyes. "Perhaps, but a lady cannot be too careful. Now that I'm thinking more clearly, no one in his right mind would be out robbing innocent people in this weather. I should have considered that before now."

"You should have considered the danger before riding alone into the mountains." He held out his hand, kicking his foot out of the stirrup. "Grab on and step in there. I'll pull you up."

"What about my horse?" she asked, settling in behind him.

"He'll be fine. Probably on the—"

"*She*. She's a mare."

He cast a quick glance in her direction, thinking she was kind of prickly. "*She's* half way back to Santa Fe by no' Miss . . . ?"

"Mrs.," she corrected, adjusting her skirts. "Mrs. Wellington."

Chapter Three

"What in tarnation?" An old man muttered another complaint as he rode out of the trees. He was followed by two
younger men. The old man nearly bumped into Ira as he
jerked his battered hat off his head, then gave Ira a hug,
darned near falling off his horse in the process. The old man
quickly collected himself, swiping at the moisture in his eyes.
He looked just like the pictures Sarah had seen of
cowpunchers. Only his hat was smaller than their big ten-
gallon hats, and he didn't have on fuzzy chaps. In fact, none
of the men were dressed like the pictures, nor did they have
handlebar moustaches or muttonchop sideburns.

"Well, I'll be a—" The other man's voice drew Sarah back
to the present. He was much younger than the old man. She
could see the family resemblance, only this man had a thick
moustache and his hair was darker than Ira's, with a little
curl, and longer, a trifle more unkempt. He nudged his horse
closer to Ira so they could shake hands. "Gosh darn, but you
a sight for sore eyes," he said with genuine emotion. "We
en't sure you'd come."

How are you, Cole." Ira returned his brother's handshake.
e youngest of the trio came over, impatiently waiting
others to move aside. Like his brothers, he was lean,
d, with Ira's tawny-colored hair. "Ira . . . I—" He
finish, and by the moisture glistening in the young
s, Sarah sensed he struggled to keep his composure.

34

Ira reached out and took the young man's hand in a firm, lingering grasp. "Last time I saw you, little brother, you were still wet behind the ears." They both laughed, then Ira let go of his hand, leaning a little to allow them all a better view of Sarah. "Mrs. Sarah Wellington. This is my Uncle Jeb, my brother, Cole, and this is my baby brother, Adam."

"How do you do?" she replied, smiling when both his brothers yanked off their hats and nodded.

"I ain't no baby, Ira," Adam replied, flashing Sarah a wide grin when both brothers corrected his English in unison. "We're pleased to meet you, ma'am."

"Did you happen to see another rider go by here a little bit ago?" Cole asked.

"I did, indeed." Sarah gave them a confident nod. "He nearly ran over me. Is he one of your hands?"

"No, ma'am," the three said in unison. Jeb finally remembered he was still holding his hat and shoved it back on his head. "We was chasin' him."

"Adam, the lady has lost her horse." Ira cued Dakota to walk on. "Mrs. Wellington has come all the way from Santa Fe to pay us a little unexpected visit. I'm sure she'd appreciate it if you'd go back down the trail and see if you can find her horse."

It was obvious that Ira and Cole traded glances, but she could not discern if it was a negative or positive exchange. Adam didn't seem to notice as he pushed his hat down on his head, gathered his reins and left to do as his brother asked.

The narrow trail was steep and forced Cole and Jebson to fall in behind Sarah and her escort. A little while later, she noted they were coming to the head of the trail. Unlike the small shack she expected, their home was large, a two-story house surrounded by ancient evergreens.

Once at the hitching post, Cole dismounted then reached

up to help her down. She placed her hands on his forearms and was somewhat surprised at how easily he lifted her down. Both brothers were tall and free with gentle smiles, but there was a sense of sadness too.

"Please, come inside and warm up by the fire," Cole offered. "Jeb makes a pretty mean cup of coffee."

She would have thanked him, but Ira swung down from his horse, drawing her attention. Oddly enough, just the sight of him—the fluid way he moved—filled her with a sense of foreboding. It was an unexplainable emotion she quickly contributed to his fearsome reputation. "Thank you for the ride, Marshal Farrell," she murmured, avoiding his vivid eyes.

"I don't remember you being so tall," Cole said, shaking his head as he held Ira at arm's length, before giving him a back-pounding hug. Cole stepped aside when Jeb tapped him on the shoulder.

"You don't know how glad we are to see you, son. What's it been, two years since your last letter?" Sarah noticed sorrow glistening in the old man's eyes as he gave his nephew a fierce bear hug.

"I'm sorry, Jeb. I should have written more often."

The old man swiped at his eyes and then forced a sad smile. "Come on inside. Cole'll take care of the horses, won't you, boy?"

"Sure. Go on in and make yourselves at home."

The interior of their home was even more impressive than the outside. As Sarah unbuttoned her coat and removed her hat, she glanced around. Though the walls were rustic logs, knots and all, it was apparent that a woman had, at one time, resided here.

Descriptive mountain-peak paintings adorned the walls, accented by several carefully stitched, colorful patchwork quilts. The quilts were sewn with various animal shapes depicted on each diagonal square. If a bear was done in green, the same color diamond surrounded it, blending with the browns, oranges, and earthy tones of the two huge braided-rag rugs.

A large, brown bear rug, with a stuffed head and large, declawed paws sprawled out between a massive rock-faced fireplace and a brown leather sofa. To the side of the hearth, black cast iron had been shaped into an upright circle, which was filled with chopped and split logs. Though she had never seen wood stored in anything other than a box, this design seemed to fit well with the decor.

Even the tables were unique, hand carved from knotty pine, scored by a hot iron with smaller versions of the large brand she'd noticed above the front door. To the right of the enormous living room was a warm and inviting kitchen.

From her vantage point, she could see a more formal dining room on the other side of the kitchen. To her left was a sitting room. As she turned her attention back to the fire, she admired a huge rifle rack hanging above the thick wooden mantel. The mantel seemed to be part of the support structure of the entire wall. On top were small, framed portraits of children—all boys. Another was of an attractive woman and a man who couldn't be anyone other than the brothers' parents.

"Your home is lovely," she said to no one in particular as the men hung up their coats and hats on pegs by the front door. "It's not at all what I expected."

"I'll take that as a compliment," came Ira's teasing voice, and she knew instantly he was referring to their encounter in the forest. "May I take your coat?"

She turned in time to match his smile, noticing the absence of a badge on his chest. She'd read enough about him to wonder how one man could have such a fearsome reputation, starting as a young gunfighter and now working as a United States Marshal. In the west, it was a common practice to thwart lawlessness using lawless men.

She rather doubted the real story of Ira Farrell was as grand as the papers made him out to be. The articles she'd read had been written by members of the man's own gender, and everyone knew how men like to brag and blow things out of proportion.

After he hung up her coat, Ira went to the hearth and picked up the poker to stir the coals. On the rock hearth sat a brass bucket filled with smaller sticks and chunks of wood from which he chose several thin pieces. When they were in flames, he added a split log, then stood and dusted off his hands on the back of his Levis.

A quick, careful inspection confirmed her first impression. He was well built, and appeared to be solid masculine muscle. Once more a tiny jolt of uneasiness tightened in the pit of her stomach. The man was far too handsome for his own good, and when their eyes met, his were far too intense.

With a sudden rush of heat to her cheeks, she realized that while she had been studying him, he had been measuring her as well. She turned quickly back to the fire in the hopes he hadn't noticed. Yet she couldn't deny that his gaze had felt like a silent caress, one that held a hidden promise. But, of what? She might pretend to be married, but she couldn't pretend to know a man's mind.

She watched the flames lick hungrily at the bark on the log. What right did he think he had to look at her in such a manner, especially after she had informed him of her name? Was he the type to openly flirt with a married woman? The thought banished all feelings of awe and replaced them with disdain. The man after all was no more than a hired gun.

Maybe he had been empowered by the government to do so legally, but in her mind, he was no better than the outlaws he captured.

"Is there something on your mind?" he asked. She met his gaze, wishing he wasn't so handsome. It would be easier to distance herself if he looked more like the short little gunfighter she had envisioned.

She realized she'd been frowning, and forced a smile. "As a matter of fact, Marshal Farrell, there is."

He motioned to the table in the kitchen just as Cole came inside and hung up his hat and coat. "The coffee's almost ready. Why don't you have a seat, and if you feel the need, you can tell us what's bothering you."

If you feel the need, she silently fumed. He followed her to the table, but it was Cole who pulled out her chair. A moment later, Jeb placed a mug filled with steaming hot coffee before her while Ira collected a small bowl of sugar and a pitcher of cream from the counter.

After everyone was seated, Ira added a little cream to his coffee then leaned back and draped one arm over the back of his chair. "Well, Mrs. Wellington, to what do we owe the honor of your visit?"

She stirred her coffee, feeling three pairs of interested male eyes on her every move. "I've come for Emily Brighton's personal things."

A sudden heaviness fell over the room. Jeb's features grew somber. He dropped his gaze to the cup between his weathered old hands. Cole's expression changed too, but Ira's remained the same. Did this cool reserve come from years of looking down the barrel of a gun into the face of death?

"I am assuming you are family to Emily?" Ira asked when it seemed the others couldn't speak.

"Yes. She and I are . . . were cousins."

39

He paused to take another sip of his coffee. "Then you've brought proof of your claim?" he asked.

"Are you always so suspicious, Marshal Farrell?"

Cole cleared his throat, stopping his brother's retort. "I don't think Ira meant to insult you, ma'am. It's just that we didn't think Miss Emily had any living relatives."

She forced her gaze away from Ira's, and then softened her expression. "That's quite all right, Mr. Farrell. I should have realized that all you have to go on is my word. However, due to an unfortunate encounter in the forest, my horse escaped along with my identification."

"Then I reckon we'll wait until Adam returns. Then you can prove you're who you say you are." Ira rose from his chair. "More coffee?"

She forced herself to return his coy smile, but just like his, the good intent of it didn't quite reach her eyes. "Thank you."

"So," Cole began, drawing her attention. "Where are you from?"

"St. Louis."

"I remember Emily saying something about St. Louis," Cole confirmed. Again there was a definite somber tone in his voice that his friendly smile denied. "Tell us, how do you like Santa Fe so far?"

Ira sat down and she felt his gaze like one would feel the heat sitting too close to a fire. "I haven't had much time to draw any conclusions. What I know of the West has been acquired from books and other people's accounting. However," she stated, adding a little more cream to her coffee, "most of what I've read seems to be overstated."

"Really," Cole asked. "How so?"

She frantically searched for a word that she could use. What would they think if she told them that she had hoped

40

that Santa Fe would be more *wild* and more *wooly* and *exciting*—and that she was very disappointed. "It's quite . . . how should I put it . . . civilized. Yes. Santa Fe is very civilized."

"I'll grant you it's not as fancy as St. Louis," Cole defended, "but, we're trying. New Mexico isn't even a state yet."

"Who wants civilization anyway?" Jeb stated with a disgusted snort. "Personally, I like things the way they were. The more city folks start comin', the more they'll be wantin' to change everything." Jeb pushed away from the table. "I'm goin' to go finish muckin' out the barn till Adam gets back."

Cole heaved an uneasy sigh. "How far can a horse go?" he muttered, looking at his brother.

"If she was rented in Santa Fe, she'd head back that way, and without a rider, I reckon she could make it home in no time at all."

"Well, Mrs. Wellington, if Adam can't get back in time . . ." Cole glanced at the grandfather clock against the far wall. ". . . and right now it isn't looking too good, we'd like you to stay the night."

"Though I'm grateful for the courtesy, I have none of my things here, and it wouldn't be . . . it just wouldn't be proper, Mr. Farrell."

"Ma'am?" Cole asked with a puzzled frown.

"The lady's trying to tell you that it wouldn't be respectable for her to be spending the night with four unattached men and no other female around to keep us civilized. Isn't that right, Mrs. Wellington?"

The marshal's eyes danced with barely contained knavery, and she wondered again why she found him so interesting when she knew from working at the *Herald* that arrogant men were the worst kind.

41

"I suppose you're correct, Marshal Farrell." She gave Cole her best smile, thwarting any further humor on Ira's part. "Since it seems I have no other choice, I shall accept your charitable offer."

Cole stood and motioned toward the stairs. "Allow me to show you to a room."

Sarah rose, then looked down at Ira, whom she suspected had purposely remained seated. He was full of himself, all right. Probably read some of the stories written about him and believed them. She tipped her head his direction with a less-than-polite smile, then followed Cole up the stairs. A long braided rug made the hardwood floors of the wide hall seem much warmer.

"I apologize for my brother, Mrs.—"

"There's no need, Mr. Farrell. I've dealt with his kind before."

"Really?" Cole opened a door and let her walk in before him. Like the rest of the house it was wonderfully done in shades of rose and mint green. It was delightfully feminine and inviting. Cole knelt down by a pot-bellied stove. "Ira's been away a long time. I'm curious. In what category would you place my brother?"

"I beg your pardon?" she asked, caught off guard.

Cole struck a match to light the stove, and the smell of sulfur teased her nose. "You said you've dealt with my brother's type before. I was just wondering what type you think he is?"

She strolled around the spacious room, fingering the Spanish lace panels under the heavier, velvet-trimmed, brocade drapery. "Not to be discourteous, but it's apparent your brother believes he's something special. In short, Mr. Farrell, the marshal is conceited and egotistical."

Cole added several chunks of wood then closed the little

42

door and stood. "Whew, that's a mouthful, but I reckon you've hit the nail on the head."

His smile matched the humor in his eyes as he wiped his hands off on the back of his pants. "There's lots of wood in this bin if you get cold. There are clothes in the wardrobe and dresser, and I'll bet they'll fit. They belonged to Miss Emily. Since she and Zach were planning to get married, she brought some of her things up here."

He hesitated at the door with his hand on the knob. "Ira's not as bad as you think. As the oldest of us boys, and with our ma dying young, he grew up fast. If I were you . . ." He gave her one of his generous smiles as he smoothed his moustache. ". . . I wouldn't believe everything you read. I'll come get you for supper if you'd like to take a little rest."

"Thank you, Mr. Farrell, I'd like that."

"My name is Cole, ma'am. Feel free to use it."

Once he'd left, she sank down on the feather mattress, suddenly more tired than she cared to admit. So this had been Emily's room when she had visited? She ran her hand over the fluffy comforter, wishing they had been closer.

But time and distance had played havoc on their relationship, as well as the fact that all Emily ever wanted was a good man to take care of. And, having just met his brothers, Sarah suspected that Zachary Farrell had been a good man. Jeb, Adam and Cole had done their best to make her feel welcome. It was plain to see that they were suffering Emily's loss as much as they were Zach's death.

Cole Farrell was polite, Adam was shy, and their uncle, though a little cranky, did his best to make her feel welcome. But it wasn't Cole or Jeb or even young Adam that left her stewing. It was Ira.

Obviously, he was a disrespectful male who had experienced feminine adoration on more than one occasion. Not only was he openly daring, he was audacious . . . granted, in a very masculine way. However, he should have shown more respect to a married lady. Especially a lady mourning the death of a family member, she thought to herself.

She removed her boots and stretched out on the comfortable bed. Ira Farrell could hardly be blamed. Wasn't it her own gender that had staunchly enforced his high opinion of himself?

"Of course it was," she muttered as she rolled onto her side. "Women all over the world are taught from birth that they are less than men. They are expected to grovel at their man's feet, kiss his hand and be eternally grateful that he pays them any attention at all. Love, honor and *obey*," she murmured, punching the pillow.

"Perhaps it's time the rambunctious little town of Santa Fe is awakened to the women's suffrage movement." She pulled a throw off the end of the bed and covered herself, suddenly very tired. Her bogus identity caused a sly smile, but the thought of a gun-slinging marshal lingered in the back of her mind. She had a lot to do, for sure, but when the time was right, she'd write Ira's story from a woman's point of view.

Chapter Four

"Well, did you get the lady settled in?" Ira asked.

"Yes, I did." After he refilled their cups, Cole took the seat across from Ira. "What's going on between the two of you?"

"Why do you ask?" Ira countered with a teasing smile.

"Did something happen before we found you?"

"Let's just say the lady isn't as helpless as you'd think. You should have seen her when she was holding me at gunpoint. She's tougher than she looks."

"So that's it. She got the better of you, and you don't like it." He purposely didn't give Ira time to respond. "She looks a lot like Emily."

Ira knew by the shadow that passed over Cole's features that he was thinking about Miss Emily and Zach. Old unwanted memories slapped Ira in the face with such force he momentarily closed his eyes to block them out, and he heaved a tired sigh. "Where is he, Cole?"

"Up on the rise with Ma and Pa. Miss Emily's there too." Cole cleared his throat. "I didn't think you'd mind, seeing that she had no family here. And what with the wedding only a few weeks—"

"No, it's fine." Both men were quiet for several moments. "Damn, but I forgot how cold it gets up here in the fall."

"We were hoping you'd be along today." Cole got up and added more wood to the fire. "I didn't notice a badge when

45

you hung up your coat. Does it mean you might be thinking of staying on?"

Ira didn't miss his brother's hopeful expression. "It just means I chose not to wear it while I was on the trail."

"I was hoping—"

"I know what you were hoping, but I decided ten years ago that I'm no rancher."

"You're more a rancher than you are a lawman," Cole confirmed. "Ranching's in our blood, Ira."

"Maybe in yours and Adam's, but it's not in mine."

"Don't say that," Jeb ordered as he came inside and hung up his coat.

"You take up eavesdropping, Uncle Jeb?" Ira teased.

"Don't you get smart with me, boy. Your voice carries. Why you're lucky you're still alive. Hell's bells, even up here we hear the rumors—the stories about your reputation. Any day now, I expect to see a dime novel with the title of *Ira Farrell, Fastest Gun in the West*."

"You read a lot of those, do you?" Ira grinned as Jeb filled a cup with coffee and joined them at the table.

Jeb gave him a sour look. "Hell no, but I gotta say, it scares me some."

Ira looked at his cup, unwilling to lie to his uncle's face. "Like you said, they're just rumors."

"Then you deny that gunslingers don't hunt you down just to see if you're faster than they are?" Cole challenged.

"Rumors," Ira repeated, rocking back on his chair. He inwardly winced at his brother's doubtful expression, and at the same time, he worried that some young gun in Santa Fe would suddenly get brave once word got out that he was in town. He hoped not. He didn't want his family to know that what Cole suspected had happened on several occasions in Arizona.

"What's it like being a lawman?" Cole asked, taking a sip

of his coffee and drawing Ira back from his somber thoughts. "I heard you get paid more than any other marshal this side of Kansas, and that you only have to walk into a bar fight and it stops."

Ira grinned. "Not exactly. I was a starving deputy for a long time. But it got better after a while."

"You should turn in your badge and stay," Cole stated.

"Great-grandpa Ira," Jeb began, "who you were named after, case you forgot, homesteaded this land, brought cattle all the way from Nebraska. Beau's great-grandson is on the south pasture keeping up the family tradition."

Ira laughed and shook his head. "So let me get this straight. You named another bull calf Beau?"

"Not me," Jeb said, with a nod toward Cole. "Him. Reckon Cole wanted to keep up the tradition." Jeb refilled their cups then put the pot back on the stove. "Maybe now that you're back, things will settle down some."

"What kind of *things*?"

Cole leaned a little closer. "I suppose there's no easy way to tell you, but things have been going on around here the last few years, Ira. A while back, we had some of the other ranchers accuse us of blocking their water. When we went to investigate, we found that someone had tossed a bunch of old logs upstream. We settled it peaceful and all, but old man Roland, who owns the ranch south, accused Adam of tossing salt in his well. Since that time, if anything strange happens, we're the first to blame."

"Surely you can prove you're innocent," Ira added, frowning.

"We tried to, but nothing's happened to us, casting even more doubt our way. Lately, some cattle and horses are missing, a few found on our land. That just about got us in deep trouble."

"Did Sheriff Porter check it out?" Ira asked.

"Old man Porter's been gone three years. Retired and went up to Wyoming to live with his daughter. Cooper Finch is the sheriff now. Do you remember him?" Cole took a drink of his coffee.

"I don't recognize the name."

"Well, he used to have a spread south of Bear Canyon, joining our land, but he couldn't make the payments, so I bought him out. It wasn't friendly, if you know what I mean." Cole took another sip of coffee. "Cooper said he checked things out, but he's not much of a lawman, usually just sends out one of his deputies. We managed to convince the man that the animals were strays. You remember Pa's drover, Micah, don't you?"

Ira nodded. "Vaguely."

"Well, just when we thought things were calming down, something must have spooked his horse real bad. When we found him, he'd been dragged. You know how rough it is up here. We suspect he probably broke his neck in the trees."

"Do you think it was murder?" Ira asked, remembering Mayor James's suspicions.

Jeb shrugged his shoulders. "We've had a few wolves, a big cat on occasion up near Cougar Bluff, and you know how spring is when the mama bears come out hungry as hell. But we couldn't find any tracks and when we went to Hermosa Meadow to check it out, the horses didn't act like they got the scent of anything wild." Jeb scratched his chin. "However, Sheriff Finch said he found some tracks."

"What kind of tracks?" Ira asked.

"Mountain lion." Jeb shook his head and Ira knew his old uncle didn't believe it. "Maybe he did, but, when we found Micah, he was whole." Jeb went to the stove and lifted the

48

kettle. "We've been up here long enough to know if something wants to eat you, it usually does."

"So, there you have it, Ira." Cole heaved a long sigh. "A couple of the hands got nervous and left, but we've hired a few new boys, and since we pay them better than most, we've been able to keep things quiet up here."

"What about the Cattlemen's Coalition?" Ira asked, remembering how his father had organized the other ranches to keep the government from reducing their grazing rights. "I assume it's still in full force."

Cole's chair scraped on the floor as he pushed away from the table and stood. "Did I tell you that Silas Pruitt took over? Him and James Roland? Since that happened, the coalition is as useless as teats on a boar hog. I don't even bother to go to the meetings anymore. The other ranchers don't trust us like they used to."

"Regardless," Jeb said, rubbing his hand over his balding head. "Every ranch in the area is missing stock. A few of the smaller spreads have gone under. We thought about buying them out, but then knew it'd make us look guilty."

Cole raised his cup and finished his coffee, setting the mug down with a thump. "So, how long are you planning to stay?"

Ira didn't miss the worry creasing Jeb's brow, or the anxiousness in Cole's blue eyes. "A lawman from Albuquerque was killed up here about a month ago. He was kin to my boss. I'm supposed to stay in Santa Fe, ask a few questions and see if I can find out anything about it."

Cole shook his head. "I remember hearing something about a man getting mauled over by the Roland ranch now that you mention it. I didn't know he was a lawman. Seems word spread that he was one of Roland's or maybe Pruitt's hands. Didn't pay it much mind."

"That's interesting. He died kind of sudden-like, after he

wrote his wife that he'd finished his assignment and was planning on going home."

"I've got to be honest with you, Ira," Cole began, leaning against the back of his chair. "None of us trust Silas or James Roland much, and neither did Zachary. But other than just a gut feeling, I've got nothing to explain it."

"Except that, of all the ranchers, Pruitt's and Roland's spreads are prospering," Jeb added with a tinge of disgust in his voice. "The rest of us are just hanging on."

"There's something else you should know," Cole added cautiously. "The night Zachary and Emily died, Zachary told me that she'd sent him a message. I still have it if you want to see it, but all it says is that she had something important to tell Zach."

Jeb struck a match and puffed on his pipe until smoke swirled toward the pine rafters. "In her note, Miss Emily said she didn't feel safe writing it down on paper, case it got into the wrong hands. So, as soon he could, Zach went to town." Jeb stared at his cup, quiet for several long moments. "That was the last time we saw him alive." The old man sniffed then shook his head. "I still can't believe he's gone."

Ira swallowed, forcing the tightness in his throat to subside, and praying his voice wouldn't betray the pain. He'd always been the strong one—the one that told the younger brothers about their ma's death—the one that held them together. "So you never found out what she wanted?"

"No," Cole finished solemnly. "They both died in the fire. When the sheriff came out here with the news, he said they got water to it right away, but Zach and Miss Emily breathed in too much smoke."

Jeb heaved a long tired sigh and pushed away from the table. "But that don't mean someone didn't start it."

Ira frowned at his uncle's grim prediction. "Didn't Zachary have his gun?"

"Sure. He never went anywhere without it." The old man began to side off the table, tears welling in his eyes.

"I've got it and all his personal stuff in a box upstairs," said Cole.

"Did you check it?" Ira asked.

Jeb stopped on his way to the kitchen, looking at Ira over his shoulder. "Check it for what?"

"To see if it had been fired?" He silently cursed himself when he noticed Cole's stricken expression. Ira wished he hadn't mentioned it. Hell, Cole was a rancher, not a gunman.

"We never thought to," Cole answered.

"Well, we should. It might tell us something."

Jeb turned with a perplexed frown. "How's a damned pistol goin' to tell us if Zachary was murdered or not?"

Ira kept his tone nonconfrontational. "I'd like to have a look."

"Sure." Cole nodded. "I guess there's no time like the present."

Ira stood and motioned toward the staircase. "Lead the way." He followed Cole upstairs and into Zachary's room. Everywhere he looked he saw reminders of his kid brother— the Navajo blanket spread on the floor, the braided horsehair bridle hanging on a wooden peg the boy carved himself above the four-poster bed. Ira picked up his brother's hat, running his fingers over the perfectly shaped crown and flicking the eagle feather stuck in the leather hatband. That horrible knot formed in his chest again.

"It's in here."

From the tone of Cole's voice, Ira knew his brother was having a hard time too. Ira lifted the lid of the large wooden box at the foot of the bed. Another of Zach's creations, the lid had his initials on the top and it was lined with cedar.

On top of a well-worn pink-and-yellow quilt rested a couple of envelopes with feminine handwriting on them, a few pieces of women's jewelry, and Zach's silver-and-turquoise belt buckle and his holster and pistol. Ira touched the quilt. "Do you remembering Ma making this?" He didn't wait for Cole to answer. "I do. I remember Ma telling me I was going to have a new baby sister." Ira smiled at Cole. "She was so sure. That's why she used pink."

"All I remember," Cole added with a sad smile, "is when Zach got to be about four, he tucked that under the bed. I don't think he used it again after I teased him about the color."

Ira lifted the belt buckle from the box and ran his thumb over the smooth, greenish-blue stones. "I sent him this for his sixteenth birthday."

"Yeah," Cole acknowledged. "It was his favorite and for a while we thought maybe we should bury him with it. But, then I thought maybe you'd like it as a kind of keepsake."

Ira didn't look up—couldn't bear to see the grief he heard in his brother's voice.

"Neither one was bad . . . you know what I mean. The fire was put out quick enough, but the smoke killed them. We buried him in the suit Emily made him for the wedding." Cole dragged his arm over his eyes. "He sure did look nice . . . would have had our hides had he guessed we'd take the time to gussy him up and all."

Ira nodded. He wanted to say more, to comfort Cole, but couldn't find the words. Instead he thought about Zach and the way he was always the last to get dressed for any special occasion, and how, when he was a child, their mother practically had to hog-tie him to get him in the tub or to cut his hair.

"I should have come home for a visit," Ira said tightly before he realized he'd spoken out loud.

"He would have liked that." Cole picked up the holster and ran his fingers over Zach's initials. "Don't go punishing yourself for it. He never knew what it was like for you around here, but Adam and I did. If we'd been in your boots, we probably wouldn't have wanted to come home either."

Ira had to think of something else or the grief would surely kill him. "Let me see that." He took the holster from Cole's hands and then slid the pistol from its leather keeper, testing it for weight out of habit. "This is a Colt Frontier Double Action," he murmured, holding it up to check the sights before he opened the cylinder. His dark brows drew tightly together. "It's been fired."

"What are you saying?" Cole questioned, his gaze narrowing.

"There's gunpowder residue and a bullet missing. Now, I can't be sure about you or Adam or Zach, but Pa taught me that if I fired my weapon once or six times, I had always better replace the empty cartridges in case there came a time when I needed six shots in a hurry."

"Yeah, he taught us the same thing," Cole added, taking the pistol for a closer look. "Zach was always careful with this. It's not like him to leave a chamber open."

"Unless he died before he could fill it," Ira added grimly. He took the Colt and shoved it back in the holster. "Let's keep this to ourselves for now, Cole."

"Why? Where's the logic in that?" Cole demanded. "If I'm hearing what you're not saying, you're starting to think Uncle Jeb is right—that someone purposely torched the shop with Zach and Emily in it. With you here, there's four of us. We could ride into town and tear the place apart if we needed to."

"Cole, listen to me. Except for a missing bullet, we have no proof. Somebody could get hurt."

"Ira, if Zach was murdered, I'll promise you this: somebody will get hurt, 'cause I'll find him and kill him myself."

Ira sighed impatiently. "If it was that easy, don't you think I'd let you? I just lost a brother. I won't lose another one on a suspicion. Until I can find out what or who Zach was shooting at, you've got to trust me on this. I know what I'm doing. It's better, for now, that Jeb and Adam think Zach's death was an accident. I don't need their interference."

"All right. *For now*, I'll let you do things your way. But don't you think for one minute, if things get hot, that you're going to deal with it alone. I know that's how you handled things when we were growing up. How you sacrificed yourself for the sake of us, but I'm older now. I can help."

Ira put his hand on his brother's shoulder. "Just give me some time, Cole. I'll be taking a room in Santa Fe for a little while so I can conduct an investigation on the marshal that was mauled to death. I'll also be looking into what or *who* caused the fire that killed our brother. If I need you, I'll send for you."

"If that marshal was murdered, and if Zach and Miss Emily were murdered, you could be getting in over your head."

"I'll be careful." Ira gave Cole a slightly amused smile. "After all, I'm a United States Marshal. I have jurisdiction over any suspected crime in this fine country by order of our illustrious president. And if that doesn't convince the good citizens of Santa Fe to cooperate, I'll just use the old standby."

"And what's that?" Cole asked.

Ira gave Cole a teasing look. "Why, my fearsome reputation. What else?"

54

After the brothers put the mementoes back in the box, Ira went down the hall to his old room. For the second time in ten long years, he thought about the promise he'd made his father never to return. He'd kept that promise until now. Not even when the old man died did Ira feel the need to visit. But now his youngest brother was dead, buried in the family cemetery on the ridge.

Ira glanced out the window. How many times, as the oldest of the four boys, did he accept responsibility for a wrongdoing he had no hand in? Punishment was always private, out behind the barn. It was the reason he left. He had too many scars on his back and in his mind to be that forgiving. Yet he couldn't help wondering, if he had stayed, would Zach still be alive?

The deep, chest-crushing pain returned and he fought the urge to give into it.

Chapter Five

Sarah awoke from her nap to the smell of roasted meat and fresh biscuits. She swung her legs over the side of the bed at the same time her stomach rumbled. She smoothed the white blouse back into the waistband of her skirt and adjusted the small cameo at the collar. After a quick check in the oval mirror above the six-drawer dresser, and a few corrections to the curls piled on the top of her head, she stepped out into the hall, nearly bumping into Ira Farrell.

He was nicely dressed in a crisp white shirt and gold, high-fastening, brocade vest. A brown silk ascot was neatly knotted around his collar, secured with a silver-and-turquoise stickpin. In fact, he looked so dashing he could have passed for a St. Louis businessman.

"Well, good evening, Mrs. Wellington. I was just coming to tell you supper is ready."

"Good evening, Marshal Farrell." She turned to leave, but he caught her elbow.

"Ira . . . my name's Ira." His gaze raked boldly over her and even when she tried to pull away, he would not relinquish his hold. "Allow me to escort you to the table."

"If you insist," she said tersely. "However, I feel it's only fair to warn you. Since childhood, I've found I am quite capable of walking on my own."

His soft laughter surprised her.

"Was I being too assertive?" he asked with a feigned look

of innocence.

"Assertive?" she repeated as they reached the head of the stairs. "Perhaps pugnacious is a more appropriate word."

"Pugnacious?" He shook his head and gave a slight shrug. "I'm not sure I like the sound of that, Mrs. Wellington."

She gave him a haughty smile. "I'm sure."

He frowned as they started down the stairs. "Do you really think I'm *antagonistic* towards you? After all, I didn't hold *you* at gunpoint."

He stopped when she did. Unable to help herself, she stared up at him. Not only was the man a flirt, it was apparent he had achieved a higher education. Certainly more than what she thought a man of his caliber would have obtained. His expression was dubious except for the twinkle of mischief in his laughing, silvery grey eyes.

"Shall we?" he asked, motioning toward the room below. "I believe they are waiting on us."

"Yes, of course," she replied a little too quickly. After he pulled out her chair, she refused to look at him again until everyone was seated in the more formal dining room.

The table was set with fine china and highly polished silver. Two elegant candleholders with long slender candles added a rather calming effect, aided by the light from a cheerful fire in a brass and lapis fireplace. Unlike the rest of the house, the walls were plastered and painted the lightest shade of yellow, and held more paintings of the New Mexican landscape. She thought to inquire about their mother, but then decided against it. Obviously, she'd had excellent taste and insisted some civility be incorporated into her sons' daily lives as ranchers.

To Sarah's dismay, Ira took a place directly across from hers. Cole sat at the head of the table, and Adam on the other end. Jeb came in from the kitchen with a white apron on over a white shirt and dark-brown trousers. Apparently the family's cook, he placed a huge platter of roasted meat and a plate piled high with fresh biscuits in the middle of the table next to the gravy boat.

"Peas and taters are comin' out next," he stated with a nod of self-satisfaction. He hooked a forefinger into his collar and gave it a tug just before he headed back toward the kitchen.

"Wine, Mrs. Wellington?" Cole asked as he removed a cork from a well-aged bottle.

"Please," she replied. Gone were the flannel shirts and Levis, replaced with pressed trousers and freshly laundered white shirts. She had the urge to giggle. Dressed up in all their finery, they looked self-conscious—almost as if they were a group of sinners waiting for the preacher and his wife to join them for Sunday dinner.

The only one who appeared comfortable was Ira. His stately attire suited him, and she found herself wondering if it was because, as a United States Marshal, he was required to attend meetings with government officials.

Cole filled her crystal goblet, followed by Ira's, then his own, and lastly Adam's. By the absence of a goblet before their uncle's place, she assumed Jeb didn't drink wine. Feeling their gazes upon her, she took a sip, and then smiled. "Excellent."

The food was passed around, the men waiting until she had made her choices. Once more she admired the proficiency of their mother in teaching her sons etiquette in such a wild and untamed region of the West.

"So, Mr. Farrell," she began, and all four of them looked at her. She gave a small laugh, aware that they had no way to know to whom she was speaking. "May I call you all by your given names?"

They all nodded, and then she turned to the youngest. "Adam?" she asked.

"Yes, ma'am," the young man answered with a slight reddening of his cheeks. Like his brothers Adam was a handsome man, but not as quick with a smile. In the short time she had known him, Adam seemed to keep his feelings well guarded, more like Ira than Cole.

"Were you able to recover my horse?"

He dabbed at his mouth with a white linen napkin. "Yes, ma'am. She made it clear down to the fork before I caught up with her. I've bedded her down in the barn." He looked as if he had something more to say then stopped.

"Adam is our resident expert when it comes to horses," Cole said, obviously proud of his younger brother. "He's got a way with them that's hard to explain. I've seen him take a wild mustang and after only a few hours, the horse'll be eating out of his hand."

"Are you hiding apple chunks in your glove again?" Ira teased.

Sarah glanced at Adam, smiling when he met her gaze then quickly turning his attention to Ira.

"You were always good with horses," Adam replied. "I remember when you lived here, the summer before you left, you decided you wanted Dakota even though he was a rangy two-year-old and no one could ride him without getting bucked off. Remember?"

Ira gave a lazy grin. "I'll never forget. He almost killed me. I should have chosen an older horse."

Male laugher bounced around the table at a memory she wished she could share.

"Well, I remember a time that had us all mending fence for a week." Jeb stuffed his napkin a little deeper into the collar of his shirt before he stabbed another slice of meat.

Sarah enjoyed the ornery gleam in the old man's eyes. "Pray tell, don't keep me in suspense."

Jeb pointed at Ira with his dinner knife. "This one and Cole were always gettin' into trouble. One day, I guess they didn't have enough work to do or somethin' like that. Anyway, they decided to wage a little contest about who could rope a calf faster."

"Uncle Jeb," Ira interrupted. "Isn't there another story you could choose?"

"Oh, no, please," Sarah encouraged. "I shall simply perish if I can't hear the rest of it."

Ira raised one dark brow. "Well, we certainly wouldn't want that, now would we, boys?"

She ignored his sarcasm. "Tell us more."

"Well," Jeb began, "Cole bested Ira ropin' calves . . . what was it? The fastest two outta three?"

"Yes, it was," Cole replied with a rather superior grin. "I actually roped all three in the same span of time it took Ira to rope two."

"You cheated," Ira muttered under his breath. His slight smile denied any hard feelings.

"Boys, I was tellin' this story," Jeb scolded. "Well, they weren't content with calves. I reckon they weren't challengin' enough for 'em. So the next thing I noticed is that they rode over to the west pasture and were pestering the yearlings."

"I believe I won that contest," Ira said with an arrogant nod, laughter lighting up his eyes.

"Why, you did, indeed," Cole confirmed, raising his glass in mock salute. "If memory serves, I had to go borrow a rope. Someone had cut mine just deep enough to have it snap on my first try."

"Must have been an old rope," Ira countered.

"No, it—"

"I ain't goin' to tell you boys again," Jeb warned with a feigned look of annoyance. He took a sip of water, then cleared his throat. "As I was sayin', these two were very competitive. Guess it's 'cause they are only a little over a year apart." Jeb squinted at Ira. "How old are you now . . . twenty-seven?"

"Twenty-eight."

"Yeah, well, after they moved on up the line to some rangy ol' steers, I thought that maybe they were through. That is until Ira, here, threw a rope over Beau."

"Who or what is Beau, if I may ask?" Sarah could tell by Cole's and Adam's expressions they were close to bursting at the seams. She glanced at Ira. He had an ornery smile as he casually toyed with the stem of his goblet.

Jeb made a great show of putting down his knife and fork. "I'll tell you what Beau is. He's plumb near thirteen hundred pounds of mean, ornery, male bovine. In other words, Mrs. Wellington, he's one son-of-a-buck, ill-mannered, contemptuous, disrespectful, stubborn bull."

She stifled a giggle. "Oh, I see." She met Ira's gaze, then gave him one of her best smiles. "Stubborn you say . . . sounds like someone I've met recently."

"Allow me to explain," Cole interjected. "Beau, at least the Beau back then, was never confined in any manner. There wasn't a rope made that could hold him—no rope, no corral, no fence. The only thing that kept him on our property was the abundance of cows my father kept in Beau's pasture."

"My, a conceited male . . . bovine, how interesting."

The men grinned at her good-natured taunt.

"That there is God's truth," Jeb confirmed with a nod. "Well, Cole told Ira that no man alive could rope ol' Beau, then dared Ira to try it."

"And did he pick up the proverbial gauntlet?" Sarah asked, turning her attention once more to the subject of the story. "Even after you knew the bull couldn't be restrained?"

"I'm a stubborn man," Ira replied, meeting her gaze. "If anyone says it can't be done, I'm usually tempted to try it."

"And he did," Cole added. "But what's worse, he talked me into helping him."

"Yup, he did for sure," Jeb agreed. "Well, these two knuckleheads lassoed that cursed animal. And let me tell you, Beau was not at all impressed. The first toss of that massive head yanked Cole and Ira right outta their saddles. The second toss pulled the rope right out of Cole's hands, but Ira didn't let go until *after* he'd been dragged over a hundred feet of mountain pasture. But that didn't stop ol' Beau, no ma'am. Once he shook free of Ira, Beau charged on and tore down plumb near a mile of barbed wire fence. Finally he got both ropes hung up in a bunch of broken fence posts where we were able to catch up, doctor his cuts and scratches, then set him free, and then we darn near got trampled. Me and their father were madder than two roosters in a cock fight."

Adam laughed, then shook his head, looking at Ira with a hint of admiration. "I'll bet you couldn't sit down for a week."

"Yup," Ira replied. "It was at least a week."

Sarah thought to add an insult of her own, but when she glanced at Ira, the humor in his eyes had faded. A quick look at Cole conjured up even more curiosity. Cole's expression had changed from amused to sympathetic. Even Adam suddenly looked a little uncomfortable.

Ira pushed away from the table, gathered up his plate and turned toward the kitchen. "Let me help you collect these dishes, Uncle Jeb. Then we can serve the pie and coffee."

"What's got him all riled up?" Jeb muttered with a dumb-founded expression.

Cole shook his head. "I guess we remember it a little differently, Uncle Jeb."

"Well, it was funny, if you ask me. Come on, Adam, pick up those plates and help us in the kitchen." Jeb and Adam got up and carried several dishes away.

"More wine?" Cole asked with a genuine smile.

"No, thank you." She put her napkin down then teased the edges. "I apologize if I encouraged your uncle to reveal something he shouldn't have."

"No, it wasn't you. It's a good story. It's just that Jeb and Ira have two different opinions on the ending."

"Dare I ask you to elaborate?"

"Our father was a harsh taskmaster." Cole added some wine to his glass then set the bottle down and took a sip before finishing. "Pa used to—" Cole hesitated, staring at his glass. "Ira's the oldest and he used to take the blame for Adam and Zach more times than I care to remember."

"I see." She toyed with the stem of her glass. "May I assume he also took your punishment as well?"

Cole's smile didn't quite reach his eyes. "Yes, ma'am, he did, and I think he still would if the occasion ever presented itself."

"Cole Farrell, what secrets are you disclosing now?" Ira asked as he carried in a tray filled with cups of hot coffee. "I knew I shouldn't have left the room." He put a cup before her, winking when their gazes met, then turned away and set one in front of Cole, thwarting any opportunity she might have had to remind him she was a married woman.

"You didn't tell her about the time I turned over Mrs. Pruitt's outhouse, did you?"

Cole laughed. "Was that you? All these years and I never knew for sure."

"Is that something you do often, Marshal Farrell?" Sarah asked, adding a little cream to her cup.

"No, ma'am, just on special occasions. If I remember correctly it was Easter Sunday."

She had to laugh at his contrite expression. Apparently he was over whatever had bothered him before. Never in her life had she met a man capable of presenting so many different facades. During the course of the evening, she had witnessed genuine humor, sensed his sadness, and just moments ago, had been the victim of his brazen flirtation.

"I assume, since Adam found my horse, that my saddlebags were also retrieved?"

"Yes, ma'am. I did." Adam came into the dining room with three plates of apple pie, placing one before her, then Cole, then sat down with his own. "They're in the living room over the back of the chair. Shall I get them for you?"

"If you wouldn't mind."

"My pleasure," the young man replied as he hurried to do her bidding.

A moment later he returned with the bags. Sarah thanked him, and then in an effort to locate the envelope containing her counterfeit identification, she placed her sketchpad on the table. Adam quickly snatched it up.

"Did you do this?" he asked.

"Yes, I did. It's—"

"Elk Mountain. Look, it's Elk Mountain." He turned the pad around and held it for everyone to see. "It's darned near perfect. Are you an artist?"

She gave a soft, disbelieving laugh. "No, I just like to draw."

"What else do you like to do?"

64

She didn't need to look up to know that the question came from Ira. He was relentless, reminding her of a wolf circling a herd of ewes. One false move and she was sure he'd be there to gobble her up.

"I like to read," she replied. "Here it is." She lifted out an envelope. "I believe, Marshal, you were asking for proof of my identity before. Perhaps this will satisfy your curiosity."

He accepted the paper and after he read it, folded it then passed it on to Cole. "It appears we have a genuine lady dining with us tonight." He took a sip of coffee. "Tell me, what does your husband do, Mrs. Wellington?"

She paused. She never really gave it much thought. Frantically she searched her memory. Her boss had mentioned that a Lord Watkins he knew was a captain on a sailing vessel. She gave her opponent a satisfied smile and replied, "He's in shipbuilding, Marshal Farrell."

"They build a lot of ships in St. Louis?" Ira asked with a skeptical lifting of one dark brow.

She inwardly groaned at her ridiculous choice, then gave a slight, nearly pathetic laugh. "Of course not. He owns a shipbuilding company in . . . in London and another in Boston," she added as an afterthought, toying with her coffee cup. She silently offered a small prayer that he wouldn't ask any more questions.

"That must be exciting," Adam replied, unaware he had come to her much-needed rescue.

"Yes, it is," she agreed.

"I expect your husband must do a lot of traveling?" Ira questioned.

She took a calming breath, and then turned to meet his relentless gaze. "Yes, he does. Why, he's on a ship bound for England as we speak."

"Then that explains why he left you to come all this way alone."

Did he place more emphasis on the word "alone," or was it her imagination? She forced a stiff smile. "As I said before, Marshal, I'm quite capable of taking care of myself. Did I mention that I'm considered to be an expert shot?"

She felt like frowning when Cole nearly choked on his coffee. Yet she was profoundly pleased when Adam smiled with approval. But much to her frustration, Ira, on the other hand, didn't seem overly impressed.

"Really?" he began, leaning a little closer as he cradled his cup between his hands. "What exactly do you shoot?"

"Bullets, Marshal Farrell. What do you shoot?"

Again Cole nearly choked, hiding his laughter behind a pretense of clearing his throat. "Yeah, Ira, if you don't shoot bullets, what do you shoot?"

"Maybe he shoots off his mouth," Jeb added as he came in and set a plate of pie before Ira.

For a moment, Sarah didn't know how to react. Her relief was nearly visible when Ira laughed with his brothers. "I reckon I deserved that one," he admitted.

Once again his gaze fused with hers. "Let me rephrase the question. Do you hunt or is your expertise in paper targets?"

"I've gone hunting before, though I must admit, I derive no pleasure in killing helpless criminals . . . I mean animals," she quickly corrected, inwardly cringing. She glanced at Jeb in hopes he'd change the subject, but he was intent on eating his dessert. There'd be no help from him. She tossed a pleading glance toward Cole who seemed to be clearing his throat an awful lot. "I-It's getting late, and I'd like to see my cousin's things."

Chairs scraped on the floor as all three men stood. As she expected, Ira stepped around the table and offered his arm.

"I'll show you where they are," he said, and instead of his voice pricking her ire, it caressed her like mink. "Cole has them in Zachary's room."

"There's really no need. You can just point me in the right direction and I'm sure I'll be able to find it."

He took her hand and folded it over his arm with a reassuring smile. "I insist."

Once they were away from the others, Sarah pulled her hand free. "Are you always this forward, or are you saving your worst behavior for me?"

"Ma'am?"

"Don't 'ma'am' me. You know exactly what I mean. I've a feeling, Marshal Farrell, that women are your primary source of entertainment."

His smile was neither abrasive nor soothing as he led her upstairs. "If that's your roundabout way of asking if I enjoy female companionship, then I must confess, I'm guilty as charged."

"Even *married* females?" she snapped.

"Married women are not prone to be as sociable, but on occasion, especially when I'm held at gunpoint, I tend to find them intriguing."

"So that's why you've badgered me all evening." She gave an impatient sigh. "You're still angry with me for refusing to trust you?"

"No, ma'am. That's not it at all. I find that you're very interesting to talk to. I've never had the pleasure of conversing with a real *titled* lady. Now, when I return to Carefree, I'll have an engaging story to tell . . . about you, and Lord Wellington's shipbuilding business."

She accepted his answer, wondering if she had misread his intentions. "I'm flattered," she replied without emphasis.

He escorted her down the hall to the second door on the

right. He pushed it open, motioning for her to enter. "This was my brother's room."

Sarah stepped inside. Unconsciously, she wrapped her arms around herself while Ira touched a match to a lamp. He then went to the wardrobe and opened it. She wondered if he'd light the stove, as each room seemed to have one, but instead, he retrieved a wooden box and placed it on the bed.

"Zach's things are in here too." He opened the box and lifted out a gun belt. "Just let me know when you're through." He would have left, but she stopped him. There were too many questions she wanted to ask.

"Marshal—"

"Ira," he corrected.

"Please, stay. I'm sure there's nothing here you need not know about."

He didn't speak; he just nodded then took a step closer. When she lifted out a beautiful belt buckle, he told her how he had it specially made for his brother's birthday. She was touched by his thoughtfulness. She opened a small envelope and a button fell from it, but he caught it before it landed on the floor. Instantly, she recognized it—had seen several in St. Louis.

"This is different," Ira said, taking a closer look. "I don't think I've ever seen another like it." He placed it in her hand. "Are those lion heads?"

"Yes, they are." She almost told him that one of the men she worked with had a jacket with the same buttons, but quickly revised her story. "My husband's associate told me his tailor got them from a shop in San Francisco. They're hand carved, and because of their exorbitant price, they're rather rare."

"Cole said that the things in this box are the things Miss Emily and Zach had with them at the time of their deaths."

His dark brows drew together. "Why would your cousin have this type of button?"

Sarah shook her head. "Perhaps she was working on a man's coat?" She closed her mouth and shrugged.

"Why do you say that?" Ira asked.

"It's just a speculation."

"May I?" he asked.

"Certainly," she replied, dropping the button in his hand.

"I'd like to keep this for a little while, if you don't mind?"

"I can see about ordering some for you, if you'd like."

His smile was back, dancing in his eyes—eyes that she could drown in. "I don't think I can afford them."

She dragged her gaze away and began to look through the box once more. "I've read articles about your proficiency with a gun. You've dispatched some rather notorious outlaws to their deaths. Surely you're paid well for what you do? Why else would you do it?"

He went to the window and moved the curtain aside, but it was dark and she wondered what he could see. She turned back to the box, jumping slightly when he spoke. "I suppose there are several reasons I chose to wear a badge. Not all of them as exciting as the newspapers make them out to be."

"Newspapers?" she repeated, worried that in some way she had let her secret out. "I think I read it on the train . . . in a novel someone left behind."

"I wouldn't believe everything you read," he countered.

"I shall endeavor to remember that." She glanced at Emily's will, not really paying any attention to it, but trying to look busy and keep her wits about herself. Why was it just being in this man's presence made her feel so self-conscious? "I did see something in the *Kansas City Sun*, though it was more about gunfighting than keeping the peace. Gunfighters must have a different view on what is and what isn't exciting, don't you agree?"

"I wouldn't know." His voice was flat, his tone conclusive. "I'm not a gunfighter."

"Really? Then by what name do you call it, Marshal Farrell?"

"I wish you'd call me Ira. There's no need to be so formal."

"Perhaps, but when I look at you, I see *Marshal* Farrell, the man who earned his notorious reputation gunfighting, according to the *Kansas City Sun*, of course," she added with more conviction than she felt. He only shrugged, his silence encouraging her to continue. "If that word offends you, I apologize. However, I should think you'd be used to it by now. It seems every time I've turned around over the last five years, I've been reading your story. It appears that on this side of the Mississippi, you're a journalist's favorite subject."

"I'm flattered that you know more about me than I would have expected a married woman of your status to know."

His insult didn't go unnoticed.

"I hate to disappoint you, but I've hardly filled my days reading about your prowess at gunning down criminals and reckless young men who challenge your status as *the fastest gun in the West*. Surely not all the men that have died by your hands were ruthless law-breakers."

"No, ma'am." His expression was expertly controlled. She suddenly felt a different kind of cold—not just from the chill in the room. "If I'm threatened, I will defend myself, regardless of the opinion of newspaper journalists and titled, temperate ladies."

She stared at him, trying without success to understand. "So I have read. However, I'm curious how a man of your ilk sleeps at night." The moment she spoke, she regretted her forwardness, but thankfully, he seemed to ignore her brazen question.

"Are you through? It's cold in here."

Somewhat relieved their verbal tug-of-war had ended, she gathered up several envelopes. "Yes, I'll read these in my room and return them tomorrow."

He placed the gun in the box, and then put everything back in the wardrobe. He crossed the room to the door, opened it and motioned for her to go before him. Once more he followed her down the hall, opening the door to her room and pushing it aside, but he caught her elbow and held her captive.

"You asked me how I sleep at night, and I'd like to answer that question now, if I may."

She lifted her chin to protest, but instead inwardly winced at the torment visible in the depths of his striking eyes. "I-I don't know what got into me, Marshal Farrell. I had no right to be so impudent."

His gaze never left hers. "I sleep soundly, Mrs. Wellington, with the knowledge that what I do helps innocent people like you to sleep soundly as well."

He lifted her cold hand and placed a chaste kiss on the back. "Pleasant dreams."

He was gone before she recovered enough to answer.

Chapter Six

Ira went back downstairs and joined his brothers for one last cup of coffee. He lifted the pot and filled his cup then topped off Adam's. "I appreciate you not telling Mrs. Wellington that her horse was tied to a tree. Our mysterious horseman was, at the very least, a gentleman."

Adam took the last bite of pie, chewing while he nodded. He swallowed, taking the time to have a sip of coffee. "Strangest thing I've seen in a while."

"Doesn't make any sense," Cole added.

"Sure it does." Ira reached for the cream and sugar. "I'm thinking this man was on Farrell property *without* permission." He paused as his brothers muttered their agreement. "So there he was, snooping around. You boys got close and scared him off when Mrs. Wellington rides up, blocking his retreat. Then Buster made matters worse. Our intruder acted out of fright and left by the fastest path—the cleared trail to our ranch."

Adam leaned back in his chair. "Why didn't he just stay in the trees? Apparently no one could see him."

"Buster saw him."

Cole put down his cup. "Why run, unless you're doing something you shouldn't?"

Ira took a sip of coffee then put down his cup. "Why'd he take the time to catch a horse and tie it up?"

"Who knows?" Cole answered. He glanced at Adam.

72

"You and I better do a little fence checking tomorrow. I've a feeling we've got some wire down." Cole turned his attention back to Ira. "You were coming up the trail. Did you see anything?"

"Wish I could say I did, but I'd taken Dakota off the path to let him have a drink from the river. When I heard Mrs. Wellington scream, I got there as fast as I could, but she was alone, and our trespasser was long gone." Ira stood, and stretched. "I'm bushed. I'll be leaving for town early." He pushed his chair underneath the table. "I don't know what's going on around here, but until we find out, we'd better watch our backs."

It seemed like only moments of blissful sleep had passed, when an obnoxious rooster perched himself on the fence outside Sarah's window and started crowing his lungs out. Muttering under her breath, she got up and threw up the sash, blinking at the burst of pink and yellow sunlight that filled her room. Spellbound by the glorious sunrise, she forgot all about the annoying rooster and drank in the sight of the golden leaves of the aspen trees, shimmering in the cold mountain breeze.

She hurried to the wardrobe and found a warm velvet robe. Shrugging it on, she hesitated a moment, thinking she might add another chunk of wood to the stove, but then thought better of it. It would be a waste of time and wood as she wanted to get an early start for town. She quickly made the bed. After she tightened the belt around her waist, she opened the door in search of the nearest outlet to the privy. She was just about to step into the hall, when Ira came upstairs, clad in blue shirt and sinfully tight blue jeans.

Her heart hammered against her breast. She quickly closed the door and leaned back against it. Damn the man for his fortitude. She cringed when he knocked. For a few torturous moments she thought about pretending to be asleep, but then he spoke. "Are you hiding from me, Mrs. Wellington?"

She inwardly groaned. Apparently, she'd been seen. "No, I'm not *hiding;* I'm simply not dressed appropriately to be out in public."

"From what I saw, you were dressed well enough."

She pictured his handsome features, the lazy, arrogant smile—a certain self-confidence that was ever present in his eyes, and shivered, thinking that she should have put some wood in the stove after all. "If you're in need of something to do—" His soft laughter fueled her courage. "Perhaps you could ask Adam if—"

"Adam's already left."

"Then if it isn't too much trouble, you could find Cole and—"

"He went with Adam. You and I are the only ones here. Everyone else has left."

She heaved a frustrated sigh. Now what was she to do? She had hoped to be spared the pleasure of Ira Farrell's company, but apparently he had stayed behind to act as her escort. Once again she had his mother's refinement to thank for her present situation. However, at the moment, Sarah didn't feel so appreciative. Pretending to be exceedingly self-assured was becoming tricky. Dare she admit she wasn't sure how to proceed?

"I shall be several minutes, Marshal. Perhaps you could wait for me downstairs."

"Yes, ma'am."

She pressed her ear against the door to listen.

"Should you have a *need*, Mrs. Wellington, there is a stairway from this floor at the end of the hall."

She closed her eyes in embarrassment, grateful for the sound of his footfalls fading away. She dressed quickly, and after she peeked to make sure it was safe, went in search of the door.

By the time Sarah returned to her room and finished dressing, the smell of bacon cooking made her mouth water. She added the finishing touches to her hair, then made her way down the stairs. She came into the kitchen just as Ira turned with two plates.

"Good morning," he said with a smile that could melt solid ice. He seemed to tower over her for just a moment, but it was long enough to awaken something worrisome in her stomach. "Hope you're hungry."

She slipped into the offered seat, surprised that he could cook, but even more surprised that she was beginning to enjoy his company. "This smells wonderful," she exclaimed while he filled their cups with hot steaming coffee.

"Why, thank you," he said, taking his seat.

They ate in silence for several moments, then, after she took a sip of coffee, she met his gaze. "How soon can we leave?" she asked, taking a moment to smear honey over a piece of toast.

"As soon as we're finished eating. The horses are already saddled and waiting."

She finished and stood, then carried her plate to the sink. "If it's possible, I'd like to visit Emily's grave before we go."

"Sure," was all he said.

Twenty minutes later, Ira guided her up a winding path that had been laid in flat stones. They came over the steep rise into a clearing sheltered by surrounding pines, aspens and spruce. A small graveyard enclosed by a stone-and-rail fence, was filled with a dozen marble headstones of different shapes and sizes.

In the far corner, a towering fir sheltered a single mound of fresh soil. She hesitated, composing herself until Ira grasped her elbow and somberly walked toward the grave, taking his hat off and holding it in his leather-gloved hand.

"You're probably wondering why there aren't two separate graves, but we thought . . ." He hesitated, then cleared his throat. When she cast a quick glance at him from under her lashes, she saw that a tiny muscle jumped spasmodically above his jaw.

"There's two separate caskets, but only one grave. Cole figured they would have wanted it that way—to be buried side by side." The raw edge to his voice caused tears to sting the back of her eyes. "Uncle Jeb's ordered a marble headstone. It's coming from Kansas City."

Sarah knelt by the grave, blinking back tears. She touched a pine wreath that had been tied together with colorful ribbons. She remembered how full of life her cousin was. "Emily would have liked it here," she murmured. "Thank you."

"Don't thank me. Jeb and Cole took care of things." She stood and gazed into his eyes, disturbed by the glimpse of torment she thought she saw. "If you'd like a few moments alone—"

"No," she hurried to say, feeling as wretched as he looked. "No, thank you. I'm ready."

He jammed on his hat. "Then we'd best get started."

While he led their saddled horses out of the barn, Sarah tried to justify her feelings of guilt. Emily had faithfully sent a letter twice a month, while Sarah barely found the time to send one monthly. On several occasions she had thought to accept Emily's invitation to visit, but never did, making up excuses about the demands of her job.

She swallowed past the ache in her throat, wishing she could have been more like her cousin and not so determined to make a name for herself in a man's world. As it was, she doubted anyone at the *St. Louis Herald* missed her.

Only when Ira's voice drew her back from her melancholy thoughts, did she realize he was trying to take her saddlebags so he could tie them behind her saddle.

"I can do it," she replied, brushing past him to do it herself. Before he could help her into the saddle, she mounted the horse and gathered up her reins. Sure that her emotions were firmly back in control, she chanced a glimpse of him, and wished she could return his compassionate smile. She took a deep breath, telling herself she was simply acting like a married woman and wasn't trying to be impolite.

"It looks like it's going to be a little warmer today."

His was the kind of voice that women dreamed about when they were alone at night in their beds.

"I beg your pardon?" she replied tersely, caught up in her own disturbing feelings.

"I said, it looks like it's going to be a nice day."

When she looked at him, he had turned his attention away from her and to the business of adjusting his own reins. Clad in his leather chaps, wool coat and cream-colored Stetson, he looked harmless enough. Yet the moment her gaze fell upon the revolver strapped on his hip, she knew that under those lazy, flirtatious smiles, there dwelled a dangerously powerful man.

She followed him down the path, all the while trying to avoid thinking about how she should have accepted Emily's invitation. They rode quietly through the forest for nearly an hour when his deep voice permeated her troubling thoughts.

"I expect you'll be returning to St. Louis now that you've settled Miss Emily's affairs?"

"No. I've decided to stay a little while longer," she said, relieved to have something other than Emily's death to think about. For the first time since leaving the homestead, she glanced around, amazed how fast the dusting of snow had melted in the warm October sun. "I suppose you'll be leaving for Arizona straight away. I can only imagine the mischief that occurs in a boom town if left too long without its marshal."

He turned slightly in the saddle, his expression tinged with arrogant amusement. "I'll be staying in Santa Fe for a while myself."

"For what purpose?" she asked, wondering if he, like her, suspected something shady about Zach's and Emily's deaths.

"I have some business to tend to."

"Really? What kind of business?" she inquired, wishing she could be less obvious, but unwilling to play the part of an acquiescent female. She was almost certain that if she were a man, she could ask any question she wanted and it would be answered. She studied his expression. Had she witnessed a flash of mistrust flickering in his gaze, or had it simply been her imagination?

"Well, for one thing," he began, "I'd like to find out more about a certain marshal that died near here a month ago. Then I'd like to see if someone owns a jacket with buttons like the one we found in your cousin's things. Whoever it belongs to might shed some light on how Zach and Miss Emily died."

The thought that they shared a common purpose sent a jolt of hope shooting through her. "Then you suspect there has been some foul play?" she asked, seeking another straightforward answer. She wasn't disappointed.

"Let's just say there are a few things that don't make a whole lot of sense."

She urged her horse a little closer, eager to continue this

course of conversation. "I feel the same way. Perhaps we could pool our resources." Her enthusiasm withered under his doubtful expression. "Do you think you're the only one who can harbor such thoughts, Marshal Farrell?"

"No, ma'am, I don't, but I am more qualified than you are to carry out an investigation."

"Really, why is that? Let me guess," she replied sarcastically, cutting off his attempt to answer. "Because you're a man and I'm a woman?"

"With all due respect, Mrs. Wellington, dressmakers don't usually double as Pinkerton detectives."

"Do not underestimate the ability of a determined woman. You might be surprised."

He pushed his hat off his forehead, smiling. She knew she should let the matter drop, but his expression goaded her on. "Did I say something amusing?"

"Determined? I'm thinking stubborn is a better word." He scratched his horse's neck and added, "Besides, won't your husband insist on your punctual return . . . to St. Louis?"

She didn't miss his implication. "Contrary to most men's beliefs, my husband does not own me, Marshal Farrell. I am my own woman, entitled to live my life as I see fit without male dominance."

His grin was patronizing. "That's a real strange way for a married woman to talk. Unless, of course, she's not really devoted to her husband."

She forced a laugh. "Do you think that devotion is exclusively a female sentiment?"

He guided his big roan gelding around a sharp rock that jutted up from the slightly muddy path. "No, ma'am, I don't, but if my wife wanted to live apart from me, I wouldn't allow it."

"Why do you think you could stop her?" she challenged. "Wives are no longer men's chattels."

Once more his smile was spontaneous. "I'd make sure she felt loved enough to want to stay."

His confession was startling, almost unbelievable coming from a man with a reputation of being an unfeeling enforcer of western justice. "And what does a man like you know about love?"

"Do you think love is only a female sentiment, Mrs. Wellington?"

Her gaze narrowed. "Certainly not. However, in my experience, a man's idea of love is often confused with ownership."

Her escort remained silent for several moments, before saying, "I own Dakota here, and I suppose I have grown to love him as man can love an animal. However, I think the love of a good woman is much deeper, and much more binding."

His gentle smile did much to further ravage her emancipated beliefs.

"Binding," she scoffed. "Most men marry so they can have someone wash their clothes and prepare their food. In my marriage, I am my husband's equal, not his servant."

The trail narrowed and she was forced to fall in behind him, thwarting any further debate on the values of marriage. Nevertheless, his comments were as disturbing as the man himself. Was it the look of doubt in his expression, or the easy manner in which he took her often-scathing insults? She couldn't be certain, but she didn't think it was either of those things.

An hour passed by with few chances for any meaningful dialogue. Her horse followed his passively without the aid of rein or heel, allowing Sarah the opportunity to let her thoughts wander. She made a mental note that upon their arrival in Santa Fe, she'd make her presence known to the local merchants. She'd politely introduce herself as the new dressmaker, soliciting their business with the promise of business in return, while trying to learn more about Emily's accident. In addition, she'd wire St. Louis, and have her solicitor send out the remainder of her possessions, especially her typewriting machine.

There was no time like the present to share her views on women's rights. However, she'd have to establish herself as a capable journalist first. *And* the best way to do that would be to write some exciting stories. Though Cole's story would be interesting back East, Ira's would draw many more local readers, especially with his extended stay in town. She'd learned early in the newspaper business that people flocked to absorb all they could about myths and legends like Ira Farrell. It mattered little if what they read was true.

Lost in thought, she was unprepared when Ira pulled his horse up and motioned for her to be quiet. Slowly, he pointed toward a small opening between the trees. A large herd of elk grazed leisurely in a not-too-far-off meadow, oblivious to their human intrusion. After a moment or two, Ira cued his horse onward. Once more she was filled with a troubling sense of awe. She found it rather unsettling to think of Marshal Ira Farrell as a man of peace—a man who would stop to watch wildlife feed.

"If you need a place to stay in town, I know—"

"I have a room," she interrupted. She didn't want to discuss her lodging arrangements in case he'd feel obligated to see her settled in. The trail widened and she was able to ride alongside him. "Like you, I have some unanswered questions, and until I get the answers, Santa Fe will be my home."

He stopped his horse again. "I'm only going to say this once. Stay out of it. Let me do my job."

She bristled like a bantam rooster, just like he knew she would.

"You're arrogant to a fault, Marshal Farrell."

Damn, but she was pretty when she was angry. Andrew Wellington had to be a fool to let her out of his sight.

"How many times do I have to ask you to drop the formalities, *Mrs.* Wellington? You use my title as if you relish the sound of it."

He enjoyed the way her vibrant blue eyes narrowed when he awakened her ire. He also enjoyed the way she had the tendency to pull herself up to her full height of barely anything.

"If you think you can stop me from conducting my own inquiry, then you are sorely mistaken."

"Not only can I stop you, I can have you put in jail." He inwardly winced at the look of utter astonishment that colored her cheeks.

"H-how dare you threaten me," she stammered.

He gave her a very confident smile. "It's no threat." He reached into his saddlebags and pulled out his badge. "This gives me the authority to conduct my investigation without being hindered by a goody two-shoes woman who, if she had any sense, would drop all notion of getting involved in what could be a triple murder. Take my advice, and get on the first train back to your shipbuilding husband—if you can find him."

The entire time he was talking, her eyes were alive with the fiery need to interrupt, and her tempting mouth was open in what could only be described as total astonishment.

"How dare you speak to me in such a manner! That badge you're so eager to flaunt does not give you the right to be rude."

He matched her glare. "I'm not being rude. I'm being

honest. This isn't St. Louis. Nor am I the kind of man who would allow an unsuspecting woman to put herself in danger. I don't know what kind of a man your husband is, but I can only conclude he's either a fool or a coward to let you come out here alone in the first place."

"Leave him out of this," she stormed. "This isn't about my husband. It's about your arrogant attitude—that because you're male, it's presumed you can do a better job than I. Admit it, Marshal Farrell, it's not that I may be a capable investigator. The truth of the matter is, because of my gender, you feel the need to coddle me."

Somehow she had risen up in her saddle, and now her face was mere inches away from his. She thought to sit back down, but didn't want to appear as if she was cowering. She swallowed apprehensively when his gaze left hers and lingered seductively on her mouth.

"You're damned right about that," he said with cool authority. The next instant, he pulled her close and captured her mouth in a ravishing kiss—so utterly intoxicating, she momentarily lost the power to resist. The feel of his warm lips moving over hers sent her senses whirling. She had allowed herself to be kissed before, but never, never like this. The next instant she remembered her lie—the husband who, if he existed, would surely put this womanizer in his place. She shoved Ira back as hard as she could, furious that he had so effortlessly shaken her confidence.

"How dare you?" she hissed, and tried to strike him, but he caught her hand and leaned a little closer. She expected him to apologize, but felt her cheeks heat with color when he didn't. She should have known better. The way he had held her—kissed her—denied he felt any remorse.

She jerked her hand free, then quickly turned away from the hunger in his hooded gaze. "You've overstepped yourself," she heard herself say, hardly recognizing her own breathy voice. "If-if my husband were here, he'd—"

"He's not."

She matched his stare for several more uncomfortable moments, wondering if he'd seen through her false title. Angrier with herself than with him, she gathered up her horse's reins, pressed her boot heels into its flanks and galloped off.

Chapter Seven

"You need a room, *senor?*" the elderly proprietor asked, turning the book around.

"Yes, Mrs. Baca," Ira replied, taking off his hat. "I do."

"*Eee-ho-la,* Ira, Ira Farrell, if you ain't a sight for sore eyes," the woman replied in heavily accented English.

Sarah hesitated on the landing on her way to her room. Taking care not to be seen, she stayed close to the wall, hidden but with a clear view. The proprietor came around the counter and gave Ira a big hug.

"Blessed Mother, the last time I saw you, you were barely old enough to shave. Now, look at you, all grown up and a famous marshal to boot." She hurried back to the wall behind the desk and took a key off a small brass hook. "Here, this is the largest room I have. It is upstairs and to your left." She gave him another motherly hug. "You stay as long as you want, *si?*"

Sarah groaned inwardly and shifted her heavy saddlebags to a more comfortable position over her left forearm. She'd hoped he would be housed elsewhere—at the small hotel down the street—but now it seemed he'd be taking the room directly across from hers. "Damn it," she whispered.

Avoiding him would be difficult. No, she amended wordlessly, it would be impossible. With the sounds of his boots on the stairs, she hurried to her door. The knob was old and the screws holding it a little wobbly. She jabbed at the keyhole and missed.

"Need some help?" The sound of his voice directly behind her intensified her determination to get inside as quickly as possible.

"No, thank you. I can manage." She rested the saddlebags on her shoulder, but each time she tried to steady the wobbly knob with her hand, they slid down and covered the lock. She felt his gaze, and the more he watched, the more her fingers fumbled with the key. After another failed try, she cast him a sideways glance. His smile was instant, rich with male amusement, as he lifted the saddlebags from her arm.

"At least let me hold these."

The moment the weight was removed, the key slid into the lock. "Thank you," she said, turning at the same time she pushed open the door. She reached for her bags, but he held them slightly out of her reach.

"Perhaps you'll do me the honor of having supper with me tonight? Cole said there's a very good restaurant at the other end of town."

"I think I'll just have something sent up." She grabbed the saddlebags and would have shut the door, but he blocked it with a firm hand.

"Look. I don't usually apologize, but I'm sorry."

She raised one brow, but apparently didn't feel like letting him off the hook too easily.

"I was out of line . . . behaved badly, and I'd like the opportunity to make it up to you."

"There's really no need."

"Yes, yes, there is. Let me buy your supper as a kind of peace offering."

She shook her head and tried to close the door, but he held

it firm. "I should warn you, Mrs. Baca isn't a very good cook."

When she glanced at him, he smiled. "Really, she's a nice lady, but . . ." He shook his head and gave her a doubtful grimace.

"I'm rather tired. Perhaps another time." Once more she tried to close the door.

"You'll sleep better on a full stomach. Besides, where's the harm in sharing a meal? I hate eating alone."

It didn't surprise Sarah one little bit that his invitation was followed by another friendly smile. A smile that erased some of the embarrassment and anger he had stirred up on their ride down the mountain. She hesitated for a moment, thinking it would be best if she avoided the man, but he'd made a good point. She didn't know anyone in Santa Fe, and, like him, she really hated eating alone.

Once more she matched his gaze. "Very well. I'll meet you in the lobby at seven."

She quickly closed the door.

Ira clicked the gold lid to his pocket watch closed. It was five minutes before seven. He heard a door upstairs close, and then a moment later watched Mrs. Sarah Wellington descend the stairs. She was a looker, that he couldn't deny, and there was no doubt in his mind she wasn't even slightly aware of it. The tight fit of her royal-blue gown was more alluring than he wanted to admit, and even though he tried to ignore her feminine appeal, the heavy feeling in his groin would have no part of it.

"You look stunning," he said as he took her matching cloak and draped it over her shoulders. The sweet aroma of her perfume rose up and assaulted his already heightened senses.

Sarah hoped he couldn't hear the rapid beating of her heart, or see how her limbs trembled when his hands lingered at her shoulders a moment too long. As much as she wanted to resist the urge to gaze upon his manly form, she couldn't do it. He was utterly dashing in a charcoal jacket. It was cut long in keeping with the latest style, yet open to reveal his high-cut, silver-brocade vest where his badge covered his heart.

He wore a dove-grey pin-strip ascot. Instead of the turquoise stickpin, a ruby twinkled in the lamplight, and she knew without looking that it matched the ones holding his cuffs. Such finery was uncommon among most men, but then he wasn't a common man. His black trousers clung to his muscular thighs, brushing the arches of his highly polished black boots. When he lifted a black Stetson from the hat-rack by the door, she decided Ira Farrell was not your usual lawman. He had the grandeur to equal even the most renowned aristocrats of St. Louis.

"Shall we?" he asked, his voice as soft as silk as he offered his arm.

A gust of cold air washed over them when he guided her out onto the boardwalk, and she pulled her cloak a little tighter. "Were you able to learn anything about the fire today?" she asked.

He covered her cold hand with his warm one, apparently in no hurry to get to their destination. "Somehow I knew you'd ask," he countered as they walked along.

"Why shouldn't I?" Even in the muted light from the street lamps, he was sinfully handsome and seemed almost too sure of himself. "Well, did you?"

He smiled down at her, patting her hand. "No. Can't you tell? I went shopping." He touched the brim of his hat, amusement twinkling in his eyes. "This type of hat doesn't fit too well in a pair of saddlebags. And, since I'm going to be here a while, I needed some clothes."

"Very well, since you seem reluctant to speak about the fire, how do men feel about shopping? Do they like it as much as most women do?"

"I like to dress well, if that's what you're asking."

She purposely let her gaze slide boldly down his full length. "I can see that, but do you look forward to going out and making your purchases?"

His laugh was spontaneous.

"No. I prefer to have my money stay in the bank, but it's important to maintain appearances." A gust of wind caught his coat, revealing his engraved, ivory-handled Colt .45 nestled in the familiar, richly carved, black leather holster.

"Is Santa Fe so wild and wooly that you must arm yourself simply to walk down the street?"

"There was a time when I had the liberty to walk down the street like any other man," he clarified. "But, that was before I became proficient with a gun."

"So the rumors are true?" she asked as he stopped before the door to the restaurant.

"What rumors?" he asked, motioning her inside.

She would have persisted, intended to as soon as they were seated, but for now, her inquiry could wait. Ira took her cloak and hung it with his hat on the rack by the door as an attractive blond waitress approached. She led them to the table before the window, but Ira declined, nodding toward a small table in the corner at the back of the room.

"Ira?" A man's voice stopped them. When Ira turned toward him, Sarah recognized Mr. Pruitt, the banker. He sat at a round table with two women, one old enough to be his wife, the other young enough to be his daughter. The pretty young woman gave Sarah a slight smile then stared dreamily at Ira.

"Silas," Ira acknowledged. "Mrs. Pruitt, Miss Pruitt. It's nice to see you ladies are still as lovely as ever."

The plump woman giggled. "Oh, Ira, I see you're still a tease." Her daughter's cheeks turned a very becoming shade of pink.

"This is Mrs. Wellington."

"Please, Sarah will do." She extended her hand to the banker. "We had the pleasure of meeting when I arrived." She shook Silas's beefy hand then smiled at his wife and daughter. "Pleased to meet you both."

"Silas was telling me you plan on opening the dress shop again." The women cheerfully smiled.

"Yes. That's correct."

Mrs. Pruitt patted her daughter's hand. "That's wonderful news, isn't it, Laura?" Both women nodded, then Mrs. Pruitt turned her attention back to Sarah. "We shall be looking forward to your grand opening with bated breath. Laura and I will be your best customers, I'm sure."

"I'm sure," Sarah repeated with a generous smile.

"Your table is ready," the waitress interrupted.

"Don't let us spoil your evening," Silas stated, clearing his throat. "Nice seeing you again, Ira, Mrs. Wellington."

"Same here." Ira took Sarah's elbow and guided her toward their table. After he helped with her chair, he took the place across from hers, and picked up the menu. "Would you like some wine this evening?"

"Yes, but only if you would."

The waitress appeared and, after taking their order, gave Ira a flirtatious smile, then hurried away. Sarah slipped her hand into her reticule and pulled out a pad and pencil. "Would you mind if I jotted a few things down as we speak? My husband's terribly interested in anything concerning lawmen and outlaws."

A flicker of wariness sparked in his gaze, but his words denied it. "Not at all. Now, where were we?"

"We were speaking about your reputation."

"We were?" Ira asked in feigned innocence.

"Yes, we were."

"As what, cattle rancher, protector of the weak, or my ability to sweep innocent young women off their feet with just a glance."

She laughed, aware that he had noticed Laura's lovesick expression as well. No wonder he was so arrogant. It seemed every woman in the building had glanced his way.

"I was speaking of your reputation as a gunfighter. You're armed. Isn't it uncomfortable wearing a gun everywhere you go?"

"I never wear it to bed," he said with an ornery grin.

"I'm trying to be serious."

"*Seriously,* I'm uncomfortable without it," he teased.

"Do you really have such a high opinion of yourself that you believe you're in constant danger?"

His smile never faded. "It is not that I have a high opinion of myself, but that over the years I have developed a low opinion of many I encounter. Present company excluded, of course."

The wine arrived and like an expert, he opened it, tested it, and then filled their glasses.

He raised his glass and waited until she raised hers. "To a pleasant evening."

And it was. The food was delicious, and Sarah enjoyed it so much she insisted her compliments be given to the chef.

"We don't have no chef," the pretty waitress said, turning her attention and her smile toward Ira. Sarah inwardly groaned. Wasn't there a woman in this town who could look at him without melting?

"We just got Granny Hill doing the cookin'," the young woman added while she cleared away their plates, then left to bring coffee.

"See what I mean?" Ira confirmed.

She shook her head. "No, I don't see what you mean."

"The absence of a chef." His expression was almost comical. "The food was expertly prepared, don't you agree?"

"Unequivocally."

"And, to any who didn't know about Granny Hill, they would have made the same assumption you did. Agreed?"

"I suppose," she said with a tinge of caution in her voice.

"Well, then, why am I not given the same courtesy?"

Her eyes narrowed. "What do you mean?"

He leaned forward and caught her hand in his, keeping his voice intentionally low. "You've passed judgment on me, Mrs. Wellington, because of how I appear, helped along a little by what you've read."

He leaned back as their coffee was served, waiting until she used the cream and sugar before he helped himself. He wondered if she realized the same thing was happening to her—that the moment they were seen together, folks had jumped to conclusions. He expected that by noon tomorrow, after the ladies shared morning tea, most every citizen of Santa Fe would know that their prim and proper new dressmaker had shared her prestigious company with an unmarried man rumored to have a rather lecherous reputation.

"*Touché*, Marshal Farrell. You win this round, but I'm not beaten yet. My paper is blank and I promised my husband."

"If your husband is like most, it will hardly matter if the information I give you is fact or fiction."

"Why do you say that?" she inquired.

"Of all the articles and dime novels I've seen, not one author have I ever met."

"Your point?" she countered.

He leaned back in his chair and pondered her question for a moment. "Well, let me see. I think it's kind of like me writing a book on . . . let's say . . . shipbuilding. I don't know a lick about it."

"So you're saying that everything written about you is fraudulent?"

"Not everything."

She couldn't avoid his taunting gaze or his wily smile. "Very well, I remember reading somewhere that you carry a slightly different weapon than most lawmen. Is this true?"

He nodded. "It is and I do."

"Other than derringers and smaller caliber pistols, I have little experience with hand guns. Would you care to enlighten me?"

She watched intently as he removed a small leather thong from the hammer of his Colt then placed the weapon on the table where she could have a look. The front half of the trigger guard was missing.

"Is it broken?" she asked, touching it with her finger.

He smiled ever so slightly. "No, I had a gunsmith make it like that."

"Why?"

"It's easier to find the trigger when you're in a hurry." He didn't miss the way her gaze flickered to his before she returned her attention back to his gun. Since she appeared interested, he continued. "This is a short-barrel Colt .45, referred to as a Peacemaker. The barrel is four and three-quarter inches long, whereas the usual length is seven inches long. I have one in my room back at the boarding house if you'd like to see it later tonight."

His gaze was scandalous. She ignored the tiny thrill of excitement his insinuation sparked and made a few notes.

"How many weapons do you carry at one time?" she asked, somewhat surprised that he spoke about deadly weapons as if they were old friends. He picked up his pistol and slipped it back into its holster.

"Usually just one, and a rifle on my saddle. The gun in my room is for Adam. It'll be his birthday in a few weeks."

"How thoughtful, but why not get him a replica of your own? It's obvious he holds you in high esteem." She jotted down another few words.

Ira took a sip of coffee. "I almost did, but then I decided against it. You see, the length of the barrel is important. The shorter the barrel, the faster the draw. Adam has no need to be fast with a gun, but he might need to pick off a rattler or stop a coyote from tormenting a calf. The longer the barrel the more accurate the shot."

"I see. That's really very interesting." Again she wrote something down, but her handwriting was barely better than a scribble and even though he was curious, he could not read upside down. Much to his surprise she also made a quick sketch of a cowboy.

"Why do I get the feeling you're not being very honest with me?" he asked when she looked up.

She blinked innocently, a very feminine gesture that tugged at his insides. "I'm not sure I understand your meaning."

"Will there be anything else?"

Sarah inwardly sighed with relief, thankful that the waitress saved her from having to answer.

Ira glanced up at the waitress. "No. I believe we're through." He stood and helped Sarah with her chair. They stopped at the mayor's table only long enough to be polite. After Ira paid the bill, he retrieved his hat and her cloak, and they stepped outside.

They had only gone a short distance when the door to the

restaurant opened. "Marshal?" the blonde called. "You forgot your pad."

He accepted it with a nod of thanks, but when Sarah reached for it, he held it out of the way. "Well, let's see what you've written." Ira flipped through the pad.

"That isn't fair," she said scornfully. "I told you, they're just notes, little tidbits of information to put in a letter to my husband."

"I'll believe that for now, but then I'm curious why your husband needs a sketch of two men drawing down on each other." He gave her a wary glance then handed her the pad.

She quickly tucked it back into her reticule, then pulled her cloak a little tighter and began to stroll with him down the boardwalk. "Thank you for the delicious meal."

"The pleasure was all mine," he replied.

At that moment a star shot across the sky. "Oh, my. Did you see that, Marshal Farrell?" she asked.

"Yes, I did." Aware she was watching, he kept his attention directed at the sky for several moments. When he met her gaze, she quickly looked away.

"I see that the rumors are true about western skies. There must be a million stars out tonight."

Ira smiled at her clever attempt to hide her brazen inspection. He'd had women look at him—mostly with unbridled hunger like the little waitress at the restaurant, others with dreamy half-smiles like young and innocent Laura Pruitt. Female admiration came with the badge.

But no woman, not even Ginger back at Carefree, ever made him feel like Sarah when he caught her watching. She wasn't schoolgirl shy, but neither did she have the salaciousness of the experienced women he knew.

"Let's make a little bargain," he began. "You call me Ira, and I'll call you Sarah. We'll pretend that we're *equals*."

She seemed to weigh his suggestion, then nodded. "Fair enough," she agreed with a dazzling smile. She wasn't even aware that her behavior was borderline scandalous for a lady of her standing. That's what excited and bothered him the most. Was she so caught up in her own liberation that she'd intentionally soil the good name of the man she married?

The thought of her husband aroused another question. A shipbuilder in Boston was believable. A shipbuilder living in St. Louis, sailing for England, was not. A man allowing his wife to come to the untamed territory of New Mexico alone wasn't believable either. Ira gazed down at the beauty by his side with the stark realization that she was a very good liar, and he knew just how to prove it.

"Well, we're here," he said, pausing before they got to the door of the hotel.

The evening breeze had loosened a few golden curls, and he brushed them back behind a very delicate ear. He should have ended it there, but his instincts told him his hunch was right, and if that were the case, there was no Mr. Wellington to make him feel guilty about seducing his wife.

Ira stepped a little closer, his left hand reaching out to possess her waist while the knuckles of his right grazed her silky cheek. Instantly she stiffened, as if preparing for an attack; at the same time her gaze fused with his—the innocent allure in the way her tongue darted out to nervously moisten her soft, full lips.

He had a need to touch her, to feel her satiny skin against his palm. He pulled her closer and caught her chin, holding her still while he bent his head and captured her mouth.

He was unprepared for the slow burn that started in his chest and spread through his body when she molded her soft, feminine shape to the hard contours of his. He deepened the kiss, teasing her lips to open, plundering her mouth the moment she complied. He tasted every recess, pressing her closer until he felt as if she were part of him.

Sarah closed her eyes and leaned toward him. Was he so dangerous that she couldn't tear herself away? His hands were hot, possessive, his mouth seductive, working like an aphrodisiac to drive her mad with new and intoxicating sensations. No wonder women threw themselves at his feet. Did he make them feel as wild and wanton as he made her feel?

He had said they were equals. Did he think she was as untamed as she thought him to be? She couldn't deny that his kiss was even more exciting than his fearsome reputation. Was she attracted to Ira the man, or Marshal Farrell the legend? All at once she felt incredibly ashamed, but not for the reasons she should. Slowly, she pushed away, pressing her fingertips against her lips.

"I must insist," she murmured, unable to look at him. She was supposed to be married, a lie of her own choosing, but he didn't know that, and it was a pretense she needed to assure her success. "I must insist that when we're together, you conduct yourself in a more appropriate manner."

Slowly, he dragged his fingers down her flushed cheek, then across her moist bottom lip. "Out of respect for your husband, I'll try not to let it happen again, but I won't make any promises."

"You . . ." He turned away before she could think of anything more to say, but even then she wasn't sure she would have if given the chance. Deep down inside, the whole time he'd held her, she knew what was happening—she knew he wanted her and she had used that knowledge to get exactly what she wanted. And, once she'd gotten it, she realized that her freethinking antics had encouraged his audacious behavior. Wordlessly, she let him escort her inside where he took off his hat and bade her to sleep well.

"Good night," she repeated. She started up the stairs then cast a puzzled glance over her shoulder, wondering why he put his hat back on. "Are you going somewhere?"

He gave her a lazy smile. "I've a mind to go over to the saloon and have a drink. Care to join me?"

She knew she should refuse, but her willful curiosity surfaced and for reasons she didn't want to explore she returned his smile. "That sounds . . . delightful." She gathered a fistful of skirt and descended the stairs. "I've always wanted to see the inside of a frontier saloon."

She placed her hand on his offered arm.

"Then by all means, allow me to be the first to show you."

Chapter Eight

Ira pushed aside the swinging doors, motioning for Sarah to enter. She paused for only a moment to meet the glances of the men and women who turned their way. Ira grasped her elbow and guided her inside, nodding at a tall, dark-haired man with a neatly trimmed moustache and a star on his chest. Emily's letter, which Sarah had safely put away in her room, came to mind. Perhaps the sheriff was a man she could trust.

"You must be Sheriff Finch," Ira said, extending his hand.

"And you must be Marshal Farrell," the sheriff replied. "Pleased to meet you." The sheriff turned his smile on Sarah at the same time he removed his hat. "And you are?"

Cooper Finch was a handsome man, with dark hair and dark eyes, but Sarah figured he was at least ten years Ira's senior. She held out her hand, but before she could speak, Ira introduced her.

"This is Sarah Wellington, *Mrs.* Sarah Wellington."

"You don't say," the sheriff acknowledged. "Is your husband coming by later?"

She smiled to herself, fully recovered from her earlier imprudence. It was very male of the sheriff to assume her husband wasn't far away. She decided not to complicate matters with an explanation. "No. Marshal Farrell is acting as my escort for the evening."

"Andrew Wellington, Sarah's husband, and I are old

friends," Ira replied. He motioned toward the bar. "Can I buy you a drink, Sheriff?"

"No, no thanks. I've got rounds to make." The sheriff touched the brim of his hat. "I hope you enjoy your visit, Mrs. Wellington. Ira," he added then turned and left.

"You needn't feel you must make excuses for me," Sarah chided as she followed Ira to the elegant bar. "I'm not so fragile that a few odd looks will damage my . . ." She paused, staring up at a huge gilt-framed painting of a nude woman lounging on a velvet chaise. ". . . my dignity," she finished in a rather breathy voice. She quickly cleared her throat and looked away. An attractive woman sat atop a piano, exhibiting a liberal amount of long, slender legs. For a moment their gazes met.

"That's Lily Barker," Ira explained.

"The owner?" Sarah asked. The feathers in Lily's hair were the same vibrant red as the tight-fitting satin gown she wore. Out of the corner of her eye, Sarah saw Ira nod a silent hello.

"You know her?" Sarah asked, shifting her gaze to meet Ira's.

"We were friends . . . a while ago." That lazy smile directed at another woman filled Sarah with a rare and confusing envy. Disturbed, she glanced around the saloon. A bald man played a lively tune, and after Lily gave Ira what Sarah thought to be a rather sultry smile, the woman began to sing. Several drunken patrons joined her in song.

Watching intently, Sarah was only vaguely aware that Ira tossed some money on the brass-and-marble counter. She heard him speak and finally glanced his way. He picked up a bottle and two glasses. Once again he motioned for her to take the lead, nodding toward a table in a corner of the noisy room, where Sarah assumed he could observe others in the room without calling too much attention to their presence. She accepted a seat and continued her inspection of the saloon and its patrons.

"So, since this is your first time in a saloon, what do you think?"

"It's different than I imagined," she replied as he opened the bottle and filled their glasses.

He lifted his glass, waiting until she did the same. "To your health."

She watched him toss it down his throat, and then copied his actions, gasping for breath the next moment. By the sound of his soft laughter, she realized he had done it on purpose.

"Good heavens," she rasped. "You actually enjoy this?"

He refilled their small glasses. "Don't you?"

She looked at her glass. "I suppose it's an acquired taste."

"I suggest you sip it this time," he recommended as he finished his second shot.

"Had I known it would set fire to my throat, I would have *sipped* it the first time."

He grinned, and she wondered if the warm feeling that came over her was entirely from the whiskey. Had her thoughts not been centered on her escort, she would have missed how his expression changed. His right hand slipped from the tabletop to rest on his right thigh—closer to his gun.

Instantly she scanned the room, wondering what or who had caused such a subtle reaction. Her gaze landed on two men standing in the doorway, lingering between the swinging doors. "Do you know those gentlemen?"

"They're hardly what I'd call gentlemen," Ira replied softly. "Jonah and Joshua Pruitt."

Though it hadn't been her intention, when Sarah glanced at them again, she accidentally caught their attention. The taller of the two was neat and clean, wearing navy blue trousers and a charcoal grey coat. He was an ordinary-looking man, and she decided that the only thing attractive about him was the red, velvet-trimmed vest he wore. To her untrained eye, he appeared unarmed.

Though both brothers had light brown hair and green eyes, the shorter one looked as if he hadn't bothered to shave that day. He wore trail-dusted Levis, a red plaid shirt and a brown leather vest. A pistol hung from a plain holster strapped low on his thigh. She stared more than she thought was polite, but if memory served, she'd read something about the Pruitts in one of Emily's letters.

"Well, well, well," the tall one began with a slightly surprised smile. "Ira Farrell—"

"Not just Ira Farrell," the short one corrected. "Marshal Ira Farrell." Though the short man smiled, it wasn't friendly. He pushed his hat back off his forehead and grinned. "And who is this?"

"Mrs. Sarah Wellington," Ira began. "This is Josh and this is Jonah Pruitt. Their father is Silas Pruitt."

"How do you do," she said formally.

"Mrs. Wellington," Jonah replied, taking off his bowler. Jonah turned to Ira. "What brings you back to these parts, Ira?"

"I swear, Jonah," Josh replied before Ira could answer. "You might have yourself a fancy college education, but sometimes you don't use your head." Josh turned his dark, contemptuous gaze to Ira. "Zachary burned up in the fire last month, remember?"

Sarah blanched at the man's vulgar attitude. It was apparent there was some deep, underlying discord between the oldest Pruitt and Ira. Obviously younger, Jonah appeared very uncomfortable, and didn't seem to harbor the same animosity. Much to her surprise, Josh grabbed a chair, turned it around then straddled it.

"Aren't you going to ask us if we want a drink?"

Ira caught a pretty barmaid's attention, and when she approached, he took two more glasses off her tray.

"Come on, Josh," Jonah urged. "I thought we were going to play a game of pool."

"Sit down, Jonah," Josh encouraged, then turned his attention back to Ira. "One little drink to catch up on old times, right, Ira?" Josh turned his attention to Sarah. "So, how come a nice-looking lady like you is keeping company with the likes of Ira here, in a place like this?"

"The marshal was kind enough to allow me the opportunity to appease my curiosity," she replied with a knowledgeable smile. "However, I had no idea I would be exposed to such an abundance of vulgarity."

The short man frowned, and then scratched his head. "Are you talking about that painting?"

"Not exactly," she purred, and then purposely looked at Ira. She wasn't too surprised by his slight smile as he filled the brothers' glasses. Josh gulped his down and pushed it forward to be refilled, dragging his right knuckle across his mouth. "Don't be stingy now."

"I'm sorry about your brother, Ira," Jonah stated, taking a sip of his drink. "I didn't know him very well, but he always seemed like a nice kid."

"Kid?" Josh scoffed. "Hell, he was two years older than you."

Feeling Josh's eyes glide down her body, Sarah bit back a sharp remark. Where was the wisdom in inviting herself to this spot? Josh Pruitt was obnoxious and disgusting, and had she been any place but the Crystal Slipper Saloon, she would have dealt him a scathing reprimand. But this was a man's domain into which she had intruded, and in doing so she had unknowingly placed herself and Ira in peril. If Josh Pruitt made any sort of ungentlemanly advance, she was certain the marshal would come to her rescue, regardless of the danger.

"My cousin also perished in the fire," Sarah added, hoping to alleviate some of the tension.

Jonah seemed genuinely concerned. "You and Miss Emily were cousins?"

She nodded, then took a very small sip of her drink, feeling a little more at ease since Josh no longer stared at her. Thankfully, he'd turned his attention to his glass.

"I'm very sorry to hear that," the younger brother replied. He also took another sip of his drink, then turned to Ira. "How long are you staying in town?"

"I'm not rightly sure. It all depends on how long it takes me to determine if Miss Emily's and Zachary's deaths were accidental."

Josh choked on the whiskey, while Jonah's brows came together with genuine concern.

Sarah gaped at Ira and, from his expression, she concluded that he had just issued an unspoken accusation. She'd thought he would have been more subtle. As a journalist she'd learned the importance of being diplomatic.

"What makes you think it wasn't an accident?" Jonah asked.

"Hell's bells," Josh sneered. "Who cares. He's gone and nothing you can do, Ira, will bring him back." Josh tossed the last of his drink down his throat, then stood. "Knowing how you spent most of your time protecting your brothers, that's gotta stick in your craw, doesn't it? Guess you should have come back a little sooner, or taught your baby brother not to play with fire."

Sarah didn't dare move, transfixed by a tiny muscle

ticking above the tight set of Ira's jaw. Though he didn't respond, his gaze never wavered from Josh as the short, stocky man walked out of the saloon, leaving his brother behind.

"I apologize for my brother," Jonah began. "Ever since I've been back from school, he's been like that."

"Like what?" Ira asked with cool authority. "I don't see any difference in the way he is now compared to the way he was ten years ago."

Jonah gave Sarah an uncomfortable glance, and then finished his drink, waving Ira away when he went to refill it. "I know you and Josh have had difficulties in the past," Jonah began, his voice a little strained. "However, that doesn't mean we wanted anything to happen to your family." Jonah stood, turned the chair around and pushed it back under the table. "All of us—Ma, Pa, and myself—we're all real sorry about your brother." He put on his hat, and then touched the brim of his black bowler. "Mrs. Wellington, Ira, please extend my sympathies to your families."

Sarah sensed if she hadn't been there, Ira would have followed Josh and finished whatever there was between them. She was about to ask a few questions when the woman from the piano came up behind Ira.

"Don't let Josh Pruitt bother you." The woman's voice was as smooth as Kentucky bourbon, directed at Sarah even though she put her hand on Ira's shoulder. "Josh has always been one step lower than a pig."

"Lily Barker, meet Mrs. Sarah Wellington," Ira stated with a lazy smile.

"How do you do?" Sarah replied, uncomfortably aware Lily's hand was making slow, seductive little circles on his shoulder. Lily dragged her gaze from Sarah's, then smiled at Ira.

"Aren't you going to buy an old friend a drink?"

"Bartender," Ira called. "Another glass for the lady." Ira stood and pulled out a chair, catching Lily's hand to place a chaste kiss on the back. "It's good to see you again, Lil."

Lil? Sarah repeated to herself, refusing to accept that the little jolt she felt was jealousy. Except for a few lines near the corners of Lily's eyes, she was still a very beautiful woman. Her lips were painted crimson, her hair worn up with several, fiery red ringlets caressing one bare shoulder. Sarah wondered if the low cut and tight fit of Lily's gown hugged curves Ira remembered. Then instantly she told herself it didn't matter if he did.

"I heard rumors that you were in town, but that you'd left again." Lily sank down into the chair with a grace that belied her age. "What brings you back to New Mexico, especially this part of New Mexico? I thought the last time we were together you swore you were leaving for good?"

Lily reached over and brushed her finger over his smooth chin, then moved his coat aside and briefly touched the star pinned on his chest. "I'd also heard you were wearing a badge." Her smile was almost sinful. "You sure have grown into one hell of a good-looking man."

Sarah felt invisible as the bartender plunked down a glass and Ira filled it.

"Zach's dead. I came back to pay my respects."

Lily's smile faded. "I heard about the fire. I'm sorry, Ira, real sorry. I know how much your brothers mean to you."

"If you know anything . . . any detail about it, I'd be obliged." He picked his drink up and swallowed it down.

Sarah frowned, even more curious than before. Had Josh hit a nerve when he ridiculed Ira about protecting his brothers? Did Ira somehow feel responsible? Each time he spoke about Zach, a barely visible sadness clouded his expression.

"How long you staying?" Lily asked.

"Don't know. I just got here."

"If you're lonely, I've got a real sweet girl who could take your mind off of your problems a whole lot better than that whiskey."

Sarah felt the heat of a blush work its way up her neck. Though she knew Lily meant well, the thought of Ira accepting her offer was almost more than she could bear. Though she wished she could enlighten the woman about feminine emancipation, it could wait. However, if Ira left, how could she learn anything about the fire? She was about to ask Lily a few questions, when a glance from Ira stopped her.

"Thanks," he began, "another time maybe. I offered to show Mrs. Wellington what a saloon looks like inside. Since we've done that, we'd best be leaving. I want to make sure she gets back to the hotel safely."

"I'm in no hurry," Sarah replied with a small smile.

Lily gave her a lingering glance, then finished her drink and stood. Ira stood with her, apparently not offended when Lily stepped so close her breasts brushed against his chest. "It's getting late and I need to check on my girls. If you change your mind, Ira, my door is always open."

She reached up and kissed his cheek, then gave him another provocative smile before she glanced at Sarah. "Nice meetin' you, honey."

Sarah watched her ascend the stairs while Ira capped the nearly empty bottle. Though disappointed, she agreed with Lily. It was late, and the air in the room was stale and smoky, and she suspected that the whiskey was the cause of her slight headache. Thankfully, the singing had stopped and all that could be heard were muffled male voices as they played a game of pool in the adjoining room.

Ira paid the bartender and then escorted her outside, stepping off the boardwalk. "You're right," he said as he took a long, deep breath and glanced at the sky. "There are a million stars out."

"It took you long enough to come out of there."

At the sound of Josh's voice, Ira spun, shielding Sarah with his body. Instantly his stance changed to that of a predator, his right hand poised over the butt of his gun. "Don't push me, Josh," he ground out. "I'm just not in the mood tonight, especially not in front of the lady."

"If she's with you, she's no lady." Josh stepped out of the shadows, his hand just inches away from the revolver strapped to his hip. "What's the matter, Ira? Lost your nerve?"

"Go home, Josh. I promised Mrs. Wellington that I'd take her home. I intend to keep that promise."

"I don't think she'd mind a little excitement. After all, if she came to this side of town, she's probably expecting some." Josh took another step, his fingers moving ever so slightly over the handle of his gun. "I've been doing a little practicing. Why don't you try me, right here and now?"

Sarah's mouth went dry. Somehow, a crowd had gathered, peering at them over the top of the saloon's swinging doors. Though she'd been too terrified to notice, Ira had carefully moved her closer to the doorway, keeping himself in front of her. Her confidence vanished. Never in her entire life had she felt so vulnerable. She was more than willing to hide behind Ira's back, even though it made her appear cowardly.

"Go home, Josh," Ira repeated. "Your ma will be worried."

Josh cast an angry glance at the crowd when several guffaws of laughter drifted out of the saloon.

"Josh Pruitt?" The sheriff stepped out of the shadows.

"You'd best get on your horse and go back to your daddy's ranch. There will be no gunfighting in my town tonight."

After several moments of silence, Josh slowly relaxed his threatening stance. "You know, Sheriff, ol' Ira's right. There isn't any sport in gunning down a man who's trying to protect a lady." Josh pushed his bowler off his forehead. "When you've tucked her into bed, why don't you come back around."

Sarah breathed a sigh of relief the moment Josh shoved aside the patrons of the saloon and disappeared inside. A quick glance made her wonder what exactly the crowd expected to see. Had she had a choice, she would have taken cover. Even now her throat was dry and her knees felt weak.

"Marshal Farrell, I would suggest you keep your distance from Josh Pruitt while you're in town." The sheriff came closer, touching the brim of his hat as his gaze fell on Sarah. "Ma'am, are you all right?"

"Yes, thank you," she managed to say in a voice much calmer than she felt.

"We'd best be heading back," Ira said as he gently gripped Sarah's elbow.

Ira waited until Sarah went into her room and locked the door before he descended the stairs, nodding at Mrs. Baca as he left the boarding house. A short time later, he entered the saloon, strode directly over to Josh and spun him around. His fist hammered into the stocky man's ribs. Josh buckled over and would have fallen, but Ira grabbed his collar and pulled him up. "If you'd like to try your hand with me now, you son of a bitch, I'll be waiting outside."

Jonah appeared in the doorway of the other room then came up behind his brother. "That won't be necessary, Ira. Josh and I were just leaving."

"The hell I was," Josh gasped, trying to catch his breath. "Give me five min—"

Jonah took a bottle off the bar and crashed it over his brother's head. Josh would have hit the floor, but Jonah grabbed his brother's arm, and then hoisted it up and over his shoulder, supporting the half-conscious man. Without another word, he carried Josh out of the saloon.

Ira watched them leave, and then returned to the table he'd shared with Sarah and retrieved the bottle still sitting there. "Tell Lily I'll pay for this tomorrow."

Ira stood at the window in his room. He didn't know, nor did he care, what time it was, though he figured it was late. It was quiet outside. The citizens of Santa Fe were sleeping, the lamps put out for the night. He thought about what Josh had said, then his thoughts drifted to Zach, and then to his other brothers. Did they think he'd let them down? Ira took a long drink, refusing to believe it. Yet in his heart he knew he'd let himself down. He'd run away from his past and would probably still be running if it hadn't been for Zach's death.

Ira held up the whiskey bottle and stared at it as if it could justify his feelings of guilt. He took another drink, then glanced up at the sky for the second time that night, only this time he saw Zach's boyish face as he remembered it ten years ago. Swearing under his breath, Ira took another swig, but nothing, not even the whiskey, could ease the ache in his heart.

Chapter Nine

"Good morning, Marshal Farrell," Sarah called.

Ira inwardly groaned. He'd tried to sneak out to use the privy, but damn it all, she was out and about early. He raked his fingers through his tousled hair, painfully aware that he had on the same clothes he'd worn last night. They were now a bit crumpled.

"My, my. You look terrible," she said, and he had the feeling she was enjoying the fact that she'd caught him in such a state. "Are you all right? Is there anything I can do to help, Marshal?"

"No, ma'am," he replied, feeling some satisfaction that two could play her game of formality. "In answer to your question, ma'am, I feel like hell, but I reckon I'll be doing much better later this morning, but thanks for asking . . . ma'am." He added the last one as an afterthought—like shooting an animal that's already dead.

"Did you realize you called me *ma'am* three times in that sentence, *Marshal?*" She lifted his hand and examined his bruised knuckles, then shook her head, even though she wore a smile.

"No, ma'am, I did not," he lied as he snatched his hand away. His mouth tasted like someone had driven a herd of cattle through it and when he turned away too fast, pain exploded in his head. He went back to his room, but she followed him inside and before he could protest, went to the

111

window and pushed aside the heavy draperies, flooding the room in brilliant sunlight. Squinting, he went to the basin and splashed his face with cold water, fumbling for a towel. She grabbed it first.

"I thought we agreed to be less formal." She held it out to him with what he thought was another superior smile and raised her chin ever so slightly—a sign he recognized instantly as her way of expressing an unspoken challenge. And damn, but if her eyes weren't the prettiest shade of blue.

"I seem to remember something on that order." He took the towel and dried his face. "I believe we had an agreement. You were to call me Ira." He paused for effect, then continued before she could answer. "And in turn, I could call you Sarah. Sarah suits you much better than Mrs. Wilmington, and is much easier to remember."

"Willington," she corrected, incorrectly.

"Willington?" he repeated, raising one dark brow. "Don't you mean *Wellington?*"

"That's what I said," she hurried to confirm. "You weren't listening."

He pressed his fingertips to his pounding head thinking there was far too much sunlight in the room to allow him to argue about it. And did her smile suddenly vanish? For a moment, he thought to call her on it, but he didn't want to stir her up much more. He only wanted to prick her a little, as she did him. No, sir. His head hurt too much to go poking at a wasps' nest with a short stick.

"Well, since we've settled that," he replied dryly. "It's like I was saying. Sarah is easier to remember . . . for both of us."

She seemed to accept his surrender. Her smile returned as she strolled toward the window, stretching as she glanced outside. He wondered if she knew how radiant she looked, or how the sun bathed her creamy skin in pristine morning light.

112

He expected she didn't. She was too unaware of her feminine allure, and far too liberated to admit it. Except as he stood there and thought about it, had she showed him a more sensual side last night when they kissed . . . or had he dreamt it?

"By your appearance, it's safe to assume you returned to the Silver Slipper last night and enjoyed a little more of Miss Lily's hospitality."

"Crystal Slipper," he corrected. "If I didn't know you were a married woman, I'd think you were jealous."

Her eyes narrowed, and at that moment, he knew she was.

"Jealous? Jealous of what? I dare say a woman who has to . . . *tend* to the wants and needs of men to make a living these days must have a very low opinion of herself."

"Really? Maybe they just know how to use what God gave them more proficiently. How much do you get paid to make a dress?"

He inwardly smiled. He'd caught her off guard and was enjoying every minute of it.

"Well, ah . . . it depends." She frantically tried to think what a fair price might be. "Something simple is usually about ten to fifteen dollars."

"That much?" he scoffed. "Well, then, how many dresses do you make a week?"

Again, she didn't have a clue . . . she was a journalist, pretending to be a dressmaker. "I don't know yet. I haven't opened—"

"If your shop were open," he corrected, impatiently.

"One . . . or two."

He eased back down. "So, if I'm hearing you correctly, and let me be the first to admit that my head is still cloudy, you're saying that you might make about thirty dollars a week?"

"On the average," she confirmed.

"That's not bad," he admitted. He could tell she was mighty proud of herself by the way she gave him another smile—the kind that goaded him on. "Miss Lily and her girls bring in about five hundred a night. Of course," he paused for effect, "I don't know that for sure."

Her smile vanished. "Of course," she replied tightly.

"However," he continued, enjoying their little game. "I think it's safe to say that tending to the wants and needs of women is more respectable than tending to the wants and needs of men . . . even if it doesn't pay as well. Don't you agree?"

Sarah cast him a sideways glance, undaunted. "What does a marshal earn these days?"

His soft laughter turned into more of a groan. He looked awful in his rumpled clothing. He was pale, his eyes slightly red when they were open. There was still a hint of the musky cologne he had worn last night. Enough to send those cursed butterflies residing in her stomach into nervous flight.

"Not near what dressmaking pays, that's for sure," he replied honestly, flexing the fingers of his bruised right hand.

Feeling sorry for him, she filled a glass with water from the pitcher on his bureau. "Here, maybe this will make you feel better."

He accepted the glass. "Thank you." After he finished, he handed it back with a request to close the curtains.

"What you need is fresh air and sunshine," she confirmed with a stubborn nod.

"What I need is darkness and solitude."

"Then perhaps I should have the sheriff put you in jail for public drunkenness."

"If it's dark and quiet, I'll go peacefully."

She smiled at his pained expression when he went over to the bed and reclined upon it. Then, almost as if acting out of habit, his hand fell to his side and he felt for his gun belt then glanced around the room until he found it.

"Don't you remember putting it on the chair?" She frowned, wondering why he seemed edgy without it. "Surely you don't sleep in it?"

He muttered something about sleeping, but she interrupted him before he said something she didn't want to hear. "You're safe with me," she teased. "I won't let anyone in."

"That's good, 'cause I think Josh Pruitt took a liking to you last night." Ira closed his eyes, pressing his thumb and forefinger against the bridge of his nose. "He's not very smart, but if I remember correctly, he's persistent. I wouldn't want him calling till I can—"

"Stand without help?" she finished mockingly. "I suppose it is difficult to draw down on your opponent, lying on your back."

He looked at her then, and something other than pain flicked across his gaze. "He's not the kind of man a lady like you would want to get mixed up with." Ira rose to a sitting position. "He's hated me for years. He could easily murder two innocent people, especially if one of them was a Farrell."

Sarah frowned. Though she wanted to deny it, Ira's confession had shed a new and unwanted light on her cousin's unfortunate demise. Had she died because she suspected that someone in a position of authority was corrupt? Or had she simply had the misfortune of being too close to a legend's brother? She glanced at the man on the bed—now, more than ever, disturbed by the way he was never without the means to protect himself. Obviously he felt the need, and now she realized he had good reason.

He was a legend. Storytellers proclaimed him to be one of the fastest guns in the West. Wouldn't it be understandable for him to be a target for a young, ambitious gunslinger looking to make a name for himself? And what of the families and friends of the men Ira had arrested, or those he had sent to an untimely death on the gallows? It wasn't unreasonable to assume they might seek revenge.

She shivered as she recalled their encounter the previous evening. If she hadn't been there, would Josh Pruitt be dead?

"If it isn't too much to ask," Ira stated a little impatiently, "I'd like to wash up and change my clothes."

Drawn back from her thoughts, Sarah agreed, then gladly stepped outside, pulling the door closed as she left. Troubled, she decided to take her mind off their discussion and go to the train station to see if her supplies had arrived. After she donned her coat and bonnet, she started down the stairs just as the sheriff came through the front door.

The tall, attractive man smiled and took off his hat, revealing thick, curly, black hair. Once more she thought to divulge her concerns, but decided against it until she knew him better. "Good morning, Sheriff." She offered her hand. "It's nice to see you again."

"Good morning, ma'am. Pardon my glove," he said as he took her hand in his. "You can call me Cooper, ma'am." His teeth seemed excessively white under his coal-black moustache. The handsome sheriff motioned upstairs. "I was told Ira was staying here. I didn't know you were staying here too." He cleared his throat as if embarrassed. "If you don't mind me asking, how'd you come to know Ira?"

"Miss Emily was my cousin. I met Ira when I went to the Farrell ranch to visit her grave."

He frowned as he nodded, digesting the information. "Have you seen Ira today?"

"Why do you ask?" she countered.

"Earl from the telegraph was at the saloon last night. He

said Ira broke a bottle over Josh Pruitt's head in a scuffle. Jonah must have taken Josh home 'cause they're not in town, but since Ira's here, I thought I'd come by and get his story."

She met Cooper's gaze. "If you don't mind me asking, how do you know the marshal?" she asked.

"I don't. Not really. I had a small spread close to his father's, but for years they never paid me much attention. In fact, by the time they did, Ira had already left. Anyway, after my wife died, Cole made me an offer, I pulled up stakes and would have left, but the mayor offered me a job. Santa Fe needed a sheriff, so here I am."

"I'm sorry," she said. "About your wife, and the loss of your ranch."

"Don't be. It's been almost six years now. Ranching's hard work for one man. Besides, I enjoy what I do."

"Sounds like you made a wise choice." She gave him a cheerful smile. "Now, if you'll excuse me, I'm expecting some supplies to arrive at the train station."

"I'll walk with you. Perhaps I can be of some use."

"I thought you came to see Ira," she said as he opened the door.

"I did, but spending some time with you is much more appealing than spending it with Ira." Humor danced in his dark brown eyes. Once they were outside, he put on his hat and walked beside her. "Silas Pruitt told me that you have plans to reopen Miss Emily's dress shop. Does that mean you're staying?"

"Yes, that's correct."

"I assumed as much when Silas asked me to help him find some carpenters. They can start later today and I reckon the renovations will be finished by the end of the week."

"Really?" Sarah replied with a puzzled frown. "Then there wasn't as much damage as I expected."

"No, ma'am. Just to the roof. Adobe doesn't burn, and the fire was put out quickly."

"Did you know my cousin?" Sarah asked as they strolled down the boardwalk.

"Yes, ma'am. She was a real nice lady."

"Did you know that she was engaged to Zachary Farrell?"

"I had heard the rumors," Cooper said.

"Rumors?"

He looked a little sheepish. "Yes, ma'am. Miss Emily and Zachary had what most folks would call a troubled relationship."

"Really? In what way?"

"They fought a lot. One minute they were sweethearts, the next she was threatening to sell up and move back to St. Louis."

Sarah frowned. She didn't remember anything in Emily's letters about a tumultuous relationship. Suspicious, she carefully glanced at the sheriff's coat. Though it was neatly tailored, the buttons weren't anything out of the ordinary, nor was it the quality of Emily's work. Her hopes plummeted, yet she felt a tinge of relief. The man seemed very pleasant.

"You look sad. I'm sorry if I said something to upset you."

She met the sheriff's gaze, wondering if his concern was genuine. "Well, here we are," she replied with a smile. When she returned, it was with the news that her packages would probably be on tomorrow's train. She gave an impatient sigh. "Probably. That's not really an answer, is it?"

"Well, maybe not for a big city like St. Louis, but for us, it's the best we can hope for." He touched the brim of his hat. "I'll be around here in the morning just in case."

Sarah spent the rest of the morning investigating the different shops, stopping at the mercantile for a few supplies and to see what kind of ready-made dresses hung on hooks at the back of the shop. An older man was there with his daughter, and by the man's garments, he was more accustomed to being on a horse than he was at encouraging his daughter to try on a dress.

Though Sarah tried not to eavesdrop, it was difficult not to. The girl had no desire to trade in her Levis and boots for lace and petticoats, complaining more and more with each selection her father made. Finally her father pulled one out and held it before him, asking the girl's opinion.

Sarah smothered a giggle when his daughter stood back and seemed to give it a careful look. Then with a defiant flick of her head, she turned abruptly and walked toward the door, calling over her shoulder that she thought it looked good . . . *on him* and suggested he buy the matching bonnet as well.

"Damn it," the man muttered, hanging the dress back on the hook. He turned and nearly bumped into Sarah, yanking off his hat. "Excuse me, ma'am. I didn't mean to offend you."

Sarah smiled. "You didn't." She cast a quick glance at the open door where the man's daughter stood on the boardwalk, feeding her horse something she'd pulled from a pocket. "If you don't mind my saying so, I was rebellious when I was her age." She nodded at the man's skeptical expression. "Really, I was. I'm the new dressmaker, Sarah Wellington." She held out her hand.

"James Roland," the man replied, shaking her hand. "That's my daughter, Liberty."

Again Sarah smiled. "She certainly suits her name."

"Yes, ma'am, she does for sure. Her ma's been dead for some years now, and I guess I let her get away with dressing like a boy for too many years. Now, I'm afraid she's never going to dress like a proper young lady."

"There's hope, I assure you. I'm the new dressmaker. My shop isn't quite ready, but why don't you bring Liberty by in a week or two, and maybe I can make something she'd like."

The rancher gave a sigh of relief. "If you think it'll do some good, I'm willing to try." He nodded his farewell, then put his hat on and left Sarah to finish her shopping.

By evening time, Sarah had introduced herself to most of the other shopkeepers. She especially liked Mr. Moya, the editor of the local newspaper, who seemed genuinely interested in the possibility of publishing some of her stories in spite of the fact that she declined to let him know of her journalistic background.

She had a quick bite to eat, purchasing a small sack of cookies for a snack later. Once back in her room, she kicked off her shoes and with a pencil and paper, curled up on the chair and jotted down a few ideas, deciding that her decision to stay in Santa Fe was a wise one. In time, she'd hire a seamstress, leaving her free to devote all her time to writing.

Ira splashed cold water over his face, washing away the last of the soap from his shave. He found a towel and dried, then began to dress. Whatever Mrs. Baca made him drink, helped his headache, regardless of the terrible taste. His head still hurt when he moved too fast, but he couldn't afford to waste any more time. Clad in black trousers and silver vest, he slipped on a matching black jacket, pinned on his badge and picked up his new hat. Once outside, he winced a little as the setting sun stabbed at him while he made his way to the telegraph office.

"Where to?" the little, balding man asked, picking up a pad of paper and a pencil, pushing it toward Ira.

Ira finished his note and handed it to the man. "First one goes to Mrs. Ginger Carson, Carefree, Arizona." He wrote another. "This one goes to Richard Granger in St. Louis, and this goes to Mayor James, Carefree, Arizona."

"Where can I find you when I get answers?" the man asked, pulling up the stool to sit down.

"I'll check with you tomorrow, or you can leave them at Mrs. Baca's boarding house." Ira paid the man, then decided to talk to a few merchants to see if he could find anything out about the fire.

Chapter Ten

The next day, Ira headed toward the sheriff's office shortly after ten. He wanted to read the sheriff's reports and see if there were any details the man found when he did his investigation. Ira had just stepped up on the boardwalk when he spotted Sarah walking with a man. The man carried too many boxes for him to see his face clearly.

"Well, good afternoon, Marshal," Sarah said, pausing before the dress shop.

Ira touched the brim of his hat. "Mrs. Wellington." He remembered mispronouncing her name and was about to comment on it, but then the man shifted the boxes. Sunlight glinted on the badge pinned to his shirt.

"Sheriff," Ira stated, extending his hand.

The sheriff shuffled some boxes then returned his handshake. "Marshal Farrell. I see you're no worse for wear after your scuffle with Josh."

They stepped aside while several men carried in a heavy crate. Though it seemed a friendly exchange, Sarah sensed an underlying tension between the two lawmen.

"By the way, my condolences to you and your family," Cooper added.

"Thanks," Ira said, his brows drawing together. "I was on my way to talk to you about the fire."

"Why don't I meet you over there in a few minutes?"

"Why don't we just talk here?" Ira countered, following

them into the shop.

"Do you think that's wise in front of the lady?" Cooper asked as he set the boxes on the counter.

Sarah raised one fair brow. "Gentlemen, please," she replied tersely. "Whatever information you may have concerning my cousin's accident, it is information I have a right to hear."

Much to her surprise, Ira wasn't as subtle. "I don't think it was an accident."

Cooper Finch's smile faded. "What else could it have been?"

"Murder."

The sheriff pushed his hat off his forehead. "That's rather a serious accusation, isn't it, Marshal?"

"Perhaps. Did you investigate that possibility, look for any clues before they were buried?"

By the sheriff's expression, Sarah knew he hadn't. She expected him to be offended, but he didn't seem particularly bothered.

"I didn't see the need," the sheriff responded dryly.

"As one lawman to another," Ira said, "I would have expected a search, maybe an inquiry or two, just in case someone might have heard something or seen something."

"It was late, Marshal. A storm was brewing. There weren't many folks out that night."

"So I've discovered. Anyway, I'd like to see your report," Ira said, his tone neither terse nor affable.

The sheriff smoothed his moustache. "Very well, come by my office in an hour." He touched the brim of his hat. "Good day, Mrs. Wellington. If you need anything . . . anything at all, my door is always open."

The moment he left, Sarah rounded on Ira. "What was that?" she demanded. "I thought you told me to keep quiet about our suspicions. You . . . you very nearly insulted him, implying he didn't do a thorough job. And what about the night before last? You practically accused the Pruitt brothers of purposely setting the fire."

Ira's frown lessened, but when he met her gaze, his was filled with cool authority. "I did what I had to do, Sarah. I—"

"You attacked him."

"I challenged him. There's a difference."

"Hardly," she scoffed. "Now that you've told him what you suspect, all of Santa Fe will know."

"I'm fairly sure they already do. That's the plan."

"The plan?" she questioned, still seething.

"Yes. As each suspect learns I'm on the hunt, someone's going to get nervous. Nervous men make mistakes." He heaved an impatient sigh. "Now what are you doing for dinner tonight?"

"Is that all you think about? I'm dining alone," she countered, stepping outside.

"Sarah, please," he said. It was the second time he seemed genuinely apologetic. "I didn't expect to run into Sheriff Finch on the street. I had no intention of embarrass—"

"Embarrassed?" she replied with a rebellious toss of her head, turning to lock the door the moment he stepped out. "Is that what you think? That I'm embarrassed?" She gave a disbelieving laugh. "I'm not that . . . that childish. I'm angry. I'm angry that you tell me one thing then do another. You asked me to trust you, and I have, but then you go forward with your plan as if my opinion doesn't matter. In short, you have not been very honest with me."

Ira looked as if he were weighing what she said and was about to speak when a young boy ran up to him.

"Marshal Farrell?" The boy thrust out two telegrams. "These came for you. I was going to take them to the hotel, but then I saw you talking"—the boy grinned at Sarah—"to this pretty lady."

Ira reached into his pocket and pulled out a nickel, dropping it in the child's hand.

"Gee, thanks, Marshal."

Sarah stewed while Ira read them both, noticing his expression change when he finished the second. Gone was his look of remorse, replaced with his usual arrogance as he caught her elbow and none too gently ushered her toward the hotel.

"Where are we going?" she asked, trying to pull free, but his fingers tightened and she realized she couldn't get away without making a scene. Ira nodded politely as they passed several couples and two older ladies.

"Afternoon, ladies," he said, touching the brim of his hat, then he leaned closer to Sarah's ear. "Someplace private."

"What for?" she demanded as he opened the door of the hotel and practically pushed her inside.

"To talk about honesty," he countered tersely.

"*Hola,* Ira. You feeling better, Ira?"

Ira flashed the *patrona* a smile. "Yes, Mrs. Baca, I'm feeling much better." He urged Sarah up the stairs. "Thank you for asking."

Once inside his room, he let her go then leaned back against the door, barring her escape. There was something in his manner, something menacing—almost as if she were a tender morsel of meat and he a hungry predator. His steady gaze bore into her then slowly slid down her body, lingering on the swell of her breasts until she nervously fingered the cameo pinned at her throat.

"Let me go, Ira. It isn't proper for me to be in your room like this."

"Why's that?" he asked, his voice smooth and seductive.

The smoldering flame she saw in his eyes made her shiver. "It's no worse than us dining together, or having a drink together at the saloon, or sharing a kiss on a darkened street." The last was stated slowly, purposefully.

"It's perfectly obvious. I-I'm a married woman and you-you're a single man." She inwardly cringed at the breathy sound of her voice as he pushed away from the door and came closer. She yelped when he caught her around the waist and pulled her tightly against his chest, so close his breath mingled with hers.

"You're trembling," he murmured, brushing his knuckle across her cheek. "Are you afraid of me?" he whispered close to her ear. "Are you afraid of what I'd do if I found out that you weren't being honest with me—that you can look me square in the eyes and lie?"

"I-I don't know what you're talking about." She tried to shove him back, but his warm hand explored the small of her back, drawing her even closer.

"Tell me something, Sarah. Does your husband make you tremble?"

"Yes . . . no. Stop this instant."

His manly scent washed over her as he held her captive and placed several gentle kisses on the sensitive place below her ear. He lifted his head, caught her chin. "There is no Andrew Wellington, is there?"

She was rendered speechless by his question.

"Answer me," he murmured. Slowly his fingers slipped down her chin to caress her throat.

"No, damn you, there isn't," she said defiantly.

He kissed her again, teasing her lips until she opened for him. His tongue plunged inside, tasting, toying, dueling with hers until she moaned and leaned into him. His mouth was ravenous, and before she realized what was happening, she slipped her arms around his neck, kissing him back with all the passion he so expertly stoked to life. She gasped a protest and tried to move away, but he wouldn't let her.

His kiss deepened almost savagely before he grabbed her shoulders and held her away from him. His expression changed again right before her eyes. Slowly as realization penetrated the passion between them, she recognized the torment in his. He turned away then, raking his fingers angrily through his hair.

"You lied to me. Your name is Sarah Brighton and you're a female newspaper reporter." The last was said as if it left a bad taste in his mouth.

She blinked several times. "H-how did you find out?" She took a step closer, stopping when he turned.

"In my business," he replied bitterly, "I've made a few influential friends—friends that owe me favors, who have other friends who owe them favors. I sent a wire to a certain mayor who sent one to a certain senator. Seems there's no record of a Lord and Lady Wellington residing in St. Louis, or in all of Missouri, for that matter. However, there is a Sarah Brighton, who works for the *St. Louis Herald*. A woman who's made quite a name for herself . . . back in St. Louis."

He stared at her for several long minutes, then went to the bureau and filled a glass with water. "I'm wondering why you're here. I'm wondering why you felt the need to hide your true identity, but mostly I'm wondering what you hope to gain by opening a dress shop so you can learn more about Zach's and Miss Emily's deaths." He took a drink, but she knew he wasn't through. "Perhaps you're looking for a good story?"

She clutched her hands tightly together. "I can explain."

He nodded. "Please do."

She took a calming breath then moistened her dry lips. "It's true, at least some of what you said. I find that pretending to be married improves my ability to gather information necessary to write good articles. I also find that it helps me avoid the . . . the complication of being pursued." She gave a small laugh. "However, that didn't seem to stop you. I lied about who I am, and even about what I do, but when you hold me and kiss me . . ."

She dropped her gaze to her tightly clasped hands for a moment then lifted her chin and matched his steady gaze. "I won't lie about the fact that I'm attracted to you." There, she admitted it, and it felt quite liberating. "Perhaps I shouldn't be here, but I have as much right as you to learn the truth about what really happened."

Her heart hammered against her breast as he came to her, clasping her arms in a firm grip. There wasn't time for any more thoughts as he pulled her close and thoroughly kissed her.

"You're right," he murmured against her lips.

Her eyes fluttered open and she blinked several times as if to clear her head. "I-I am?"

"Yes," he agreed, but she sensed he was mocking her.

"About what?"

"You shouldn't be here. But I can see that you've already made up your mind to stay." He looked at her for a long time, then turned and picked his hat up off the chair. "If you had any sense, you'd pack your things and leave. This isn't St. Louis."

"Any sense," she shot back. "You have no right to speak to me like that. I want to be here. I have a right to be here," she confirmed a little desperately. "I'm a grown woman, Ira. I make my own decisions. And, one of them is to learn the truth about my cousin's accident."

His smile was almost menacing as he walked to the door. "Then you'd best not get in my way."

He left before her anger surfaced. She picked up a glass and thought to throw it, then stopped herself, taking a long deep breath to help gain control of her rampant emotions. After a few moments she was composed enough to return to her shop. Taking up a piece of paper, she searched around for a bottle of ink and a pen. What had Ira said? Nervous men make mistakes? More determined than ever, she began to write.

Ira spent the next two days talking to more of the local merchants, and though most of them were sympathetic, none could offer any information that didn't coincide with Sheriff Finch's report. He stopped by the Crystal Slipper to talk with Lily, only to learn that she had taken some food to a sick friend. Making the most of his situation, he had a cool glass of beer before heading toward the hotel.

Rounding the corner, he saw Sarah at the depot, speaking with one of the conductors. By the stiff set of her shoulders, and the tight set of the man's jaw, Ira concluded the two were having an argument. He'd been on the receiving end of her sharp tongue and almost felt sorry for the older man. Sarah Well—Brighton, he mentally corrected—was about the most confusing woman he'd ever met. In between giving him what for, she had slipped in a little confession. *I won't lie about the fact that I'm attracted to you.*

That little bit of news had just about rocked him back on his boot heels. So much so, that he'd replayed the scene over and over in his head and finally came to the conclusion that he could have handled it a little better. He was used to women falling all over themselves to get his attention, but none had ever had the courage to just come out and say it.

But Sarah wasn't like his usual kind of woman. She was clever, well-educated, determined and . . . a lousy liar. She obviously had her pride, as he had his, and at the time, it was his pride she was stepping all over by insisting that she could help with his investigation.

The memory of their argument slowly faded, replaced with a more pleasant one of how she seemingly melted in his arms. He frowned, watching the pair argue, thinking he had successfully avoided thinking about her—until now. He hesitated for a moment, and then strode purposely toward the depot.

"Afternoon, Mrs. Wellington." Ira touched the brim of his hat when she spun to glare at him. She was surrounded by several wooden crates. None were overly large, but there were several she couldn't handle by herself.

Sarah stopped in mid-sentence, and nodded. "Good afternoon, Marshal." She turned back to the older man. "As I was saying—"

"Excuse me," Ira interrupted. "Are these your boxes?"

She cast him a sideways glance, raising one brow. "They are."

"May I assume you might need some assistance with them?" he asked. Before she could answer, the older man nodded enthusiastically.

"Yes, Marshal, I was just explaining to . . ." The man gave Sarah a rather weak smile. ". . . to the lady here, that I've done all I can do. Most of the heavy stuff's been delivered, and I don't have any more time to spare. She'll just have to find someone else to help her take the rest of these to her shop."

"Then the problem's solved," Ira concluded. He stepped up on the platform and lifted one of the larger boxes marked Singer Company. "Lead on, Mrs. Wellington."

She gave him another cool stare, then hoisted a smaller

130

box and took off quicker than he expected. It was several moments before he caught up. "What's in here? It weighs a ton."

"Nothing that you should be concerned with," she snapped. "If it's too heavy, take this one and let me have it."

"On the contrary, I'd rather wreck my back than yours," he teased, following her into the shop. He placed the box on a new table and took off the lid. "Well, I'll be," he muttered with a skeptical edge to his voice as he lifted out a black sewing machine and placed it on the table next to the box. "Do you really know how to use this thing, or was that—"

"I can sew," Sarah declared as she opened one of the boxes already on the floor, the one containing her typewriting machine. "Although it's really none of your business, I type better than I sew, and I enjoy writing articles more than making dresses. I will probably hire a seamstress to help me with any orders. However, I shan't need any help expressing my opinions on women in business, visiting saloons and the horrible taste of whiskey."

The painters were still busy, but she didn't seem to notice as she opened several more boxes. "Don't you have something more important to do, Marshal?"

He thought to goad her further, but decided against it. "Yes, ma'am, I do. But first I'll just go over and collect the rest of your packages." When he returned with the last two, she motioned toward the back of the room through a door leading to a little apartment where she had already stored some of the bolts of colorful wools and ginghams while the painted shelves dried.

A desk had been placed in the back of the room, away from curious eyes, along with another box of paper, and that's where she placed her typewriter. At the sight of a bed, nightstand and two trunks, Ira realized that she planned on living there.

"Do you really think this is a good idea?" he asked.

She spun, apparently still angry.

"Listen," he began calmly. "I don't mean that you can't, I just mean that it might not be safe."

"I'm not worried," she replied, and by the softening of her stance, he felt confident that he'd smoothed a few feathers. "I have my gun should anyone dare to disturb me."

He thought about that for a moment, thought about how useless her gun would be against someone with murder on his mind. But then he had no real proof there had been a murder. "Is there anything else I can help with?" he asked, trying to keep his tone nonaggressive.

She gave him a skeptical glance. "I suppose, if you can spare the time from your investigation, I could use some help measuring the windows." She nodded toward the corner where a ladder leaned against the wall. "Speaking about the investigation, have you discovered who murdered my cousin yet, Marshal Farrell?"

Ira put the ladder next to the front window. "Now, now, Mrs. Wellington . . ." he lowered his voice, "or should I say Miss Brighton? You shouldn't be jumping to any conclusions, especially in front of strangers." He nodded toward the painter as the man finished the last few strokes. The moment the painter left, Sarah rounded on Ira.

"There's something you should know," she began, holding the ladder while Ira measured the width of the window. She had decided a little lace would make the place look more feminine. "Emily sent me a letter about a month before I received notification of her death. I didn't realize it at the time, but now that I've come to Santa Fe, met a few of the people she mentioned, I think she suspected something."

Ira shook his head in disbelief. "You've been keeping this from me?"

"I didn't mention it before, because . . . well, because I wasn't certain I could trust you."

"Where have I heard that before?" he muttered under his breath. "What did she say?"

"It's rather vague, and as I said, I didn't think too much about the letter at first, but then after . . . well, afterwards, when I reread it, I realized that something she said was rather intriguing, almost as if she suggested that there was some sort of conspiracy going on."

"Four feet, six inches," Ira said as he climbed down.

She made a hasty note. "Good, thank you."

"Do you still have the letter?" Ira asked.

"Yes, it's in my room back at the hotel."

Ira picked up the ladder and carried it into the back room, dusting off his hands when he returned. "Did she name any names?"

"Not any I recognized until I met the Pruitts."

"Are we done here?" Ira asked.

Sarah glanced around and smiled. "Yes. I believe so."

"I'm starving. Why don't we have a look at Emily's letter then get some supper?"

"Do you think that's wise," she said with a worried frown.

"Reading the letter or supper?" he teased. She melted a little inside at the arrogant humor that glittered in his laughing grey eyes. Apparently he'd forgiven her faster than she'd forgiven him.

"Supper," she confirmed.

"Let me see. You've had supper with me, gone to the Crystal Slipper Saloon *with me,* and now you're worried what people will think if they see us together?"

She gave him a firm look. "Nevertheless, it might be best if I keep up the pretense of being Mrs. Wellington for just a little longer."

133

He heaved an impatient sigh. "As much as it pains me to leave you alone, I agree." He put his hand on the knob. "I'll be in my room later if you feel like coming by." His expression was scandalous.

Ira opened the door and was stunned to see Billy Carson standing outside, his hand raised to knock. "Marshal Farrell, boy I'm glad I found you. I was just over at the mercantile delivering their order when I overheard some men talking. When I heard your name, I thought maybe I'd come and talk to you about a matter of utmost importance. Is there a place we can get a drink?"

Ira quickly composed himself, tossed a glance over his shoulder at Sarah, and then stepped outside, pulling the door closed. "Yeah . . . sure."

Ira ushered Billy over to the saloon. Four men played cards at a round table close by, but other than recognizing the proprietor from the mercantile and the old man who ran the telegraph, Ira didn't see anyone he knew. Once they got to the bar, Ira ordered two beers. "What's on your mind, Billy?"

"Ginger. I don't know what to do, Marshal. All I know is that if I catch the varmint Ginger's been sleeping with, I'm going to kill him with my bare hands."

Ira nearly choked on his beer. He had forgotten all about Ginger. Hell, he hadn't even looked at another woman since meeting Sarah. Though he wasn't proud of himself, he didn't see the need to confess his sins. "Well, I don't know how I can help you, Billy. Adultery isn't exactly against the law, but I will give you some friendly advice."

"What's that?"

"If Gin—Mrs. Carson is straying some, perhaps she's lonely . . . feeling kind of left out."

"Left out of what?"

"Out of your life," Ira said with more conviction than he

felt. "If she were my wife, I'd pay more attention to her. Why . . ." He hesitated, searching his mind for something else, but he couldn't think of a way to make the short little man any more appealing. ". . . I'd—"

"Take her a present."

Ira turned, relieved to see Lily standing behind them.

"Pardon me, boys, for eavesdropping." She gave Billy her best smile. "Do you travel away from home a lot?" she asked with a concerned expression on her face.

Billy nodded. "Yes, ma'am, I do."

"Well, if I were married to a handsome man like you and he was never home, I'd get plumb lonely too. Now I'm not saying your wife was right to share her attentions."

Lily looked at Ira for a moment, then turned back to her prey, flicking the man's bow tie with a painted red nail. "What I'm saying is maybe you need to make her feel special. Take her a present. Buy her something black and desirable to wear. Give it to her when you're home next, if you know what I mean." She winked, then bumped him in the groin with her hip. "Lucy over there can help with your selections, if you need it."

Billy glanced at the enticing blonde clad in a black lace gown. At the same time his cheeks turned bright red. "Y-yes, ma'am. Th-thank you, ma'am." Billy looked at Ira. "Thanks for the beer, Marshal, but I've got a hankering to do some shopping and get on back to Arizona." He touched the brim of his bowler and damned near ran out the door.

Ira leaned against the bar and pushed his hat back on his head. "Whew," he said with a sheepish grin. "Thanks for getting me out of that little mess."

"Ira Farrell, I thought I told you never to get involved with married women. Jealous men are dangerous and sometimes even desperate enough to do harm to the culprit seducing their wives." She cupped Ira's smooth chin. "And that would be a crying shame."

Ira laughed, then turned around and took another sip of beer. "Believe me, Lily, I tried to take your advice."

"Speaking of married women, I've heard rumors about you and that Mrs. Wellington you brought in here the other night."

Ira tried to look contrite, but knew Lily knew him too well to believe it. "You know how people like to talk. This town's full of gossips. Just remember, Lil, not everything you hear is true."

"Well, if you won't take my advice, then at least be discreet." Lily fingered the red lace of her cuff. "If her husband has money, he's even more dangerous."

Ira gave her a skeptical look. "How fast with a gun can a shipbuilder be?" he replied with a teasing twinkle in his eyes.

"He doesn't have to be fast. If what you say is true, he has the money to hire someone to do his dirty work." She turned to the bartender. "Ira's beers are on the house, Sam."

Ira watched her walk away, and then finished his beer. He pushed his hat down on his forehead then nodded at the men playing cards. Ira touched the brim of his hat on his way out the door. "Gentlemen."

Sarah glanced at her watch. She'd been putting things away in her shop and now it was nearly suppertime. She quickly put on her coat, and after locking up her store, headed toward the boarding house. She spoke briefly with Mrs. Baca, then hurried to her room to retrieve Emily's letter. Glancing around to make sure none of the other guests were about, Sarah hurried down the hall and knocked softly on Ira's door.

"You look too good to be eating alone," he said, pulling

her into his arms. He kissed her, and at the same time took the envelope from her slack fingers.

"Are you always so thorough?"

"What?" he said, opening the letter.

"You know what I mean," she chided.

"Do I kiss all women like that?" he teased, scanning the page. "Mostly just you."

"Mostly me?" she repeated. She would have scolded him further, but his expression changed to one more serious. "What? What do you see that I didn't?"

From the letter, his gaze flicked up to hers. "Emily says here that the sheriff was sometimes distressing." Ira raised a brow questioningly. "You're a woman, what does that mean?"

Sarah shrugged. "I assume he was interested in her, and since she was in love with your brother, she found his attentions rather *distressing*."

"She seems to have the same problem with *Mr.* Pruitt," he added. "But, she doesn't say which one."

"Yes, I noticed that, and I wish I knew."

Ira folded the letter. "Do you mind if I show this to Cole?"

"Is he in town?" she asked. The thought of a story about cattle ranching skittered through her mind. The local newspaper might not be interested, but she was sure her old editor back in St. Louis would be.

"No. I'd like Cole and Jeb to see Emily's letter. Maybe they can help me figure it out." He didn't tell her that he'd noted the corral down by the train station seemed to have a few broken boards, as if it had been filled to overflowing with cattle. "It's also close to Adam's birthday, and I have to deliver his present."

He put his knuckle under her chin, lifting her face to give her a soft kiss. "Promise me, you won't ask too many questions. For now, it would be best if you just kept to your dress-making."

"I suppose," she replied despondently when he let her go.

"You still have that little shooter you pulled on me, don't you?"

"Of course." She slipped her hand into the bag and drew on him with a superior smile. "See?"

He pushed her hand down. "Good, keep it in your bag. I'll sleep better knowing that you've got your gun." He cupped her cheek and grinned. "How did you put it that day? 'I warn you, Mr. Farrell, I am an excellent shot.' "

She smiled at his terrible attempt to mimic her voice. "Well, I am, and you'd be wise to remember that." He opened the door, hinting that she should leave. "My, how you've changed," she admonished, disappointed that they wouldn't be having dinner together. "When you thought I was a married woman, you were relentless. Now that you know I'm not, you've become quite cautious."

His eyes darkened and made her tingle inside. "That was before . . . when I thought you were someone else's wife." He took a step closer, his hand slipping around her neck as Sarah found herself pulled close for a short, yet intoxicating kiss. When he lifted his head, his gaze pierced her heart. "But, now it's different." His breath was warm on her moist lips as he hesitated for a moment. She wanted him to kiss her again, but instead, he held her back. "Now I care what people will say. It will look better for you if you avoid me."

"You're asking the impossible," she murmured, tucking a loose curl into her neat chignon.

"What did you say?" he asked. His smile was sinful.

She met his gaze. "I said, *you're* impossible."

Chapter Eleven

Sarah moved the dress shop lamp a little closer, and then typed away on her first story, using some of the notes she'd made when she and Ira had supper that first night. Tomorrow she would go and see the editor of Santa Fe's only newspaper and see if he'd print her story. If not, there was always St. Louis. She paused, thinking about her old job, but then her thoughts turned back to Ira. She had another problem. She needed to figure out how she was going to tell the citizens of the bustling little town that she was soon to be *widowed*.

Someone knocked on the door to her shop, and after she quickly checked the little watch pinned on her dress, she picked up the lamp and went to the door.

"Sheriff Finch," she said with a cheerful smile. "Come in."

"I hope I'm not intruding, Mrs. Wellington, but I saw your light while I was making my rounds and thought I'd make certain everything was all right."

She motioned around the tidy shop. "As you can see, everything is in order."

His smile was generous. "Have you had supper yet?"

"No, as a matter of fact."

"Then perchance you will do me the honor?" Cooper asked.

"I suppose there's no harm in dining with the local sheriff," she said with a smile. Perhaps if she were seen with

Cooper, it would knock the town gossips off the scent of her and Ira. She put the lamp on the table and blew it out, using the light from the street lamps to lift her coat from the hook. "Shall we?"

Unlike Ira, the sheriff didn't care where they sat, choosing a table in the center of the room. "How's the shop coming?" he asked as he assisted her with her chair.

"Very well, thank you."

"If you're as talented as your cousin, you're bound to be busy." The waitress came over and took their order. At the same time, Ira came in and took a table in the far corner. The waitress went over immediately, and though Sarah tried not to notice, it appeared that Ira flirted with her. Whatever he said caused the woman to laugh before she went back into the kitchen.

"I'm surprised to find Santa Fe so civilized," Sarah commented, dragging her gaze away from Ira to focus her attention on the sheriff. "I'm not much of a cook and to find a restaurant of this caliber is quite liberating."

The sheriff smiled and smoothed his moustache. "Liberating?"

"Yes. Having a place to eat, delivers me from the kitchen." She gave him her best smile, hoping Ira watched.

"I see," Cooper began. "I thought I heard you typing when I came in tonight. One of those boxes was pretty heavy and I'm thinking you have one of those new typewriting machines."

"Yes, I do," she confirmed reluctantly. "I suppose there's no harm in telling you that I often write articles for local newspapers."

He took a sip of coffee. "Really, about what?"

"Things that I hope my readers will find interesting."

"Such as?" Cooper asked.

"Well, such as what it's like in a saloon from a woman's point of view."

Cooper grinned. "So that's why you were at the Crystal Slipper." He put down his cup. "I was wondering why Ira would take a lady like you into a saloon."

"I don't think he really wanted to, but I can be very persuasive at times." She cast a fleeting look Ira's direction. He had finished his meal rather quickly, stood and retrieved his hat. He stopped only long enough to pay his bill then left without glancing her way.

"I can only imagine." Cooper leaned back while their food was served. "When will your husband be arriving? I'm looking forward to meeting him."

She matched the sheriff's steady gaze. "My husband won't be joining me . . . at least for a while."

"I see. Well, allow me to offer my services should you need anything in his absence."

Sarah would have responded, but the sheriff motioned for the waitress to bring more coffee. Though he was pleasant enough company, she sensed there was something underlying his concern for her welfare. Her thoughts returned to Ira and the suggestive way they had parted. When at last she and the sheriff were through eating, she accepted his offer to walk her back to the hotel.

"When can I expect to read your first article in the *New Mexican*?" Cooper inquired.

"I'm not sure. It depends if the editor finds it interesting."

"What's it about?" An older man nodded as he walked past them. Cooper touched the brim of his hat, but didn't stop to talk.

"I'm sure you're aware that Marshal Farrell is rather well

known in this area." She glanced over at the sheriff. "I think his story would attract readers, don't you agree?" He met her gaze and grinned.

"Yes, I do." His smile slowly faded. "I sure don't understand why he's going around spreading rumors about Miss Emily and Zachary. I can understand he's upset over their loss, but murder? That just doesn't make any sense at all."

"Why do you say that?" Sarah asked, hoping to learn anything that might reveal something that Ira might have missed.

"Well, for one thing, the fire was started when a lamp got knocked over. There's a lot of stuff that can catch fire real quick in a dress shop. I'm thinking it just got too hot too fast before Zach could put it out. It was the smoke that killed them."

Sarah was quiet for a little while, thinking about the button and why Emily would hold on to it if she and Zach were trying to put out a fire. "It seems to me that Emily would try to go for help while Zach stayed to fight the fire."

"That's what I thought, but I guess we'll never know."

Sarah wanted to ask more questions, but they were at the hotel. "Thank you for supper," she said politely, standing outside the door. She glanced up at the second floor, surprised to see a light in Ira's window.

The handsome sheriff touched the brim of his black hat. "It was my pleasure."

She returned his smile, then slipped inside the lobby, leaning back against the door for several moments to collect her thoughts. Mrs. Baca poked her head out of the back and upon seeing her, bade her to lock the door and turn out the lamp.

"Good night," Sarah called as she went upstairs. She stood in the hall thinking of all the reasons she shouldn't go to

Ira's room. In St. Louis, her friends often divulged their sexual experiences with men. Free-spirited as she, they felt no shame in describing in detail how much they enjoyed it.

She closed her eyes and relived his kiss—the promise it held. Memories of his warm hands pressing her hips to his arousal made her feel as if she were in control. The feeling was exhilarating, and once more she glanced at Ira's door.

There was only one thing holding her back. She cared for him. Enjoyed his company. As liberated as she was, could she willingly share her body with him, and then afterwards pretend their relationship was purely physical?

She was about to go to her own room when Ira opened his door. Their gazes fused. His shirt was open at the neck, rolled at the sleeves. He looked different, seductive—more exciting than any man she had ever known.

"I was getting worried." He stepped aside. A subtle invitation, but nevertheless one she couldn't refuse. The faint aroma of his cologne washed over her. "Did you enjoy your supper . . . with Cooper Finch?"

He had noticed, and he sounded jealous. "Yes, as a matter of fact, I did. He's very nice."

He took a step closer, drawing her into his arms as he pushed the door closed. "How *nice?*"

"Not nearly as nice as you, of course."

No more words were needed. She knew what they both wanted, what their bodies cried out for. She looked up at him, her heart hammering against her breast with excited anticipation. His gaze turned her knees to liquid, sent moist heat flowing to the junction between her legs. Slowly, purposefully, he bent his head, nipping at her lips, while he loosened the pins in her hair.

Ira slipped his hands around her back. His low groan thrilled her, and she realized the power he had over her was nothing compared to the power she wielded over him. His body hardened, his kisses became more demanding. Her fingers tingled with the need to feel his bare skin, to touch and be touched. As if he could read her mind, he began to unbutton her dress. He moved tortuously slowly, taking his time as each piece of her clothing fell away.

"You're beautiful," he whispered, standing back at arm's length.

She stood before him, naked to his gaze, as his warm hands followed the path of his eyes. He cupped her breasts, circling her taut nipples with the pads of his thumbs, then his hands moved lower, to her waist, over the soft swell of her hips, slipping over her thighs then back up, caressing her bottom and finally the small of her back. He lifted her into his arms and carried over to the bed.

The sheets were cool on her bare skin, but he followed her down, his mouth claiming hers. She writhed beneath him, anxious to feel his flesh against hers. She pulled at his shirt, tearing at the buttons, until she could push it off his broad shoulders. When he stood, his gaze was dark and sensual, his mouth moist from her kisses.

While she watched, he undressed. His gaze never left hers as he pressed her back into the mattress with his masculine weight. His hands gently kneaded her breasts, hot and nearly as potent as his mouth, exploring her, tasting, touching every recess. He rolled to the side, holding her back when she tried to follow. He brushed her hair away from her face with his knuckle, and then dragged his fingers down her cheek, along her throat then between her breasts.

She reached over and cupped his cheek, sliding her hands lower over his shoulders then across the bunched muscles of his chest. When he moved and took a nipple into his mouth, she moaned and closed her eyes, sinking her fingers into his thick hair. His tongue circled and flicked as his hands glided over her belly to the curls between her legs.

"Ira," she gasped, drawing his mouth to hers.

His tongue entwined with hers in an age-old dance that drove them both to the brink of sensual insanity. His hand pushed against her thigh and instinctively she opened for him. He took his time, sharing his attention between her breasts while his fingers found her feminine folds and began a different type of torment. He lifted his head, his expression so intensely tender she could hardly bear it. "You've never been with a man before," he said, his voice flowing over her like a hot desert breeze.

Her tongue darted out to moisten her lips. "No," she whispered honestly. "Not until now. Not until you."

Her tone was raw with yearnings equal to his. He caught her chin, forcing her to look at him. "Sarah," he whispered hoarsely. "Damn it, Sarah, you're a virgin."

"Not for much longer," she panted.

He looked as though he wanted to scold her. "If we do this, there's no going back." His gaze was intense, his expression more serious than she could ever remember.

She smiled. "This is what I want . . . what you want."

He smoothed his hand over her cheek. "Yes, I want you, but you need to listen to me. You need to understand that I mean what I say. There's no going back."

Her brows crinkled in puzzlement. "I want you, Ira. I want to feel you inside of me."

His breathing was harsh, his voice was husky. "Ah, God, Sarah, you don't understand."

She pressed her fingertips against his mouth. "Shush," she whispered. "I'm my own person, Ira. I know we've only known each other for a short while. I'm stronger than you think. I'll be fine. You don't have to make any promises—I don't expect you to. I want you. I want what you're doing to me. That's enough for now."

She reached up and kissed him with all the longing she felt. He growled his resignation, rolling on top of her. The weight of him was more intoxicating than she expected. His hand slipped between their bodies, finding the sensitive flesh between her thighs. With the touch of an expert, he stroked the embers of her ardor into a flaming inferno. He spread her with his knee then she felt him—hard, yet soft, like velvet-covered steel.

"It's going to hurt," he breathed near her ear, his voice raw with compassion. "Just a little at first, but then it will get better, darlin', I swear."

He entered her tight sheath at the same time he kissed her, stifling her painful gasp. She was small, tight. Though it was torture, he held perfectly still, whispering her name and how special he felt to be her first. He kissed her, cupping her face between his palms as he drowned in her innocent gaze. When she relaxed he moved ever so gently, then slowly withdrew, kissing her as he eased back inside.

This time she arched her hips as her arms entwined around his neck. His mouth plundered hers, his body went deeper and deeper with each powerful thrust of his hips. His hands slipped down and under, holding her to the hard length of him. She was slick and hot. Her wetness surrounded him, throbbing against him.

"You're beautiful," he whispered, watching her as her eyes mirrored the wonder of her first climax.

"Oh, God," she breathed, arching up against him, clinging to the bunched muscles of his back and shoulders.

The scent of her womanly essence wreaked havoc on his mind and body. He squeezed his eyes tightly closed, withdrew and spread his seed on the sheets.

A few moments later, Sarah pulled the covers a little higher and rested next to Ira, content and happy, though a little confused. Back in St. Louis she often protested against male dominance over the weaker sex, she was strangely pleased with the way Ira had applied his masculine strength. He rose up on his elbow, taking the time to move a curl from her cheek, tucking it behind her ear.

"You're beautiful. Your hair's as soft as . . . ," he grinned, "as a newborn calf's."

She smiled up at him. "Calf? My my, Marshal, you do have a way with words." She moved to her side so she could more easily see his face. "Is this how it always is between a man and a woman?"

A shadow momentarily darkened his eyes. "Mostly."

Her smile was shrewd. "Then tell me, Marshal, why are there little children walking around?"

He smiled then, but it didn't quite reach his eyes. "Babies come from the sky . . . dropped down the chimney by big white birds." He rolled to his back, tucking his arm under his head. "I would think as a big city journalist, you'd know that."

"Really?" she scoffed, tracing a small pattern on his chest. "Didn't your father ever take you behind the barn and give you the talk?" A flash of memory arced across her mind—the touch of pain—the feel of a scar. With stark awareness she remembered several scars.

Ira caught her hand and kissed it before getting out of bed to put on his pants. He had his back to her, and her suspicions were confirmed a minute before he shrugged on his shirt. "My father and I didn't get along so well."

He tugged on his boots then looked up and flashed a smile. "So, until I learn differently, I'm just going to be careful and make sure no big white bird nests in your chimney."

She sat up, tucking the sheet over her breasts. "Where are you going?"

"I've got a few things to do before I leave for the ranch." He tucked in his shirt, then rolled down his sleeves and fastened the cuffs. He knew she would be hurt if he left, but he had to leave before he made love to her again. And again. Though he was fairly certain he pulled out in time, there were no guarantees. No guarantees except that an unwanted child would most likely ruin her independent life.

"Where?" she persisted. "It's late. I was hoping you'd stay here . . . with me."

He raked his fingers through his hair and sighed. "I need some air, Sarah. I need to think a few things through." He turned away, steeling himself against what he saw in her eyes. How could he explain that something happened to him as he gazed down at her in the throes of passion? How could he tell her how he felt when he couldn't find words for it? He wanted her in more ways than just to ease his need. He wanted her to adore him as he adored her.

But Sarah Brighton was a free spirit. No doubt a pampered rich brat caught up in the latest rebellion—the one that pitted woman against man. What had she called it? The woman's suffrage movement? Hell's bells, he was the one suffering.

He heard her get up, and by the rustle of clothing, knew she was getting dressed. Hating himself for what he had done, he turned toward her just before she put her hand on the knob. "Sarah, I'm sorry."

She gave him a small smile, lifting her chin as rebellious fury danced in the depths of her eyes. "You're sorry?" she repeated. Her skeptical laughter gnawed at his heart like a rabid animal. "Whatever for? You didn't do anything I didn't want you to do. I'm the one who should leave. After all, this is your room."

She turned, but he caught her arm. "Are you going to be all right?" he asked with genuine concern. "I'm going to the ranch tomorrow, but I won't go if—"

"I'm fine . . . no," she corrected, "I'm better than fine." She pulled her elbow from his grasp and opened the door. "Don't flatter yourself, Ira. I'm perfectly capable of getting along without the assistance of man."

Ira tied Dakota to the hitching rail in front of the sheriff's office then stepped inside.

"Morning," Cooper Finch said as he looked up from some papers on his desk. "What can I do for you, Marshal? Want some coffee?" Cooper went to the stove in the corner, picked up a pot and refilled his cup.

Ira pushed his hat back off his forehead. "No, thanks."

The sheriff resumed his seat and nodded to the chair at the side of his desk. "You look like a man with something on his mind. Sit down and tell me why you're here."

Ira motioned toward the door. "I can't stay long. I've got my horse outside. I'm going back to the ranch for a few days, but there's something I need to find out."

"Speak your mind." The sheriff took a drink of coffee.

Ira relaxed in the chair, resting a booted foot on his knee. "What do you know about Bob Phillips?"

The sheriff looked puzzled, then shook his head. "I don't know the name."

"Is that so? I was told you took his body back to his widow."

Sheriff Finch put down his cup and matched Ira's stare. "Why don't you quit beating around the bush and just say what's on your mind?"

"Bob Phillips was a marshal out of Albuquerque. He was up here investigating a suspected cattle rustling ring, but he died before he could solve the case."

149

"All I know is that one of the Pruitt hands brought down from the mountain a body . . . a body of a man mauled to death by a mountain lion. No one ever told me his name or said anything about him being a lawman."

Ira stood and walked over to the window. "Maybe I got my story a little mixed up." He turned when he heard the sheriff stand. Ira was certain Cooper knew more, but didn't press him further. "Well, I'd better get started."

"Since you're going to pass the Pruitts' place on your way to your ranch, why don't you stop by and speak to them?"

"Maybe I'll do that. In the meantime, Sheriff, if I were you, I'd get me some men together and go hunting. It sounds like you have a man-eater loose, and we both know it's liable to strike again once it's tasted blood."

"Yeah, I'll just do that," the sheriff replied.

Chapter Twelve

Ira knocked on the Pruitts' front door as he pulled his collar up a little higher against the cold wind that blew down from the nearby snow-covered peaks.

"Why, Marshal Farrell, what a surprise," Mrs. Pruitt said with a rather strained smile. "My husband isn't here, if you've come by to see him. He's out checking on the cattle with Josh."

Ira took off his hat. "That's too bad. I was hoping to speak to him about the murders and the marshal that was mauled to death."

"Murders?" she gasped.

"Mother?" a male voice asked from somewhere behind her.

"Please, Marshal, come inside." Mildred Pruitt stepped aside as Jonah came into the foyer. "Jonah," the older woman replied with a worried frown, "Marshal Farrell is here. He said someone's been murdered and a man was killed by a mountain lion."

"Calm down," Jonah said, patting his mother's shoulder. "Why don't you have Rosa serve some coffee? I'll speak with Ira." He waited until his mother left the room. "Marshal," Jonah motioned to the parlor. "Let me take your coat."

"That's all right," Ira stated. "I can't stay long."

"There was really no need to upset my mother with your misguided allegations about the fire. But, I suppose it's too late to ask you not to do it now. And, did I hear you say something to her about another body?"

Ira related his story, watching Jonah's reaction closely. "So, here I am. Is there anything you can tell me?"

Jonah frowned. "I don't know anything."

"Where were you and Josh the night of the fire?" Ira asked matter-of-factly.

Jonah gave a disgusted snort. "Here, playing cards with our parents."

"Do that often?" Ira asked sarcastically. "I'm assuming they'll confirm your story?"

"Look, Marshal, your brother's death was as much a surprise to me, to all of us, as I'm sure it was to you. And I assure you, I'm even more in the dark concerning Marshal Phillips. Josh found him. He takes care of the ranch. You might just want to speak with him."

"When do you expect him back?"

"You know how the ranching business is. He's up in the mountains rounding up strays. He could ride in any moment or be back after dark. Who's to know?"

Ira fought against the urge to question Jonah further. He'd gotten what he came for. "Well, thanks anyway," he said as he strolled toward the door.

"Come anytime, Marshal," Jonah offered.

Ira hesitated with his hand on the doorknob. He couldn't resist one more question. "Have you been missing any stock?"

Jonah pursed his lips then shook his head. "Not that I know of. Like I said, Josh is mostly in charge of running the ranch."

"Are you leaving so soon?" Mildred Pruitt asked as she came back with a tray of coffee. Mildred placed it on the foyer table just as Laura came down the stairs. She blushed when Ira nodded his acknowledgment with a brief smile.

"I've got to get going, but before I leave I should caution you ladies not to travel without an armed escort."

"Really? What in heaven's name for?" the girl asked.

"A man was mauled to death by a mountain lion a month ago." Ira put on his hat. Laura and Mildred followed him outside. "You know what they say. Once a big cat tastes human blood, it usually hunts for more."

Ira untied his horse from the hitching post, touched his fingers to the brim of his hat and mounted. "You ladies have a nice day . . . and remember, be real careful till that cat is found and destroyed."

The week Ira was going to be gone turned into two, giving Sarah time to get her shop in order. She kept busy making a few dresses, but mostly she made time to write. The editor of the *New Mexican* had agreed to publish her story about Ira, promising front-page coverage.

But even the anticipation of seeing her work in print didn't lift the heavy weight from her heart. At night she lay awake in her bed thinking about Ira—remembering the tender way he treated her, then remembering the terrible way they parted. She'd felt something good and wholesome in his strong arms.

And something more. She'd felt protected and cherished.

She squeezed her eyes tightly closed. Why could a man take a woman and feel nothing, and on her first time she fell hopelessly in love?

"So much for equality," she muttered as she punched the pillow and tried to get some sleep. Maybe tomorrow he'd come back . . . and maybe she'd tell him how he made her feel.

Maybe.

Maybe not.

Ira had told the story of his visit with Jonah Pruitt to his brothers and his uncle the night he arrived. As soon as they learned that Jonah used the dead marshal's name, even though Ira had never mentioned it, they all wanted to ride back to Santa Fe immediately and get to the bottom of things. But Ira insisted they wait. "I need more information before I can make any arrests," he'd said after the trio calmed down. "No one's going anywhere, and besides, I don't want my family involved if there's going to be trouble."

"Trouble?" Uncle Jeb had nearly choked on the word. "What in the blazes is family for if'n it ain't to help when there's trouble?"

It had taken Ira several moments to make his uncle and brothers see his side, but finally they all agreed to wait. Meanwhile, they'd keep their eyes and ears open for anything unusual.

"Like what?" Adam asked.

"Like a herd being moved."

Since that conversation, Ira had made several trips into the mountains, riding fence with his brothers, searching for signs of mountain lions *and* cattle rustlers. Today he headed for Cougar's Bluff. The piece of land that separated their ranch from the Rolands' was rugged, steep in places, with a treacherous drop-off on one side. The ride was long and cold, but as he got closer, there were more tracks than he expected. A horse whinnied from somewhere below. Just to be on the safe side, he dismounted and tied Dakota to a tree well away from the bluff. Once near the edge, Ira crawled forward to peer over the cliff. What he saw didn't surprise him. Who he saw did.

Ira didn't get back until late. All lights were out except for one small lantern in the kitchen. Ira walked in, took off his coat and hung it by the door.

"Hungry?" Jeb asked as he came out of the kitchen in his nightshirt. "Well, you took long enough," Jeb muttered. "Sit down. I fixed a plate for you. Want some coffee?"

"If it's hot," Ira answered, pulling out a chair. He sat, suddenly very hungry.

"Well, did you find any clues?" Jeb asked, sloshing some coffee into a couple of mugs. He fetched the cream and sugar then took the seat across from Ira.

Ira took a mouthful of fried potatoes and chewed. He swallowed, and then matched his uncle's stare. "I got what I was looking for," he replied calmly.

He added cream and sugar to his coffee before taking a sip. He stabbed a chunk of leftover roast and popped it into his mouth.

"Ain't you gonna tell me?" Jeb asked, frowning.

"Nope," Ira stated over a mouthful.

"Why in blazes not?" Jeb demanded, his features growing even more fierce.

Ira swallowed his food, looking at his uncle for several minutes before he spoke. " 'Cause I don't want you hurt."

Ira got up early the next morning to give Adam his present. As Ira expected, Jeb gave him several stern looks at breakfast, but didn't press him for any more information. Later that day, Ira took Adam out behind the barn to teach him how to shoot, pleased that the young man seemed a natural.

"Getting shot at for collecting taxes is part of the job," Ira stated, showing Adam the safest way to reload. "Serving arrest warrants can be tricky too, especially when you collect your pay and find out that you nearly got killed for a lousy seventy-five bucks a month."

"Is that all they pay you?" Adam asked skeptically.

"Nope, but that's the going rate for a lawman starting out." After an hour of shooting, Ira and Adam went back into the house. Ira showed Adam how to take apart his new Colt, clean it and where to oil it. "This is for your protection, not to line your pockets."

"Sure, Ira. I understand." Adam rubbed the Colt with a soft rag, then placed it in the holster. He strapped the gun belt around his waist and lifted his arms. "Well, how do I look?"

"I mean it, Adam. The last thing I want is for you to get a silly notion that being good with a gun is a quick way to make it rich. It's also a quick way to end up on the hill behind the house. Shooting a rabbit is a hell of a lot different than shooting a man. Rabbits don't shoot back."

Later that night, Ira stared up at the beamed ceiling in his old room in his father's log house. His thoughts were filled with so many things he found it difficult to sleep. He replayed Adam's lesson, hoping he'd done the right thing in buying the boy a gun.

He thought about Zach, inwardly wincing at the ache that stabbed his heart, wishing he'd taken the time to come and visit. Then he thought about the cattle being held in the rocky canyon near Cougar's Bluff. He'd ride up at first light and see if the herd had been moved. He had to be patient. He had a gut feeling that James Roland wasn't acting alone.

He rose, and after he added several chunks of wood to the stove, went to the frosty window and stared out into the dark. Sarah's image lingered in the back of his mind. How she looked, how she felt, everything about their lovemaking haunted him. Was she so wrapped up in her struggle for equality, she couldn't see they were perfect for each other?

He dragged his fingers through his tousled hair. Maybe when he got back to Santa Fe, he'd sit her down and tell her just how he felt. He went back to bed and heaved an irritated sigh.

First he'd have to take care of business—the conspiracy involved more men than he'd expected. He'd need help if he were to round them all up without someone getting hurt. Then he'd have to find the right words to tell Sarah exactly how he felt. Both things were going to be difficult.

"Oh, my goodness," Laura Pruitt exclaimed. "Why, this is the prettiest wrapper I've ever seen. Wait until the girls at my boarding school see it."

Sarah stood up from pinning the hem, resting her hands on her waist. "Blue is definitely your color."

"I'm sure all my friends will want one, Mrs. Wellington."

"You flatter me, Laura."

"I can hardly wait for school to start. After Marshal Farrell stopped by a few days ago with news of that man getting killed—why I've been having nightmares almost every night."

The door to the dress shop opened and Mildred Pruitt came in, smiling the moment she looked at her daughter.

"Mama, do you like it?"

"Oh, yes. It's just beautiful." Mildred put her coat on the coat tree. "Sarah, you've done a wonderful job."

"Well, thank you," Sarah replied, then gave Mildred a worried look. "Laura just told me that she's been having nightmares."

"Yes, she is, and Marshal Farrell's to blame. He stopped by the homestead a couple of weeks ago. He was real concerned for our welfare. He said that a man had been killed over a month ago in the mountains."

"Really?" Sarah asked, thinking she might learn something that would give her another good story.

"Yes, indeed. The marshal said the man was mauled by a mountain lion."

"That's terrible. Why didn't someone put it in the newspaper?" Sarah asked with a worried frown.

"That's exactly what I was thinking," Laura added. "Your stories are always so interesting. Why don't you put a notice in the paper about the mauling?" Laura turned to look at her reflection in the long, oval mirror. "How are we to protect ourselves if the men keep things from us?"

"That's not the worst of it," Mildred continued. Her features hardened. "The marshal seems to think that your cousin's death might not have been an accident." Mildred gave a shake of her head. "I had gone to get coffee, but when I came back, I heard him questioning Jonah. Let me tell you, I got the distinct impression he was trying to implicate my boys in some way."

"I don't like it, Cooper. This isn't how things were supposed to turn out."

The sheriff watched as James Roland paced the small confines of his office.

Roland cast a quick glance over at Silas Pruitt then continued. "Ira knows what's been going on. I'm sure of it."

"Calm down, Jim. Getting all riled up isn't going to help us." Cooper sat at his desk and rested his feet on the top. "Now, tell us what you mean."

"I *mean,* my daughter was out riding a few days ago. Up by Cougar's Bluff." James paused, but Cooper remained silent.

"So what?" Silas asked. "All you had to tell her was those cows we're holding are strays from our ranches and that we're just keeping them there until—"

"I'm not worried about my daughter and those damned cows," James growled, curling his fingers into fists. "She spotted a big roan horse tied to a tree. That roan is Ira Farrell's horse."

"Did she see him?" Cooper asked, sitting upright.

"No. She didn't. She got spooked and went back to the ranch. I didn't find out about it till supper that night." James turned to Silas. "There's no telling what he was doing up there, but I'll bet you he recognized some of the brands as his own."

Cooper waited while Silas tried to calm the rancher down, walking him to the door and promising that Cooper would take care of things. It took some persuasion, but the rancher finally agreed to go back to his ranch and stay out of town for a while.

Silas closed the door and turned to the sheriff. "We're in too deep. My business associates on the other end are expecting a shipment. First we had that pesky marshal from Albuquerque nosing about, now we have Ira making public accusations about you and my boys, and now he's snooping around our land. Why, he even had the gall to go up to the house. He's got Mildred and Laura in a tizzy claiming there's a rampant cougar roaming the mountain. And now they've gone and babbled it to that fancy lady dressmaker." Silas nodded toward the paper on the sheriff's desk. "Have you read that this morning?"

"Nope. What's it say?"

Silas heaved an impatient sigh. "There's plumb near a half page in big, bold print warning the citizens of Santa Fe to beware of a man-eating mountain lion."

Cooper laughed. "No kidding?" He picked up the folded paper and opened it. "Well, I'll be damned. This is very interesting. Almost as interesting as Ira's story." He shook his head. "And, it's almost believable. She writes well." Copper tossed the paper back on the desk then went to the pot-bellied stove and poured himself a cup of coffee. "I've got a couple of men out hunting. All we need to do is

159

bring in a big cat, and our problem with that dead marshal is solved."

"How can you say that?" Silas demanded, red-faced, waving away the offered coffee.

"Think about it," Cooper said. "It's just like I told you. Someone's going to kill a mountain lion and start bragging that they killed the man-eater. Mrs. Wellington doesn't know it, but she's helped us out by printing this story. Just like she helped us by printing Ira's."

Silas stopped pacing, his frown slowly turning into a sly smile. "I suppose you're right."

"The good marshal can snoop around all he wants. In a few days, if he hasn't got bored and left for Arizona, it'll all be over anyway. If he stays, I'll take care of him—just like I take care of everything."

Silas gave him a firm look. "Farrell's not a nobody like that other marshal. He's known in these parts. Well enough that the governor might feel compelled to investigate. I don't want to arouse any more suspicion."

"Don't worry, Mr. Pruitt. There's absolutely nothing going to happen that would implicate any of us, including your boys."

"You'd best be damned sure about that." The banker pulled out a long white envelope from an inside pocket and tossed it to the sheriff. "I assume this will cover any expenses you might encounter?"

Sheriff Finch opened it and counted the cash inside. "This will do nicely," he said with the glitter of contempt in his voice.

By the end of the second week, working on dress orders had lost its appeal. Sarah felt confined, and her fingers hurt from the multiple needle pricks. She tied on her bonnet and slipped on her coat. A cold November wind splattered a few raindrops against her window, but when she looked for her umbrella, she realized she must have accidentally left it at the hotel.

She pulled up her collar and stepped outside, locking the door to her shop. She glanced at the sky, thinking they were in for some snow. Though the thought of Ira getting snowed in at the ranch before he could return was dismal, winter in New Mexico paled in comparison to the winters she had experienced in St. Louis.

It wasn't uncommon to see men on horseback riding up and down the street, but for some reason a rider caught her eye as he came out of the mercantile, adjusted his horse's cinch strap, and then mounted the big bay. She stared, thinking it was the man's pale hair and pale moustache in harsh contrast with his black clothing that made him stand out from the others.

"Morning, Mrs. Wellington." The barber stuck his head out and smiled, drawing Sarah's attention away from the stranger. "Liked your article about Marshal Farrell. I sent an extra one to my sister in Tombstone."

"Thank you, Mr. Harper."

"They killed that cat yet?" he asked.

"No, I don't believe so." She tugged her collar up a little higher, nearly bumping into Mrs. Pruitt and her daughter.

"Good morning, Sarah," Mildred Pruitt said with an instant smile. "Laura and I were just talking about you. That article you wrote about the woman's suffrage movement in yesterday's paper just inspired us so much, we've decided that Silas and the boys can start fixing their own breakfast on Saturday mornings. Mrs. Smith and Mrs. Porter are doing the same."

Sarah forced a stiff smile, frowning as the black-clad

stranger rode past. The wind caught his coat, exposing a pair of six-guns buckled around his waist. With each step his dark horse took, the man's silver spurs tolled like tiny bells.

An eerie sound on a gloomy day, she thought. He looked like a Kansas City gambler, only more profane, and when he turned down the road toward the unscrupulous part of town, she had no doubt that she had drawn the correct conclusion.

Instantly Ira's crafty smile popped into her mind. *You've passed judgment on me, Mrs. Wellington, because of how I appear, helped along a little by the stories you've read.*

"Did you hear me? We are all so impressed."

Sarah finally took her gaze off the gambler and turned to smile at the women. "I'm glad you liked it."

"We not only liked it, my dear. We're starting our own affiliate of the one you belonged to in St. Louis. Our first meeting is this Saturday. Would you do us the honor of being our very first speaker?"

"Please, Mrs. Wellington," Laura pleaded. "We would so enjoy listening to your views on equality. It's going to be over at the town hall, ten o'clock, Saturday morning."

"Why, I-I'd be honored. I'll type up a handbill to inform all the ladies about the meeting."

She watched them leave, pulling her collar up, then hurried toward the hotel.

"Where can I find the sheriff's office?"

Lily watched from the landing above the bar as a black-clad stranger sipped a cold beer.

"You need to speak with the sheriff?" the bartender asked as he put the stranger's money in a cash box. He motioned toward the other room. "There's no need going over to his office. The sheriff's in there shooting a game of pool with Josh Pruitt."

"Who's that?" Lily asked as she approached the bar.

"Nobody you should hook up with, Lily."

"Really? Why not? He looks like he could afford me." Her smile was sly.

"Yeah, I bet he could, but that there's Dawson Yates."

Lily shrugged her shoulders. "So?"

"He's a gunfighter. I was in Kansas City before I came out here. I saw him and some other young gunfighter face each other down. Let me tell you, the young buck that challenged him was dead before he hit the ground."

"What's Yates doing here?" Lily asked, her smile gone.

Sam picked up a cloth and began to polish some glasses. "He said he wanted to speak to Cooper, but my guess is somehow he got wind of another fast gun being in town."

"You think he's looking for Ira?" She didn't wait for his answer. Instead she grabbed her cloak and headed for the door.

"Hey!" The bartender watched her leave. "Where are you going?"

The moment Sarah stepped inside the door to the hotel, Mrs. Baca begged her to stay so the elderly woman could run a few errands. Sarah graciously agreed, and went about straightening some papers on Mrs. Baca's desk. She accidentally knocked a pencil on the floor. When she stooped to pick it up, the bell above the door jingled. Sarah straightened, surprised to see Lily Barker standing at the counter in a red satin, fur-lined cloak.

"May I help you?" Sarah asked, eyeing Lily cautiously. The saloonkeeper appeared nervous, almost agitated.

"I need to get a message to Marshal Farrell. He told me he was staying here."

"He did?" Sarah cleared her throat. "I mean, he was, but

he left town two weeks ago." Sarah forced a stiff smile, trying to be polite.

Lily heaved a relieved sigh. "Good. I thought maybe he was back by now, but it's good he isn't." Lily turned to leave.

More than a little irked that a woman of this caliber knew Ira at all, Sarah wanted more information. The knowledge that Ira had shared his plans with her was even more troublesome. "If I may be so bold." Sarah suddenly felt small under the woman's scrutiny. "Why were you looking for him?"

"To warn him, honey." Lily came back to the counter. "Ira and I go back a long ways, and I wouldn't want anything to happen to him."

"What could possibly happen?"

Lily leaned closer, placing her glove on top of Sarah's hand. "He could get himself killed, honey. That's what could happen. But, since he's not here, I reckon there's no chance of that."

Lily's gaze washed over Sarah and then she smiled. "If they don't pay you enough here, you come see me over at the saloon. With your looks, we could take in a hundred dollars a night."

Chapter Thirteen

Another cold day passed and so did the rain, leaving behind the wind to erase any signs of moisture. Sarah glanced out the window and watched as a dust devil skittered by, kicking up dirt and bits of debris.

She added a few chunks of wood to the stove, holding her hands before the open door to warm them a few moments before opening for business. The tinkle of the shop's little bell caused her to turn around. Ira's tall frame was silhouetted as he stood before the glass door, dressed as elegantly as he'd been the night he took her to dinner.

"Hello, Sarah," he said, taking off his hat. His expression was guarded, his smile slightly forced.

"Ira, when did you—"

"Late last night. Mrs. Baca said you'd moved in here. I would have come by last night, but I was sure you were sleeping."

She wanted to run into his arms, to have his inviting mouth claim hers, but instead, she smoothed the material of her skirt, then tucked a wayward strand of hair back into the bun at her nape. "It's nice to see you again." She felt inexplicably awkward and uncomfortable. "Come in, please. Laura Pruitt brought some cookies yesterday. Would you like one?"

He hung his hat and coat on the rack by the door. "No, thank you. I didn't come to have cookies. I came to see you."

He stepped close—close enough that if she wanted, she could reach up and kiss him.

"How are you?" he asked, his deep voice awakening the butterflies resting in her stomach. "I missed you."

She looked at him then, moistening her suddenly dry lips. "I-I—" She lowered her gaze from his to linger on his mouth. "I'm fine . . . keeping busy." She turned away, motioning to several colorful dresses hanging on hooks on the walls. "See, I told you I could sew."

"You can write too," he added. She knew immediately that someone had given him a copy of the story she wrote.

"Did you like it?" she asked, matching his gaze. "I tried not to be biased."

"I'm flattered. However, I wish you'd told me about it first."

As much as she was thrilled about his return, she felt a spark of anger ignite in her breast. "I didn't think I needed your permission," she countered. "You didn't ask mine when you practically told the whole town that you thought Zachary and Emily were murdered. Besides, you know I'm a journalist."

Something flickered in his vibrant eyes. "That's not what I meant. I just wish you'd told me so we could have discussed it . . . as equals. You as the writer, me as the topic."

"I didn't think to. I'm used to—"

"You're used to doing what you want whenever you want to, without thinking about the consequences."

She raised her chin a little higher. "Consequences?" she repeated. "What harm could come from a little story about a famous man? I thought I gave my readers a more factual accounting than I've read in other newspapers."

"You did. It's one of the best I've seen."

"Then why—"

"Dawson Yates liked it too."

"Dawson Yates?" she repeated, her confusion reflected in her eyes. "I don't know him."

"He's a gunfighter," Ira said flatly. He lifted his watch out of his vest pocket and opened it. "I've got an appointment with him in about ten minutes."

She felt the blood drain from her face. "An appointment?"

Ira nodded, his expression unlike any she'd seen. "He's here for a reason. He's been spreading rumors around . . . rumors about me and a certain married woman. I don't care what he says about me, but I care a hell of a lot for the woman."

Sarah sank down in her chair. "Oh, my God." She was about to speak when the door burst open. A young boy came inside, but kept a hand on the door, holding it open. The child's wide eyes were filled with unbridled excitement.

"Marshal? There's a man outside. He gave me a five-dollar gold piece to tell you that it's time, and if you don't come out in the next five minutes, he's going to come in after you. He says he's been waiting for you and that he aims to kill you either way . . . in here or out there."

Sarah flinched when the door slammed shut, rattling the glass. In the distance she could hear the boy shouting, his voice high-pitched.

Ira's gaze fused with hers a moment before he moved to the window. Keeping to the side, he looked through the lace curtain. Curious onlookers had already gathered in alleyways and in doorways. "It will be dangerous outside." His tone was flat, void of emotion.

"This can't be happening," Sarah said in a small voice. "There must be some mistake."

Ira met her gaze. "There's no mistake. What did you think would happen when you printed your story?"

"What has this got to do with my story?" she asked frantically, searching his face.

"You're a smart woman, Sarah. Don't pretend you didn't think there was a chance that something like this could happen." He shook his head in disgust, but she knew it wasn't directed at her. "Hell, practically all of Santa Fe is out there to see the show."

He removed his pistol and checked it, making sure everything was as it should be, then grabbed her arm and walked toward the back room. When he turned her to face him, that's when she saw the hurt deep in his eyes. "You must stay inside, away from the windows, do you understand me?"

"Why? I—"

He gave her a little shake. "Do you understand me?" he ground out. "I won't worry about you if you stay here."

"You won't worry about me?" she cried incredulously. "I'm not the one facing that man out there."

Ira pulled her into his arms. His expression tore into her heart as he bent his head and kissed her with an urgency that jolted her whole body. When he pulled away, he stared at her for several heart-wrenching moments, his fingers pressing into the soft flesh of her upper arms. "Promise me, you'll stay inside."

"I promise," she whispered, swallowing to ease the ache in her throat.

He would have left, but she stopped him. "Ira. You can't be serious. You can't go out there. There's a back door leading out to the alley. You can get away."

He gave a dismal laugh. "Do you really believe that?"

"Farrell?" came a man's voice from outside. "Don't keep me waitin'."

Ira put on his hat. His body shielded her from a cold blast

of wind as he pulled the door open. He glanced back at her for several aching moments, then stepped outside.

Sarah ran to the window and peered out. Her mouth went dry. The darkly clad stranger she'd seen before stood in the middle of the street about forty feet away. Strapped to his hips was a pair of matching pistols.

Without thinking about her promise, she lifted her coat from the rack and carefully slipped out the back door. She made her way to the front of the building using the alley between her shop and the one next to it. She tried to stay out of sight, standing behind several men. Ira was already in the street, walking purposely toward the stranger, his coattail billowing out as a gust of wind swirled by.

The street was packed with townsfolk. Mrs. Baca came out of the hotel at the same time several other businessmen poked their heads out of doors to see. As Ira walked closer to the stranger, some folks scattered, mothers grabbed their children and pushed them in the nearest doorway.

Sarah's stomach rolled. Ira had called it a show. Now she realized this was some kind of wild entertainment. Understanding settled in her breast like a lead weight. This was why Ira was hurt and angry—this was also why he couldn't run away. The blow to his pride and reputation would have been too great.

"Ira Farrell," the man sneered. "I say you're a yellow-bellied, wife-stealing coward, and I'm itching to drop you where you stand."

Wife-stealing coward? Sarah blanched at the man's insinuation. Dawson Yates had only just arrived. He had no first-hand knowledge that she and Ira had spent time together.

"This isn't necessary, Yates. You can take back what you said and walk away. I'm not the type to hold a grudge."

Sarah felt as if she couldn't breathe. Ira appeared calm, returning the man's taunts as if this were some kind of game. Gone were all the tender virtues of the man she loved, replaced with the proficiency of the predator she knew he could be. He slowly lifted the little leather loop from the hammer of his pistol. His stance was poised, yet strangely relaxed.

Yates kept walking, unwilling to back down. His long coat had been pushed aside, gently flapping in the breeze. He stopped about thirty feet from Ira. "On the count of three, Marshal."

"One."

Sarah blanched at the arrogant smirk on his face. Her knees felt weak and her mouth was so dry she couldn't swallow.

"Two."

Afraid of what she'd see, Sarah forced herself to look at Ira. His gaze was steady, cool and confident as an unnatural silence fell over the crowded street.

"Three!"

Ira's pistol seemed magically to appear in his hand. The sound of two shots fired simultaneously hurt her ears, and reflex made her cover them as she stifled a scream. The crowd groaned in unison. At first she thought both men had missed. A breath of a moment later, Dawson swayed, then fell backwards to the ground.

A roar of approval blended with the howl of the increasing wind. The dusty street came alive. Men ran toward the fallen man, while others swarmed around Ira. Some even exchanged money while several women and some of the older children applauded.

Stunned, Sarah watched as Ira slowly holstered his smoking gun. He seemed to search the crowd until finally his gaze fastened on hers. He stared at her for what seemed like an eternity before he turned and walked away.

★ ★ ★ ★ ★

Ira sat at a table in the saloon, breaking the seal on a new bottle of whiskey. He filled a small glass, then tossed its contents down his throat. Staring at the empty glass, he replayed every event up to the fight. He put the glass down, then glanced at the tear in his left sleeve, just above his elbow.

"A close one this time?" Lily's voice penetrated his dismal thoughts as she came up behind him. She rested her warm hand on his shoulder.

He glanced up, then motioned for her to take a seat, but she refused. He refilled his glass, finished it, and poured another. "Dawson's fast, just not accurate."

The swinging doors burst open and Sarah rushed inside. She was flushed from the cold weather, and several strands of coppery hair had come loose from her bun. He watched her hesitate for a moment, her rebellious gaze impaling Lily before she purposefully strode to his table.

"Did you have to kill him?"

Lily quietly backed away, turning toward the bar where she softly asked the bartender for a drink.

"Well?" Sarah demanded. "Answer me."

"If I hadn't he would have killed me," Ira replied flatly.

Anger and remorse smoldered in her eyes as she leaned on the table with both hands. "How do you know that? You're the best, Ira. You could have shot him in the arm."

He stood and grabbed her, pulling her closer. He gave her a little shake. "Is that what they do in St. Louis? Did I offend your sense of propriety?" he ground out through clenched teeth. "Did you think Dawson gave me time to choose where I put my bullet? If you did, you're a fool, Sarah. I have seconds to measure a man—to try and look in his eyes and see if he's got what it takes to put a bullet in my chest. And Yates did. I saw it. Something else you should know. Just in case you want to put it in your next story. I can *feel* it, Sarah. I can feel the depth of his hate by the way he looks and by the way he stands. Yates was a professional. I did him a favor. I made it quick and painless."

She jerked away, then slapped him. "Don't say that," she cried, trembling. "It could have been you."

"You broke your promise," he said softly. The change in his expression from anger to hurt nearly rendered her speechless.

"I-I had to make sure you'd be all right." She stifled a sob. "Ira, you could have died out there."

"I only hope when I do, it'll be as quick and as painless."

Stunned by his confession, she watched him reach down and toss his drink down his throat. He looked at her for several tense moments, and once more she caught a glimpse of torment in his eyes. He started to speak, but didn't. Instead, he strode from the saloon, leaving her to stare after him.

"So you're the one." Lily picked up her drink and came over to the table.

Sarah slowly sank down on Ira's vacated chair, aware that Lily had poured some whiskey into Ira's glass.

"Here, drink this. You look like you could use it."

Like a child, she obeyed, choking as it scalded her throat. "T-the one what?" she asked, her voice a raspy whisper.

"The one he's in love with." Lily sat down. "Don't take this so hard, honey. If you love him back, you're going to have to get used to his way of life. When you're fast, you're a target."

"I'll never get used to it," Sarah said with a slight tremor in her voice. "He could have walked away. It was his choice to kill that man, just like it's his choice to wear a badge—to continually place his life in danger." She met Lily's dauntless gaze. "He could quit his job and go back to ranching."

"Do you really believe that?" Lily asked with a skeptical laugh.

"I-I don't know what to believe anymore." Still trembling, Sarah brushed a strand of hair away from her face.

"You didn't hear what Dawson said about you," Lily stated.

"I don't care what he said," Sarah replied furiously.

"Well, I can tell you, they don't come any better than Ira Farrell. But he's not as tough as you think. If you believe something like this doesn't affect him, then you don't know him very well. It was close. Real close. If you don't believe me, just take a good look at his sleeve. There's a bullet hole plumb through it." Lily filled the glass, then tossed it back, staring at Sarah the entire time. "You're thinking you're better than me. I can see it in your eyes. Yet you're a married woman chasing after a single man."

Sarah blanched. She didn't want to be so obvious—didn't like hearing out loud how opinionated she was, in spite of the fact that her pretend marriage was a lie. Lily's assessment went against what she wanted to believe about herself. The open defiance she'd felt moments ago dimmed, replaced with repentance.

Lily's smile was quick and forgiving. "Don't fret, honey. I quit worrying what people think about me a long time ago. Maybe what I do isn't exactly respectable, but I own this saloon, and just between you and me, it's most likely my money in ol' Silas's bank. Money he lends out to proper folks like you when they need a loan."

Lily leaned back in her chair. "I've read your articles about women's rights. They're good. Ira's story was good too. You may come from a big city, but I'm guessing you've been protected from the bad things. Most likely, you've been surrounded with good things. I bet you had a loving family, a mama and a papa that took real good care of you." Lily nodded as if she'd just made a discovery. "You're a little bit of innocent and a whole lot of naïve. That's why he loves you."

"I don't know what you mean," Sarah lied, even though her heart did a little somersault.

"Did you ever ask Ira why he left ranching?"

Sarah shook her head, muttering a miserable "no."

"Ira's pa used to beat him when he was a boy. I don't mean he'd backhand him for being rude. I mean he'd take a buggy whip and lay into him until his back was bleeding. When you're treated like that by the one person you look up to, it changes you."

Sarah swallowed, remembering the night she and Ira had made love—her fingertips gliding over the tiny scars on his back—his reaction when she asked if his father had ever taken him out behind the barn.

"Ira took his brothers' punishment as well. He'll put himself in danger first before he'll ask anyone else to do it. That's why I love him too." Lily shook her head. "Oh, don't. Don't you dare look at me like that. And, don't you dare go thinking anything bad about him. What we had was a long, long time ago. Ira needed a place to stay when he quit his pa. I gave it to him. Ira's one of the few good things that ever happened in my life."

Lily stood. "If you love him, and I think you do, you're going to have to get used to him being protective . . . or go back to your husband."

Sheriff Cooper Finch and Silas Pruitt both stared down at the body on Doctor Hensley's table. A single bullet hole showed dead center in Dawson Yates's left breast. The doctor had all the blood cleaned away. "Clean as a whistle," the doctor muttered just before he moved away. "Probably dead before he hit the ground."

Dawson's hair had been combed and his moustache smoothed by the photographer. The man stood several feet away, fumbling with his equipment, getting ready to take the dead man's picture for the newspaper. "Anyone want to stand next to this fellow?" the photographer asked just before the flash went up in smoke.

Silas glanced at the sheriff, speaking softly while the man gathered up his camera. "Is there anything you can do? Can't you arrest Farrell?"

Cooper shook his head. "Nope. Half the town was watching. It was self-defense." He took one last look then pulled up the collar of his coat and walked to the door.

Silas walked out with him. "Well, now what do we do? Farrell's bound to figure out what we're doing sooner or later. It isn't bad enough that Ira might have found the herd when we had them up by Cougar's Bluff. Josh said he spoke with both Adam and Cole just before they damned near stumbled on the boys moving the herd to my ranch." Silas threw up his hands. "I can't hold off on the shipment. The longer those cows stay at my ranch, the more likely someone's going to find them. I've got men waiting to drive them to the stockyard, but not with the marshal staying in town."

The sheriff jammed on his hat. "I reckon we'd better arrange a meeting of the town council."

Saturday arrived, and although Sarah was ready, it had been difficult to focus on giving a speech after her confrontation with Ira. She glanced at her notes. She didn't really need them. For the last few years she'd lived what she would preach, and knew that once she stood before the ladies of

Santa Fe, she would easily recite her beliefs and share her knowledge.

She donned a deep-green brocade gown with black velvet trim. As usual her golden-bronze curls were piled high on the top of her head and fixed with a ribbon and short, feathered clasp. She checked her appearance one last time, then shrugged on a matching cloak before stepping outside.

She had only taken a few steps when she had the urge to glance over her shoulder. Ira was a little way back. Her heart gave a jolt as she realized he must have been coming to see her, and had apparently been delayed when Mr. Harper stepped out of his barbershop to talk.

Taller by a head, Ira looked past the little man. Her gaze met his for the briefest moment. Late for her meeting, she forced herself to look away, then, feeling wretched, she hurried down the street toward the town hall.

Casting one last glance over her shoulder to see if Ira had followed, Sarah took a deep breath and opened the door. Two dozen women sat on chairs placed in a semicircle near the back of the room. Another dozen stood conversing and turned when she entered. Laura Pruitt ran up to her and took her coat, placing it on one of the many racks near a table that was loaded with a variety of small cakes and cookies.

"Good day, ladies," Sarah began, feeling a little awkward as she made her way to the opposite end of the room. She put her paper on the lectern, next to a glass of fresh water. She glanced around the room. Mrs. Pruitt and Laura were there in their fur-trimmed velvets and satins.

There were several ranchers' wives, the waitress from the hotel restaurant, and many more she didn't recognize. Sarah's gaze fell on several women sitting by themselves on the back row. Though they were dressed much more conservatively than they'd been in the saloon, Lily Barker and her girls were in attendance. The sound of female voices slowly came to a halt as they turned their attention to the podium.

Sarah cleared her throat. "Mrs. Pruitt has graciously asked me to attend the first meeting of the Ladies Liberty Association. I hope what happens here today becomes a monthly occurrence." She paused while they applauded.

"The eighteen-nineties have seen many new and exciting changes for women. Back east there is a widening circle of opportunity for our advancement. There's the Women's Building at the World's Columbian Exposition in Chicago, the first of its kind, funded, managed and designed entirely by women. Abroad, New Zealand has granted women the right to vote." Sarah waited for several more moments of applause to quiet down. "However, even with these giant steps toward gender freedom, many of us are still suppressed. Many of us are stifled by men who constantly remind us that they can do better than we can."

"Hear, hear," Milly Pruitt cheered, clapping and nodding.

Sarah's audience was so engrossed in her speech, they didn't bother to turn around when the door opened. Nor did they notice the infamous Marshal Farrell quietly remove his hat as he leaned back against the wall. But Sarah noticed. So much so, she nearly forgot what she was going to say. When the room grew quiet, she quickly took a sip of water, then cleared her throat for the second time. "F-for centuries, women have been taught from birth that males are dominant over females. We're told men are stronger, smarter and more capable than women. Men have held us hostage under the pretense that we are the weaker sex."

While several women clapped and verbally agreed, Sarah chanced a quick glance at Ira. Much to her surprise, he smiled and nodded, as if offering her his endorsement.

She swallowed hard, and then dragged her gaze away to look at several of the woman. "I ask you, how many in the room have children?" Almost all raised their hands. "I shall also ask, why do you think childbirth is called labor?" Several women laughed.

"Let me give you an example of how male society views our feminine capabilities. I am confident all of us have been accused of being hysterical at one time or another." Again she had to pause as several ladies heartily agreed. Sarah checked her notes. "The word *hystera* is Greek for womb. *Hystera* is considered by many prominent physicians of our modern day as a woman's disease. Now, I ask you, have any of your men every ranted and raved?"

"Yes," many said in unison.

"Have any of your men ever acted irrationally?"

Again female voices rose in mutual agreement.

"Do men have wombs?"

"No," they cried in a fevered pitch.

"Then why is *hystera* labeled a woman's disease?" Sarah took another drink of water while she waited for the women to calm down. "There is a great deal of injustice toward women in our country. Women who have affairs and are divorced by their husbands, are required to forfeit their property, even though they may have brought it into the marriage in the first place. Men under the same circumstances may retain their property. Now I ask you. Is that fair?"

"It most certainly is not," cried Milly Pruitt.

"The road to gender freedom will be long and tedious, but we will prevail. Education is the door to social freedom. Yes, ladies. Education is the door, yet many of the same prominent physicians preach that women who seek a higher education can harm their delicate health."

Sarah felt Ira's gaze heavily upon her, but she chose not to look his direction. Instead she focused on several women in the front row. "How can this be? Mrs. Pruitt, when you read a book do you suddenly feel faint?"

Several women laughed.

"No, I certainly do not," Milly confirmed.

"Of course not. Education isn't harmful," Sarah responded with a frown. "Ladies of Santa Fe, now is the time to cast aside the bonds of male superiority. We must challenge the balance of power and enter into a social revolution. We must rise up and unify against domestic slavery. It is time that our men rid themselves of their fanciful ideas that we, as wives, are their property. Instead, we must force them to accept us as their equals."

All of the women stood at once, applauding and voicing their total agreement. Sarah was swarmed with compliments and questions. When she finally glanced at the back of the room, Ira was gone. A glass of punch was pressed in her hand and as refreshments were served, the ladies stood around and conversed, voicing their ideas about how they could apply Sarah's suggestions.

In the midst of all the attention, Sarah found herself feeling a little doubtful. Her night of passion with Ira still lingered in the back of her mind. Ira was a strong man, yet he was considerate as well. Though she wasn't as experienced as she wanted everyone to believe, she didn't think that many men would have been so protective of her welfare. Nor would they have held back their sexual enjoyment as Ira had done for her.

Sarah believed with all her heart in what she preached, but did she really want to practice it? *Of course,* she answered silently. She would never willingly yield to a dominant man. Would she?

Ira ordered a beer from the pretty little blond barmaid, then walked to a corner table where Lily worked on a ledger. "Can I buy you a drink?"

"No, sweetie, I'm sticking to coffee till I get these damned books to balance."

"Are you too busy to talk?" he asked, removing his hat.

She laid down her pencil and motioned to a chair with a wide smile. "I'm never too busy for you. Saw you at the meeting of the Ladies of Liberation." Lily's eyes glinted with amusement, making Ira even more proud of Sarah and her beliefs. "That woman of yours sure knows how to get her point across. Me and the girls are all new members. Of course, Sarah had to convince some of the more *proper* ladies that we're all equals."

"Do I congratulate you?" he teased.

"What do you think?" Lily laughed. "Honey, I was liberated before it was fashionable."

Ira grinned. "Personally, I like freethinking women."

"Yeah, I bet you do." Lily tucked a red curl back into place. "Tell me what's really on your mind. Your face is smiling, but your eyes are telling me something different."

Ira took a seat and heaved a long sigh. "Zach, the fire, several things I've learned."

She leaned a little closer, giving him her full attention. "What things?"

"When I first got here, I thought I was coming to say goodbye to my brother and try and find out why a marshal ended up on his wife's doorstep in a closed coffin."

Lily raised one red brow. "Are you speaking about the man who got mauled? I wasn't aware he was a lawman until I read it in the paper."

"I saw a copy. It was a good article." He took a sip of beer.

"Bob Phillips was murdered. He was killed because he was too inexperienced to know what to do when he stumbled on some cattle rustlers."

Lily looked around the saloon. "Ira, you've got to be careful. There's those that don't take kindly to your accusations."

"Lily, I don't give a damn. The man was murdered. So were Zach and Miss Emily."

Lily sighed, and then leaned back in her chair. "I can see it ain't no use arguing. Maybe one of my girls knows something that can help you. We get a lot of loose-mouthed cowboys in here. Me and my girls are good listeners. Our policy is don't ask and don't tell, but in this case, I'll make an exception. Meanwhile, you need to watch yourself. If memory serves, you pretty near got yourself killed just a few days ago."

"That had nothing to do with this," Ira stated tersely. "Sarah wasn't thinking when she printed that article."

"Maybe it wasn't her article." Lily pursed her red lips, looking down at the ledger. "Some say Dawson got here awful quick after Sarah's story was printed. Maybe too quick, if you know what I mean."

The doors swung open and Josh Pruitt strolled inside and walked to the bar. Lily nodded and smiled, then watched while he ordered a beer and went into the other room to play pool. She finished her coffee and motioned to Sam for more. "Another beer?" she asked Ira.

Ira shook his head. "Thanks, but I've got to get going. I've got some business to tend to with the sheriff." He stood, but Lily caught his hand.

"I reckon you'd better talk with Cole about Cooper Finch. Rumor has it that there's bad blood between him and your family."

Ira nodded. "Be careful, Lil."

She gave a soft laugh. "You do the same."

Lily waited until Ira left, then motioned for Sam to sit down. "Call a meeting for later today before the saloon gets too busy. Make sure all my girls are there." Sam stood, but Lily caught his arm. "Keep it real quiet, Sam. I don't want anyone knowing what's going on."

Her bartender patted her hand. "Don't you worry none, Miss Lil. I'll take care of everything.

Ira walked out of the saloon. Lily had no cause to worry. He wasn't the type to go off half-cocked. Nor did he want to involve his brothers. He stepped off the boardwalk and headed toward the telegraph office. Before he talked to Cooper Finch, he'd take Mayor James up on his offer to send some men to Santa Fe to help.

Ira paid the little man for sending the telegram then headed for the jail. The door was open when he got there so he walked on in. "I'd like to talk to you, Sheriff."

Cooper looked up from some wanted posters. "What's on your mind, Marshal?"

"Stolen cattle."

Ira only divulged the whereabouts of the stolen cattle, keeping his suspicions about who might be involved to himself. Cooper had already lied to him about who had brought in the dead marshal's body. If Ira's hunch was right and Cooper was trying to protect Josh Pruitt, the sheriff would warn Josh about the herd. Ira knew his brothers would keep a watchful eye out for any suspicious activity and send word if they saw anything. A herd that size wouldn't be easy to move without being noticed. Ira took a deep breath, pleased that a plan had finally been put into motion. Now all that was left to do was wait.

He glanced up at the clear blue sky, a blue that reminded him of Sarah's eyes. They hadn't parted on the best of terms, and he itched to set things right. He pulled out his watch and checked the time. It was nearly noon, the weather was unusually warm, and by the lack of clouds in the sky, it held the promise of staying that way. Thinking he'd take advantage of it, he headed toward the restaurant with a definite purpose in mind.

Chapter Fourteen

"I love this material," Laura Pruitt stated. Sarah waited patiently while Laura twirled around. "Isn't it pretty, Mama?"

"Yes, it is," Milly said with a proud smile. She turned to Sarah who had several pins between her teeth. "I want three more in different styles. My little Laura will be going back east to finishing school right after Christmas."

"Hold still," Sarah ordered even though it was difficult to speak. She caught the hem and finished pinning it, then stood up. "This shade of yellow is perfect for her, but I think a little ivory lace would soften the neckline. Perhaps a little around the cuff as well, what do you think?"

"That's a wonderful idea," Laura added.

"You do whatever you think is necessary," Milly said. "Nobody's going to say my little girl isn't well dressed. Laura, honey, run along and change. I told your Papa we'd meet him for dinner over at the restaurant while we're in town."

"But, Mama, it's only noon, can't we be a little late?"

One look from her mother, and Laura's slender shoulders sagged. "Very well. Thank you, Mrs. Wellington. You seem to know exactly what I like. I only hope you have time to finish them all."

Sarah inwardly agreed. She was beginning to hate dressmaking. She pasted on a smile. "Don't worry, Laura. I promise to have all your dresses finished before Christmas."

After the Pruitt ladies left, Sarah heaved a tired sigh and

started to pick up the scraps from Laura's gown. Sarah had purposely stayed busy in hope of keeping her thoughts from Ira. Not because she was still angry, but because she was ashamed. She smiled to realize that it had taken Miss Lily to open her eyes about Ira, and her very own speech to remind her how she really felt.

When the little bell jingled, she continued with her task and didn't bother to look up. "Did you ladies forget something?"

When they didn't answer, she turned around. Ira leaned against the door, braced by his right hand, the thumb of his left hand hooked casually over the gun belt he wore around his hips. Her heart did a little backward somersault at his lazy smile. His hat had been pushed off his forehead, giving him that boyish, teasing appearance that always made her insides turn to mush. She couldn't deny the instant and absolute attraction, and felt her cheeks color under the intensity of his gaze. "Ira . . . h-how are you?"

"I'm restless, and a little hungry. How about you?"

Restless? Just looking at him made her tingle to feel his warm hands on her body. And did he say hungry? She had to chew on her lip to keep from smiling. When it came to Ira Farrell, her hunger was insatiable.

"That depends," she replied with a cunning smile. "If you want me to fix something for us to eat, then I'm sorry to disappoint you." She gave a little shake of her head. "I'm a terrible cook."

He pushed away from the door, took her left hand in his and led her to the back room. Once out of sight from anyone passing by, he pressed her back against the wall, his face just inches away from hers, his hands possessing her waist.

"I was thinking we'd do something different," he whispered, his breath warm against her cheek and ear.

Sweet anticipation flowed over her with such intensity it nearly took her breath. "W-what do you have in mind?"

He caught her chin between his thumb and forefinger, holding her as he gazed deeply into her eyes. "I was thinking we can go some place where we can be alone, away from all the busybodies in town."

He kissed her then and she nearly melted against him, kissing him back. Shivers of delight followed his fingers as they slipped from her chin and inched around to the back of her neck. He held her captive, his persistent mouth coaxing her lips to open.

When they finally parted, she was breathless, hungry for more, but he turned her toward her room and gave her a little pat on the bottom. "Now, hurry up and go change into something warm and more suitable for riding."

Sarah doubted that riding out of town twenty minutes after Ira left would curb any dedicated gossips. However, she agreed to play along, finding her anticipation growing with each mile that passed. Off the road and over the rise in a sheltered copse of evergreen trees, she spotted the rump of his big roan.

"I was beginning to think you'd changed your mind," he said as he lifted her down from her horse. He took the reins and tied the animal to a tree. When he turned, there was strength as well as vulnerability in his eyes. "I want you to know something. What I said to you the day of the gunfight, was wrong of me. I had no right. You're not to blame. I am."

She would have interrupted, but he shook his head, preventing her from doing so. "It's something I didn't consider when I was young and eager to make a name for myself. And now that I'm a marshal, it's part of the job. Even in Carefree, I've been called out a few times."

As if it were a natural occurrence between them, he laced his fingers through hers and pulled her along. He didn't speak, nor did she feel the need. Just being with him, away from the critical eyes of the townsfolk, was enough for now.

Several yards ahead, where the sun warmed a patch of ground, he had spread a blanket on the winter-dry grass. On the blanket sat a small cloth-covered tin box and a bottle of wine. "I'm here to ask for your forgiveness, and to ask you if you'll share this feast with me." His smile was back to teasing. "Nothing mends fences better than good food. Do you like fried chicken?" he asked with a boyish grin.

"Indeed, I do."

He urged her to sit down, then sat across from her, Indian style, and picked up a little sack she hadn't noticed before.

"Here," he said as he pulled out two tin cups then filled them from the bottle. He studied her appreciatively for several moments before tapping his cup to hers. "To us," he said.

She repeated his toast and then they drank. When he put his cup down, he lifted the cloth from the tin. The food looked wonderful. After she made her choice, eating with her fingers, she declared it tasted even better out of doors.

"When you were a boy, and after you left the ranch," she began, "what did you do?"

"Well, let me think." He tossed a bone into the trees, then licked his fingers at the same time he gave her a sensual smile. A ruffling of butterfly wings began in her stomach.

"When I left the ranch, I was young, but I didn't think of myself as a boy. I was a man, and I had to make a living. I didn't know anything but roping steers and branding calves, so I rode down to Magdalena. I hired on with an old man named Ortiz."

"Was he a rancher?" she asked, taking a sip of wine.

"Nope. He owned a cantina. He needed someone to do dishes and empty the spittoon."

She grimaced. "That must have been delightful."

His laughter was spontaneous. "Yeah, well, it paid fifty cents a day. I could stay in the shed out back. It wasn't a hard job, at least not to my standards, and I had a whole lot of spare time on my hands."

He stretched out, leaning on his left elbow. "One day a man came in dressed like a New York banker. He had two of the fanciest pistols I'd ever seen strapped to his hips. He ordered food and a bottle of whiskey. He gave me a twenty-dollar gold piece for serving him."

"My goodness, that's a lot. Was he a lawman?" she asked.

Ira gave a nod. "He was. He was one of the fastest guns in Dodge City in his day. He was passing through town on his way back to Kansas to visit his brother."

Ira leaned over and refilled their cups. "I reckon he saw something in me I didn't know was there, and decided to stay on for a time. He played cards at night. During the day he taught me how to use a gun."

"So you followed in his footsteps to become a lawman?"

Once more Ira gave a little shake of his head. "Not exactly. I was still pretty young and pretty reckless. I learned real quick that a fast gun filled my pockets with gold. Lots of gold. Most of it from collecting bounties and drawing down on other fast guns."

She nearly choked on her wine. "You were a bounty hunter?"

"For about four years. I traveled a lot. Went down to Texas and ended up in El Paso for a time. Now there's a wild town. Got a bullet in my thigh from some bushwhacker I never saw."

She looked at him with a mixture of awe and disbelief. "How old were you when all of this happened?"

"Twenty-two. I remember because I got shot on my birthday." His grin turned scandalous. "Do you want to see my scar?"

"Ira," she scolded. "How can you tease about something as serious as getting shot?"

He shrugged his shoulders. "I'm more careful now. I don't sit close to doors or in front of windows."

She remembered how he had asked for a table in the back at the restaurant. "Were there other injuries?"

"Just a nick here and there."

"A *nick* here and there?" she repeated. Unexpectedly, another flash of memory startled her. She saw Ira in the middle of the street, facing down a man who could have easily ended his life. She remembered Lily telling her to look at his sleeve. The moment she did, she saw the small tear.

"After I recovered, I headed west into Arizona. I landed the position of deputy sheriff under the watchful eye of Sheriff George Ruffner." Ira took another drink. "He was a smart man—smart to still be alive when most lawmen his age weren't. I worked for him close to three years. His brother-in-law was the mayor of a wooly little town called Carefree, but the town wasn't big enough to support a full-time lawman. They were having a lot of trouble with horse thieves and rustlers. Mayor James had a few senator friends in Washington and before I knew it, the president appointed me a United States Marshal."

"So here you are," she murmured with a half smile. "I've read many stories about men like you, and until now never thought they were factual, just made up to impress the reader."

He frowned. "Is that good or bad? I can't tell." He finished his wine, then picked up the remains of their picnic, but when she went to stand, he caught her wrist and pulled her down. "Let's not go yet."

His touch was strangely reassuring. When he folded her in his arms she returned his kiss. As he brought her senses to life, she decided not to think of his past; instead she would focus on the present.

He placed her bolero aside at the same time he unbuttoned her blouse. His mouth seared a path from just below her ear to the taut peaks of her breasts, where he circled each nipple with his tongue, nipping and suckling until she moaned his name. He kissed her on the mouth again, then worked at the buttons on her skirt, sliding the garment off her hips. He slid his fingers under her frilly bloomers to caress her hips and thighs.

The gentle massage sent icy-hot currents of pure delight to the very center of her being. Soon she was naked to his hungry gaze. She shivered. Not from the temperature, but from expectation. He frowned, and she knew he worried that she was cold.

At once he stripped, then stretched out beside her, drawing the edges of the blanket over their bodies. "Better?" he asked in a husky voice.

"No," she said, reaching up to pull him on top of her. His hard length filled her. "Now I'm better," she gasped, accepting his kiss. He braced his weight on his elbows and began to move his hips in harmony with hers—torturously slowly at first then harder and more urgently until she felt as if she could reach out and touch the highest mountain peak.

Ira slipped one hand under her bottom at the same time he kept most of his weight from crushing her. He held her to him as he sank deeper into the tight folds of her feminine flesh. She was slick and hot, matching each urgent thrust. She writhed beneath him, urging him on. When he felt her body clench around him, he squeezed his eyes tight, trying to hold back to allow her the precious time to experience every blissful moment. Not until she took a breath did he begin to move within her again.

Much to his surprise, she arched her hips, driving him deeper. The tension in his body grew and expanded. Again, he had to concentrate to keep from exploding inside of her. Yet she wouldn't stop, grinding her hips to his. He felt her throb again, her soft flesh convulsing around him. He had to pull out, but when he tried, her hands clutched his buttocks, holding him to her.

"Ah, God," he growled, in agonizing bliss. He had no sooner regained a small portion of control when she climaxed again, crying out his name. The lusty sound of her voice—the call of her body was too great. Groaning with the most powerful climax he had ever experienced, he drew her so close he felt as if their hearts beat at the same time. With her warm body next to his, their arms entwined, he knew he couldn't live without her.

Snuggled close to his side, Sarah floated slowly back to reality and rested until she could breathe normally. A cool breeze ruffled her hair as Ira slowly lifted his head and stared at her. His expression was troubled, his gaze filled with concern. She cupped his cheek, then traced her fingertip across his smooth lips. "I wanted it this way," she murmured, then kissed him.

He rolled to his side, taking her with him. "But it's a risk—"

She stopped him with another kiss. "A risk. That's all, but I know my body and I think we're safe." She gave him a wily smile. "You take worse chances every time you strap on your gun and pin on your badge."

He brushed a curl away from her cheek. "Marry me," he said, gazing deeply into her eyes.

Her heart stopped for a breath of a moment. Afraid he felt obliged, she shook her head. "Ira, I know what you're feeling. You don't have to worry. The chances that—"

"Sarah." Ira placed his fingers against her mouth, searching her face. "Sarah. If you really want to know how I feel, then be quiet and I'll tell you." He cupped her face and kissed her again, teasing and tasting, a thorough, staggering kiss.

"I've been with other women. You know that. But that was different—a physical need. There was never any chance that I'd fall in love. I thought it was something I could avoid. Then you came along and changed everything. I tried to tell myself what we shared was that *physical need,* but something inside told me differently. You've become a part of me. It scares me some, and I don't know why."

Happy tears pooled in Sarah's eyes. "It scares me too," she whispered with a tender smile, "but I'm more frightened of living without you."

He gave a soft laugh, and then shook his head. "I reckon we'd better do something about it, don't you?" He kissed the tip of her nose. "Now, I'm only going to ask you this one more time, and I'm not letting you out of my arms until you give me the answer I want." He grew more serious. "Sarah Brighton, marry me, and then maybe, when we're *together,* we won't be so scared."

Cooper Finch picked up the gavel and banged it loudly on the table in the secluded room behind the mayor's office. Pruitt and his sons, as well as Earl Watts from the telegraph office were there. James Roland from the Rocking R Ranch had arrived with Louis Peters, owner of the mercantile.

Doctor Hensley had come in a moment ago, grumbling something about having to check on Mrs. Johnson's sick baby, but Finch paid him no attention until he handed Jonah a jacket.

The two men talked for several moments, and then the doctor showed Jonah a tear in the left sleeve. Cooper waited until they were through, then he banged on the table several more times.

"Gentlemen, it's late," Finch began, but the men in the room appeared not to hear. They were all talking at the same time. "We can't proceed till you quiet down. This meeting is called to order."

Silas Pruitt stood up and the voices died down. "Now that we're all here, I have some concerns to be addressed." He reached into his inside pocket and pulled out a piece of paper. "My first and utmost concern is Ira Farrell. This is a telegram Earl was supposed to send to Carefree, Arizona. It's asking the mayor to send some lawmen up here to assist Ira with his investigation. Thanks to Earl's fast thinking, it never got sent. My second concern is the cattle shipment. It's overdue *because* of Ira Farrell." Silas's frown deepened. "None of us can afford to have more lawmen snooping around."

Everyone started to speak at once, and Cooper had to re-apply the gavel. "Quiet down."

"Quiet down?" Doctor Hensley repeated. "If we're not careful, we'll all quiet down on the gallows."

"I'm with Doc," the rancher agreed. "When I first decided to enter into our little agreement, all I had to do was get a few boys together, steal a few head of cattle, drop a little salt in some wells, and make sure the Farrells got blamed. That was all right. No one got hurt. Then I get wind of a man dying in the mountains. Some foolishness about him getting mauled to death. And if that isn't bad enough, some damned dress shop burns down with the marshal's brother in it. I would like to know what the hell is going on."

Once more the sound of male voices talking over one another filled the room. Cooper sat back, surprised to see Jonah stand. Until now, Pruitt's youngest hadn't played much of a role in their scheme.

"Gentlemen, please," Jonah pleaded. "Nothing will be gained if we panic."

Cooper raised his hand, motioning for the rest of the men to be quiet. "I think you all should know the marshal came by my office today to tell me he found a herd of stolen cattle up in the canyon by Cougar's Bluff."

"That's been taken care of," Josh stated matter-of-factly. "They've been moved. Ira won't find them this time, and even if he gets wind we're hiding them at the ranch, I'll have the brands changed in another day or two."

"Well, that's just fine," the doctor countered sarcastically, leaning back in his chair. "Since you're so clever, why don't you tell us what you're going to do to fix our little problem with the dead marshal? A hot iron won't change the fact that he's dead. Nor will it change the fact that Ira believes one of us killed his brother and Miss Emily."

"Yeah," Louis and Earl agreed in unison.

"That's precisely why we called this meeting," Silas stated, pacing before the others. "We can't count on anyone but ourselves. Therefore, I'm suggesting—"

"Wait just one minute," the rancher interrupted. "How many more men have to die before we're through?"

"Just one," Cooper replied flatly. "Ira Farrell."

James Roland stared at the sheriff, then shifted nervously. "Arranging a fair gunfight and just gunning a man down are two different things. If something suspicious happens to Ira, Cole and Adam might look in my direction."

"None of us are immune," Silas muttered as he took his seat by Cooper. "No telling how many people saw my son call the marshal out in front of Lily's place a while back. Like you, James, my ranch borders theirs on the southern tip. We've had our share of skirmishes. And what about Cooper?" Silas asked. "We all know he lost his ranch because of the Farrells. That's good enough for some people to think he'd have reason to get even. Pretty near every man in this room has a good cause to want Ira dead."

"I've no beef with the Farrells," Earl stated nervously. "Especially a man like Ira. Don't forget, the marshal's got friends in high places. Friends that could bring every lawman in the territory down on us like flies on horseshit. If anyone is to blame for our predicament, it's your boys, Silas."

Cooper inwardly smiled. Old Earl had a way of hitting the nail on the head.

"There's no need to accuse my sons," Silas warned, shaking his head. "Everyone here knows that what happened with Miss Emily and Zach was just an unfortunate accident."

"Father," Jonah interrupted. "Please. We've got a problem to solve." Jonah's gaze moved around the table. "I say to you all, consider this carefully. If Ira has seen those cattle, and it's my understanding he has, it won't take long for him to implicate each and every one of us." Jonah leaned forward, his expression grim as he looked at the rancher. "James, you said murder is different from cattle rustling, but according to the law, they're both hanging offenses."

"What's your point?" the doctor demanded, tugging at his collar.

"My point is this. It won't matter if Ira can't prove we killed the marshal. We will still hang."

Cooper nodded, standing to get the men's attention. "If

Ira's dead, he's no threat. I suggest we arrange for him to have a little accident."

"Like what? Another fire?" Earl said with a worried frown. "We gotta do something quick. The marshal's going to get real suspicious if those deputies he sent for don't show up."

"I'll take care of Farrell," Josh stated with a sinister smile. "I've got no problem dropping him where he stands."

Jonah stared at his brother. "You're no gunfighter—"

"I ain't planning on meeting him out in the street," Josh sneered.

"All right, boys, settle down." Cooper rubbed the stubble on his jaw. "Suppose you gun down Ira, then what?" He didn't give anyone time to answer. "Every lawman in the territory will join forces with Cole and Adam and be all over this town. Like your father so carefully pointed out. You've already called attention to yourself."

"I'll just make sure I have an alibi," Josh countered.

Cooper scoffed. "Who? Jonah? Hell's bells, you've got to come up with something better than that or you'll be swinging from the nearest tree." Cooper glanced at James, but the rancher just shook his head.

"Don't look at me. I'm no shooter. Can't hit the broad side of a barn."

The doctor heaved an irritated sigh. "Then I propose, gentlemen, and believe me, I use the term lightly, that we take Josh's offer and simply pray we find some poor unfortunate drifter to take the blame."

"Yeah," the owner of the mercantile piped up. "If we have a shooter, Ira's family and friends will have no reason to get involved."

The sheriff looked at the storekeeper and shook his head. "Are you an idiot, Louis? Who in the hell would believe someone other than the men in this room would have a reason to gun down the marshal?" He scanned the men's faces. "You're all plumb crazy."

"I-I think I know of a man who we could blame," Earl Watts said weakly, taking out a clean handkerchief and dabbing at the beads of sweat on his brow. Everyone in the room gave him their full attention. "Louis, you know the man who brings you that liniment?"

"Sure do. He got in town yesterday. His name's Billy Carson. Brings me some every month, but this month he's early because of something special coming up . . . I think he said it was his wife's birthday."

Cooper heaved an impatient sigh. "Who in the hell cares about this man's wife?"

"I-I do," Earl stammered. The elderly man flinched when everybody spoke at once.

"Let's hear him out," Jonah chided. "Go on, Earl."

"Well, if we blame Billy, then after things settle down, we can say he escaped. No harm done. He'll never show his face in these parts again."

"Why in the hell would a traveling salesman want Ira dead?" Cooper asked with a disgusted edge to his voice. James Roland and Doctor Hensley agreed.

"Tell us what you're thinking, Earl."

"A-a couple of weeks or so ago, me and some of the boys were playing cards over at Miss Lily's." Earl looked at Louis. "You remember, don't you?"

"Now that you mention it I do. The marshal and that snake-oil salesman came in and had a drink at the bar. I thought it was kind of odd that they knew each other, but then someone told me they both live in the same town."

"That's right, Louis, they do." Earl gave a satisfied nod. "Well, I overheard Billy Carson telling the marshal that his wife was messing around on him. I never paid it no attention. Then I got to thinking, and—"

"For God's sake, Earl, are you going to drag this out all night?" the doctor grumbled.

"I'm getting to it, I'm getting to it," Earl said defensively. "A few days before, as far as I can recollect, the marshal came over to the telegraph station and sent out a whole bunch of messages. One of them was to a woman. It said something like he was real sorry—that he didn't think he was going to be back in Carefree anytime soon."

"So the marshal has a lady friend. So what?" Cooper muttered, drumming his fingers impatiently on the table.

Earl Watts scratched his balding head. "The lady's name was Mrs. Ginger Carson. I reckon she's Billy's wife, and quite possibly the marshal's lady friend."

Sarah didn't see Ira the next day, and she knew he was making every effort to keep the townsfolk from drawing too many unfavorable conclusions about her. Although she wasn't particularly bothered by their opinions, she thought it was sweet of him to be so protective.

She said a little prayer that they would solve the mystery surrounding the fire soon. She had lied to Ira again. *Not really,* she quickly corrected, hoping to ease her conscience. She had simply stretched the truth. She had no idea if she carried his child or not, and wouldn't know for another two weeks. But, the sooner she could stop pretending to be Mrs. Andrew Wellington, the sooner she could become Mrs. Ira Farrell. Just the thought of being his wife and having his baby gave her happy goose flesh.

"Excuse me."

She started then looked up to see Jonah Pruitt standing near her. It was after five, and she thought she'd locked the door. She quickly put aside her work and stood. "Y-yes?" She fingered a curl back into place with a puzzled frown. "How did you get in here?" she asked as she tried to calm her pounding heart. Had she been so engrossed with thoughts of Ira that she hadn't heard the bell?

"The door was open. I'm sorry. I didn't mean to startle you." He placed a jacket on the counter top then jerked off his bowler. "I'm Jonah Pruitt, remember?"

"Yes, of course," she replied, trying to smile.

"I came to see if my sister's dresses are ready. She told me they might be."

"Yes, two are." She stepped around the counter to fetch Laura's dresses. "I left them hanging in the back. If you don't mind waiting, I'll get them."

His smile was warm and friendly. "Not at all. Shall I stoke the stove for you while I'm waiting? It's kind of cold in here."

"Ah . . . yes. Thank you." She found Laura's dresses and carried them into her shop. "Here they are. Let me wrap them for you."

"They're lovely," Jonah said. "Laura and my mother have only good things to say about you." His smile was friendly, yet she felt his eyes roam over her body. "However, I must admit that lately my father is a little upset with my mother. It seems she is becoming more and more independent."

Sarah raised her chin and matched his stare, feeling strangely uneasy. "Your mother's independence shouldn't upset your father. He should be proud of the example Milly is setting for Laura."

"Really? I hadn't thought about it much."

"Laura's going back East soon. She'll need an abundance of self-confidence if she's to succeed in today's society."

Jonah nodded thoughtfully. "I assumed she was attending finishing school to attract a suitable husband."

Sarah scoffed. "Laura is attractive enough to do that without obtaining a higher education." Sarah shook her head. "Your sister's a free spirit. Once she see all the opportunities available to her, there's no telling what she will accomplish."

Jonah laughed. "She'd do well just to find a good husband. After all, it isn't up to her to rediscover the world. She's the type to be content raising children and seeing to her husband's needs."

Sarah gave him a sad smile and shook her head.

"What? Why are you looking at me like that?" he asked with an arrogant smile. "Isn't that every woman's dream?"

"I hardly think we women spend our nights dreaming of washing clothes, fixing meals and changing diapers." She finished wrapping the paper around the dresses and reached for the string, but he pulled some from the roll for her.

"Here, let me help you."

His smile was steady, but once more his gaze roamed down her length before he turned his attention to the string. He quickly tied the ends into a knot. "I almost forgot." He spread the jacket on the counter, showing her a tear in the sleeve. "Can this be fixed?"

Sarah's mouth went dry. The buttons on the jacket were tiny lion heads.

"Mrs. Wellington? Did you hear me? Can this be fixed?"

Sarah quickly collected herself, and then pretended to examine the sleeve. She gave a silent prayer that her voice wouldn't reveal her shock. "Y-yes, I believe I can mend this. But, you'll have to leave it."

"I intended to," Jonah replied, flicking the small tear. "Strange thing, this. Doc Hensley gave it back to me last night. He said I must have left it at his office, but I can't fathom why I would have been in his office in the first place, nor can I recall how I damaged it." He looked up and smiled. "I suppose that's of no interest to you. When can I pick it up?"

Sarah swallowed to calm her nerves. "I-I'm terribly busy right now, but I think I can have it ready next week . . . provided I can order such an unusual button."

"I can help there. I had this made in New York. Harrington's Tailor Shop." Jonah picked up his sister's package and tucked it under his arm. "Laura says to put this on our account. Good evening, Mrs. Wellington."

"Good evening," she managed to say. After he left, she quickly locked the door, then leaned against it for several moments trying to think what she should do.

Chapter Fifteen

Sarah was still leaning against the door when someone knocked. Trembling, she moved the lace curtain, startled to find Ira standing on the other side. She threw open the door. "Ira," she gasped. "You frightened me."

Ira stepped inside. "Something's bothering you. What is it, Sarah?"

She turned away from his piercing gaze and hurried to the counter. "Jonah Pruitt came by a little bit ago and brought this to be mended. Look at the buttons."

Ira's slight smile vanished. "Did he hurt you?"

"No, no. He just walked in and put it on the counter. He said he couldn't remember how he tore it." Sarah took a ragged breath. "Ira, he . . . he must have . . ." Tears pooled in her eyes and she couldn't finish. The moment Ira took her into his arms she melted against him, grateful for the comfort. After a few moments, she lifted her head from his shoulder. "I-I was so frightened, I didn't know what to do."

"It's all right, Sarah. You did just fine." He held her close for several moments, resting his chin on the top of her head. "It's late. There's nothing we can do till morning. Why don't you get a few things together and I'll take you back to the boarding house."

Sarah recalled her conversation with Lily—how the wise woman said Ira was obsessed with protecting his brothers from his father's cruelty. Now he was trying to protect her, and Sarah loved him even more for it.

She gave him a worried smile. "I'll just be a minute." She hurried to the back room, returning with a small satchel. "I'm ready."

Ira glanced out the window. The weather had turned bitterly cold. Frozen rain pelted the glass. "I sent Mayor James a note yesterday, and if everything goes as planned, it could all be over soon."

He turned and gave her a reassuring smile. "I've decided I'm going to give up my badge and hang up my gun as soon as we're married."

Stunned, she could only look up at him.

He took her satchel and the key to the shop from her cold fingers. "All I need is a good woman to keep me on a straight path—one who I'll treat as my equal," he added. "After all, it wouldn't do to make the first speaker at the meeting of the Ladies of Liberation my slave."

He put her satchel on the boardwalk, locked the door, then shoved the key into his coat pocket. "I'm thinking you ladies wield much more power over us men than you give yourselves credit for."

"We do," she said, slipping her arms around his waist.

"That's why I love you," he said softly. When his warm palm caressed her cheek, she leaned into it, covering it with her cold hand.

"I love you more," she murmured just before reaching up to kiss him.

Ira kissed her back, and then lifted his head. "Come on, darlin', it's downright cold out here." He moved her aside to retrieve the satchel.

It almost sounded like a crack of terribly loud thunder, but the glass in the upper part of the door near their heads shattered. Ira shoved her down, shielding her with his body as his gun appeared in his hand.

"Stay put," he ordered as he hovered over her, searching the night for a sign of the shooter.

Another crack and wood splintered, showering Sarah with debris. Ira fired two quick shots at the rooftop across the street, then turned and kicked the ruined door open. He pushed her inside, following her to the floor just as a third shot ricocheted through the deserted street. She heard his painful grunt, but it didn't immediately register on her terrified mind. He crawled to the window, then grabbed her and pulled her close. Both of them sat on the floor amidst the broken glass, their backs against the wall under the window. Except for their labored breathing, an eerie silence fell over them.

"Are you all right?" he asked. His voice sounded strange, urgent. Instantly she knew something was wrong.

"Yes," she whispered, trying to catch her breath. "Who's shooting at us?" When he didn't answer, she began to tremble even more. "Ira?"

"Sarah, I'm hit."

Though the words were said calmly, cold dread settled in her heart. She looked at him then, and in the muted light from the street lamp, she saw a dark wetness seeping through his coat on his upper right chest. His right hand rested in his lap, his fingers slack over the butt of his gun. "Oh, God," she rasped. "H-how bad is it?"

"That's not important now. You have to listen to me," he ground out. "Put my pistol in my left hand."

She obeyed without question.

"Now, go . . . go out the back. Stay low. I'll draw their fire—"

"No," she nearly shouted. "I-I can't . . . I won't leave you."

"Ah, God, Sarah, please don't argue . . . you've got to get help. I-I can't protect you." His voice faded into a whisper. "Trust no one."

Sarah stared at Ira—at the blood on his coat. Somewhere in the deathly quiet town a dog started barking, and then another picked up the howling crescendo. Slowly, lights appeared in windows, and men's voices could be heard, shouting warnings and bellowing for the sheriff.

"Ira?" she said, hating the fragile sound of her voice as she touched his face. She reached up and grabbed several scraps of cloth from the counter, then moved aside his coat, stuffing the wad inside his shirt. "Ira," she cried hysterically. "Ira," she repeated, over and over again as she cradled his limp body in her arms. "Somebody help me," she screamed between heart-wrenching sobs. "Please, somebody help me."

Josh Pruitt cursed then leaned back against the brick chimney on the roof of the mercantile. He could only hope that one of the three bullets hit his target. He peered around the chimney, trying to see if he had time to fire off a few more rounds, but the street was rapidly coming alive. "Shit," he muttered, yanking his sheepskin coat tighter around his body. He was trapped. But only for a little while. As he shivered against the cold, he wished he'd had the foresight to bring a flask.

Sarah clutched Ira's gun belt to her breast, watching in stunned silence as the doctor donned a clean white apron. He was older than she expected, probably fifteen or twenty years her senior. He moved quickly, yet not too quickly, rolling up his sleeves before taking a pair of shears to cut away Ira's bloody clothes. She swallowed down the urge to be sick at the sight of so much blood, willing herself to be strong for Ira's sake.

"Do you want me to take that for you?"

Sarah slowly turned to see Sheriff Finch hold out his hand. She vaguely remembered him coming into her shop and asking some men to carry Ira to the doctor's office. Other than that, everything else was a blur. "No," she murmured. She looked down at Ira's holstered gun, then back at the table where he lay. "No. He'll want it close by when he wakes up."

When Ira heard Sarah's voice, he tried to open his eyes, but he didn't have the strength. He felt weighted down, as if his arms and legs were tied to a table. White-hot pain burned through his back and into his chest. Each breath made it worse.

"Mrs. Wellington, there's nothing you can do here. You'd better go on home," someone said.

No. Sarah, don't go. I need you. Ira drew in another painful breath and tried to speak aloud, but couldn't form the words.

"I'm not leaving," came her sweet voice.

"Then go into my kitchen and boil some water." More pain coursed through Ira as someone pressed down on his chest.

"Why the hell did you bring him here, Cooper?" the faceless voice demanded. The man removed something sticky from Ira's chest, replacing it with a dry cloth, pressing down hard. Ira groaned aloud.

"Can he hear us?" the other voice asked cautiously.

"Can't be sure. He appears to be in a semiconscious state. No matter. In his present condition, I doubt he'll remember anything that's happened." It grew quiet, but the pain intensified for several moments then ebbed. "The wound looks clean." Quiet again, then the voice was barely above a whisper. "You should have left him. With a hole this size, he would have bled to death in a very short time. Now I have no choice but to patch him up."

"Here, doctor. What do you want me to do with this?"

Ira concentrated on Sarah's voice, willing her to stay. He tried again to open his eyes, but the voices grew farther and farther away.

Sarah put the basin on the table beside the doctor, and then took several steps back, staring at Ira. She could already see a change. He was covered in a fine sheen of sweat, and his cheeks were void of any color. When the doctor had Cooper roll Ira on his side to wash his back, fresh blood trickled from the wound on his chest, and suddenly she realized he could still die.

She glanced at the two men. A doctor she'd never met and the sheriff. *Trust no one.* Ira's words floated in and out of her thoughts, filling her with doubt. When the doctor gathered up a large needle and some thread, Sarah turned away and tried to collect her thoughts, wishing she'd brought her derringer.

"Not much longer now," the doctor replied. "I'll just bandage this good and tight."

Trust no one. Sarah couldn't get the sound of Ira's voice out of her head. Those three words were the last he'd spoken, and he'd done so with great effort. Instinctively she knew they were said to protect her. Or were they? Maybe he knew he was badly wounded. Maybe he'd said them so she would protect him.

"When you're finished, I want him taken to his room at Mrs. Baca's boarding house," she said, drawing herself up to her full height. Both men frowned, looking at her as if she'd lost her mind, but she didn't care. All she cared about was getting Ira back to the safety of his room. "You heard me,

Doctor. Finish with the bandage, then have some men take him to his room."

"There's a bed in the other room that I use for my patients, Mrs. Wellington. I'd advise against moving him that far and out in the cold night air." The doctor exchanged glances with the sheriff. "However, if you insist."

"I insist." She raised her chin and met his gaze. "Mrs. Baca and I are perfectly capable of taking care of Ira. More so than you, since we'll be able to stay with him around the clock. If we need your services, we'll send for you." She stared him down, refusing to yield.

Doctor Hensley heaved a loud resigned sigh. "Very well, Mrs. Wellington." He looked at Cooper. "You heard her. I have a stretcher in the other room. Can you and your deputy help the lady?"

The sheriff looked as if he wanted to ask her to reconsider. But she gave him a look that thwarted any protest he might have voiced.

"Yeah, sure," Cooper replied tersely. "I'll go get him."

Sarah jumped when the front door slammed. Once more she wished she had her derringer.

"Since I can't change your mind, maybe you'll accept some advice."

"I'll do whatever is necessary."

"Good, because it will be touch and go for a while." He opened a glass-faced cupboard and took out two bottles, adding them to several clean cloths he said were for extra bandages. He lifted one of the bottles. "This one is for the pain, and trust me, he'll have a lot of it when he wakes up . . . if he wakes up at all," he added with a shake of his head. "A teaspoon in a little water should keep him comfortable. It kills the pain, but it puts him to sleep. Don't be alarmed if he can't seem to stay awake. This one is to help the fever—"

"What fever?" she demanded, trying her best to appear calm and composed.

The doctor gave an impatient sigh. "Well, he doesn't have a fever . . . not yet, but, trust me, it'll come. It always does with wounds as serious as this. Now pay attention. A capful in a half glass of water or tea. Anything you can get down his throat should help the fever. Of course don't forget to use cold compresses. If his fever gets too high, he'll die. Do you understand me, Mrs. Wellington?"

"Completely," she managed to say, matching his stare even though her knees quaked.

"Good. It's very important that you follow my instructions if you want to keep him alive."

A few minutes later, the sheriff returned with his deputy and another man Sarah had seen around town. After they had Ira secure on the stretcher, she followed them out.

The moment she was gone, Cooper rounded on the doctor. "Why in the hell did you let him leave?"

Doctor Hensley gave a snort. "It's perfectly simple. Farrell's wound is very serious. There's a real good chance he won't make it through the night."

"We could have made sure of that if he'd stayed."

"And could quite possibly be blamed for his death," the doctor countered. "No, trust me. It's better this way. Much better."

Sheriff Finch arrived just as his men were leaving. Though Sarah's attention was focused on Ira, she heard him greet Mrs. Baca as he took off his hat. "You ladies take good care of the marshal, and I'll take care of everything else. Don't you worry. I put a man in the lobby downstairs to make sure no one bothers you." After covering Ira, Sarah turned to face the sheriff. "My deputy and I will be checking out the buildings across from your shop. You can send Mrs. Baca if you need us for anything."

"Thank you. That's very kind." Sarah closed the door and leaned back against it for several minutes feeling as if a great weight had been lifted off her shoulders.

"Did they get the shooter?" Ira asked, startling her. She rushed to Ira's side. Tiny beads of sweat dotted his brow and his jaw clenched each time he shifted his weight.

"I didn't know you were awake," she said as she brushed his hair off his forehead. "Not yet." He inquired about her welfare twice, and twice she told him she was all right, that he was the one that needed attention, not her, but he grew increasingly restless.

He shivered violently. "I can't move my arm."

"The doctor tied it down. He said it would heal faster this way."

Ira seemed to accept her answer, resting back against the pillows. He shivered again. The room was warm, overly so. Mrs. Baca had just added two thick chunks of wood to the stove in the corner of the room. Sarah cast a frightened glance at Mrs. Baca when she came to the other side of the bed. The kindly older woman leaned over and pulled the covers a little higher over Ira's chest. "I will go get another blanket, and a pillow and blanket for you as well."

Ira tried to sit up when the door opened and closed. "Sarah?"

"I'm here," she reassured. She urged him to be still, and told him he was far too sick to move. Finally, after he focused on her face, he appeared to relax, but his eyes were cloudy with pain.

"Please, try to sleep," she pleaded.

"I hurt too much to sleep," he murmured, taking hold of her hand. "Stay with me. Stay close, where I can see you."

She forced a smile. "I'm right here. I'm not going to leave this room, I promise." She placed his left hand on his chest. It felt warm to the touch. "I'm just going to get some water."

She picked up the brown bottle the doctor had given her for the pain. She had heard of laudanum, knew it could be habit-forming if used too often, but also knew it would take away Ira's pain. Medicine the doctor gave to her expressly for Ira. She glanced at Ira and her heart clenched as she imagined his pain. She put the bottle down and filled a glass with cool water.

She returned to his side and brushed her knuckles against his cheek, reviving him. His eyes slowly opened. "Can you drink a little water?" she asked with a concerned smile. He nodded, then clenching his jaw, tried to sit up. She helped him as best she could, but he only took a few sips.

"Where's my pistol?" he asked, and she sensed with his right hand bound to his chest he felt vulnerable.

"It's there, on the chair. Would you like me to get it and put it on the bed?" She didn't wait for his answer. Instead she picked up his gun belt and placed it on top of the covers where he could feel its weight by his side. "There. Now rest. Everything's going to be all right. The sheriff has a man guarding the door downstairs."

"Sarah?" There was a slight tremor in his voice, and once more she was reminded how serious his situation was.

"Yes?" she said, fighting back the urge to cry at the weakness in his voice and the way he trembled.

"Send for Cole. He'll be able to . . . keep you . . . s-safe."

The doctor's prediction came to fruition. By dawn, Ira was hot to the touch. He hovered between illusion and reality, talking off and on in his sleep. When he grew restless, it took both women to hold him down. He said things Sarah

211

didn't understand about people she didn't know. He often called for Cole and Adam.

Then his voice would change to a low, agonizing whisper as he apologized to Zach. Between bouts of delirium he was lucid, asking for water and warning her not to leave or go anywhere without her little gun.

She reassured him several times that Mrs. Baca's son had gone into the mountains to fetch his family, but that news didn't seem to help. He was restless, fighting to stay conscious. She and Mrs. Baca worked in shifts, bathing him with cold cloths, encouraging him to take sips of broth for the fever and watered-down whiskey for the pain.

Ira was finally resting a little more peacefully when someone knocked on the door. Sarah was napping on a chair next to the bed, but before she could get up, Mrs. Baca put her knitting aside, went to the door and asked the intruder to identify himself.

"Cole Farrell."

Mrs. Baca threw open the door and stepped aside as the three Farrell men stepped inside. "We just got into town," Cole stated, taking off his hat and coat and tossing them at his younger brother. Jeb didn't bother to take off his coat before he hurried to Ira's bedside. The older man placed a weathered hand on Ira's forehead, frowning more than Sarah had ever seen. As she glanced at Ira's brothers, their expressions were guarded as well.

"I will go make some coffee," Mrs. Baca said, softly pulling the door closed when she left.

"How bad is it?" Cole asked, his brows pulled tightly together as he lifted the cover and inspected the thick bandage on Ira's chest.

Sarah took a weary breath. "He was shot in the back. The bullet went completely through his shoulder. Nothing's broken, but the doctor said it was serious and that . . . well, we wouldn't know for the first few days."

Adam visibly blanched, but Cole was more like Ira, able to keep his feelings hidden. Jeb never looked up. Instead, he wrung out a wet cloth and placed it on his nephew's forehead. Except for the slight clenching of the old man's jaw, Sarah didn't see any change in his expression. Jeb carefully tucked the quilt back around Ira's shoulders, then sat on the left side of the bed and reached for Ira's hand. "I knew somethin' like this would happen. I just knew it."

Cole stared at his brother lying motionless in the bed. "Did the sheriff get who did it?"

"I-I don't know," Sarah said softly as she pulled her shawl tighter. "I haven't left his side since it happened."

"Why is he here instead of at the doc's?" Jeb asked. The old man rose to face her.

Sarah pressed her fingertips to her forehead. "I-I didn't think he'd be tended as well."

Cole exchanged a worried glance with his uncle before turning to Adam. "Hightail it to the livery and rent a buckboard. Ira can't stay—"

"What?" Sarah stepped aside as Adam did what he was told without further question. "What are you going to do?" she asked nervously. "If you're thinking that you're going to move him from this room, you're mistaken."

Cole's expression never changed. "We can't leave him here. It's not safe." Cole's gaze never left hers. "I thank you for helping with my brother, but we'll take care of things from here."

"Really?" she replied with a mixture of hurt and sarcasm. "Then I'm dismissed?" She inwardly cringed at the confused look on Cole's face.

"I'm sorry, Mrs. Wellington. I didn't mean to sound like I

wasn't appreciative. It's just that I thought you'd want to get back to . . . to dressmaking."

Nearly exhausted and close to tears, Sarah took a ragged breath. "I'm in love with your brother."

Jeb put down the cloth. "Well, I reckon there's no easy way to say this, so I'll just be as blunt as you are. I didn't like that trash you wrote about my nephew's reputation, about him being a cold, calculating gunfighter. And, I don't like you being here with him now, giving the nosey bitty-bodies somethin' else to gossip about." Jeb glanced down at Ira for a brief moment. "He's a grown boy, and what the two of you are doing ain't no business of mine. But, while he's down and can't take care of hisself, he's our business, and I believe I speak for the whole Farrell family when I say we don't want no more trashy rumors about him socializing with a married woman. Do I make myself clear?"

She swallowed back her heated retort. "Yes, you do, but your concerns aren't valid."

"Not valid?" Jeb repeated incredulously. He would have said more but she planted her fists on her hips and matched his glare.

"Although it's none of your business, as Ira's uncle, I feel I owe you an explanation." She fastened her gaze on Cole. "You, also."

"We're listening," Cole countered.

"You have my permission to call me Sarah. You see, my real name is *Miss* Sarah Brighton. I'm not a dressmaker. I'm a journalist, and I used to write for the *St. Louis Herald*. And there's something else. I'm not really married . . . not yet."

The trip to the ranch was long and tedious. Cole and Adam had filled the buckboard with straw and covered it with several blankets. Cole was strong enough to lift Ira without difficulty, placing him in the middle of the wagon. Sarah climbed in, tucking the multiple blankets around Ira as she settled herself by his side. Jeb and Adam followed on horseback while Cole drove the two-horse team.

Upon Jeb's insistence, they stopped several times to force water down Ira's throat. Finally, as the sun appeared like an orange ball of fire between the peaks, Cole pulled up to the Farrell home.

Sarah lifted her head from Ira's left shoulder where she had been sleeping. "Thank God," she murmured as Adam helped her down.

"We'll take it from here," Adam said with a kind smile, adding that she would probably enjoy a little time to freshen up. Sarah took one look at her wrinkled gown and agreed.

An hour later, after Sarah had changed into one of Emily's calicos, she found Ira in bed in his old room. He apparently never awakened, even when Cole had carried him upstairs. By Cole's expression, Sarah knew this had caused them all great concern. After Jeb finished changing Ira's bandage, he gave Cole several orders about fetching firewood and blankets. Jeb put an arm around Adam and led him out the door with instructions to slaughter a rooster for soup. Weary to the bone, Sarah silently hoped it'd be the rooster that woke her up so early the last time she visited.

"He's still too damned hot," Cole said grimly after he'd put his hand on Ira's forehead.

"The doctor gave me some medicine, but—"

"But what?" Cole asked, dropping the cloth in the basin of cold water. "What is it, Sarah? I've a feeling you've been hiding something."

"I'm not really hiding anything. It's just a feeling I have." She sank down on a chair Cole had placed by Ira's bedside.

"Before Ira passed out, he tried to get me to leave, but when I wouldn't go, he told me to trust no one."

Cole added a small log to the kindling then closed the stove door. After he dusted off his hands, he faced Sarah. "That's not so strange, considering he'd just been ambushed."

"I suppose," she said listlessly. "That's why I wouldn't let the doctor keep Ira at his office."

"I doubt Ira meant you couldn't trust Doc Hensley, but that don't matter so much now. Ira's better off here anyway. Jeb's a regular mother hen when it comes to tending us when we're sick."

Chapter Sixteen

Sarah stood in Ira's room staring out the window on the second day after Ira was shot. A light snow had started to fall, trying to stick to the pane, dusting the roof of the barn in white. The room was warm, the lamp turned down to add a soft yellow glow.

Ira's fever was worse. He was delirious most of the time, barely able to take even the smallest amount of fluids without choking. A little while ago, Cole had brought in several buckets of ice. With Adam's help, they'd lifted Ira and placed him on a canvas tarp, then proceeded to pack ice around his body. They were careful to keep his bandaged shoulder dry. Though worried, Sarah hadn't interfered, sensing that they knew what they were doing.

"I remember when Zachary got a bad fever years ago." The sound of Cole's voice drew her away from the window. Cole sat by his brother, his brow drawn together as he wrung out the wet cloth, then placed it back on Ira's forehead. "It was early spring, and we didn't have the icehouse then, but Uncle Jeb said we had to cool him off or he'd die. Adam and Pa were out hunting. I had a broken arm at the time and wasn't much help. And, Jeb wasn't strong enough to lift Zachary. Anyway, Ira picked Zach up and we all went down to the river. The snow had just begun to melt upstream. Ira paid no attention to the frigid temperature. He just waded right in and sat down, holding Zach's head above water."

Cole heaved a worried sigh, then smiled for the first time that morning. "That water was so cold, I don't think Ira got warm till summer. Now that I think about it, he had an aversion to swimming after that too." Cole took a handful of crushed ice and dropped it in the basin, then rewet the cloth. "My little brother's fever broke in about a half-hour's time. I'm hoping the same will happen for Ira."

Sarah smiled weakly at the look on Cole's features, completely aware that he was trying to ease some of her distress. A moment later Jeb came in with two cups of steaming hot coffee. He bent close to Ira and whispered something they couldn't hear, then straightened up and, with tears on his wrinkled cheek, headed for the door.

Sarah sank down on the chair. "Do you remember when I wanted to see Emily's things the night I stayed at the ranch?" she asked, taking a sip of coffee.

Cole nodded while he bathed Ira's forehead. "Yes, ma'am. I do."

She was thankful for his presence and his patience. "Ira and I found a button in an envelope. Not an ordinary button, but one that's rare, that can only be specially ordered for men's jackets and coats."

Ira shifted restlessly, drawing her attention while Cole urged him to rest. "Go on," he said once Ira settled.

"The night Ira was shot," Sarah began, "Jonah Pruitt brought in that jacket and asked me if I could mend it. When Ira came by, I told him about it. He said there was nothing we could do until morning. He also told me he'd sent a telegram to someone in Carefree asking for help."

"I'm not sure I'm following you," Cole replied.

"There has to be a connection. Did anyone say where the button in Emily's things was found?" She chewed her lip, watching Cole tend his brother when Ira became more restless.

"Easy, Ira."

Ira's eyes fluttered open, but they were glazed and red. "That steer has broken down the fence."

"I'll catch him. Don't you worry none." Cole's patient compassion was endless even though she knew he had to be exhausted. He was quiet for several moments—so many, that Sarah wondered if he'd heard. She was about to repeat her question when he stood and faced her. His expression was grim, his eyes glinting with something similar to pain.

"I found it in Miss Emily's hand," Cole said solemnly as he picked up his coffee and took a drink, staring out the window. "We came down from the mountain to take them home the moment we heard about the accident. I didn't want no undertaker messing with my brother, and since we all knew and loved Miss Emily, I brought her home as well. Jeb and Adam were too torn up to handle what had to be done, so I took it upon myself to bathe them and change them into some nice clothes."

"That must have been difficult for you," Sarah whispered.

Again he fell silent for a long time, sipping his coffee and watching the snow. "Tell me again about this coat."

"The button you found in her hand came off of Jonah Pruitt's coat. I think he must have tried to assault her."

Cole turned and faced her. "Why would he do something like that? Everyone knew she and Zach were planning on getting married."

"I don't know. Perhaps he was sweet on her," Sarah said a little desperately. "All I know is the button you found came off his coat."

Sarah pressed her fingers to her forehead, trying to think. "I'm guessing that maybe Jonah tried to kiss her and Zach must have walked in on them. Somehow Jonah managed to overpower him, then set the fire to hide what he'd done."

Cole put down his coffee. "I can hardly believe Zach would let Jonah get the upper hand. Even if it happened like you say, and somehow Jonah knocked Zach out, why didn't Miss Emily scream for help?"

"Maybe she did," Sarah added sadly. "Maybe she couldn't."

Cole raked his fingers through his dark hair, his expression one of disbelief. "Jonah's got a good education. Could he be that cold-blooded?" Cole's brows snapped even tighter together. In two strides he was at the door.

"Where are you going?" she asked frantically.

"To pay a little call on the Pruitts."

"No Cole, please don't. Ira said he sent for some help. I'm sure some deputies are on their way. We're not even sure about the fire. It could have been an accident, now that I think about it. There could have been a scuffle. A lamp could have been knocked over."

"That hardly justifies Jonah leaving them there to die."

Sarah's shoulders slumped. "True, but it doesn't make him a murderer either."

Cole looked at her for several tense moments then heaved a tired sigh. "All right. For now," he emphasized, glancing at Ira, "I'll wait until I can speak with my brother."

A soft knock sounded on the door.

"Come on in," Cole muttered as he pulled it open. Sarah looked past Cole, shocked to see Lily Barker. She was as beautiful as ever, her dark red curls piled high, partially hidden beneath a fur-lined, hooded cloak. There was one thing different. Instead of her usual color choice of red, her cloak was as white as the snow.

"Cole," she acknowledged. "I came to see Ira."

"Come in," Cole replied as he stepped aside.

Lily went directly to the bedside and gently brushed a

gloved hand over Ira's cheek. "How is he?" she asked, her voice barely over a whisper.

"He's holding his own," Cole answered.

Sarah inwardly winced at the tears glistening in Lily's eyes when she turned. Slowly, Lily pushed back the hood then went to the bureau and lifted the bottle of whiskey Cole had put there. "May I?"

"Help yourself." Cole's expression bordered on shock, and Sarah knew he was as curious as she to find out why Lily came all this way in a storm. Lily poured a little into a glass then took a sip before returning to Ira's bedside.

"This is most likely my fault."

"Why's that, Lily?" Cole asked, voicing Sarah's thoughts.

Lily swiped at her tears then looked at Cole. "Ira came to my place two days ago. He and I had a nice long talk—that is, until Josh Pruitt walked in." Lily's hand trembled when she lifted the glass and took another sip. "I told Ira I'd ask my girls if they knew anything about the marshal that was killed." Lily's gaze locked with Cole's. "I'm thinking Josh heard us talking. I'm thinking he thought I might have told Ira something I shouldn't have." She tossed the rest of the whiskey down her throat then looked at Sarah. "Cooper said they caught the man who did it, but I don't believe him."

"Why not?" Sarah asked.

"The man they said did this didn't look like he could swat a fly." Lily turned back to Cole. "Late last night, they drug Billy Carson out of his hotel room and put him in jail."

"Who in the hell is Billy Carson?" Cole asked with a scowl.

Lily cast a quick glance at Sarah before answering Cole. "He's a traveling salesman." Lily walked to the door. "I just wanted to make sure Ira was . . . that he was safe. I've got to be getting back. Why don't you walk me out and I'll tell you everything I know."

When Cole looked at Sarah, she wanted to protest, but then realized someone had to stay with Ira. "You go on," she replied. "You can tell me later."

Once outside Ira's room, Lily lowered her voice and walked with Cole toward the stairs. "I didn't want to say anything in front of Sarah, but I think the sheriff is using Billy to protect the real culprit."

"I still don't see the connection." Cole grasped Lily's elbow and started down the steps.

"Billy Carson travels a lot, selling snake oil to anyone who'll buy it. He lives in Carefree and knows Ira. They both came into the saloon a little while back. Billy was really upset, kind of loud and easily overheard. Naturally I was interested, so I listened to their conversation. Seems Billy found out his wife was having an affair when he was out of town. He wanted Ira to help, but I could see Ira was in over his head. I offered to help, and Billy left shortly after we talked."

"What's all this got to do with Ira?" Cole asked at the base of the stairs.

Lily strolled with Cole to the door, stopping to give him a cool smile. "Ira was the man fooling around with Billy's wife."

Cole was just about to open the door, but her revelation caused Cole to stop in his tracks. "What?"

"You heard me." Lily's expression confirmed she was speaking the truth.

"Then Billy had reason," Cole stated flatly.

"He had reason, but he didn't do it." Lily pulled the hood of her cloak over her hair and slipped on her matching gloves. "The Pruitts had something to do with this. Remember when I said I told Ira I'd ask my girls if they knew anything about the marshal that was killed?"

"Yeah, I remember," said Cole.

"Josh Pruitt killed that marshal from Albuquerque," she replied, "and then bragged to some of my girls about how he made it look like an accident."

Sarah paced at the foot of Ira's bed. She'd noticed the look on Lily's face when she was talking about the man Cooper arrested. Lily had something more to say—something she wanted only Cole to hear. Who was Billy Carson, and why did he shoot Ira? When the door opened and Cole stepped inside, she gave a small sigh of relief. Maybe now she'd get some answers.

"Well?" she asked Cole, after he checked on his brother. "Are you going to tell me what Lily had to say?"

"Lily thinks they got the wrong man."

"I know that," Sarah replied impatiently.

"I'm not so sure." Cole took a patient breath. "I'm thinking this man, Billy Carson, might have had good reason to try and kill Ira."

"Good reason?" Sarah repeated in disbelief. "How can there be any reason good enough to shoot a man in the back?"

Cole raised his hands. "I know . . . I know. But, I think this fella, probably *thought* he had good reason."

"What did Lily tell you?" She frowned when Cole looked extremely uncomfortable. "Cole, please."

"Look, Sarah. It's plain as day that you and Ira are in love, but I don't want to hurt you. It would be better if Ira told you himself."

Sarah put her hand on Cole's arm. "I have a right to know," she said quietly.

"Billy Carson lives in Carefree and knows Ira."

"Then he's a gunfighter?"

"No—"

"An outlaw? Did Ira lock him up once and he felt the need to get even?"

"No. Billy Carson's a traveling salesman." Cole looked away then heaved an impatient sigh. "It seems Ira knows his wife . . . intimately."

"I-I see." Ira had seduced another man's wife. The shock of it stabbed into her heart and clouded that little place where she kept the ridiculous, naïve thought that he was hers and only hers.

"I'm sorry, Sarah, but even in my book that's reason enough to gun a man down."

Stunned, Sarah only nodded as Cole gave her a sympathetic smile. "At least we have the shooter. As far as Miss Emily and Zach are concerned, we're just going to have to wait until Ira is better." Cole hesitated for a moment then turned to leave. "I'm going to go get some more ice."

Alone with Ira, Sarah swallowed down the urge to cry. She took a deep breath, and then turned to check on Ira. She dampened a cloth and dabbed at the beads of perspiration on his forehead. It wasn't logical to be so upset, she told herself. Ira had confessed he'd been with other women, but she had assumed they were young and single, free spirits like herself. Even so, if Ira seduced another man's wife, it had happened before she knew him . . . and . . . and she was certain he hadn't been with anyone else since they met.

Yet a seed of doubt sprouted in her breast the moment Lily's beautiful visage flashed in her mind. The way Lily's hand had rested possessively on Ira's shoulder the day of the gunfight when she had found them together in the saloon— Lily's expression when she went to his bedside a little while ago.

Sarah squeezed her eyes tightly closed. Though she tried to be forbearing, the thought of Ira with another woman very nearly crushed her heart. Once more she dabbed at the per-spiration on his forehead, noticing for the first time he was sleeping peacefully.

"Oh my," she murmured, pressing the back of her hand to Ira's forehead. "Oh my," she said louder, rising and flinging open the door.

Ira opened his eyes. He remembered having nightmares—remembered being so hot he thought he'd died and gone to hell, but now all he felt was a dull pain in his shoulder and back, and an overwhelming thirst.

"Well, it's nice you decided to join us." He heard Cole's voice. In fact, now that the fog was lifting from his head, there were voices all around him. He recognized Sarah's, Jeb's and Adam's. As someone picked up his hand, he struggled to see who it was, but couldn't keep his eyes open long enough.

"He's coming around," Uncle Jeb muttered.

"Are you sure? He's still so pale," Sarah said, her voice pushing Ira to open his eyes. He remembered being shot at, the fear in Sarah's vivid blue eyes. But that was all. Everything else was just a blur, like his vision.

"Sarah?" he said in a voice that sounded as if it belonged to someone else . . . someone sick and feeble. His efforts were rewarded with a brilliant smile from the woman he loved. Too soon she moved away and Cole and Adam stood before him, grinning down at him.

"How are you feeling?" Cole asked.

"Like hell," Ira answered hoarsely. "I need water."

Adam hurried to fill a glass. Ira gritted his teeth when Cole helped him sit up, bracing his weight while he drank. After-ward, Cole eased him back down. When Cole got up, Sarah returned. Ira waited until the pain eased a little, then asked, "What happened? Why do I hurt so bad?"

"You were ambushed," Cole replied.

"I'll tell you what happened," Jeb scolded. "You damn near got killed. I warned you not to leave the ranch without us. Some yellow-bellied son of a buck back-shot you. I hope they hang him from the nearest tree."

"Uncle Jeb, he's hurt. Let up on him," Adam said with a worried frown.

Ira concentrated on the warm fingers entwined with his to keep the room steady. He needed to hold on to reality, to tell them about the danger, and something important, but he couldn't remember what it was.

"Are you doing all right, Ira? You don't look so good," Adam replied.

"Just tired." He had to rest again, to try to search his memory. "Did . . . did they get the shooter?"

"They caught him," Adam hurried to say.

"Gentlemen, please," Sarah admonished. "It's too soon for so many questions. He needs peace and quiet and lots of rest. I suggest you go get some coffee." The last words came out like an order.

"She's right," Jeb confirmed. "We'd best let this boy get some sleep."

Cole glanced down at his brother. "We'll come back a little later, after you've rested."

Ira caught his sleeve. "Cole," he said urgently, collecting the last of his waning strength. "We need to talk . . . about Zach and the fire."

Cole leaned down close to Ira. "Miss Lily came by to see how you were doing. We had a nice long talk, Ira, and I think when you're better, we'll have everyone involved behind bars."

Ira started to protest, but Cole put his hand on his brother's uninjured shoulder. "You've done all you can do

226

for now. Concentrate on getting better. Leave the worrying to me and Adam. I'll be back a little later to check in on you. If you're stronger, we'll talk some more."

Ira nodded and closed his eyes. He listened to his family as they gave Sarah strict orders to send for them if she needed to. When the door clicked shut, he lifted heavy lids. "There's something I needed to tell Cole, but I can't remember what it was." Ira was quiet for a long time, but she knew by the pressure on her fingers he wasn't asleep. "The shooter . . . who—"

"It isn't important, Ira. What's important is that—"

"Sarah, please," he rasped. "I know they caught the man who shot me. I need to know his name."

"I'm not sure you're well enough." Another squeeze and she gave in. "Very well, Cole said it was . . . Billy Carson."

She cringed at Ira's painful growl when he tried to rise. "What are you doing?" she said in a mixture of shock and fear.

"Where's Cole?"

"He's not here. He told you to rest," she cried. She pushed Ira down on the pillows, and for a few seconds she feared she would lose the battle to keep him there. "Ira Farrell, if you don't lie down, I swear I'm going to tie you to this bed."

"You don't understand. I-I've got to—"

"Over my dead body," she replied rebelliously. The next instant, he gave in, but not before he had depleted his strength. She gazed down at him, her heart thumping from her efforts to keep him in bed. His eyes were half closed, but he seemed resigned to the fact that he was still too weak to move. A moment later he was sound asleep. Sarah smoothed a lock of hair off his forehead, then wiped her cheeks at the sudden onset of tears.

Two days later, Sarah was still feeling sorry for herself. Though she tried not to judge Ira for what he had done, she couldn't quite bring herself to forgive him. After Adam came to sit with Ira for a while, she went downstairs and took her coat off the hook.

What she needed was some fresh air to help clear her thoughts. Outside, she pulled her collar up against the cold, noticing a horse and buggy tied to the rail by the barn. At first she thought to turn the other direction, but her curiosity wouldn't allow it. When she stepped inside, Jeb was there, tossing some straw into one of the stalls. Miss Lily was watching him.

Clad in a dark blue riding habit and matching short coat, Lily looked more like an English lady than a saloonkeeper. Sarah hoped she hadn't been seen, but Lily turned and smiled. At that moment, something snapped inside Sarah. Instead of feeling betrayed, she felt a spark of anger. Lifting her chin, she marched forward.

"Uncle Jeb," she began, "if you don't mind, I'd like to speak with Miss Lily . . . alone." Jeb started to say something, but Sarah stared him into silence. "I think Ira was asking for some soup."

Lily sank gracefully down onto a bale of straw, pulling a piece to chew on the end. "Well, I'm all ears, honey."

Sarah moistened her dry lips. "I-Ira is mine."

Lily's soft laughter did nothing for Sarah's nerves.

"This isn't a laughing matter," she said stiffly. "Ira has asked me to marry him, and I intend to do just that, but you should know that I will not tolerate my husband sharing his attentions with a mis—"

"Hold on, honey," Lily said with a smile. "Did Ira tell you that I was his mistress?"

"Not exactly, but I saw the way you looked at him, and—"

"And, nothing." Lily shook her head and laughed again. "I won't lie to you. I loved Ira, but it was a very long time ago.

And you know something . . . I still love him. I tried to start things up with Ira when he came back, but he'd have no part of it. He hasn't spent one night with me since he came back. You see, it's hard for a woman like me to admit it, but he never did love me." Lily tossed the stalk of straw to the ground, then stood and dusted off her skirt. "But he loves you, and has asked you to marry him. I've been honest with you, so why don't you be honest with me?"

At first Sarah thought to avoid answering any questions, but by the look on Lily's face, she knew it was no use. "My name is Sarah Brighton, and I'm definitely not married. Mrs. Wellington's just a name I invented so I could learn more about my cousin's accident." She leaned over the top rail of the stall, watching Ira's horse munch on some hay.

"There's something else bothering you, isn't there?" Lily asked with a concerned smile.

"I don't know," Sarah sighed. "I guess I'm a little confused."

"Talking about it might help." When Sarah didn't reply, Lily added, "Come on, honey. Us women, we have to stick together, don't we?"

Sarah looked at Lily for a long time. "If Ira's the kind of man to seduce a married woman, then he must be the kind of man who doesn't believe in fidelity, and if that's the case, how can I believe he really loves me?"

"How can you say that?" Lily challenged. She stepped closer and patted Sarah's back. "I've been dealing with men all my life. Most of them are married, and, like you said, most of them don't love their wives. That's why me and my girls are still in business."

Sarah swiped at a tear. "I don't understand. How is that supposed to make me feel better?"

"If I had to count on men like Ira, I'd be out of business.

Ira loves you." Lily gave an impatient sigh. "He never loved me, not like he loves you, and I'm guessing he doesn't love that man's wife either. He was just taking advantage of something she was willing to give."

Sarah blinked several times. "How will I know that he won't do it again?"

"I'm thinking that even with all your liberated hokey-poky, you're cutting yourself short."

"What do you mean?" Sarah asked with a crinkled frown.

"You're a very beautiful woman, and smart too, when you're not being silly." Lily held up her hand to keep Sarah from interrupting. "Love changes a man, honey, and it's like I said. Ira's in deep." Lily motioned for her to follow her out to the buggy. "I came up here to bring Jeb a couple bottles of whiskey, but I brought a little present for you, too." Lily reached into the buggy and pulled out a small pink and black box, tied with a black satin ribbon. "It's to one liberated woman from another, but I'll guarantee it'll keep Ira faithful for a lifetime. Not that he's going to need it, mind you. Like I said, give him credit for being one of the few that has integrity."

"I don't know what to say," Sarah replied.

"Don't say anything." Lily untied the horse, and then waved at Jeb, who was sweeping the porch. "Don't open it now. Let's call it an early wedding present. Save it for your wedding night, or use it sooner, whichever you want."

Sarah felt the heat of a blush creep up her neck. "What is it?"

"Just a little something to wear." Lily stepped into the buggy and picked up the reins. The older woman's smile was filled with friendly understanding. She was about to turn the horse to leave, when Sarah stopped her.

"Lily, I'm sorry. I—"

"I know, honey. Just remember one thing. Ira loves you."

"Where's Sarah?" Ira asked when he finally awoke, more lucid than he had been in days.

Cole helped Ira sit up, bunching the pillows behind his brother's back. He was still very pale with dark smudges under his eyes. "She went out for some fresh air. She'll be back soon. Here, Uncle Jeb sent up this cup of soup with orders to make sure you drink every drop." He handed Ira the cup, then sat in the chair nearest the stove. Ira shifted his weight and swore aloud. "It's still kind of soon for you to be moving much," Cole warned. "Sarah said you lost a lot of blood."

"There's something you should know about her, Cole," Ira said, taking a sip of the soup. "She's not really married."

"Yeah, she told us." Cole grinned. "Congratulations. I hear you're getting married."

Ira gave a tired smile. "I'm glad you know." Ira moved again, muttering under his breath something about his arm and being hog-tied. "Have you got a knife?" he asked, resting his head back against the pillows.

"Yeah, why?" Cole asked, amused by Ira's complaining.

"Then cut this damned bandage off. I can't take much more of my arm being tied to my chest like this."

"Well, that's too bad. Uncle Jeb says it's for your own good. He'll be changing it later. You'll have to wait till then."

Ira heaved a sigh. He had hoped when his head cleared that Sarah would be here, but she wasn't, and even though he had no reason to think she was in danger, he couldn't shrug the feeling that something wasn't right. "Did Billy confess?" he asked.

"I don't know. All I know is what Lily told me." Cole's expression grew more serious. "She told me that Josh Pruitt killed Marshal Phillips—that Josh bragged about it to one of her girls."

231

"I suspected as much." Ira raked his fingers through his tousled hair, then dragged his hand down over his face, rubbing his beard. "How good are you with a razor?"

"I've been shaving for years without so much as a nick."

"Good, then maybe you'd do me the honor."

Cole returned with a bowl of hot water, two small towels and a cup and brush. After Cole had soap all over Ira's chin, he picked up the razor.

"Don't move," Cole warned.

"Where are Adam and Jeb?" Ira asked between strokes.

"We've still got a ranch to run. I sent Adam out to see if our rustlers have moved the herd. I thought maybe they might think they could with you down."

"I don't want either of you getting into any trouble. Ouch. Damn it, Cole, be careful."

"I told you to hold still. Here, let me wipe that." Cole's grin was nearly evil. "You can't afford to lose much more blood, so I reckon you should try and hold still. Now close your mouth and do as I say."

"What—"

"Shush. I know what you're thinking, but Adam's a full-grown man now, Ira. He and Jeb will be careful." Cole gave his brother another arrogant smile. "You're not the only Farrell that uses his head."

Ira closed his eyes, annoyed that just a small thing like sitting up and getting a shave could drain him so completely. "Did Sarah tell you about the jacket?"

"Yup." Cole dropped the razor in the bowl. "She's not so sure it's murder any more." Cole handed Ira a small towel. "You've got a little soap right there."

Ira would have liked to continue their conversation, but someone knocked on the door.

"Come in," Cole called, putting the basin and razor on the

bureau. He wiped off his hands as Jeb came inside with a pile of clean bandages and a small sack. "Ira was just saying how much he appreciated you bandaging his arm up the way you did." Cole glanced at Ira. "Didn't you?"

Cole dodged a towel, caught it and tossed it aside. "You'd better watch out, Jeb. Ira's kind of grumpy."

"He is, is he?" Jeb put the cloths on the side of the bed then rolled up his sleeves. He retrieved a small pair of scissors and a jar of salve from the sack, then cut the knot at Ira's shoulder. "Well, I see you're looking some better. When I take this off your arm, son, don't try to move it."

Jeb removed the outer bandage then carefully lifted Ira's right arm down and placed it on the bed by Ira's side. Though he moved slowly, Ira clenched his jaw tight and little beads of sweat formed on his brow.

"Now, let's have a look-see," Jeb murmured as he removed the thick pad from Ira's chest. "Cole, help me hold him more upright. This damned thing is stuck to the wound."

Cole was at Ira's side the next moment, holding him steady. Though Ira never said a word, Cole felt him stiffen when Jeb peeled away the old bandage and tossed it aside.

"How's it look, Doc?" Cole asked when his uncle frowned after inspecting the swollen and red flesh on Ira's shoulder.

"As good as can be expected." Jeb left off the salve, explaining that it was best because of the stitches. After he covered them with a clean pad, he wrapped the wounds, ignoring Ira's muttered complaint that it was too tight.

"Leave it off," Ira ground out through clenched teeth when Jeb went to tie his arm to his chest.

"Your shoulder will heal faster if you can't move your arm," Jeb said gruffly, fixing Ira with a squinty-eyed glare.

"I won't," Ira countered in the same tone. He pressed his left hand against his shoulder, apparently in pain.

Jeb glanced at Cole. "I'm going to tell you, because it's evident he ain't listening. The wound is still too fresh. If he moves, it could break open. If I tie his arm down, he can't move. It's that simple."

Cole nodded. "I know you're doing what's best, but he's right-handed—"

"Don't you think I know that?" Jeb muttered, shaking his balding head. "That's the very reason I tied his arm down in the first place." Jeb picked up the old bandages and stuffed them in the sack. He gathered up the salve and the scissors then heaved an impatient sigh. "I can see that you think I'm a mean old goat, but by sidin' with him," Jeb looked at Ira, "you're not doing him any favors." Jeb went to the door, then turned around and practically glared at Ira. "Don't move that arm for at least a few more days, or I'll come when you're sleepin' and tie it back up."

Cole waited until he was sure Jeb had left, then shook his head and smiled. "Damn, but he can be testy."

"I've been kicked by horses that had a better bedside manner," Ira muttered.

Cole went to the bureau and poured a little whiskey into a glass. "Here, you look like you could use this."

"Thanks." Ira almost lifted his right hand, then winced, swearing softly under his breath. He grabbed the glass with his left and swallowed it down, closing his eyes and resting a little deeper against the pillows.

"Maybe you should have listened to Uncle Jeb," Cole said softly when Ira gave him back the glass.

"Tie your hand to your chest and see if you can stand it," Ira growled sarcastically.

Cole gave a soft laugh. "All right, you made your point, but you can't be moving your arm for a while." He picked up the glass and put it back on the bureau, expecting an argument, but when he glanced over his shoulder, Ira was asleep. After Cole pulled the covers up over his brother's chest, he took a cloth and wiped the sweat from Ira's forehead. "Stubborn fool," Cole muttered.

Chapter Seventeen

The next several days passed by without incident. All the snow melted and the weather warmed up considerably. So much so, that when Sarah entered Ira's room that morning, she went directly to the window and opened it. "Smell that?" she asked, not expecting an answer. "It's going to be a beautiful day."

When she turned, Ira patted the side of the bed. "Come here," he said with a lazy smile. She sank down, taking his big hand in hers. "What's got you in such good spirits?"

"I was thinking we might have a spring wedding."

She could tell she caught him completely off guard as he gave her a puzzled look for a moment, then relaxed back against the mountain of pillows.

"How am I going to marry you, if everybody thinks you're already married," he asked with a twinkle dancing in his eyes. Though his statement was meant to tease her, it struck a sensitive chord. She was just about to tell him that she would rectify the situation as soon as she could send someone to town with the announcement she'd written, when Uncle Jeb came in with a cup of hot soup.

"Is this the same soup you've been feeding me this past week?"

Jeb made a face and mimicked Ira's voice. "No. It's fresh soup."

Sarah giggled at the old man's expression. "Eat, Ira. It's good for you."

When Jeb left, she leaned over to place a kiss on Ira's forehead, and his left hand slipped behind her head and he captured her mouth in a long, gentle kiss.

Sarah gazed into his eyes after he released her. "Marshal Farrell, behave yourself. While you eat, I'm going to my room to write an announcement. It's high time I informed the good citizens of Santa Fe that my marriage has been a hoax."

"Are you sure you want to do it that way?" Ira asked. "It might be better to call a meeting of the Ladies of Liberty and tell them in person."

"Oh, I'm sure that after I explain my reasons, maybe even cite an example or two where the pretense of marriage saved me from some overzealous man, the ladies will forgive me." Sarah went to the door, smiling at Ira over her shoulder. "Especially if we invite them all to the wedding."

By the end of the week, Ira was as cantankerous as a bear being poked with a sharp stick. Sarah took out the checkerboard, placed it on the bedside and arranged the pieces.

"Adam was kind enough to take my announcement into town. Look," she said, showing Ira the page of the paper where it was printed. "And look at these," she said, showing him several envelopes.

"What are those?" he asked, frowning.

"Why, these, my love, are orders for clothing from available gentlemen. And these are invitations from mothers of available young men to have Sunday dinner as soon as I return to Santa Fe."

"Well, I wish you would have waited until I was on my feet," he protested, sliding a black disk to a red square.

"Why should I have?" she countered, moving a checker piece to block his.

"Because, Sarah, I saw how the men around there looked

at you when they thought you were married." He jumped her piece and then another.

Miffed, she heaved an aggravated sigh. "I am not your property, Ira. As much as I want to be your wife, I am my own person, and I am perfectly—"

"Perfectly capable of taking care of yourself," he finished irritably. Out of habit, he moved his right arm without thinking, wincing at the revived pain. "Isn't there something we can do other than play this dammed, senseless game?"

"Uncle Jeb says if we are to sit outside for a while tomorrow, you need to be quiet and get plenty of rest today." She moved another piece and almost immediately he jumped it as well as three others.

"Crown me," he muttered.

"I'd love to," she replied tightly, placing a second black disk on the one he'd moved to her end of the board.

"Since when is Uncle Jeb the expert?" It didn't take very long before he had all but one of her pieces. She moved to the red square just to the right of his king. He followed. She moved again, trying to avoid the other black disk to her right. They continued around the board for several frustrating minutes.

"Ha," she cried, jumping a piece when it was clear he wasn't paying any more attention.

He raised one dark brow, then purposely placed another black disk in jeopardy.

She jumped it and the one behind it.

"Crown me," she said with a toss of her head. He did and the game continued until there were only two pieces on the board—his black king and her red king.

They chased each other from square to square for another few minutes until Ira moved his arm wrong and groaned in pain. The moment she looked up, he jumped her piece and snatched it up in his fist. "I win," he said with an arrogant grin.

Her mouth fell open. "You . . . you cheated. You made me think you were in pain to break my concentration."

"Sometimes, playing fair isn't sensible."

She giggled at his grumpy expression. "How can cheating be considered a viable alternative?"

He folded the board and tossed it over on the chair, then grabbed her hand and pulled her close, his mouth just inches away from hers. "When it gets the job done . . . quicker."

"And, if I may be so bold, why are you in such a hurry?"

"Because." He slipped a hand around the back of her neck and he pulled her close to receive his kiss. "I have another game I want to play."

She started to speak, but his mouth possessed hers, tasting and teasing until she leaned against his broad chest and kissed him back. When she gently pushed away and sat up, he began to unbutton her dress. His warm fingers against her skin were almost too much to bear.

"What do you think you're doing?"

"I'm undressing you," he murmured. He cupped her breast, teasing the taut peak with the pad of his thumb. Her breath caught, and for several blissful moments she relished his touch. When she couldn't stand it any longer, she pushed away and stood just out of his reach.

She glanced at him from beneath her long lashes then began to finish the job he had started. The knowledge that she could bring him to full arousal by simply exposing one creamy shoulder was almost as stimulating as his hands had been the night they made love. With each piece of clothing that fell to the floor, his expression grew more and more seductive.

"Do you like what you see?" she teased, moistening her

lips at the same time she pushed the strap of her chemise off her shoulders. She caught it just before it slipped from her breasts.

"I like everything about you, Sarah. I like the way your nipples harden with just a glance. I like the way your eyes grow misty when we make love."

Sarah gave him a sultry smile, and then let the chemise float to the floor.

Early the next morning, Sarah carried in a tray, stunned to see Ira sitting on the side of the bed, dressed from the waist down in faded Levis and his not-so-dressy brown boots.

"What do you think you're doing?" she replied with an air of cool authority in her voice as she placed the tray on the bedside table. He had shaved and apparently had even managed to wash his hair as it was still damp and neatly combed.

"I don't think I'm getting up . . . I *am* getting up." After he lifted the cloth from her tray he met her gaze with one just as determined. "Let me guess. Chicken soup?"

"Yes. Uncle Jeb said you should have lots of fluids."

He closed his eyes and breathed deeply. "I smell bacon and fried potatoes . . . and coffee. I don't want any more soup, especially chicken. The only thing a chicken is good for is eating June bugs."

He motioned to the wardrobe. "Pick out a shirt, darlin'." She set aside the tray, chose a soft blue flannel, then helped him slip it on his right arm first, holding it while he shoved his left arm in the other sleeve.

"I suppose I can't talk you out of this for a few more days," she said a little doubtfully as she fastened the buttons.

He gave a skeptical laugh. "Not a chance."

"Wait for just a moment." She hurried to her room then

returned with a large colorful scarf. "Here, put your arm in this," she ordered, tying it around his neck. "I should have thought of it sooner."

"Yeah," he replied with a hint of sarcasm. "Aren't flowers out of style?"

Sarah laughed softly. "No, they're all the rage. Now stop complaining." She folded the corner and tucked it around his elbow. She stood back and nodded. "You look absolutely dashing."

Sarah chewed her bottom lip a little as Ira pressed his palm over the bandage on his right shoulder and stood. He had to hold on to the bedpost for a moment, and by the way he closed his eyes, she knew he was still a little lightheaded. "Why don't I ask Uncle Jeb to fix you a plate and bring it up here?"

Ira's eyes opened and he gave her a patient smile. "Sarah, darlin', why don't you go downstairs and tell them to set another place."

"I think they'll do that when they see us." She hurried to his side and slipped her shoulder under his good arm. "If you're sure this is what you want, at least let me help you down the stairs."

Ira grew stronger each day, and more restless. Checkers had lost their appeal, so after he dressed, he went to Sarah's room and knocked softly on the door. "Meet me outside. It's warm and I've a hankering to take a ride."

An hour later, clad in a warm brown riding habit, Sarah's heart did a fearful little dance when she stepped outside and saw two horses saddled. "I thought we were going to take the wagon," she replied with a concerned frown.

"I tried to talk him out of this," Cole added, holding her horse while Ira gave her a boost up onto the horse's back.

"He's as stubborn as a mule. You should let me hitch up the wagon, like Sarah suggested."

"That bumpy ol' thing," Ira teased. "That's only good for going to town, and I don't think I can ride that far . . . not yet." Cole grabbed Dakota's bridle while Ira swung up into the saddle using only his left arm. Once settled, he pushed his hat down on his forehead and gathered his reins. "We'll be back in about an hour, little brother."

"Yeah, just in time for dinner, I reckon."

"Well, at least the weather's cooperating," he replied with a smile as he guided Dakota down the road, away from the house.

Adam and Cole had done wonders with the path to their home. Seeing it in the daylight, it was wider and almost as smooth as other, more traveled roads. "There's a trail a little bit ahead that'll take us over to a small meadow. Jack's Creek runs through it," Ira told her as they rode.

A cool breeze ruffled Sarah's curls as she held her mare back to stay alongside Dakota. The horses were fresh and lively and would have enjoyed a good canter, but she was careful to hold back, keeping her mare to a walk. Ira might feel better, but she knew he wasn't completely healed. Even to trot now would cause him more discomfort, and his pride wouldn't allow her to get too far ahead on the trail. They were quiet for many miles, each enjoying the other's company as they followed the trail and wound their way up the mountain.

"How are you doing?" Sarah asked as she glanced at Ira.

"I'm fine," he said. But she was sure his deep voice sounded fatigued. Just then, Dakota spooked at something off the trail. Ira instinctively grabbed the saddle horn with his right hand to keep from falling, swearing under his breath.

"Are you hurting?" she asked, glimpsing a flicker of pain in his eyes.

Ira pressed his good hand to his shoulder. "Yeah, but it'll pass in a few minutes." He glanced over at a copse of spruce. "Something's moving in those trees."

"What is it?" she said softly, following his gaze. Though she tried to appear calm, fear coiled in the pit of her stomach. It intensified the moment Ira slipped his left hand into his saddlebags and retrieved his gun.

"Ira, please," she pleaded when he carefully dismounted. She jumped off her horse at the same time he turned and pressed Dakota's reins into her gloved hand. "We're not far from the ranch. Let's go back. Whatever is out there can wait."

"Stay here, and make sure the horses don't get away."

She was about to follow when she realized that if the horses bolted and got away, Ira was in no condition to walk far. She clutched the reins even tighter, watching helplessly as Ira disappeared into the trees.

Afraid for him, she remained mute, watching and straining her ears for any sound. After what felt like an hour, but she was certain had only been a few minutes, a small calf staggered out of the trees with Ira following.

"Come help me," Ira called to Sarah.

"What do you want me to do?" she asked as she hurried toward them. "Oh, Ira, it's so cute."

"Yeah, but if we don't get her back to the ranch, she's not going to make it. She needs milk and she needs it soon."

"How do I pick her up?" she asked.

Ira heaved a tired sigh and by his expression, Sarah knew he was more than a little frustrated with his sore right arm. "Do you think you can?"

She gave a little shrug of her shoulders. "I don't know, but I'll certainly give it a try. Now, quickly, tell me what to do." With Ira's help, Sarah managed to lift the newborn into her arms. It wasn't as heavy as she expected, and she gave a proud smile as she held it while Ira mounted his horse. Together, she and Ira managed to drag it up and over Ira's saddle. He shrugged out of his coat and covered the shivering little calf. Warmer, it fell asleep with its head cradled on Ira's left arm.

Cole and Adam came out of the cabin as soon as Buster started barking. Sarah glanced at Ira and heaved a sigh of relief. He was pale and she knew the burden of cradling the newborn had drained his strength.

"What in tarnation do you have there?" Jeb exclaimed as he came out of the house, drying his hands on a checkered towel.

"Ira found a baby cow," Sarah said, as she quickly jumped down from her horse and tied the reins to the rail. Cole was at Ira's side, lifting the calf from his brother.

"Where did you find her?" Cole asked as he handed the calf to Adam.

"On the trail to Hermosa Meadow," Ira said, wincing as he shifted his weight. "She was nearly frozen. She needs some warm milk as soon as possible."

"I'll get right on it," Jeb muttered from the porch. His worried expression wasn't entirely for the calf, and when Sarah turned to help with Ira, she knew why. Ira stepped down off Dakota, but his knees buckled. He would have fallen if Cole hadn't been there to catch him.

"How are you feeling?" Sarah asked as she brushed a lock of hair from Ira's forehead. In the muted light from the lantern, he looked younger than his years. Cole had placed Ira on top of the bed, choosing not to bother his brother by undressing him. As Sarah gazed down at Ira, a flicker of pure delight shot through her as she imagined what their children would look like.

Ira glanced up at her, and she knew by his gentle smile, he was feeling better. "I guess I was more tired than I thought," he murmured. He held out his good hand. "Help me sit up, darlin'."

"Have I told you I love it when you call me that?" Sarah replied as she bunched the pillows behind his back. His warm smile was answer enough. "Uncle Jeb is fixing us something to eat."

Ira gave her a cautious glance. "You didn't ask him to make any soup, did you?"

She laughed at his expression. "No. I asked him to prepare a thick beefsteak, medium rare, and I think he said something about frying some potatoes with bacon and onions."

Ira reached out and pulled her down on the bed, rolling until he was on top of her. "That's good, 'cause I need to eat something other than soup if I'm going to make love to you tonight."

She accepted his kiss, then cupped his cheek and gazed into his eyes. "I love you," she whispered then kissed him, teasing his lips with the tip of her tongue. He groaned and pressed her closer, devouring her willing lips. He slipped his good hand down and tugged the material of her skirt up, brushing her hip with warm, exploring fingers.

Someone knocked on the door and Sarah virtually bolted off the bed. She tucked several loose curls back into place as she tried to look innocent, and then quickly smoothed her skirt.

"Come in," Ira called, grinning.

Cole opened the door. "Uncle Jeb says supper is ready."

Ira's smile was sinful. "Great. Sarah was just helping me up."

"Ah, yes," Sarah stammered, her cheeks filling with color. "But, now that you're here, Cole, I'd best go downstairs and see if I can help Uncle Jeb in the kitchen." She didn't wait for Cole's answer, but turned and slipped out the door.

Sarah took her place across from Ira, relieved that the Farrell brothers hadn't changed into more formal clothes. She had stayed with Ira the whole time he slept and didn't think about dressing for supper.

"This looks wonderful," she replied as a smaller steak was placed on her plate. "Someday, Uncle Jeb, you're going to have to teach me how to cook."

"That'll be my pleasure," the older Farrell replied as he slapped a thick, juicy steak on Ira's plate. When everyone was served he sat down and nodded to Cole. "You do the honors."

Sarah looked at Ira then at Cole, wondering what was going on. Cole picked up a very dusty bottle of wine and read the year on the label. "This bottle of wine was purchased nearly thirty years ago by my father. He planned on using it to celebrate his and our mother's twenty-fifth wedding anniversary. However," Cole continued, as he opened the wine and began to fill their glasses, "we thought tonight we'd use it to welcome a soon-to-be, newest member to our family."

Cole raised his glass, waiting until everyone else at the table raised theirs. "To Sarah. May her marriage to Ira be a long and productive one." Cole looked at her over the rim of his glass. When she met his gaze, he winked, causing her cheeks to warm with a blush.

"To Sarah," everyone said in unison. Crystal glasses tinkled as they touched then everyone drank.

Blinking back happy tears, Sarah glanced across the table at Ira. His expression was filled with love and admiration, and she could have gazed at him the rest of the night, but then he too winked and turned his attention to his steak. He frowned, then shoved his plate over to Adam. "Cut this up for me, will you?"

Adam grinned, apparently pleased that he could help. "Sure." When the steak was reduced to bite-sized pieces, Adam gave an ornery smile. "Want me to eat it for you too?"

Ira playfully cuffed his brother, and then pulled his plate back. He took a bite of steak and chewed with his eyes closed. "This is perfect, Uncle Jeb." After he swallowed, Ira inquired about the calf.

"She's going to make it," Adam offered. "Uncle Jeb got a bottle of milk down her shortly after you arrived." Adam took a sip of wine. "I'll give her another before I turn in for the evening."

"Was there any sign of her mother?" Cole asked. His previous smile was now a frown.

"No, but there were lots of tracks. Somebody drove some cattle through there recently. I'm thinking the cow got separated from its calf and since it's way early for a cow to calve anyway, the drovers never noticed."

"That's a stupid mistake," Jeb added. "Any fool knows that even if they change a brand, if we find a cow with a full udder and no calf, we've got our rustlers."

"I sent a couple of my best hands to look for her," Cole stated, cutting another piece of steak. "They're good men, good trackers. I told them if they find her, leave her be and come get us. This could be the break we've been waiting for."

"Why do you say that?" Sarah asked.

"A mama cow missing her calf will be bawling her head off." Jeb stabbed a potato and held it on his fork for a minute. "Unless they shoot her first."

Sarah blanched. "They wouldn't do that, would they?"

Ira gave her an understanding smile, aware that she was thinking of the newborn being without its mother. "I doubt it, darlin'. She's worth too much on the hoof, and most likely she'd settle down after a while." He tossed Jeb a dark look. "Isn't that right?"

"Oh, yeah. They'd want her alive for sure. Kinda hard to move a dead cow down the trail," Jeb replied sarcastically.

Cole cleared his throat. "Pass the potatoes, please, Uncle Jeb." He quickly helped himself then offered the plate to his brother. "Ira? More potatoes?"

Adam caught on right away and quickly changed the subject. "I read there was a five-hundred-dollar reward out for Dawson Yates 'cause he robbed a Wells Fargo stage six months ago. Since you drew down on him and shot him dead, won't you be getting that?"

Ira didn't miss the enthusiastic gleam glittering in his brother's eyes, or the look of utter shock in Sarah's. "I reckon."

"That must have been something to see, and to get five hundred bucks for doing it too." Adam shook his head at the same time he took a mouthful of meat.

"It wasn't all that exciting," Ira stated flatly.

"That ain't—"

"Isn't," Cole corrected. "Ma wanted us to use proper English, remember?"

Adam nodded. "The paper said you were a real hero, didn't it, Cole?"

Ira met Cole's gaze then looked back at Adam. "There's nothing heroic about killing a man, Adam." Ira picked up the biscuits. "Have another biscuit."

Sarah cleared her throat. "I have a little announcement that I think you should all hear." She inwardly smiled when Ira's head snapped up and he quit chewing. "It has to do with my cousin's estate," she replied, narrowing her eyes at him. He immediately relaxed.

"You see," she continued, "since Emily left everything she owned to your brother, and in turn he left everything to the three of you, I think you have a right to know that her estate was worth several hundred thousand dollars."

Their silence was deafening. Very happily, she picked up her wine and took a little sip. "When we get back to Santa Fe, I shall send a telegram to her solicitor and have him transfer the funds into your accounts."

The rest of the evening passed without incident after the men recovered from their shock. Cole stood up, and when the conversation died down, he suggested that they take some of the money and do something special with it in memory of Zachary and Miss Emily.

Once more glasses were raised and everyone agreed that Sarah should be the one to choose a suitable charity. Soon after, all the dishes were cleared away and Cole suggested Ira head back to his room to get some rest. Sarah sensed that it was just an excuse so the two brothers could talk, so she declined when Ira asked her to come along, stating that she should help Uncle Jeb wash the dishes, and that by doing so, he might share some cooking secrets.

"I hope, now that you're feeling better, you aren't getting any ideas about returning to town too soon," Cole began as he tossed another chunk of wood in the pot-bellied stove in Ira's room. "It'll be Thanksgiving in a couple of weeks. No sense—"

"Cole," Ira interrupted. "There's not much I can do till my shoulder heals. At least out here, I know Sarah will be safe." He sat on the side of the bed, more tired than he wanted to admit. "The day I got shot, I sent a telegram to

Carefree asking Mayor James to send some deputies to help us round up the Pruitts and anyone else who might be siding with them." Ira shook his head. "Obviously it never got sent. They should have been here by now. Even if they showed up late and couldn't find me, I'm sure someone would have told them to come out to the ranch."

Cole frowned. "Do you think Earl could be in on the trouble?"

"Makes sense now that I've had time to think about it. He was the only one who knew I'd sent a telegram to Mayor James. He was also the only one who knew that I'd sent a telegram asking about Sarah's *pretend* husband. What's got me the most concerned is I also sent one to Ginger Carson, telling her that we were finished."

"Maybe they sent for Dawson Yates?" Cole frowned. "I wanted to talk to you about that."

"It's over, and I'd like to forget it." Ira held up his hand when Cole wanted to say something more. "It happens, Cole. I don't need to hear how I should lie low or tuck my tail and run. No, sir, I've heard it all, and there's only one way to handle it, and I did."

"I'm sorry, Ira. It's just that I don't want to bury another brother."

Ira gave Cole an understanding nod. "Anyway, after this is all over, and Sarah and I are married, I plan on turning in my badge." Ira accepted a pat on the back from his brother. "It's all starting to fall into place," Ira said. "However, at the time, when Yates called me a wife-stealing son of a buck, I never thought for a moment how he could possibly have found out about Sarah and me."

Cole grinned and raised one brow, but Ira hurried on to keep his brother from speaking. "Don't say it," Ira warned good-naturedly as he massaged his shoulder. "I thought it was Sarah's story, but now I'm not so sure." Ira unbuttoned his shirt and pulled off his boots. "Let's suppose Earl is in with Silas. It makes sense that they're using Billy Carson to get me out of the way."

"And he nearly did. Mark my words, he'll pay for it," Cole confirmed.

Ira shook his head. "Billy's no shooter. Hell, I've never even seen him with a gun."

"What are you saying?" Cole asked, his dark brows snapping together.

"I'm saying I think someone else was on the roof that night, and Billy is taking the blame."

Cole heaved a concerned sigh. "Who do you have in mind?"

"Who do you know that's low enough to shoot a man in the back?" Ira challenged, his voice tinged with disgust.

"Josh Pruitt," they said in unison.

Ira tossed off his shirt then stood and undid the buttons on his jeans, stepping out of them. "If Josh is involved, then surely Silas and Jonah are in it too. After Thanksgiving, I've got to get back to Santa Fe and talk with Billy. I don't want an innocent man tried for something he didn't do."

"Ira, Sheriff Finch isn't about to let anything happen to Billy before the circuit judge can get here."

Ira shook his head. "Maybe, but I've got a feeling this whole mess is bigger than we think it is. We already know James Roland is in cahoots with Josh."

"Then Adam, Jeb and I will be riding with you. You're not facing them alone, not this time."

"I don't plan to. Tomorrow I'll write a letter to Mayor James. I'll ask him to wait until after Thanksgiving to send those men. Next time one of your hands goes to town, I'll ask him to post it for me."

"What if they try to ship the herd?"

"It's a risk, for sure. But my guess is that they won't make any moves until they're sure I'm out of the way. For all they know, I could be riding back to town any day."

"Then you think they'll try again to—damn it, Ira. I don't like this one bit," Cole ground out.

"Neither do I, but they won't try anything while I'm here, and I'm fairly certain they won't show their hand in public." Ira put his hand on Cole's shoulder. "I'm not going to make myself a target, so stop worrying, will you? I'll have lots of help when I make my stand."

"We've got a few weeks to think about it," Cole stated flatly as he walked to the door. "You can protest all you want, but the next time you go to town, Adam and I will be riding with you."

Lily Barker helped her bartender wipe down the bar as they closed for the night. She collected the cash from the steel box under the counter and put it in a little velvet sack.

"Anything else you want me to do?" the bartender asked.

"No, Sam. You'd best be getting on home." Lily unlocked the little safe hidden under the balustrade.

"Good night, Lil. I'll see you tomorrow."

"Good night, Sam." It had been a profitable night. As she slipped the cash into the safe and closed it, she heard the door squeak. She stood, expecting to see Sam. Her heart slammed into her breast when she saw two men standing just inside the door, both with cloth masks on and tan-colored dusters.

"Evening, Miss Lily." Their eyes glittered eerily from behind the holes cut into the cloth. From their size and shape, they could have been anyone, but when she glanced down at the round-toed black boots of the taller man, she knew who he was.

"W-what do you want?" she said, taking a small step toward the bar as the slightly shorter man pulled out a pair of gloves and tugged them on.

"Word's out that you've been talking too much to the wrong people."

She gave a small, nervous laugh and took another step. "What people? Sweet-talking is part of the profession." She grabbed a bottle of whiskey and two glasses, setting them on the counter, trying to keep their attention away from the Schofield .45 she kept under the bar.

She gave them her best sultry smile. "There's no use hiding behind those masks. Let's have a drink and talk about it, face to face." Her hand shook a little as she filled the glasses.

"We're not here to be sociable," the shorter man snarled as he lunged.

She grabbed the gun, but his fingers tightened around her wrist, forcing it upward, wrenching the gun from her grasp. "Now, that's just plumb foolish."

She struggled against his hold until the other man grabbed her from behind and dragged her back against his chest. A gloved hand clamped down over her mouth before she could scream. Furious and frightened, she squirmed and kicked herself free. But not fast enough. The short man backhanded her across the face. Dazed, she would have hit the floor, but the other man caught her arm. Although she tried to squirm free, he pinned her arms to her sides. The last thing she saw was the other's fist just seconds before everything went black.

Chapter Eighteen

Thanksgiving supper was one of the most enjoyable meals Sarah had ever experienced. The morning was spent gathering pine boughs and bunches of pine cones to decorate the inside of the cabin. The mouth-watering aroma of a roasting turkey blended with the pungent scent of the pine and filled her with a warm family feeling. A feeling she hadn't experienced for many years. She thought of Emily and wished that they could have spent more time together, thinking how wonderful it would be if Emily and Zach were alive and enjoying the festivities. The warm feeling of belonging gave her comfort, chasing her melancholy away.

She spent the rest of the evening cuddled next to Ira, sitting before a blazing fire, listening to Jeb tell stories of his life as a young man, and more stories of his nephew's adventures. After the fire died down, and everyone had gone upstairs to bed, Ira kissed her then stood, pulling her up. "It's late and you look tired."

Sarah covered a yawn. "I am. It was a wonderful day, wasn't it?"

Ira took her hand in his, staring into her eyes. "We'll have lots of days like this," he said just before he kissed her again. This time the kiss was long and filled with the promise of more to come. "Do you remember when you said you'd like a spring wedding?" he asked.

"Yes, I do," she answered softly, staring into his twinkling grey eyes.

He tucked a strand of copper-colored hair behind her ear, then kissed the tip of her nose. "I was thinking a winter wedding might be nice. Here at the ranch. Maybe sometime around Christmas?"

Sarah's heart did a little flip. "I'd love that," she whispered, accepting another kiss.

The next morning, after the cock nearly crowed his red head off under her window, Sarah rolled over in bed, thinking she could chop the rooster's head off herself. She tossed the covers aside and stood, then sat quickly back down. Her stomach rolled and she felt a little lightheaded. Her monthly routine was over a week late, and as she thought about it, a slow smile spread across her face.

She took a deep breath and tried not to think about her stomach as she placed a slightly trembling hand over her flat tummy, and sat there until the sickness passed. Finally, she stood and poured a little water in the basin to splash over her face.

It was a beautiful, warm day. Thinking that a little fresh air would help her, she unlatched the window and pushed it open. She chose a rust-colored day dress, humming to herself as she fastened the brown buttons. Instead of pinning her hair up, she decided to leave it down, tying it back with a satin ribbon the same color as the dress.

She was especially happy thinking about Ira, when she heard his deep voice waft in through the open window. The next moment, Cole answered him, and by the tone of his voice, Cole wasn't very pleased. Curious, she pulled the lace curtain aside and caught a glimpse of the two brothers by the woodpile. Cole held an axe. He took a log off the pile and with one swing, split it in half. He picked up the two pieces and tossed them onto a different pile.

"You should have told me what you were planning," Ira said tersely. He had his pistol strapped to his hip and he was practicing his fast draw, flexing his shoulder and stopping to massage it after each awkward attempt.

"Well, now you know," Cole countered, matching his brother's curt tone. "You're still not your old self, Ira. I didn't plan on it happening. It just did. Several of our boys rode up on them by accident. Roland's hands were changing the brands on a dozen head of our cattle. That calf's mama was one of them. The men scattered, but not before my boys caught three of them. They got the iron they were using to change the brands, too. I had them take them into Santa Fe and give them to the sheriff after we got a little information out of them."

"We knew Roland was in on it. I told you when I saw them that day I rode over to Cougar's Bluff." Ira drew again, swearing under his breath.

"Yup." Cole split another log. "But now we know for sure that Pruitt's holding most of the herd. I reckon with you snooping around, it was just too risky to drive them to the rail yard. I've posted some men to watch his ranch just in case."

"Sounds like I need to pay a visit to the Rocking R and arrest Roland."

Cole leaned on the axe. "You've got to be kidding me. You think he's just going to let you ride up to his front door and arrest him for cattle rustling?"

"I can't just hide here at the ranch the rest of my life, Cole. I've got a job to do. James Roland's no fool. He's got a daughter to think of. He won't give me any trouble." Ira drew again, and again he slammed his pistol back into the holster, obviously unhappy with his speed.

"And if he does, what will you do?" Another log was split, only this time Cole held on to one of the halves.

Ira glared at his brother. "What I usually do if I'm challenged."

Sarah's mouth fell open when Cole tossed the log to Ira. "Here, catch that."

Reflex made Ira catch the log, but it was obvious the quick movement hurt his shoulder. "Why, you son of a buck," Ira ground out through clenched teeth as he took the log in his left hand and threw it back. Cole easily dodged it. "What the hell are you doing?" Scowling, he massaged his right shoulder.

"I'm sorry, Ira."

Sarah didn't think Cole's voice sounded very remorseful.

"I'm just trying to show you that you're not ready to face Roland—or anybody, for that matter. You can barely lift your arm. How the hell are you going to draw down on a man if he challenges you?"

Sarah flinched as Ira stalked over to Cole and grabbed him by the collar. "I won't be responsible for any more Farrells dying, Cole. Do you hear me?"

Cole stood his ground. "Is that what you think? That somehow it's your fault Zach died?"

Ira shoved Cole away, turning his back on his younger brother. "Maybe. So what if I do? Fact is it might not have happened had I been here."

A lump formed in Sarah's throat. She remembered when Ira was delirious—how he had apologized to Zach. She hadn't thought anything of it then, but now she knew the depth of his guilt. She ached to run down to him, to comfort him, but knew that the brothers needed to settle this between themselves.

When she glanced at Cole, anger no longer hardened his features. Instead, he relaxed his stance and took a step toward

Ira. "You can't blame yourself. None of us can. I felt the same way at first, that if I could have been three, maybe it wouldn't have happened. But I had to get over it. You gotta get over it too. Nobody saw this coming. Nobody could have stopped it."

Ira turned back to his target and drew his pistol. Even Sarah could see he was stiff and unsure of himself. "I don't want you and Adam involved." Ira's voice sounded deadly, like it had the day he talked with Dawson Yates. "You could get yourselves killed."

"Maybe," Cole answered in the same tone. "Maybe not, but we sure as hell aren't going to let you go alone. Like it or not, Ira, we're all you got . . . at least for a little while." Cole picked up the axe. "I took the liberty and sent a man to Carefree. In a week, we should have some help."

Ira flexed his right arm once more, but his frown never lessened. "Fair enough. But, I'm going to tell you something, and you'd better pay attention." When he turned, his expression reminded Sarah once again of a predator.

"Josh Pruitt is mine."

Sarah stepped away from the window. The happiness she had felt only moments ago vanished, replaced with the knowledge that her baby might never get to know its father. Her knees felt weak as she sank down on the edge of the bed.

She remembered how exciting it had sounded to come to this wild, untamed territory. She stared at nothing in particular, yet saw Ira's face, his confident smile. In a matter of minutes, she relived the time they'd spent together—their first meeting, their first kiss, the first time they'd made love.

A sob caught in her throat as she remembered how he had been concerned for her, even though he was the one who'd been shot. She felt again the fear she had experienced when he faced Dawson Yates in the middle of the street, and again in the doctor's office when Ira was covered in blood. With stark realization, she understood why Ira was so insistent that she stay close and that his gun was always in reach even while he was recovering. Somehow he'd discovered that Zach's and Emily's accident was just a small part of a larger conspiracy contrived by powerful, dangerous men who had already murdered to keep their dirty little secret. Now, the man she loved was anxious to return to face them, even if it meant sacrificing his life.

"Sarah?"

Her breath caught and she practically jumped off the bed. "I-Ira," she said in a shaky voice. His concerned expression tore her heart in two.

"Are you all right?"

The more she looked at him the more her despair changed into anger. "I-I didn't hear you come in."

"Apparently. You're trembling." He pulled her into his arms, placing a gentle kiss on her temple as he held her for several minutes. "What's the matter, darlin'?"

When she couldn't find her voice, he held her at arm's length and made her look at him. "Sarah, something is bothering you. You have to tell me what it is."

By the way she raised her chin, he easily recognized her subtle defiance. He inwardly flinched when she turned her rebellious blue eyes his direction.

"How dare you treat me like . . . like I'm just a simple woman."

"I would never do that, and you—"

"Don't you speak to me in that condescending tone," she replied furiously, pulling out of his gentle grasp. "I-I deserve better."

"Of course—"

"I have every right to be upset with you." She began to pace, wrapping her arms tightly around herself.

Ira didn't try to speak for several minutes. Instead he let her pace, sensing that she needed to collect herself and voice her thoughts. After a few tense moments, he asked, "Are you going to tell me what I did?"

Once more she impaled him with her heated gaze. "You and Cole have plans to arrest half of the population of Santa Fe, and you didn't even bother to tell me."

Ira tried to keep his tone nonconfrontational. "I didn't want to upset you."

"Didn't want to upset me?" she repeated tersely. "Leaving me out of your plans . . . pretending that nothing is amiss . . . those kinds of things would upset a saint, Ira, especially if she's—" She pursed her lips, and a fire danced in the depths of her eyes. "Never mind."

"Never mind?" he asked with a perplexed frown. "What the hell is that supposed to mean?"

"It means, Marshal Farrell, that if I'm not important enough to you to be included in your plans, then you are certainly not important enough to be included in mine."

She strode to the window, but he knew she wasn't interested in anything outside.

"Sarah, look at me." She refused.

He took a step toward her, but sensed he'd be rebuked. Instead, he put his hands on her shoulders, taking in the sweet scent of her hair. He took a long deep breath and let it out slowly. "I can't fix it, if you won't talk to me."

She was quiet for several tense moments before she spoke. "I-I cannot believe you would even consider, for one moment, that what happens to you doesn't affect me."

"I agree." He turned her and even though she resisted, he made her look at him. He gazed deeply into her tear-bright eyes. "Did you hear me? You're right."

"Yes, I am," she replied angrily.

He put his finger gently on her lips. "Shush. Give me a chance to apologize, will you?" He put his knuckle under her chin. The hurt glistening in her eyes cut into his heart. "I'm sorry, Sarah. I guess I've been alone for so long, I've forgotten how special it is to have someone to share things with."

"That doesn't change the fact that you're planning to return to Santa Fe when you know full well it's dangerous. I want to know how many men are going to be waiting for you."

Ira took a calming breath. "All right. If I'm correct, at least five men are involved."

"Five?" she cried. Once more angry tears glistened in her eyes. "Your shoulder isn't completely healed. I haven't even taken out the stitches yet. Cole and Adam aren't lawmen. Even if they go with you, the odds are certainly not in your favor."

"I have to go, Sarah. It's my case. The deputies are coming to help me, not do it for me. Chances are, when the Pruitts see that there's no escape, they'll surrender."

"And what if they don't?"

"I can't let my brothers or my deputies risk their lives if I'm not willing to do the same. You've known all along what I am. You knew when Dawson Yates showed up, and even though you're angry with me, you can't deny that you knew from the beginning that I'd have to see this through to the end."

He pulled her back into his arms. "Some of why I love you so much is that you're a strong woman. Your notions of liberty and equality, though sometimes frustrating, make sense. Your independence is comforting to me, Sarah, because I know if anything ever happens to me, you'd be all right without me."

She pushed away from him, shaking her head. "No," she

cried, covering her ears. "I'm not. I'm a fraud. I don't want to be strong. I'm scared and . . . and damn it, Ira, I'm pregnant."

His expression went from compassionate to stunned. "You're pregnant?" he repeated.

"Yes, I'm pregnant, and if you for one moment think that I want to raise this child alone, you are sorely mistaken." She swiped at her tears. "I may be capable, Ira Farrell, but I'm not willing. I need you to take care of me . . . of our baby."

When he wrapped her tightly in his arms, she clung to him. "Don't cry," he murmured, kissing her hair. "Please, darlin', don't cry. We still have another week together."

After a few moments, he bent his head and gazed deeply into her eyes. "There's nothing to worry about. I'll be back, I promise, and we'll get married, and I'll try to be a good husband and a good father. I'll give up my badge—I'll do anything you want, but first I have a job to finish."

He cupped her face, dying a little inside at the heartbreak glistening in the depths of her eyes. "Everything will be all right, Sarah. We have to believe that."

She finally took a calming breath, then went to the pitcher and added a little water to the basin to bathe her face. "I'm better now."

"Are you sure you're—"

"Yes. I'm better."

"No, darlin', are you sure about the baby?"

She blinked up at him. "As sure as I can be this early."

"Are you feeling well enough to take a little ride? I could go saddle a couple of horses and we could have a picnic. I'll bring extra blankets."

His grin was back to being sinful, and even though she was still frightened, she couldn't refuse such a delightful way to spend some time alone with the man she loved.

Ira tossed a saddle on Jeb's old buckskin gelding, thinking about what Sarah had said. She was pregnant. He was going to be a father. On one hand, he blamed himself for not being more careful. On the other, he was happier at that moment than any man had a right to be.

Deep down inside, he knew when he'd asked her to marry him he'd wanted her to bear his children. He pulled the cinch tight, then took down the stirrup, wondering what he'd do when the baby arrived. Very soon he was going to have a wife, and shortly after that a baby. What kind of father would he be? A picture of his own father came to mind, and uncertainty gnawed at his insides.

He didn't know a lick about children. Hell, he didn't even know a lick about providing for anyone other than himself. He was a gunslinger turned lawman. What kind of life was that? No wonder Sarah was frightened.

"Ira? Are you all right?" Cole asked.

Ira glanced up, suddenly aware that he'd been leaning on the saddle staring out into space. "Yeah," he replied quickly, pretending to check the cinch that he'd just fastened.

Cole came around with a pair of saddlebags and a couple of Navajo blankets. "Uncle Jeb said you and Sarah are going for a ride. He packed some food."

"Thanks," Ira said as he tied the bags behind the cantle on Jeb's gelding.

Cole tied the rolled blankets on Adam's stallion. "You must be special to get to ride Warrior."

Ira picked up the gelding's reins, still frowning. "Yeah, Dakota threw a shoe."

"Are you going to tell me why you're looking so serious?" Cole asked as he untied Warrior.

Ira met his brother's gaze. For a moment Ira thought to

keep the baby a secret, but then he felt the need to share the news, hoping that Cole might offer some advice. "I just found out that Sarah's pregnant."

Cole's concerned gaze never wavered. "By your expression, I'm not sure if congratulations are in order, or if I should go get a gun and put you out of your misery."

Ira relaxed a little and grinned. "Did I look that bad? I didn't mean to, it's just that I never thought much about being a father."

As they led the horses out of the barn, Cole put his hand on Ira's back. "I don't think it's something we actually think about, it's just something we do. Hell, quit worrying. You'll be a great father."

Ira gave a skeptical laugh. "How can you be so sure?"

Cole's smile was encouraging. " 'Cause, you've been like a mother hen to Adam and me for years."

Ira grinned sheepishly at his brother, then spotted Sarah waiting on the porch. "She's beautiful, isn't she?" he said quietly.

"Indeed she is," Cole confirmed.

Ira caught Cole's sleeve, searching his face. "If anything happens—"

"Ira, nothing's gonna happen."

"Cole, listen to me. I have to know that if it did, you'd take care of her. She's stubborn and has some crazy ideas about equality and how she sees her role in society." Ira searched Cole's face for a sign of understanding—relieved to see it in his brother's brown eyes. "Deep down, she's scared and naïve. I'd feel a whole lot better if I knew you'd be there for her."

Cole was quiet for a long time. "The moment you chose her to be your wife, she became part of our family. We Farrells always take care of our own, remember?" Cole put his hand over his brother's and gave it a firm squeeze. "Now, get. You're wasting a good day jawing with me when you should be spending it with her."

Chapter Nineteen

Sarah put away the small basin and scissors. She had just removed Ira's stitches and was pleased to see the wound was healing nicely. Afterward, he pulled her into his arms and said that instead of being a journalist, she should think about becoming a nurse. He'd kissed her soundly, then dressed and gone downstairs to help his brothers saddle their horses.

The week had passed too quickly, Sarah thought dismally, focusing on all the pleasant things they had done together. The night after their picnic—after they both agreed to share their secret with Uncle Jeb and Adam, Ira announced to his family that he would soon be a father, and even though she felt a little embarrassed, his family bombarded her with a thousand suggestions, down to what kind of cradle would be the best, to whose name selection did she like the most.

"I think Zachary might be nice if it's a boy," she had said with a cautious smile. "And, maybe Emily if it's a girl." Her trepidation had only lasted a second as glasses were raised and her decision was finalized at the supper table. With every day that passed, she had felt more and more a part of the family, but only after Adam had told her that the calf they found had been named Little Sarah, did she really feel accepted.

"I'm flattered," she had said truthfully.

"Well, that's good, 'cause she's got those big ol' eyes that kind of reminded me of you."

Ira and Cole had nearly choked on their coffee that morning, but after a scathing glance from her, they were able to control themselves. She had thought the matter was settled, only to realize she was wrong. Later, when the sun was resting on the treetops, and she and Ira sat on the porch swing under a warm blanket, Ira pulled her into his arms and looked deeply into her eyes. "Did I ever tell you that . . . that you have the prettiest cow eyes I ever did see?"

She smiled again at her memories, remembering how he'd dodged her elbow, but was laughing so hard, he almost fell off the swing. Even now, as she watched the brothers tie their saddlebags on their horses, she recalled how Ira insisted she feed Little Sarah the day Adam went to fetch the calf's mother.

"Come on, darlin'," Ira had said to her with an ornery grin. "This will be good practice for you."

"Somehow I don't think feeding a calf will be anything like feeding a baby," she had protested. But to no avail. He took her to the straw-filled stall where the calf was curled up in a little brown-and-white ball.

The moment Ira had opened the gate the baby clambered to her feet and started bawling. The hungry calf fed so voraciously, Sarah had to hold the bottle tightly with both hands or have it tugged from her grasp.

But that was two blissful days ago.

Now, Ira was on the porch gazing down at her, and she quickly pushed the past away. With her heart in her throat, she pasted a cheerful smile on her face and entwined her fingers with his. Together they walked to where his brothers waited. Like Ira, both Cole and Adam had six-guns strapped to their hips, and all three saddles had rifles nestled in the rifle boots under the left stirrups. "I'll send word as soon as I can," Ira said softly. "In the meantime, you're in good hands with Uncle Jeb."

Ira gently grasped her chin and held her while he kissed her. "Are you going to be all right?"

"Yes," she lied, feeling cold deep down inside.

He gave her a confident smile. "There's nothing to worry about," he encouraged, giving her a little squeeze. "My deputies will probably ride into town the same time we do."

Unashamed, he wrapped her in his arms and kissed her again, molding her to his hard body. When he pulled back, his eyes glittered with confidence. "I can't wait till spring to marry you," he murmured close to her ear. "Think about what I said before. When I get back, I want to start planning our wedding."

He pulled her back into his arms for one last hug, holding her close, while she tried not to worry. Even when he moved away with one of his lazy smiles, the ice that had settled over her heart didn't thaw.

"You boys watch your backs," Uncle Jeb called as they rode away from the cabin.

Ira turned, and when he gave her an arrogant grin and touched the brim of his hat, a little of the ice melted.

Sheriff Cooper Finch leaned back in his chair, waiting for another meeting to begin. He already knew the topic on the agenda—had known what it would be when Ira and his brothers rode into town that afternoon and stopped at the jail. Cooper had managed to appear calm. Hell, he'd even managed to look eager to help. His act had worked, too.

Ira had told him everything, all his suspicions, even told him help was coming from Carefree. Ira also told him there was a jacket in Sarah's shop with a lion's head button missing. Cooper could still hear Ira's voice. *Find the owner and you'll find the person responsible for Zach's and Miss Emily's deaths.*

Cooper dragged a hand down his face, wondering when Ira's deputies would arrive. Wondering if there was any hope to save his own skin. Cooper almost sneered as he glanced around the room, thinking that he was looking at a bunch of dead men.

"Where's Roland?" Silas asked, checking his watch.

Cooper pushed his hat off his forehead, leaning his elbows on the table. "Well, let's take a guess," he started, with a disbelieving shake of his head. *Could Silas really be so stupid?* "Last week James Roland shipped his daughter off to some relative in Wyoming. He and some of his boys were supposed to be here yesterday with the herd, but they never showed. I'm guessing he's halfway to Mexico by now."

"I always thought he was a yellow-bellied coward," Josh Pruitt grumbled.

"Some could say the same about men who beat up women." The moment Josh stood, Cooper's hand fell to his side and rested on the butt of his gun. Jonah Pruitt caught his brother's arm, muttering something before dragging Josh back down. Cooper stared at Josh for several more moments then gave a dry laugh. "Ira's not going to be too happy when he finds out what you did to Miss Lily."

"Me?" Josh countered. "You were there too."

"Yeah," Cooper agreed. "But we were just supposed to scare her, not beat her half to death." Cooper looked at the men sitting around the table. "If any of us were smart men, we should all be thinking real hard about skedaddling down to Mexico with Roland."

"Fighting among ourselves won't get us anywhere," Jonah chided, tugging his coat back into place.

Doc Hensley took a clean handkerchief out of his pocket and dabbed at the beads of sweat on his upper lip. "Who in the hell stoked the stove?"

"It's hotter than this in hell," Cooper teased morbidly. "I reckon we'd all better get used to it."

"Will you shut your goddamned mouth?" Silas snarled. He gave the sheriff a dark look then banged the gavel on the table. "All right. We've got ourselves some trouble, but it isn't the end of the world." Silas paused to collect his thoughts. "The only thing Ira has on any of us is those three cowboys over in jail."

Cooper laughed again. "That's all he needs. Them and the iron they were using. It's just amazing how easy it is to turn an F into a P."

"Don't forget Billy's over there too," Earl added. "He's bound to talk to Ira as soon as he gets the chance."

Silas shot Earl a dark look then began to pace. "We've got to stay calm."

"I say we cut our losses and get out of town." Louis practically jumped out of his chair. "You boys know how to handle guns. All I know about is running the mercantile. I'm through. You can have my share of the loot we got stashed in the bank. I'm packing up my wife and my two kids and I'm leaving tonight." He jammed his bowler on his head and almost ran for the door.

Josh got up out of his chair, his hand reaching for his pistol. Once more Jonah caught his brother's arm. "Let him go. We don't need him."

Earl cleared his throat, rising slowly to his feet. "I-I'm just an old man. I'm like Louis. I don't know nothing about guns." Earl swallowed hard. "K-keep my share, but don't ask me to stand up to the Farrells, 'cause I just don't have the guts to do it. Your secret is safe with me. I'll watch the office. If I get any telegrams for the marshal, I'll bring 'em to you for sure." He spun and headed toward the door. "I'm just gonna lie low till this blows over."

After the door closed, the doctor shook his head. "Blows over?" he repeated tersely. "He's a bigger fool than I thought if he thinks this is going to *blow over*. It's going to blow up in our faces, and every man in here knows it."

Cooper heaved an impatient sigh. "There's still five of us and only three of them."

"For how long?" The doctor turned his full attention on the sheriff. "I thought you said some deputies were on their way?"

"There are, but Ira wasn't sure when they'll arrive. He and his brothers are holed up in the boarding house. They won't do anything stupid. They're just going to sit there, waiting and watching till help arrives."

"Ira just waltzed in and told you that, did he?" the doctor scoffed.

The sheriff matched Doc Hensley's smirk. "You see, Doc, because I wear a badge, people tend to trust me. Hell, I even managed to convince you that I hurt my arm chasing some outlaw. But, that wasn't the case . . ." He looked across the table at Jonah. "By the way, I borrowed your jacket. Doc has it in his office if you want it back." Cooper tried to look contrite. "I'm afraid I tore the sleeve."

Jonah's tawny brows snapped together. "You tore the sleeve? How?" When Cooper only shrugged, Jonah looked at Doc Hensley. "You never mentioned Cooper wore my jacket. You just said I left it at your office when I brought your share of the last sale."

"What difference does it make now?" the doctor grumbled.

Silas raised his hands. "Gentlemen, please. None of this is going to matter if we don't come up with a plan."

The doctor leaned back in his chair. "The way I see it, even if we tuck tail and run, the Farrells can identify every man in here. Maybe we should just give up and hope for the best."

"Hope for the best?" Cooper cried incredulously. "What exactly is that? A soft rope?"

Josh stood up. "You're all just a bunch of quitters. I say we take them down before help arrives. Five to three are a lot better odds."

Doc Hensley raked his fingers through his hair. "This is crazy . . . you're all crazy. We can't just gun down three men in the middle of the street and expect to get away with it. Besides, Cooper said they were holed up in Mrs. Baca's boarding house waiting for help to arrive."

"Hell," Cooper added with a disgusted laugh. "Even if Josh was on the roof with a rifle, chances are he'd miss."

Josh lunged at Cooper, but Jonah caught him again. "Stop it," Jonah snarled. "He's just shooting off his mouth."

Doctor Hensley stood and glanced at the men around the table, then dabbed at his upper lip. "It seems to me we have two options. The first option is to leave now, while we still can. With the money we've saved, we could live like kings in Mexico. The second option is to draw them out and fight."

"How do you propose we do that?" Jonah asked.

"What about Sarah Brighton?" Four pair of eyes turned toward Silas Pruitt. "Has anyone here thought about her? Everyone knows she's Ira's woman. It was even in the newspaper."

Sarah lay in bed staring at the ceiling, missing Ira more and more as each hour passed. She thought about going downstairs to get a glass of milk, but at night, out from under the covers, the cabin was cold.

She had just rolled over and snuggled down a little deeper under the quilt when Buster started barking. A few minutes later, she heard Jeb's bedroom door open and his footfalls disappearing down the hall. A moment later she heard the bar drop downstairs after it had been lifted from the front door.

Curious, she slipped into her velvet dressing gown and stepped into the hall. She tiptoed to the top of the stairs where she could see who was calling at such a late hour. Her brows crinkled when she recognized Sheriff Finch, holding his hat in his hands and talking with Jeb.

Ira and his brothers sat on the bed playing cards. Mrs. Baca's grandson had brought them their supper and only a few moments ago collected the tray, pleased with the five-dollar tip Ira gave him for his trouble.

Adam picked up his cards, and then tossed two matchsticks on the bed. "I'll bet you ten dollars." "Gracious sakes," Cole teased. "I think the boy must be holding aces."

"Yeah, well, I'll see your ten bucks and I'll raise you ten more. Now, how many cards do you want to go with your aces?"

Adam started to answer, but someone knocked softly on the door. Ira signaled to Adam to stand in the corner by the wardrobe. After he picked up his rifle, he did as he was told.

Cole grabbed his rifle and leaned against the wall behind the door, just before Ira opened it.

"Marshal Farrell? I'm one of Miss Lily's girls, and . . ." The attractive young woman had to pause to dab at her eyes with a lacy handkerchief. Ira gently grabbed her arm and pulled her inside, then closed and bolted the door.

"Get her a glass of water, will you?" he asked Cole before he led the weeping woman to a chair in the corner and encouraged her to sit down. After she took several small sips, she was back in control.

"The rest of the girls and me, well, we took a vote. We decided that no matter how dangerous it is to come and see you, we couldn't wait no longer. You see, some men came by several days after she visited your ranch and they beat Miss Lily within an inch of her life."

The young woman lifted her red-rimmed eyes to Ira. "We're all scared to death that they might come back."

Ira exchanged glances with Adam and Cole. "Get your coats. We're going to take this lady home."

Ira nodded at the barkeep. He gave his rifle to Cole, and then climbed the stairs, leaving his brothers to guard the front door. Removing his hat, he knocked on Lily's door. "Lil? It's Ira."

He opened the door and stepped into the dimly lit room. A scarf had been draped over the white lampshade, bathing the room in a muted shade of red. It looked much the same as he remembered, the same gold velvet chairs, the white-and-gold satin wallpaper that matched the covers and sheets on the huge brass bed.

The only thing different from what he expected was the woman in the bed. She looked small and frail, her red curls spread over the satin pillow in disarray. Her face was turned toward the wall, avoiding his gaze. He stepped closer and after he tossed his hat on the chair, slowly sat on the side of the bed.

"Lil?" He reached over and picked up her hand, pressing it between his own. When she still wouldn't look at him, he gently grasped her chin and forced her to face him. He felt as if someone had punched him in the stomach. Though the bruises and cuts were over two weeks old, they were still painfully visible. One eye was still swollen and bloodshot.

"Don't look at me," she cried softly, trying to turn away, but he wouldn't let her. He scooted closer and picked her up in his arms, holding her protectively against his chest the moment she began to weep. He knew by the bandage around her ribs, that the damage hadn't been limited to her face.

"Is there anything broken?" he whispered.

"No," she replied in a small voice. "I'm just sore . . . and ugly."

He held her away and made her look at him. "Never ugly," he said with a smile. "Just bruised, and bruises heal."

He bunched the pillows and she rested back against them with a weak smile. "I knew you'd come," she began. "My girls were supposed to keep this a secret, but then I guess when you got back to town, they figured you'd be the only one who'd help."

Ira cupped her cheek, brushing a tear away with his thumb. "Who did this to you?"

"I can't be sure. They wore masks, but—"

"They?" Ira interrupted. "How many?" he asked, his voice deadly calm.

"Two." Lily pressed her fingers to her forehead. "I knew the Pruitts were crooked, and I told you I suspected Doc, but I never guessed Cooper was in on it."

"S-sheriff Finch did this to you?" Ira asked with a sharp edge to his voice. Rage threatened his composure, cutting into his chest. While Lily recalled what had happened, all he could think about was how he wanted to drag Cooper Finch out of his office and beat the man to a bloody pulp.

"Ira?" Lily repeated, drawing him back from his menacing thoughts as she reached up and placed her hands on his chest. "Ira, you've got to be careful. I didn't know Cooper was like he is, but if he'll do this to me, it won't bother him at all to do worse to you."

Ira caught Lily's hands and held them, forcing a gentle smile. "Don't you worry none, Lil. It's all going to be over soon." He leaned over and placed a kiss on her forehead. "Sam's got a shotgun downstairs and he's not about to let anybody in that could hurt you."

He stood and picked up his hat.

"Ira, Billy Carson . . . I don't think he's—"

"I know. I'll make sure I set things right with him." Ira put on his hat and touched the brim. "You catch up on some rest. I'll handle things from here on out."

"Well?" Cole asked the moment Ira came downstairs. The look on his brother's face was unlike any he'd seen, but then Cole expected it was the way he looked each time he faced a man down.

"Cooper Finch is in with the Pruitts."

"Son of–a buck," Cole breathed.

"Is that what Miss Lily said?" Adam asked, falling in with his brothers as they left the saloon.

"That's what she said," Ira stated. "And she's got no reason to be saying it if it isn't true."

"What are we going to do?" Cole asked, glancing around to make sure they weren't being followed.

"Something I've never done before." Ira never looked up, he just kept walking. "I'm going to beat the hell out of a sheriff. Then I'm going to find Josh Pruitt and beat the hell out of him too."

Cole caught Ira's arm. "I know how you feel, Ira, but you can't do that."

Ira jerked his arm free. "Why not?"

Cole tapped his finger on Ira's badge. "Because you're not like Cooper. We'll go over to his office and if he's there, we'll put him in a cell and wait for your deputies to arrive."

"That's too easy. He needs to pay for what he did to Lily."

Cole shook his head. "He'll pay, Ira. We both know that, but it's not up to us to choose his punishment." Cole's stride matched Ira's. Adam was a step behind. Something tinkled in Adam's pocket, causing Ira to ask what it was.

Adam grinned, his teeth a muted white in the lamp light. He opened his coat, exposing a pint bottle of Lily's best Kentucky bourbon. "I thought after we're through with Cooper, we'd have us a little drink just to warm up a bit. It's a cold night."

"Sounds good to me," Cole added as they turned down Main Street toward Cooper Finch's office.

Doctor Hensley darted into the alley the moment he saw the Farrells. His heart hammered so violently against his chest it was nearly painful. He held his breath as they walked by and broke into a cold sweat. He inched forward, peeking around the corner as the brothers stopped before the sheriff's office and banged loudly on the door.

"Finch, open up," Ira called.

The doctor swallowed back his fear when a deputy opened the door and the Farrells disappeared inside. Hensley hesitated for a fraction of a moment, then ran across the street and around to the back door of the bank, praying the Pruitts were still there.

"What the hell?" Josh muttered as he pulled open the door. "I thought you were home by now."

The doctor hurried inside. "I-I was on my way, but I damned near ran into the Farrells. They're over at the sheriff's office."

"Finch is gone."

"I know that," the doctor snarled. "Don't you see? This might be our chance. We could wait until they come out and take care of them."

Jonah stepped around his brother at the same time he

pulled out his watch. "It's late. Was there anyone in the street?"

The doctor shook his head. "No. It's deserted."

Jonah grinned at Josh. "Pa's got a couple of rifles in a cabinet in his office. I'll get them."

Sarah kept herself out of sight as she strained to listen to what Sheriff Finch was saying. She heard Jeb as he explained that Ira told him to stay at the ranch no matter what.

"Yes, and I can understand you're doing as he asked, but he's been hurt. I'm not sure he's going to make it this time. Cole and Adam are with him. Neither one of them wanted to leave, so they asked if I'd come."

Sarah's mouth went dry and her palms grew moist, but Jeb didn't seem to believe him. He asked the sheriff to give him more details.

"Yes, the men arrived from Carefree. We got the Pruitts in jail, but there was a gunfight and Ira was hit in the crossfire."

Sarah ran to her room and dressed as quickly as she could, shoving her little derringer into the pocket of her coat just before she stepped back out into the hall. She hurried down the stairs, but Jeb caught her before she could leave. "Uncle Jeb, please. Let me go. If Ira's hurt I need to be with him."

"Sarah, if Ira's hurt that bad, there's nothing you can do. He made me promise I'd keep you here until he sent word himself."

"He can't," Cooper replied tersely. "He's hurt too badly." Cooper turned to Sarah. "I've got a horse waiting. Can you ride?"

"Yes." She tried to pull free, but Jeb's grip on her sleeve was relentless. To her horror, the sheriff drew his gun and brought the butt down on the back of Jeb's head. The old man sank to the floor. She tried to see if he was all right, but Cooper yanked her up.

"You're just like your cousin," he growled, giving her a little shake.

She looked at him as if he lost his mind.

"Since you're going to die with Farrell, I suppose there's no harm in spilling the beans now."

"I-I don't know what you're talking about," Sarah said as calmly as she could.

"No, I reckon you don't." Cooper pulled her a little closer. "It really was an accident. The fire, their deaths. None of it was supposed to happen."

"How-how do you know?" she managed to ask, even though her mouth had gone dry.

"I know because I was there."

"You and Jonah?"

Cooper laughed. "I didn't think it would work, but apparently it did."

"W-what worked?" she asked, hoping to learn the truth.

"Jonah wasn't there. I took his coat and wore a mask. I wanted Miss Emily to think it was Jonah, but then she wouldn't cooperate, and things got out of hand."

Sarah struggled against his hold. "You bastard. You killed her."

"I didn't want to, it just happened. I tried to warn her to stop snooping around, but she tried to stab me in the arm with her damned scissors. I shoved her away, but she fell back against the table and knocked over the lantern."

"You could have saved her," Sarah cried.

"I was going to. But Zach showed up and I knew he'd blame me. I'm the damned sheriff. I couldn't go to jail. Zach gave me no choice." Cooper shook his head. "After the fire started, I ran to the doc so he could tend my arm. I never noticed the button missing until after Cole collected the bodies. Even then I wasn't too worried. It was Jonah's coat." Cooper laughed, and then started toward the door. "Let's go," he growled.

She managed to pull free. "No. I won't go with you," she said breathlessly. His lecherous smile caused her knees to quake. Drawing her little gun, she raised her chin and matched his stare. "Get out before I call for help."

"There's no one around to help you, Sarah. Jeb just said all the hands are gone." Cooper took a step closer. "You're not the kind of woman who could shoot a man."

"Stay away from me," she warned.

Cooper grinned again and shook his head. "No, you're too much of a lady to gun a man down."

The next instant he lunged. She fired and he hollered as the small-caliber bullet tore into his sleeve. "Why, you little bitch." He took another step and she fired again, her second shot catching him in the leg. He hollered again, but as he fell, he caught the hem of her coat. Frantic, she tried to get away, but he pulled harder until he dragged her to the floor.

Terrified, she raised her foot and kicked at the bloodstain on his arm. Her stomach rolled in disgust, but his grip slackened enough that she could pull free. She scrambled to her feet and backed against the wall, her cold fingers brushing against Uncle Jeb's old twelve-gauge shotgun.

Cooper lay on the floor breathing heavily and swearing as he slowly dragged himself up. At the same time, a bitter memory flashed in her mind. *Do you think Dawson gave me time to choose where I put my bullet? If you do, you're a fool, Sarah. I have seconds to measure a man—to try and look in his eyes and see if he's got what it takes to put a bullet in my chest. And, he did. I saw it. And something else you should know, just in case you want to put it in your next story. I can feel it, Sarah. I can feel the depth of his hate by the way he looks and the way he stands.*

Her breath caught in her throat and her hands began to shake as she realized shooting Cooper Finch in the arm and leg wasn't enough. Praying he'd just go and leave them alone, she grabbed the shotgun and raised it.

"Get out," she screamed. Yet she knew with sickening assurance he wasn't the kind of man to give in. "Please," she sobbed. "Just leave."

"It's all right, Sarah," he said, wiping the sweat from his eyes. "It's my fault . . . I shouldn't have forced you. Don't make the same mistake your cousin made."

The whole time he spoke, the fingers of his right hand curled over the butt of his gun.

She squeezed her eyes closed and tightened her finger over the trigger. The blast was deafening. Shoved backwards from the recoil, she hit a chair, then crashed to the floor, never letting go of the shotgun. She lay on her back with the weight of the gun on her chest as she tried to catch her breath. A deathly calm fell over her. She could feel her heartbeat, hear it in her ears, but she couldn't move. She closed her eyes, trying not to think of what she had done.

Chapter Twenty

"Evening, Marshal, Cole, Adam. What brings you boys to town?" The young deputy smiled nervously. The way he wore his hat on the back of his head reminded Ira a little of Adam. "You all look like you're getting ready to do some hunting."

Ira walked over to Finch's desk and glanced at some papers. "Where's Finch?"

"Sheriff Finch . . . he ain't here." The young man's eyes darted around the room as if he were looking for a fast way out.

Ira stared at the boy. "I can see that. Where'd he go?"

The deputy swallowed and shifted his weight. "I don't know, Marshal, he just told me to get over here and watch the prisoners. He—"

Ira caught the boy by the collar and backed him up against the door leading to the cells. "You're lying. Want to know how I can tell? 'Cause you won't look me in the eyes, that's how."

The young man never took his eyes off Ira, he just started to shake. "He said he h-had to leave t-town for a while. H-he didn't say where he was going, only that he'd be back by morning."

"I think he's telling the truth." Cole matched Ira's steady gaze. "He's got nothing to do with this, Ira. Let him go."

"I c-can't go," the deputy stuttered. "I'm on duty."

Ira slowly released the boy, then glanced at the star on the young man's chest, admiring him for at least being loyal to the badge. "I'll watch the prisoners. You go on home."

Cole stepped over to the door and opened it while the deputy shrugged on his coat. A rifle shattered the silence and everyone hit the floor.

"Douse the lamp," Ira ordered, watching as Adam reached up and carefully turned it down.

The deputy was on his side with his head at an awkward angle. "Shit," Cole growled under his breath. "He's been hit."

Ira crawled toward Cole and together they were able to drag the deputy inside. Cole kicked the door closed just as two more bullets ripped through the wood. Ira moved aside the deputy's coat. There was a hole in the boy's shirt just under the badge. Ira checked the boy for any signs of life, but shook his head.

"Saints, Ira. Who's shooting at us?" Adam asked with a tinge of fear in his voice. He scooted closer to the window and peeked out.

"See anything?"

"No good," Adam murmured. "Someone's doused all the street lamps."

"There's a full moon. Keep your eyes open."

"What's going on?" came a frightened voice. Ira glanced at the door leading to the cells.

"Billy? Is that you?"

"Marshal Farrell? I'm innocent. I'd never—"

"I know it, Billy," Ira interrupted.

"Who in the hell's shooting?" another voice called. Someone else asked to be freed.

Adam glanced at the door between the rooms. "Those are the rustlers we brought in."

"Cole, you and Adam take the deputy to the back and put him in one of the empty cells."

While they carefully dragged the boy out of the room, Ira leaned his rifle against the wall, and then shoved the desk over on its side. It was an old desk, made of thick, dark wood, and with three heavy drawers on each side, it would provide adequate cover. After he pushed it against the front door, he turned around to assess their situation.

The walls were solid adobe. Other than a double-planked wooden door, there was only one other opening to the outside. A small window faced the street, but it was barred and had heavy wooden shutters that he carefully reached up and closed. All in all, Ira decided they were as safe as could be expected under the circumstances. He could see no reason to leave. Standing, but staying low, he went to the pot-bellied stove at the back of the room, flicked open the door and added a few chunks of wood from the bin. A warm orange glow filled the small office, but it wasn't enough light to be seen through the shutters on the window.

"What are you doing?" Cole asked as he and Adam crept back into the room.

Ira sat on the floor near the stove. He'd taken off his coat and had it bunched behind his back, looking quite at ease with his rifle cradled on his lap. "Since we're staying, we might as well get comfortable."

"What do you mean, we're staying?" Adam asked, sitting down on the floor like his brother.

Ira motioned around the room. "This place is a fortress. Look around. The walls are a foot thick. There's no way out except through that door, and someone's got a rifle, just waiting to use it."

"So now what?" Cole asked, making himself a little more comfortable against the adobe wall across from Ira.

"We wait." Ira lifted out his pocket watch, tipped it toward the tiny light around the door on the stove, and then read the time. "We've got about six hours till dawn. Hopefully my deputies will arrive by then." He snapped the watch closed and slipped it back into his pocket.

"What if they don't?" Adam asked.

"I don't think our shooter is crazy enough to stay around when the good citizens start waking up."

Ira massaged his stiff shoulder. "Where's that bourbon you bought?"

Adam pulled it out of his pocket. "Right here." He tore off the seal then pulled out the cork. "Here's to your deputies arriving bright and early." He took a sip then passed it to Ira. Ira took a sip then passed it to Cole, who followed suit. He gave it back to Adam with an appreciative smile.

"That's smooth, and about the best I've had."

"You've been sneaking into town and drinking?" Cole teased. The bottle went around again then Adam capped it and set it aside.

"Ira?" Adam began, then his voice faded off into the stillness of the night.

"What's on your mind?" Ira asked, keeping his voice low.

"With Cole and me helping you like this, does it mean we're your deputies?"

Ira laughed softly. "Do you want to be my deputy?" He glanced over at his youngest brother, suddenly very proud of the man that Adam had grown to be.

Adam shrugged his shoulders, a little embarrassed. "I wouldn't mind it none."

"Then consider yourself deputized. You are now Deputy Adam Farrell."

"Son of a bitch," Josh ground out through clenched teeth. He was hiding with Jonah in the little alley between the dress shop and the barbershop. The doctor and his father were across the street behind some barrels in front of the mercantile. "Why aren't they coming out? It's been damned near an hour and nothing."

Jonah gave a disbelieving laugh. "Well, why do you think?"

"All right, Mr. College Man, what do you suggest we do now? In a few hours it's gonna be daylight and everybody and their brother's gonna be out here to see what all the shooting's about."

Jonah braced his rifle against the wall, then pulled the collar of his coat a little higher. "All I know is that we're out here freezing our asses off while they're in Cooper's office where there's a stove." Jonah gave an irritated sigh. "Whose bright idea was this anyway?"

"Doc Hensley's," Josh muttered. "Wish we could start a little fire to keep warm."

Jonah glanced over at his brother. It amazed him sometimes that they had the same parents. Josh's manners and ways of thinking were so backward, it was often irritating. Even now, he had no clue that by suggesting they build a fire it had given Jonah an idea. He tapped his brother on the shoulder. "Come with me."

"Where to?"

A few minutes later they were in the alley where Jonah shot the lock off the back of the dress shop.

"Now what?" Cole asked, scooting over to the window. He carefully pushed the shutter aside and peered out.

"See anything?" Ira asked

"No. The whole town looks deserted."

Ira frowned and joined his brother. "I wonder why our shooter fired his pistol." He rose and carefully glanced around, but just as Cole had said, there wasn't anything moving. He crawled back to his place and hunkered down where he was a little more comfortable. "We'd best take turns watching while two of us try to get some sleep. Adam, you're first."

Adam gave Ira a disgruntled look. "Why me?"

Ira shrugged. "You're the youngest."

"Gee, thanks."

Ira grinned, then pushed his hat down over his eyes. "That's thanks, *Marshal Farrell,* to you, and you're welcome. Let this be a lesson to you."

"In what?" Adam grumbled.

"Well, in respect, and in choosing a profession. Sometimes it just doesn't pay to be one of my deputies."

Lily Barker got out of bed and slipped on a satin robe. It was late, and only a few of her steady customers were at the bar. She stepped out onto the balcony overlooking her saloon and met Sam at the head of the stairs. "Did you hear what I heard?"

Sam nodded. "Yup. Gunfire. I was just coming to tell you that Doc and Silas Pruitt have the Farrells holed up at the jail."

"You can bet Josh and Jonah are there too," Lily spat.

"I reckon."

"Are there any men down there willing to help?"

Sam gave a disgusted shake of his head. "Nope. Nobody's sticking their heads out, and from what that man over there said, the whole town is locked up tighter than a drum." Sam met her worried expression with one of his own. "It don't sound too bad, Lil. I'm thinking the Farrells will just sit tight till morning."

"What happens then?" Lily asked.

"I heard some rumors that the marshal's got some men

coming to help. Besides, if it is the Pruitts, they ain't going to hang around long after the sun comes up."

Lily heaved a despondent sigh. "I suppose you're right. What time is it now?"

Sam pulled out his pocket watch and flipped it open. "One-thirty."

"What are you planning?" Josh asked as he and Jonah stepped inside Sarah's dress shop.

"I'm looking for a lantern and some matches."

A small flame brightened the back room. "Here's some—"

Jonah slapped the match out of his brother's fingers. "You idiot. Give me those, and grab that lamp."

"We're going to set fire to the jail?" Josh asked. "Adobe don't burn. Don't you remember?"

"That's right, but the roof isn't made from adobe, is it? And we both know smoke kills just as good as being burned to death. It's cold, and I'm tired. I don't feel like standing around all night until the marshal's deputies ride up and arrest us. Now, go up front and get ready. Wait until you can see the flames on the roof, then fire a couple of rounds at the door."

"What for?" Josh asked.

"I want the fire to get going. If they're busy watching the front door, they won't suspect anything until they smell smoke. By then, it'll be too late." Jonah led his brother out of the shop. "Now go on. I'll join you in a little while." Jonah made his way along the alley behind the buildings until he was several doors away from the jail. He silently cursed the full moon. Staying to the shadows as best he could, he carefully crossed the street. He paused for several moments to catch his breath, then worked his way through the alley behind the jail. He put the lantern down on the ground then lifted the glass globe. He blew on his fingers to warm them, and then he struck a match, touching the small flickering flame to the wick. After he replaced the glass, he took several steps back, and then tossed the lantern up and onto the roof.

"Ira, wake up," Adam whispered.

Ira sat up, flexing his shoulder. "What?"

"I thought I heard something."

"Where?" Cole asked, lifting his head up. Adam motioned toward the room where the men were sleeping in their cells.

"Go back to the window. I'll check it out." Ira crawled toward the door then slowly got to his feet. He pulled out his pistol and slowly opened the door. The room was inky black, filled with the sounds of men snoring. Quietly, he backed out, then, staying low, joined Adam at the window. "Everything's nice and peaceful."

"I don't know about you, but I sure as hell can't sleep," Cole grumbled.

"You boys just aren't used to this kind of work. I was sleeping like a baby," Ira replied with a grin.

"While you were sleeping, I found a deck of cards in the desk. How about we have a little game of poker?" Adam suggested, holding the cards up for the others to see.

"Sounds good to me." Cole scooted closer. "What should we bet with?"

"There's a box of matches by the stove. I'll get them." Ira grabbed the box then sat by Cole while Adam dealt the cards. "Each match is worth ten bucks."

"Only ten bucks? Why not a hundred bucks?" Adam asked. "What do we care? It's not like it's real money."

Ira nodded. "All right. I bet two hundred dollars."

"So," Cole began, nodding at Adam to toss in his bet. "I reckon we'll be uncles some time in July."

289

"Yeah," Adam said with a proud smile. "That's something to drink to, isn't it?"

Cole nodded his head. "Why, I do believe you're right, little brother."

"Well, I don't," Ira stated firmly, taking the bottle out of Adam's grasp. "All I need is two drunk deputies." He put the bottle on the floor, and then looked at his cards. "It's your bet, *Uncle* Cole."

"I bet you're a bunch of fun to work for," Cole teased. He tossed several matches on the pile. "I'm calling your bet and raising you three."

"Uncle has a real nice sound to it," Adam replied, looking at his cards. "I fold."

"Fold?" Ira repeated. "You can't fold."

"Why not?"

" 'Cause he was winning," Cole replied with a grin. "I fold too."

"That's not fair," Ira grumbled. "You know I like to see how badly I beat you." He reached down to pull the pile of matches over to his little stack. His smile faded at the same time he glanced over at the stove. "Do you smell smoke?"

Cole gave a good sniff. "I think it's just the stove. I'll go check it." Cole went over to the stove. Everything looked all right. He opened it and added another chunk of wood before he rejoined his brothers. "I think it's just a little windy outside, blowing some smoke down the chimney." He leaned back against the desk next to Ira. "What time is it?"

Ira heaved a tired sigh. "Two."

"Hey, out there!" came a man's voice from the back room. "There's smoke in here."

Ira and Cole exchanged quick glances then Ira got up and, crouching down, moved quickly to the door and yanked it open. Thick smoke hugged the ceiling and began to drift into the office. "We've got trouble," Ira muttered. "Cole, grab those keys."

Cole reached up just as another burst of gunfire splintered two more places in the door.

"Break that window," Ira ordered and Adam instantly obeyed, firing his own rifle out the window. Almost as soon as the glass was broken, a bullet slammed into the frame, barely missing Adam's head.

"Now what?" Adam asked, a little desperately.

"Stay there and keep your head down. Cole, get those cuffs then come with me."

They ran into the back room, and while Cole held his gun on the three rustlers, Ira opened the cell door and ordered them to hold out their arms. "So you're the famous Marshal Farrell," one of the men said with an arrogant smirk.

Ira slapped the shackles on the man's wrists, then turned to the other men and did the same. Once the prisoners were secure, Ira shoved them toward the front of the building. A quick glance confirmed his fear. Flames were already starting to burn through the ceiling and scorch the top of the inner wall. Ira slammed the key into the lock and threw open the last iron door. "Come on, Billy," Ira hollered over the hiss of the expanding fire.

After he followed Billy into the main office, Ira motioned for the prisoners to sit on the floor. The front door was riddled with holes. "You boys listen, and listen real good. The only way out is through the front door. Now I'm thinking your boss is out there with a rifle, just waiting to drop anything that moves. You can stay here and I'll do my best to get us out of this mess, or you can leave. It's up to you. If you decide you want to leave, I suggest the moment you go through that door, hold up your hands and pray they don't shoot."

The three rustlers looked at each other for several frantic moments. "I ain't going out there," one of them said.

"Me neither," the other two replied.

"Then sit down over there by the stove, and keep your heads down." Ira turned to Billy. "You better get down. That door won't stop a bullet."

Billy scrambled to the other side of the room, huddling down. "Marshal Farrell, you've got to believe me, I didn't shoot you."

"I know that, Billy," Ira muttered as he tried to think of a way out.

"We're going to burn up in here," Billy cried. "You've got to do something."

Ira ignored the man's desperate plea. He cast a quick glance around the room, then crawled over to where Cole had taken a position behind the desk. "What's next door?"

Cole shook his head. "I don't know for sure. I think it's just a shed, but there's a small alley behind us. Why? What are you thinking?"

"Do something, Marshal," one of the rustlers pleaded.

"Yeah, you're supposed to protect us . . . it's your duty," the other one grumbled.

Cole motioned to Adam to follow him as they crawled closer to Ira. "I've got an idea. If it works, it could buy us a little time and some fresh air. You stay here."

He was up the next second and ran across the room. Another shot rang out but it smashed harmlessly high on the opposite wall. Using the stock of his rifle as a club, Ira broke the lock on the gun case. After he tossed several boxes of shells to Cole, Ira tossed two rifles to Cole and two to Adam, taking the last one for himself.

"Billy, get over here," Ira ordered as he dove down and

rolled. Once in position, he grabbed a box of shells and handed it to Billy.

"Fill your pockets."

"B-but I don't—"

"Just do it," Ira ground out.

Ira motioned to his brothers to return to the window. "Shoot and keep shooting."

Cole's and Adam's rifles exploded, and soon the smell of gunpowder mingled with the acrid smell of smoke. The moment they started shooting, bullets began to fly from the street, slamming into the wall and pulverizing the door. When one rifle ran out of ammunition, it was tossed to Billy to be reloaded and another was picked up. A bullet zinged past Ira's head, clanging loudly as it glanced off the stove. Billy cried out in fear, dropping several bullets.

Two of the prisoners started coughing and complaining that they couldn't breathe. When Ira glanced in their direction, the third man was slumped over. A dark red stain spread in the area of his heart.

"Hold your fire," Ira shouted. He moved toward the front of the office. Lying on his back, he took both feet and moved the desk far enough from the door where he could reach up and open it. As soon as that happened, bullets began to fly. Several tore into the old desk, but it seemed to block them rather well. Ira rolled out of the way and waited until things quieted down. Smoke poured out of the doorway, buying them a little time.

When he felt it was safe, he shoved the desk out the door and onto the boardwalk. Again a barrage of bullets splintered wood all around him, but by placing the desk sideways in the opening, he had successfully provided a small obstacle behind which one or two men could hide for a short while. Then, with any luck, they could make it to the shed and then to the alley behind the burning jail. From there, they had a chance to escape, but only if they could reach the alley.

The smoke streaming out the door provided further cover. After Ira told the others his plan, he motioned for Adam to be the first out the door. "Get going and stay low."

"No, I'll cover you, you go."

"Damn it, Adam, don't argue." Ira crawled over to his brother and grabbed Adam's coat. "I said, get going." Ira ignored Adam's protest and shoved him out the door. "Cole, cover him." Ira shouted, rapidly firing his own rifle. After Adam was safe behind the shed, Ira nodded at Billy. "Go!"

Certain Billy was with Adam, Ira scrambled over to the other two men and told them to move. "Come on," he shouted after the first one left. The second man hesitated, shaking from head to foot.

"Move it." Ira pushed the last man out. "Cole, you're next." Ira picked up another rifle and emptied it into the street. When Cole was behind the shed, Ira pulled his neck scarf up over his nose. He was just about to leave when he heard a strange crackling sound. He only had a second to cover his head as the wooden wall between the cells and the office exploded in flames.

Chapter Twenty-one

Sarah held her breath, listening as someone groaned. "Uncle Jeb?"

She waited, but he didn't answer. Afraid Cooper Finch was still alive and would try again to kill her, she scrambled to her feet, lifting the shotgun for another blast.

"H-hold on," Jeb rasped. He was on his hands and knees, trying to stand up.

"Oh, Jeb!" Sarah cried. She put the gun aside and knelt by the old man. "The sheriff tried—" Sarah covered her face with her hands and began to shake uncontrollably. She didn't resist when the old man pulled her into his arms and held her for several minutes, both of them on the floor.

"There, there," he muttered softly, patting her back as if she were his child. "Everything's gonna be fine. You just wait and see. Before you know it, it'll be fine and dandy."

After Sarah calmed down, she raised her head from his shoulder. "Are you all right?"

"Sure. We Farrells are known to have hard heads." Jeb rubbed the back of his neck. "It's gonna be a little sore, but I'll live."

Sarah helped him up, and then tried to make him sit down on a nearby chair so she could examine his skull, but he'd have no part of it. Instead he took her trembling hand in his and asked her to wait in the parlor, giving her strict orders not to come out until he said so. She sat there, trying to keep her thoughts in check so she wouldn't be sick. But there had been so much blood. She shivered, nauseated by what a shotgun can do at close range.

She was just beginning to get worried that Jeb might have collapsed, when he came for her. He had dressed and donned his hat and coat. "Come on," Jeb muttered, placing his arm around her as he led her toward the front door. Sheriff Finch's body had been covered with a Navajo blanket, but still she couldn't draw her eyes away from the dark pool of blood beside him on the wooden floor.

"Don't you think about it," Jeb said as he encouraged her to keep moving. "I know how you feel, but just don't you go thinking about it too much, 'cause it'll do no good." He took her hand and pulled her out the door. "No, sir, you listen to your Uncle Jeb. There's no good worrying over things you can't change."

Sarah glanced up and saw two horses saddled. With a gentle smile, Jeb helped her to mount then handed her the reins, catching her trembling hands between his own. "You just hold on to the saddle horn and follow me. I've been up and down this mountain so many times in the dark that I can do it with my eyes closed."

"I'm not afraid," Sarah replied with a strained smile.

"No use to be," Jeb agreed as he climbed into the saddle. "Are you warm enough in that coat?" he asked. "Want a blanket?"

She shook her head. "I'm warm." *Warm,* she thought. She'd just killed a man. With that realization, she thought it would be a long time before she ever got warm again.

"Now, while we're on the subject," Jeb's gruff voice broke into her morbid reverie. "I don't want you thinking that what the sheriff said has anything to do with us going to town." He turned in the saddle and looked at her. "Understand?"

"Yes, Uncle Jeb," she said softly, drawing in a deep breath of cold mountain air to help her queasy stomach.

"Are you doing all right?" Jeb asked for the second time as the horses made steady progress along the steep and winding road leading down the mountain. Under the full moon, it wasn't as dark as she expected. Now that her vision had adjusted, she could clearly make out the trail.

Shivering more from nerves than the cold, Sarah nodded. "I'm fine."

"It's nice having a full moon, ain't it?"

"Yes, it is," Sarah replied, even though she didn't feel very much like talking.

"Going into town . . . well, it's just a precaution. I'm thinking we'd be better off with the boys around. It's like I've always said, us Farrells, we stick together, and I should never have agreed to let them go without us."

Sarah continued to follow the old man down the trail, listening to him ramble on. His voice had a soothing effect and kept her mind off of the terrible things the sheriff had said about Ira and her cousin. As Jeb continued to tell her his thoughts on a number of things, she offered a silent prayer that when they got to town, everything would be just as Uncle Jeb said it would be . . . *fine and dandy.*

Ira tried to draw a breath, but the smoke was too thick, the heat unbearable. He had to get out and get out fast or burn to death. Flames were already licking across the wooden floor. He cautiously checked the street. It was empty. Only a few shots rang out now and then, but they were directed at the shed, not at the opening of the jail.

Drawing his pistol, Ira rolled out the door. A barrage of bullets splintered the wood of the boardwalk, and slammed into the wall directly above. He paid them no mind. Scrambling to his feet, he ran toward the shed. Cole was there waiting, firing his rifle several times to draw the other men's fire.

"What now?" Cole said, a little winded as he handed Ira a rifle. "We can't stay here. The fire's too hot. Some sparks have already spread to those crates blocking the alley." Cole glanced around with a worried expression, and Ira knew what he was thinking

"Yeah, it's only a matter of time before this place goes up in flames." He dragged his hand down his face, wiping some of the sweat from his eyes. "At least we can breathe. Adam?" Ira called, and the next instant Adam was there, waiting for instructions, as was Cole.

Ira looked at them for several indecisive moments. "I'm sorry I got you into this mess, but I can't change it now. We got three men counting on us to get them out alive. Two of them, I don't particularly care about, but nevertheless, they're my responsibility. I don't want anything happening to Billy. I think he's been through enough."

"What do you want us to do?" Cole asked. The back of the shed burst into flames. The men were silhouetted for several moments.

Shots rang out. They hunkered down as several bullets flew above their heads, sending sparks flying when they hit the burning wall.

Ira peered around the side of the shed. Nothing moved, then moonlight glinted off a rifle barrel. "We know there's two shooters hiding behind the barrels in front of the mercantile, and more in the alley by Sarah's shop. After this shed burns, there's nothing to use as cover on this side of the street that we can reach safely." Ira glanced at the flames devouring the dry wood at the rear of the shed. Already the sparks from the roof of the jail had spread to the roof of the shed. "We're lit up like firecrackers here. We've got to move."

"The only place left is the telegraph office up the street," Cole said, flinching as several more shots zinged by their heads.

Ira glanced up the street. The telegraph office was a small building several yards away from the train station. It was the closest building, but getting to it exposed their backs. He tried not to think about it—about losing another brother—but he knew it was their only option.

"How far is that? A hundred feet?" Adam grinned. "I can make that easy."

Ira looked at Adam. The young man had a lot of the same features as Zach. Ira felt his gut wrench. He hadn't been able to help Zach, but he sure as hell could help Adam. "All right," he said gruffly. "It's our only chance."

Ira checked his pistol. "Cole, you take the two prisoners and head up the street. Don't be a hero. Protect yourself. If they want to live, they'll keep up with you. It'll be hard to return fire. Your backs will be exposed, so just concentrate on getting there. Adam and I will cover you."

"Got it," Cole answered.

Ira put his hand on Cole's shoulder. "Just remember what I said, take care of yourself first."

Cole told the two prisoners the plan, and when they were in position, Ira and Adam began to rapidly fire their weapons. The two prisoners burst from the shed. Cole raced after them. In spite of Ira's and Adam's rifle fire, a shower of bullets still rained down on Cole and the two men, kicking up dirt and slamming into some nearby hitching posts. Cole lunged the last ten feet and rolled behind a horse trough. One prisoner made it safely into the building, but the other stumbled. The prisoner howled in pain as a bullet caught him in the arm.

Ira swore aloud, watching as Cole scrambled up and,

firing his last three rounds, grabbed the man and dragged him to safety.

Ira pulled Adam back, then quickly reloaded his pistol before shoving it back in the holster. Billy came over with two rifles and a box of bullets in each pocket.

"These are all that's left, Marshal." Billy gave them both a handful of shells. He coughed a little from the thickening smoke, then handed Ira a freshly loaded rifle. "This building is about to collapse."

"It's your turn, Adam. Take Billy. Shove him along if you have to." Ira gave Billy the extra rifle then pointed at the telegraph office up the street. "Cole's kicked in the door to the telegraph office. He'll cover you. Do your best to stay close to Adam. All you have to do is make it to the trough. The rest is easy."

"I-I can't," Billy cried, shaking his head. "I don't know how to use a rifle."

"Don't try to shoot. Just take it and run. Cole needs it, and those shells you have in your pocket." Ira gave Billy an understanding smile. "I know it looks like a long way, but you can do it."

The flames from the fire were starting to get uncomfortably warm. When the building groaned, all three men froze for several seconds. Sparks and ash from the roof floated down on them, burning tiny holes in their coats.

"Ira, I—" Adam swallowed hard. "You're coming next, right?"

"Yeah." Ira looked at his brother, terribly proud of the tough young man he was. "Promise me, if I go down, you'll stay inside. There's no use two of us getting shot up."

Adam visibly swallowed. A spark of anger ignited in the depth of his grey eyes. "I can't do that, Ira. Even if I don't try, Cole will. So I suggest you make it, hear me?"

Ira closed his eyes for a split second, riddled with indecision. On one hand, he couldn't bear losing Adam, but on the other hand, he knew his brothers would never leave him behind. Ira heaved a ragged sigh. "I hear you. Now, get."

He didn't give Adam any opportunity to argue; he leaned around the corner, momentarily making a target out of himself, and then began to shoot, dodging return fire. A quick glance told him Cole was trying to lend as much cover as he could, but Billy was slow, and Adam wouldn't leave him.

"Shit," Ira muttered when Adam went down. He turned toward the mercantile, took aim at where the shot came from, and then fired. A man cried out and fell backwards from the barrels. More shots came from the alley, and Ira turned his rifle that direction—pulling the trigger, cocking, pulling the trigger, cocking, repeating the process over and over again until his smoking weapon emptied.

A quick glance up the street confirmed his efforts had been worth the risk. Cole had gotten Adam and Billy safely into the other building. Trying to breathe past the thick smoke was agony, as was not knowing how badly his brother was hurt. Winded, Ira leaned back against the wall. Too late he realized the shed was crumbling. A burning piece of debris fell onto his leg. He lunged toward the only escape—the street—rolling as soon as he hit the ground, but his pant leg was on fire.

"Damn it," Cole murmured as he caught sight of Ira. "Cover him," he shouted as he and Adam began to fire. A man stepped out from the alley, aiming his rifle at Ira, but Cole's well-placed shot shoved him back against the hitching post where he collapsed in a heap near the boardwalk. Ira lay in the street, no longer on fire, but pinned by his assailants.

He had covered his head, lying outstretched and as low as possible while bullets slammed into the dirt around him.

"Is he moving?" Adam asked, wincing as he dragged himself closer to the door where he could see.

"I can't tell." Cole cursed aloud again, then glanced at Adam. "You gonna be all right?"

Adam patted the makeshift bandage Cole had tied around his leg to stop the bleeding. "Go. I'll cover you." Wincing, Adam positioned himself by the open doorway and started shooting.

"Jonah?" Josh called, dodging several bullets. "Jonah," he screamed when his brother didn't answer. Josh swiped at his eyes wondering why he was sweating when it was cold outside. His brother was wounded, or worse. "You son of a bitch," he ground out. In a rage, he emptied his pistol at Ira, ducking back behind the wall of Sarah's shop to reload. "Pa?" he called desperately. He inched closer to the corner of the building, trying to see if his father was still alive. "Pa, can you hear me?"

"Yeah, son. Stay down."

"Pa," Josh cried, his voice breaking. "They shot Jonah. I think he's dead." He waited for several moments for his father to answer. "Pa, what do we do now?"

Silas leaned back against the barrel trying to think. Doc Hensley was several feet away, bleeding and unconscious. The acrid smell of gunsmoke burned Silas's nostrils, and the rifle he had in his hands had grown heavier. His hope that Sheriff Finch would arrive in time had dwindled along with his hopes of killing all three of the Farrells. "Goddamn them," he spat, so angry he couldn't see straight.

His youngest son was wounded—possibly dead. And it

was their fault. They were to blame for his present situation. Weary, he closed his eyes for a moment, wishing to God he'd left for Mexico. His thoughts turned to his wife and daughter for only a brief moment.

Thankfully he hadn't involved them in anything illegal. They'd be all right. He doubted they'd even miss him—until the money ran out. He gave a snort, silently cursing Sarah Brighton and her fancy notions. Hell, he even had to make his own goddamned breakfast.

Mexico came back to mind, and for several moments he imagined how wonderful his life would be if he could get there. Several shots shattered the temporary silence, causing him to flinch. He pulled the gold watch from his vest pocket and popped the lid. In another hour or so it would be dawn. The town would wake, and his life as he had known it would be over. He glanced out at the deserted street. The jail stood stark and scorched, smoke billowing out the crevasse that was once the roof. The shed on the side of the jail had been reduced to a pile of smoldering ashes. His gaze drifted toward the bank. If he could get there, he'd have enough money to spend the rest of his days in total comfort. *With the money we've saved, we could live like kings in Mexico.* Silas glanced at Hensley, thinking he'd take Doc up on his suggestion. Silas looked over at the bank again, and then called to his son.

"Hensley's hit. He's not moving. It's just you and me, son."

"What'll we do, Pa?" Josh called back. "Should I come over there?"

"Hold on, hold on. Give me a moment to think."

It seemed to Cole that all of a sudden the shooting stopped the moment he stepped out of the building. Adam kept up a steady assault, successfully thwarting any return fire. Cole wasted no time getting to Ira, grabbing Ira's coat and yanking him up.

"Took you long enough," Ira ground out through clenched teeth. "My leg," was all he had to say before Cole jammed his shoulder under Ira's arm and half dragged, half carried his brother back to the telegraph office. Once inside, they both fell to the floor.

Ira groaned in pain then rolled to his back as he took a few seconds to catch his breath. "A-Adam?"

"I'm here, Ira."

Ira closed his eyes and offered a prayer of thanks, then rose up on his elbows to have a look around. Billy sat in the corner on the floor, cross-legged. The prisoners also sat on the floor, the wounded one cradling his injured arm. Adam was by the front door, propped up by a box of unused telegrams. "How bad are you hurt?" Ira asked his brother.

"Not so bad," Adam replied.

"He took a bullet in the leg," Cole added gruffly. "Let's have a look at you."

Ira tried to stop Cole, but his brother was determined, moving aside the singed material of Ira's jeans. In the dim light, Cole visibly blanched at the burn on Ira's leg.

"Damn it, Cole," Ira muttered. "That hurts. Leave it alone and help me up."

"Ira, you're hit," Cole stated with a worried edge to his voice as he helped Ira stand. Ira sucked in his breath when Cole's searching hand brushed against his side. "Give me your scarf."

"What for?"

"Your side, damn it. It's bleeding."

Ira glanced down. His shirt stuck to a small wound on his side. There was also a bloodstained tear in his jean, just below his hip, but both wounds were superficial, although painful.

His leg felt as if it were still on fire, causing his patience to wear thin. "Will you stop fussing, Cole?"

"Can't you wait until I see how badly you're hurt? You can't afford to lose any more blood."

"I'll take my chances," Ira said tightly. "I don't know which hurts worse, getting shot or you poking around in the dark."

Ira limped toward Adam. Adam's pant leg was soaked in blood. Ira took off his scarf. Ignoring his own pain, he knelt down on one knee and added the scarf to the old bandage as best he could. "Are you certain you're all right?"

"I'm all right," Adam said wearily. "It's not as bad as it looks, but we sure could use those deputies of yours . . . *I quit.*"

Ira gave a soft laugh. "Yeah, you'll live." He rose slowly, then limped over to the window and staying to the side, glanced out. "It's going to be light soon."

"Do you think we can get some help from the townsfolk?" Billy asked.

"Everyone's stayed inside, afraid they'd get shot, but Silas and whoever else he's got out there can't take the chance of being seen." Ira leaned back against the wall while he lifted his pistol out of his holster. He took the last six bullets out of his belt and slid them into the cylinder. "Silas Pruitt?" Ira shouted, shoving his pistol back into his holster. "I know you can hear me."

"I hear you, Marshal Farrell."

"I've got a little deal for you." Ira noticed Adam and Cole exchange cautious glances.

"What kind of deal, Marshal?" Silas asked.

"I'll let you and the others live if you give yourselves up." Ira heard Cole stand up, sensed he was standing right behind him.

"Think they'll take it?" Cole asked.

Ira shrugged. "Who knows?"

Several moments later Ira recognized Josh's voice. "That's no deal, Pa. He'll just gun you down the moment you show your face."

"That's not true," Ira said. "I'm not the judge and I'm not the jury, but I'm sure as hell the man who's going to bring you in. It's your choice how you want to do it—dead or alive. It don't matter to me." Ira waited for a moment, but when Silas didn't respond, Ira added, "I suggest you and the others toss out your weapons and give yourselves up."

Ira noticed the top of Silas's bald head as he peeked over the barrel, and then disappeared. "Sounds like you think this fight is over."

"If not now, it will be very soon," Ira countered. "My men will be here any minute."

"I suppose you're wondering where Sheriff Finch is at?"

Ira glanced at Cole then answered, "Apparently he's not out there with them." Ira turned back to the door and Silas. "You could say I thought about that a time or two."

"I reckon he'll be riding into town any time now."

"Then he'll be given the same opportunity that I'm giving you. Surrender and no one else has to get hurt."

Silas laughed out loud. "You haven't asked me where Cooper went. Come on. Take a guess."

"Let me tell him, Pa."

Ira heaved a sigh. "Well, Josh is still alive."

"Yeah, unfortunately," Cole added.

"He went to pay a little call on Miss Sarah," Josh shouted.

Ira had a quick and frightening thought. He leaned back against the wall as the memory of Lily's battered face floated before his eyes. His fingers tightened over the handle of his

Colt. For several seconds he felt as if he couldn't draw a proper breath.

"Ira. It's a trick," Cole said. "They're just saying it to get you out there so they can gun you down. Jeb wouldn't let anything happen to Sarah. You know that."

Ira took a long deep breath. What Cole said was true. But what if something had happened to Jeb? Ira pushed that thought aside. "It won't work, Silas. There's no way Finch could get to Sarah."

"Now, Marshal, you're always so damned sure of yourself. But, how do you think your uncle and your woman would react if Cooper told them you were dying?"

Ira groaned and dragged his hands down his face. "Son of a bitch."

"What's the matter, Marshal . . . cat got your tongue?" Josh taunted.

A horse whinnied in the distance, and when Ira glanced toward the end of the road, a group of riders was 300 feet away. Even in the predawn light, he instantly recognized Deputy Harris's big grey gelding.

"Why'd it get so quiet?" Cole asked.

Ira had been staring at the riders, but still thinking about Sarah. When he heard his brother's voice, Ira turned with a relieved smile. "She's here," he said, his tone tinged with disbelief.

"Sarah?" Cole asked before he cautiously looked out the door. "Where?"

"They just went around the corner toward the livery. Sarah's with them. Jeb and Sarah are with them."

Before Ira could stop him, Billy ran out the door, hollering and waving his arms. "Over here! Hey! Over here!"

Ira instantly grabbed up his rifle and stepped outside, prepared to shoot the first person that showed. "Get down!"

At almost the same time that Ira shouted his warning, Billy realized his mistake and fell to the ground, covering his head. Time hung thick and heavy for several seconds, but Ira stayed planted on the boardwalk with his Winchester ready.

"I reckon they're gone," Cole muttered as he joined Ira, his rifle also at the ready. "I suppose if you're going to make a stand out here in the open, you could use a little help."

Slowly, Ira lowered his weapon. A moment later, Billy lifted his head, then scrambled up and raced after the riders. Ira and Cole went back inside and together they helped Adam to stand for a moment until Cole could pick him up and carry him outside.

"You two stay put," Ira ordered as he glanced at the prisoners. "Someone will be here in a few minutes."

"Who's that?" Deputy Harris asked, watching a man in a crumpled suit wave his arms as he ran down the street in their direction.

"Well, if that don't beat all. He looks plumb crazy." Jeb squinted past the wild man then muttered, "I'll be damned." He jerked his horse to a halt, and then almost jumped from the saddle. "Come on, boys. Those there are my nephews."

Chapter Twenty-two

Aware that Ira's deputies were systematically checking out the surrounding area, Sarah's breath caught in her throat at the sight she beheld. Cole carried Adam toward them, and Ira limped along at his side. Their clothing was dusted with soot and dotted with various-sized burn holes. Adam's right leg was covered in blood, but without a doubt, Ira looked the worst of the three. His clothes were badly singed, with half his right pant leg missing. There was blood visible on his side and on his hip.

"Dear God," Sarah cried as she began to run. "Dear God," she repeated. A second later, Ira caught Sarah in his arms, holding her tightly as she besieged him with a thousand questions. When she was sure Ira was mostly whole, she turned to Cole and lastly to Adam. "Oh dear," she said with a compassionate smile. "Let's get him over to the boarding house, quickly," she ordered.

Ira relinquished his hold on Sarah as she led Cole and Adam across the street, and Deputy Harris stepped out from behind some barrels. "You are a sight for sore eyes." Ira grinned as he shook Harris's hand. "I thought you'd never get here."

Deputy Harris pushed his hat off his forehead. "You all right, Marshal? You don't look so good." Ira walked with his deputy over to Sarah's dress shop. In the alley they found Jonah Pruitt's body. He'd been killed with a single shot to the head. While they gathered a couple of discarded weapons, another young deputy came over, out of breath.

"Marshal Farrell?" The young man's gaze went from the top of Ira's dusty black hat, down to the soot on the top of his once-shiny boots. "You all right?"

Ira gave an impatient sigh. "Yes, Tom, I'm fine, now what did you come to tell us?"

"There's a dead man over by the mercantile."

Ira identified the man as the town's doctor. "There's more," Ira said as he searched the rooftops of the nearby buildings. "Silas Pruitt, the banker, Earl Watts, and I'm not certain how many others, but in the meantime, post a man in the bell tower at the church. It's the best place to see if anyone tries to leave town. I'm fairly confident that once you question Earl, he'll provide the names of the others."

"Tell me what you want the rest of us to do," said Harris.

"I've got two prisoners over at the telegraph office. They're handcuffed and one's wounded, so even if they decided to make a break for it, they can't get far."

Ira dragged his hands down his face, suddenly tired. "Send Joe over to the doctor's office and have him bring all the bandages and supplies he can find over to the boarding house. My brother's got a bullet in his leg."

"Where are all the townsfolk?" Harris asked as he walked down the street beside Ira. "This place looks like a ghost town."

"There were a lot of bullets flying last night. I expect once they see your badges, they'll be coming out." They were standing in front of the boarding house, when the door open and Sarah stepped out.

"Deputy Harris, may I have the marshal for a while?"

"Yes, ma'am." Harris glanced at Ira. "I'll come for you if we find anything."

Ira stepped up on the boardwalk and slipped his arm around Sarah's waist. "There will be a man at the livery who knows the way to the Pruitt ranch. It would be wise to send a couple of our men up there, but be careful. Josh Pruitt is a dangerous man." Ira started toward the door, but stopped. "One more thing. Keep an eye open for Sheriff Finch. He's tall with black hair and a moustache. He's—"

"H-he's dead."

Ira turned to Sarah, frowning at the despair glistening in her eyes. "How do you know, darlin'?"

"I-I just know."

Ira exchanged a quick glance with Harris, then turned and held the door for her to enter. Once inside he pulled Sarah close as together they started up the stairs. "You know that new window you just had installed at your shop?" he asked, purposely changing the subject. "Well, you're going to need another one."

Sarah dried her hands on a towel and glanced down at Adam. The laudanum the deputy brought with the bandages had helped his pain while Uncle Jeb removed the bullet from his leg. Cole and Ira had helped hold Adam, but he was a lot stronger than his older brothers thought.

Afterwards, while she and Jeb bandaged Adam, Cole and Ira left to bathe and change. Ira was confident with the help of his deputies there wouldn't be any more gunplay. His deputies were making the rounds, keeping the peace. He and Cole entered the bathhouse with a bundle of clean clothes and some bandages. Sarah needed to stay with Adam, so she gave strict orders for Cole to help Ira wash his leg, and then apply some salve and bandage it as well as his other wounds.

"Damn it . . . ouch!" Ira muttered as Cole poked at Ira's

side, then examined his hip. Ira stepped into the tub of water, squeezing his eyes tightly closed as it burned his injured leg.

"I'm not so sure a bath is the best thing for a burn," Cole muttered as he helped his brother ease down into the hot water. "Maybe we should have waited—"

"For what?" Ira snapped, obviously in a lot of pain. "Do you think dirt is better?"

"Don't go getting uppity with me, Marshal Farrell, I'm not one of your deputies."

"No, and you're no damned doctor either."

While the water heated for Cole's bath, he soaped up Ira's hair then rinsed it. "Well, at least you won't smell like a calf at branding time."

"*Senor?*" the Mexican man called from the door. "Your bath is ready."

"Go on," Ira grumbled. "I need to soak a while, and besides, you don't smell so good yourself."

"How is he?" Ira asked as he limped into the room. He tossed his freshly brushed black hat on the chair. He'd shaved and dressed, and to Sarah he looked every bit the dashing lawman in his black trousers and gold-brocade, high-cut vest. The star that covered his heart filled her with unexpected pride. Ira bent over Adam, placing the back of his hand on his forehead. "No fever."

"He'll be fine," Jeb replied. "Sarah gave him something to make him sleep, then we washed him up some." Jeb looked at Ira. "You look better. How are you doing?"

"Good. Cole is almost as good as you are at doctoring." Ira gave his uncle a reassuring smile. "You know how we are, Uncle Jeb, you can't keep a Farrell down for long."

"That's damn right," Jeb said with a confident nod.

Ira stepped aside for Sarah as she tucked the covers

around Adam's shoulders. "How are you?" Ira asked softly, his breath warm near her ear. The moment his hands possessed her waist she leaned back and savored the feel of him—his hard chest, his cheek on hers, the way his warm fingers splayed across her ribs.

"I'm better now," she murmured. She turned in his arms and accepted his kiss, blocking everything out except the feel of him and the clean, manly scent of him.

"Gosh darn it," Jeb muttered. "If you two don't mind, I'm too old for all this hugging and kissing. Where's Cole?"

"He was still soaking in a tub of hot water when I left," Ira replied, never looking up.

"I'll find him," Jeb said, slapping on his hat. "When you're finished, Ira, we need to have a little talk. I'll be over at the saloon with Cole."

"I'll meet you there in a few minutes," Ira agreed.

"Yeah, well, don't dawdle."

The door closed and Ira pulled Sarah even closer, pressing her to him at the same time he ravished her willing mouth. She clung to him, gleaning his strength when all she really wanted to do was go somewhere far away from all the danger. When he pulled back, he gazed deeply into her eyes, and she inwardly prayed he couldn't see her fear.

"I missed you," he whispered a second before he kissed her again.

"I can tell," she murmured, pressing her hips to his hard length. His soft pleasurable groan chased away a little of her anxiety. He was everything she could possibly want, hard masculine muscle, yet his expression so gentle and tender it nearly brought her to tears.

After one last kiss, she reluctantly pushed him away. "You're going to be late for your meeting. I'll stay with Adam." She picked up his hat and gave it to him. "Hurry back."

Thirty minutes later, Sarah turned away from the window when Adam stirred. She went to the bedside, surprised to see him trying to wake. "How are you feeling?"

"My leg hurts some, but not too bad." Adam winced when he shifted his position.

"You shouldn't move too much," she said softly as she quickly checked his bandage then replaced the covers.

"W-where's Ira and Cole?"

"They're over at the Crystal Slipper with Uncle Jeb. Ira's deputies have the town surrounded, so there's nothing to worry about."

"I'm kinda thirsty," he murmured.

She filled a glass with water and helped him take a drink. After she put the empty glass on the bedside table, she dampened a cloth and was about to bathe his forehead, when someone knocked softly on the door. Assuming it was Mrs. Baca with some fresh water, Sarah pulled it open with a smile. There was no time to scream. Josh jammed the barrel of his pistol against her breast and forced her back into the room.

Adam came wide awake, but before he could move, Josh turned and gave him a sinister grin. "Come on, pal. Just try it and I'll blow her in half."

"Let her go," Adam ground out through clenched teeth.

"Oh, no. She's my ticket out of here." He motioned for Sarah to get her coat. "Where's Ira?"

"Don't tell him," Sarah cried.

"Shut up, bitch," Josh snarled, slapping her across the face. Sarah sank to the floor at the same time Adam dragged himself nearly out of the bed. "Don't do anything stupid, Adam. Of course, I really oughta kill you." Josh's smile was evil. "A brother for a brother."

in on Jonah, blaming his brother for being so smart and making him feel stupid, when he really wasn't.

She had listened, too, trying to glean something out of his ranting that she could use, but there was nothing but hate and insanity. Now, though he still muttered about his prowess with a gun, he'd dragged her to the front of the barn where he ordered her to watch for Ira.

"Word must be out," Josh said with a satisfied nod as he peered out the door. "There's not a living soul out there."

He took off his hat and raked his fingers through his hair. Sarah said a silent prayer that Ira would find her soon. She had hardly taken a breath when Ira appeared at the far end of the street. Relief flowed over her, but it quickly turned to cold fear. Instead of staying on the boardwalk where there was some protection, Ira stepped out into the street.

"There he is, in all his glory," Josh stated sarcastically as he shrugged out of his heavy coat. "I reckon I'm not as well-dressed, but then that won't matter. I'll have lots of time to clean up after."

After? She prayed Josh would get his wish. Undertakers usually cleaned up the men who died violently. They did it so their pictures could be taken for the local newspaper. And, anyone who died facing Ira Farrell would surely make the local newspaper.

She tried to remain calm, shivering a little in the bite of the wind, as she watched Ira continue toward them. Except for a slight limp, he appeared in control, calm and confident—the predator she *wanted* him to be. He walked directly down the center of the street, unafraid, and though she didn't think it possible, her heart hammered against her chest with un-abashed feminine pride. His knee-length black coat flapped in the wind as he stopped a good distance away—out of pistol range, but well within rifle range.

Sarah dragged her gaze from Ira. She gave a cautious, sideways glance at the rifle leaning against the wall just out of her reach.

"Josh?" Ira called, drawing Sarah's attention again. Josh grinned, never taking his eyes off Ira. "You once said you wanted to meet with me, man to man, fair and square." Ira slowly moved his coat aside, exposing the ivory-handled Colt .45 strapped around his hips. "Here I am. Let Sarah come out, then you and I can finish what's between us."

Josh gave a little excited laugh. "Look at the audacity of that bastard. Why, I could shoot him down like a rabid dog. I bet that would wipe that look off his face."

"W-why would you want to do that?" Sarah asked, keeping her tone nonconfrontational. "What glory would there be in that?"

Josh turned his face to hers, his foul breath hot against her face. "That's right. That's right. Anyone could do that, but only someone special could take 'im in a fair fight."

The word "fair" nearly made Sarah retch. Just a little while ago, Josh had bragged about putting a bullet in Ira's back—targeting his right shoulder. The memory of Ira practicing at the ranch made her stomach clench with renewed dread.

"All right, Marshal," Josh hollered. "Just give me a minute."

Josh turned to her then frantically looked around, his wild gaze settling on a pair of old dusty reins hanging on the wall. He shoved her toward them and ordered her to put out her wrists. All hope of helping Ira faded when he tied her hands tightly together.

"Go on," he urged, holding his pistol on her. "Walk on out there, but don't you try nothing stupid or I'll gun you down."

Sarah stepped out of the shadow of the livery, blinking

several times as her eyes adjusted to the bright sunlight. "Ira," she breathed his name and instantly his eyes fused with hers. His strength flowed over her, lifting her spirits, soothing her fear.

When they were thirty feet away, Josh pulled her back against his chest. He pressed the gun to her temple, but she wasn't afraid as long as Ira didn't look away—as long as his gaze held hers, sharing his dauntless faith. Ira slowly flexed his long fingers.

His stance was lethal, his gaze primal—unforgiving.

"He sure is an arrogant son of a bitch," Josh muttered, dragging a dirty sleeve across his sweaty forehead. "I'm gonna let you go now, and when I do, you walk on over to the boardwalk nice and slow-like. Then turn around 'cause I want you to watch me gun down the famous Ira Farrell."

Josh gave her a little push and she did as she was told.

"Do we count to three?" Josh hollered. His fingers twitched above his gun, and she knew with sickening assurance he was going to pull his gun early. "Or do we just *draw?*"

Sarah never saw Ira draw his gun, only heard the deafening blast, then Josh's painful howl. Josh fell to his knees, clutching his belly. Blood spread quickly on his shirt, spilling over his fingers. She thought it was all over, but Ira made no move toward her. Instead he holstered his gun.

To her horror, Josh staggered to his feet and raised his pistol. The impact of Ira's second shot spun Josh around. Josh took a stumbling step, and then fell face down in the dirt. Sarah gave an anguished moan then ran toward Ira. He gathered her into his arms, his hands moving over her as if to make sure she was all right, pressing her face to his chest to shield her from any more horror.

"I'm sorry, darlin', I'm so sorry," he murmured over and over again. He tore the leather from her wrists and, keeping his body protectively between her and Josh, he lifted her. She buried her face in the crook of his neck, entwining her arms around him as he carried her down the street, toward the boarding house.

He pushed the door aside, then climbed the stairs and took her to his room.

Slowly he set her on the bed, his eyes searching her face, her body, back to her eyes, as if to reassure himself that she was in perfect condition. Slowly he undid his gun belt and placed it on the chair with his hat. Her heart expanded with the need to have him love her, to feel his warm flesh under her fingertips. She wanted his body against hers, to confirm that he was whole and alive and totally hers.

Her gaze explored his then slipped to his mouth where it lingered for several moments. He groaned low in his throat and pulled her up to receive his kiss. The kiss was urgent, insatiable, so compelling that she tore at his clothing, whispering what she wanted him to do to her, and what she wanted to do to him.

When at last their clothing was in a heap on the floor, he pressed her back against the soft mattress. Her head went back and her fingers sank into his thick hair as he took her breast into his mouth, nipping, scraping his teeth lightly over the sensitive peak, drawing a soft moan from her before he moved to the other. He kissed a path to her neck then sank his right hand into her hair and lifted her to receive his kiss, while his left hand glided over her abdomen, pausing, pressing as if he were trying to tell her without words how happy he was to know she carried his baby.

Hungry to feel him inside of her, she spread her legs, inviting him to enter as her fingers floated over his muscular shoulders, kneading, sliding lower, hovering over the nicks and wounds he had sustained the night before. With a tenderness born of love and admiration, she avoided the deep gash on his hip, circling the small of his back and the tight muscles of his buttocks. Holding him she arched against his rigid manhood, breathing his name when he thrust inside.

Ira balanced his weight on his elbows and drove deep, and then withdrew only to sink back into her satiny warmth. Watching her writhe beneath him gave him such intense pleasure that he couldn't take his eyes off of her. She moaned his name and he bent his head and kissed her, plunging into the sweet recesses of her mouth. She matched each move, teasing, tasting, taking him to the summit, but he wasn't ready to end so soon what they had started, even though she reached her first climax.

Enthralled with her body's pulsating response, he lifted his head, gazing down at her for several lustful seconds before he nuzzled her neck and whispered how she was his soul, his sanctuary. Her gaze met his, and then she smiled sensually, lifting her hips to meet each slow, methodical thrust. When her palms grazed his nipples, and her tongue darted out to moisten her lips, he pumped harder, and they each attained sweet release precisely at the same time.

Long after their breathing returned to normal, they stayed in each other's arms, snuggling, whispering small secrets that only two lovers can share. She was content and secure in his arms, remembering how he had whispered his love, telling her she was his sanctuary from the world. And, now she confessed how proud she was, how utterly cherished he made her feel.

The shadows on the wall slowly faded and when it grew cold, he rose and added more wood to the stove, then slipped back into bed next to her, pulling her against the warmth of his body, and when he kissed her and caressed her, she pressed closer, offering herself completely, giving and taking, drawing as much pleasure from his touch as he did from hers. And together they climbed to the stars and touched the sun as the full moon rose.

Epilogue

A light snow dusted the shoulders of the Farrells, their many guests, and the dark overcoat of the minister as he stood before a huge spruce with his Bible in hand. Miss Lily was there in a ruby red cloak, her hair swept up and held with fur and feathers. All her girls stood behind her, dressed in green and red fox fur to keep the colors of Sarah's Christmas wedding.

Cole, Adam—leaning on a cane—and Jeb stood across from them, all in crisp black overcoats and matching Stetsons, holly berries pinned to their lapels, gloved hands clasped before them. The rest of the guests, including Mayor William James and his wife, wore their winter-Sunday best, holding pine sprigs and little velvets sacks of bread crumbs, oats and cracked corn in lieu of rice, as Sarah wanted the wild things in the forest to share in her happiness.

Sarah was warm both inside and out in her white fox fur coat over her white velvet wedding gown and warm, fur-lined white boots. Her matching fur hat was adorned with a sprig of pine and red-berried holly, matching the bridal bouquet Miss Lily held for her, while the couple exchanged their vows.

But though everything surrounding her in the pristine mountain snow was soft and as beautiful as she, Sarah hardly noticed. Her gaze was fastened on Ira, the love of her life. He was clad in a black fur-trimmed overcoat and black Stetson. Instead of the star on his chest, there was a small pine sprig tied with a red satin ribbon. He held in his black-gloved hands her white-gloved hands, and she knew by the twinkle in his vivid grey eyes, she was the love of his life, too.

"And will you, Sarah Brighton, love, cherish and honor Ira in your marriage, on earth and for all eternity?" The preacher's voice broke into her reverie.

"I will," she answered softly.

"And will you, Ira Farrell, love, cherish and treat Sarah as your *equal* . . ." The preacher cleared his throat, then glanced at the vows again to make sure he'd read them properly. "A-and, treat Sarah as your equal in your marriage, on earth and for all eternity?"

Ira raised one skeptical brow.

Sarah narrowed her eyes, squeezing his fingers lovingly.

Her feigned frown turned into a wondrous smile, when in a deep, clear voice he replied, "I most definitely will."

"Then before all who have witnessed this union, I pronounce you husband and wife."

Amidst the cheers of the men in the crowd, Ira wondered if they knew how completely happy he was.

While the ladies smiled and dabbed at their tears, Sarah wondered if Ira would like the lacy, white-satin corset Miss Lily had given her for a wedding present.

However, as soon as the preacher said, "Marshal Farrell, you may kiss your bride," all thoughts of what the others thought vanished, and Ira pulled his beautiful wife into his arms and kissed her until they were both *equally* breathless.

About the Author

Donna MacQuigg is a native of New Mexico and knows first hand what life in the west is all about. Having raised and trained Arabian horses for over 25 years with her husband and two children, she's spent many hours in the saddle, riding trails in the beautiful Sangre de Cristo Mountains. She was taught at an early age the skill of hand gunning and enjoys archery and knife throwing as well. Donna has previous published two historical romances. She enjoys receiving your comments at Knightwriter@comcast.net or visit her Web site at www.geocities. com/donnamacquigg.